Tumiko

AND THE
FINICKY
NESTMATE

BY FORTHRIGHT

FORTHWRITES.COM

Amaranthine Saga, Book 5
Fumiko and the Finicky Nestmate

Copyright © 2021 by FORTHRIGHT
ISBN: 978-1-63123-075-2

TWINKLE PRESS

because I found in you a place to sing

TABLE of CONTENTS

Fumiko

AND THE
FINICKY
NESTMATE

1

SQUEAKY WHEEL

There was a trick to the box. Fumiko remembered that much.

Seated on the second-to-last step of a spiral staircase, she turned it this way and that, admiring the pearly luster of inset tiles. She'd always liked things made from seashells. They swirled with myriad colors in the sunlight angling from the lantern room above.

"A puzzle box," she decided, running her fingers along each side, searching for seams. "Whose was it, again?"

Maybe it was hers? Everything here was, by default. But had it been hers from the beginning? It did seem old enough.

But no. As she explored its patterns and panels, flashes of memory stirred. Fumiko could see the box in the hands of a man with nimble brown fingers. Careful hands. Confident as they pressed and turned. He had known the trick to the box.

1

He was a good memory, warm with love and belonging. How had he been important?

A sibling?

A friend?

A husband?

A child?

Fumiko wasn't sure anymore, but that didn't bother her. Zuzu would remember.

Carrying the puzzle box to the wide bed with its drapery of netting and scarves, Fumiko nudged aside a green vase shaped like a fish and a striped tin filled with yellow crayons. If she also moved one of the book stacks to the floor, there was just enough space.

"I chose something, Zuzu," she murmured. "Tonight, you can tell me its story."

"Up here," came her sister's voice from overhead. "The hummingbirds are back, and they've brought friends."

Fumiko's chunky sandals rang on each metal step as she climbed to the lantern room, which was half-lost amidst her sister's branches. Only for a handful of hours in the afternoon did sunbeams reach the gallery, which boasted a spectacular view of the Pacific.

Gulls whirled upward from the beach, raucous as they squabbled over some tidbit stolen from a tourist. Pelicans soared past in perfect formation, looking vaguely prehistoric and thoroughly dignified. To the south, kites danced and spun in the stiff breeze that tugged at Fumiko's long, layered skirt and tangled her in a swirl of her own hair.

"Let me," Zuzu offered warmly.

"Thank you." Fumiko put her face to the wind and shook the mess from her eyes. Stupid hair, always growing, always getting in the way. She'd take a knife to it one of these days, just to get some relief.

"See them?" Zuzu's hands were busy braiding, but she leaned over Fumiko's shoulder, pressing their cheeks together to guide her line of sight. "They come to us because they don't like winter."

Although Portia's wards were an impenetrable barrier to problems, big and small, she'd made allowances for many species, including migrating avians. Hummingbirds darted amidst the branches, which bore clusters of fragrant purple flowers all year round. Tiny birds, bright as jewels. Most people thought of them as the smallest of birdkind. But only because they'd never seen a nippet.

"Vert nippets." Fumiko hadn't seen one in a while.

"Here to cheer you up." Zuzu's arms twined and tugged. "See? You're smiling."

"I don't need cheering."

Fumiko wished people wouldn't make such a fuss over every little thing. Didn't everyone have moody phases? She supposed it came from living with too many preservationists. They obsessed over Zuzu's pollen count in much the same way.

"I'll always smile for you," Fumiko said, lacing her fingers with Zuzu's.

They didn't look like sisters, let alone twins. But their bond was the truest thing in Fumiko's life. Zuzu was her only constant, her lasting comfort. Sisterhood defined their entire existence.

Once upon a time, they'd lived on the far edge of a vast grove, the nearest tree-kin to the reavers who'd tended this very lighthouse. Now, Zuzu's branches were strung with a thousand tiny chimes that were both remembrances and prayers for those lost.

Zuzu asked, "How long has it been since the last time?"

Fumiko immediately knew what she meant. Maybe because they were sisters. Maybe because they'd had this discussion so many times before. "Not *that* long."

"I overheard the girls talking about some men coming here." Zuzu dimpled. "A whole group of guests. That's how it starts."

"It *can't* be," Fumiko muttered, trying to think back. "Wasn't Dru here for the last time?"

Zuzu hummed in that way that meant she liked her idea better.

"And they always send a healer first. Checkups and teas and things."

Her sister immediately brightened. "A healer from a horse clan is with them!"

Fumiko's confusion doubled. "Wouldn't there be a letter?"

Zuzu vanished, only to return two moments later with her hands full of unopened mail. "One of these, you think?"

She shook her head, as if denial could make her contract go away. "I guess I'd better ask Diva."

"I hope it *is*." Zuzu peeped at her from under thick lashes. "Maybe one of them will fall in love with you. Or me. Or us."

"You're such a romantic," she accused. Not for the first time.

Fumiko wasn't sure if all trees lived and breathed love stories or if Zuzu was a special case. But reaver contracts weren't romantic. They were a practical necessity.

4

That's when a familiar rattle and squeak claimed all of Fumiko's attention. The afternoon courier had to park his truck at the entrance to Jacaranda Circle, which was a pedestrian-only zone. So deliveries were loaded onto a metal rolling cart with a squeaky wheel that protested every crack in the sidewalk.

"Umm ... I should go check." Fumiko tried to tone down her eagerness. "In case there's something for me."

Zuzu kissed her cheek and let her go.

Snagging a beaded shawl on the way through her bedroom, Fumiko clattered down six short flights of stairs, turning sideways to edge around an overflowing steamer trunk on one landing and past a bristling umbrella stand on the next.

In the gathering room, where meals were shared, one of the interns was lifting knickknacks as she dusted. Fumiko offered a breathless smile. "Hello, Antigone."

"Good afternoon, my darling. In a hurry?" There was a teasing light in the woman's brown eyes.

"Not a *big* hurry," she fudged. "Was there something you needed?"

"Yes, actually. I was wondering what you might like for dinner tonight." Antigone was sixty-something and a preservationist, but she was also into yoga and yoghurt and healthy habits in general. More than any of the rest, she fretted over Fumiko's diet.

"I don't care." Fumiko edged past a cart stacked with mismatched coffee cups. "Anything's fine."

"Did you eat lunch?"

"I wasn't hungry."

Antigone shook her microfiber dusting cloth admonishingly. "You *need* to eat. You should be eating more."

5

"I will," Fumiko called over her shoulder as she escaped out her front door.

A wide walkway skirted the low rectangular building that butted up against the lighthouse. It had been longer at one point, but nearly half of it had been dismantled a few centuries back to make room for Zuzu's expanding girth. She was bigger around than the lighthouse, now. And proud of it.

Fumiko stopped and stared at all the guesthouse's windows and doors, which were open to catch the sea breezes. The interns only ever cleaned and freshened those rooms when they were expecting company.

Was Zuzu right?

She *really* needed to check with Diva.

Easing through a crystal-frosted gate, Fumiko slipped beyond one of the barriers that hid Zuzu from passersby and prying eyes. Three establishments were arranged along a cul-de-sac. All part of the camouflage. All run by Betweeners.

Fumiko waved to the deeply tanned man with blond dreadlocks who was chasing purple flower petals with a push broom. Rafter grinned and gestured with its handle. "He went thataway!"

As if she didn't know the courier's usual route. Always the flower shop first. Then the library. And finally the office of the Wind-and-Tide Fresh Market.

Her gambit was probably silly, given that everyone in their little cooperative knew everyone else's business. But whenever Fumiko ordered things online, she'd spread out where they were delivered in the futile hope that nobody would notice how many packages were arriving.

There were always one or two. Sometimes many more.

So far, her friends hadn't teased—much—or staged an intervention. Maybe they thought shopping was a healthy outlet? It's not like she had many other options, cornered as she was, with the sea at her back.

Loitering outside of Flutterbys Flowers, Fumiko waited for the courier to finish chatting with Melody. Fumiko wasn't supposed to be seen too often. Tourists weren't such a big deal, since they came and went, but locals and regulars might remember her and wonder about her.

While she waited, Fumiko cast a worried look toward home. Her contract with the In-between was straightforward enough. In exchange for the protection they offered, she gave birth to a minimum of one child per century. When it was time, they'd usually send in four or five men for her to choose from. All with exemplary pedigrees. Each willing to do their part.

If Zuzu was right, Fumiko was about to go through it all over again.

Picking the reaver who'd father her next child.

2

JACARANDA CIRCLE

Akira spent much of the ride from the airport chatting with their driver. Candor was from a nearby enclave, though he was vague about the location—*off a ways, along the coast*. The Amaranthine people had made strides toward equality in America, but plenty still lived in hiding. Akira wasn't about to be nosy. He was too grateful that Candor was both fluent in Japanese and willing to play tour guide.

Off the expressway, everything slowed down. Buildings crowded the road, which dipped and bumped under their tires. Even though it was October, trees and shrubs were green, and flowers bloomed everywhere—pink and orange and violet.

Candor had to slow often for jaywalkers. "Tourists," he remarked with a philosophical shrug.

They passed a sign swinger whose acrobatic dance was drawing attention to a shop that rented motorized scooters. Surfers in wetsuits hefted longboards. There were dog walkers and dog joggers. Sunbaked and scruffy men snoozed in the shade of bushy palms, and a rollerblader skimmed gracefully past, dancing to the tunes blasting from a speaker clipped to their belt.

Distracted by the riot of beautiful and bizarre sights, Akira lost his bearings. "I hope you know where we are," he joked. "I'm completely turned around."

"Hard to get lost. Wherever you are, aim for the ocean. After that, the Ghost Light will lead you home."

Akira wasn't sure if Candor was serious or if they'd run up against a translation error. "Ghost Light? As in … specters?"

Candor laughed. "It's a local legend that tries to explain a mysterious light that's been seen along the shore. Some say it's a restless spirit who can't find peace. Some think it's a portal into the seelie court. There's even a contingent who are convinced it's linked to alien activity."

Juuyu was listening now.

Akira wondered if that in itself was important. "Sounds like something those cryptid chasers would have fun debunking."

With a bark of laughter, Candor asked, "You watch *Dare Together*?"

"Sure." It was the show he'd been referring to. "The kids back home are big fans. Suuzu and I read the subtitles for them. I'm always Josheb. He's always Caleb."

"Typecasting?" Candor glanced at Juuyu in the rearview mirror. "You're Spokesperson Farroost's brother, yeah?"

"I am." Curt as ever.

Juuyu had disguised his Amaranthine features so he'd draw

9

less attention while escorting Akira through traditional channels. But their driver had keener senses than humans. Some of Akira's friends were from the wolf clans—dog clansmen, too, for that matter—and they could sort out another Amaranthine just by scent. Stuff like that simply wasn't a secret. Still, Akira thought he should steer the conversation away from Juuyu.

"Suuzu's been my best friend since middle school. But what about the Ghost Light? What is it really?"

"You'll see for yourself. And be sure to count yourself lucky, since it's a sight few ever see." Idling while he waited for a crosswalk to clear, Candor nodded to an overhead sign that spanned the width of the street. "Welcome to Wind-and-Tide."

Akira eyed the houses, which crowded four and five deep, as if jockeying for position in their rush to reach the sand. Faded paint in vivid hues. Beach towels flapping on picket fences. Rooftop decks vying for views. "I thought we were in Beacon?"

"Yep. This is Beacon, California. But plenty of neighborhoods and beaches have their own names. And personalities."

"Sort of like Kikusawa, which is a neighborhood within the city of Keishi."

"Keishi, Japan?" Candor pointed his finger like he was cocking a gun. "Fan of Eloquence and Kimiko Starmark, are you? I'm a cousin ... in a roundabout way."

"Friend, actually." Akira had assumed this guy knew who they were, but maybe he was just putting together names and faces. "I want to school with Kimi and Quen."

With a low whistle to show he was impressed, Candor asked, "Ever see *Crossing America*?"

Akira shook his head. "Is that another TV show?"

"In its sixth season and going strong. It's the one with Ash and Tami Sunfletch."

"Oh! Sure, I know them." It was the secondhand kind of knowing, since his friends and family had helped pull off their wedding.

"On the show, Ash travels all over, giving good publicity to Amaranthine who are willing to *step out*, as they say." Parking in front of a line of concrete posts that barricaded a dead-end street, Candor waved a hand. "There's a flower shop over there that was featured on their show. *Tripled* this neighborhood's popularity."

A double row of graceful trees lined the street, their arching branches nearly touching over the center. Beneath them were open stalls with long tables under blue and white awnings. In a reserved spot at the end of the row, Akira spotted an antique truck with a logo on its door—RED ROOSTER FARM.

"All this part's a farmers market." Candor hopped out and opened the back of the black SUV he'd met them with. It seemed too somber for the scene. Impersonal. "Not much luggage, considering how far you've come."

Juuyu left the vehicle, distractedly remarking, "The rest is arriving later."

Akira reclaimed his backpack and drifted toward a table piled high with mesh bags of avocados. Another held corn with multi-colored kernels. He'd made it as far as the crates of pumpkins when Juuyu caught up.

"Do not wander off."

"I have the years to walk unattended," Akira replied, calm but firm.

"I promised my brother ...."

"*After* the fact." Akira treated his travel companion to a long look. "He's furious with you. And me, for that matter."

Juuyu's gaze roved the vicinity. It was hard to tell if he was avoiding eye contact or looking for threats. "We could not wait for his obligations to the Council to reach an end."

"Because they never will?" Akira asked wryly.

"You agreed to come."

"Because I wanted to see California. So let me *see* it!"

"If you are careful."

Akira caught the sleeve of Juuyu's suit coat. "I'll take whatever precautions will put your heart and mind at ease. Within reason."

Juuyu bowed his head and sighed. "You are too used to getting your way. I am *not* my brother."

"*Speaking* of Suuzu!" Akira brought out his phone. He thumbed to its camera, simultaneously pulling Juuyu down by his necktie. Going up on tiptoe to diminish the remaining height difference, he cheerfully ordered, "Smile!"

While Juuyu didn't smile, he permitted the manhandling. Only tutted a little as he put his suit back to rights. "Reassure my brother. I will meet you inside the florist shop."

"The Amaranthine one?"

Juuyu inclined his head. "There is a safehouse here. Very secret. Completely secure."

"And a ghostly light ...?"

"That was not mentioned in my briefing. Ask Sinder."

"Will do!"

Leaning against one of the rock-studded supports for the

trellises that shaded a picnic area, Akira tapped a message for Suuzu.

> **Arrived safe and sound**
> **Meeting up with the rest soon**

> **Your meetings will be more**
> **enjoyable than mine**

> **Someone droning rhetoric again?**

> **Everything is important to someone**

> **But not you?**

> **You are important to me**

Akira's smile dimmed. He *knew* that. And what a mess he'd made of Suuzu's composure with these sudden travel plans. But Boon had called in an old favor. And Akira had convinced himself that it would be all right since Juuyu would be with him.

> **Juuyu won't neglect his**
> **promises to you**

> **I wish I was there**
> **With you**

> **Soon**
> **Hang in there**

> **I will persevere**
> **Then I will come to you**

> **I'll be here**

Angling his phone so the next selfie showed the street sign on the corner—JACARANDA CIRCLE—he gave his best friend his most reassuring smile.

Who else will be in attendance?

Juuyu's team
But they're busy guys

Your hosts?

Not sure yet
I'll text you before bed
Or call?

Please

It's a promise

I will endeavor to be patient

Suuzu wasn't exactly clingy. He *couldn't* be. His position on the Amaranthine Council required a great deal of travel. But Suuzu was happiest knowing that Akira was safe at Stately House.

Any departure from their usual routines was a challenge, but Akira had never been one to shy away from new things. Suuzu insisted that Akira's more adventurous streak was admirable, that as an ambassador for his people, Suuzu needed his horizons broadened. However, the selfie Suuzu sent in return showed the barest of smiles and a wistful gaze.

Akira wouldn't apologize, but he'd keep his eyes open for a peace offering. Avians liked gifts. Maybe he'd find something to add to Suuzu's "nest," a necklace they'd been adding to ever since their last year of school.

Even though the tradition was wolvish, Juuyu wore one and had encouraged his younger brother to create his own. Suuzu's included braided hair, a tuned crystal, and other small items that served as touchstones.

Reminders and rituals had a calming effect on the phoenix brothers, who were both extremely sensitive to their surroundings.

With that in mind, Akira stowed his phone and strode purposefully toward the florist shop, which had been painted on every side with an eye-catching mural of butterfly kites dancing at the ends of their strings, streamers flying. A sandwich board out front announced their claim to fame.

FLUTTERBYS FLOWERS
AS SEEN ON
CROSSING AMERICA
WITH ASH SUNFLETCH

Akira took another selfie in front of the mural before stepping inside. It was like walking into a bouquet. He paused to admire a glossy photo of Ash standing outside the shop, black wings extended behind two Amaranthine ladies.

Juuyu was talking to the one with candyfloss pink hair now.

While Akira wouldn't go so far as to say he was fluent in English, he got along well enough if people were patient. So he caught most of what they were saying, and it didn't seem to be top secret.

"The dock? Very sensible," she said. "That will draw less attention."

Her posture shifted, and Akira adjusted his own. She glanced between them, and Juuyu inclined his head. "He is with me."

"Human?" She seemed puzzled.

Akira stepped up to offer his palms. "Human," he confirmed in

15

English. "My name is Akira."

Matching his hands in the traditional greeting, she said, "Melody Skyflutter. We must have someone lead you through the gate. Fumiko, my dear? You're there, aren't you? Come, and meet your guests."

Juuyu's gaze immediately slid to the door.

Akira turned in time to see a woman step inside. She was tallish and draped in loose clothing, all in mismatched patterns. Her long braid was decorated with purple flowers, and everything about her posture was uncertain.

Used to making his own inroads, Akira extended a hand and offered his greeting. But in Japanese this time. He realized his mistake at once and laughed sheepishly. "So sorry. Your name was Japanese ...?"

"I'm sorry. I'm American." As was her accent. Fumiko hesitated, then admitted, "I *did* understand, though. Do I know Japanese?"

Melody tapped her chin with a finger. "I think you do. Or did. Early on. Diva might know."

Akira was confused enough to wonder if something had been lost in translation. He looked to Juuyu for help, but the phoenix was contemplating his pocket watch.

"Candor is waiting." Juuyu snapped the timepiece shut. "I have a meeting at the museum next."

"This is home away from home, right?" checked Akira.

"It is."

"We're fine then." He shooed Juuyu toward the door. "Get your stuff done, and I'll see you later."

Juuyu stepped close enough to loom. It was strange, looking

16

into eyes that *should* have been orange, but weren't. Hopefully, once they were settled behind barriers, Juuyu and his team could drop all the pretense and be themselves.

"I will return before you require sleep."

Akira grinned. "I don't need tucking in."

"Perhaps not. But my brother *was* furious. And certain promises were extracted."

He couldn't believe it. But he could. And it wasn't like he minded. "Do I get a lullaby out of the deal?"

Juuyu glanced away, toward things Akira couldn't see, and said, "Yes. I believe I could sing here."

Then all at once, there was another woman in the room. Just ... *there*. And talking fast.

"Sister! You'll never guess! Please, come? There's something new!"

Her sister? Akira supposed one of them *could* be adopted. There was certainly no family resemblance. This woman was taller than Fumiko and definitely not Japanese. Her skin was several shades darker. Her hair was a rippling cascade of brown waves, and she was crowned with the same purple flowers that Fumiko wore. But more of them. Lots more.

"*Zuzu!*" Melody exclaimed, all exasperation.

Fumiko softly added, "You *know* better."

The new lady rolled her eyes. Which were a vivid shade of purple. "They're our guests."

Akira didn't need to be told that Zuzu was Amaranthine, but he was still plenty confused.

"Peace." Juuyu made a soothing gesture in Fumiko's direction. "Your twin knew it was safe to manifest here."

Not just sisters, but *twins*?

And with that, Akira caught on.

These two were tree-kin. Isla had been quizzing Suuzu about them the last time they were both home at the same time. But Akira had tuned out most of the conversation because—in typical Isla fashion—she'd insisted on conducting the entire discussion in French.

Right then, Zuzu glided over to Juuyu and just sort of inserted herself into his personal space, pulling him down into a kiss.

Akira gawked.

Juuyu didn't bat an eye. Like kissing beautiful women was all in a day's work.

Wait. Was he smiling?

Then Zuzu whirled and exclaimed, "Oh, but Sister! You really *should* come and see. There's a dragon swimming in our bay!"

3

AT THE AMORY

Nostalgia hit Juuyu with the force of a gale.

Six years had passed since his last visit home, and he'd only gone because custom demanded that he escort Suuzu and Akira.

Work was as constant as instinct, but Juuyu didn't begrudge the urgency of the tasks their team took on. Still, his sort longed for familiar patterns. And this place stirred him up in unanticipated ways.

Brine upon the landward breeze.

Waves upon a nearby shore.

And Zuzu smelled like home.

She was a tree of the same variety as Letik, whose branches had provided shelter to generations of Farroost tributes. Letik was twin to Juuyu's father, and Juuyu had raised Suuzu among his branches. The tree was their birthplace and their home. Indeed, Juuyu still carried Letik's petals in a bottle as a remedy for homesickness.

Zuzu looked as if she belonged to the grove tended by the Farroost clan. Juuyu brushed a knuckle across bark brown skin, faintly traced with fine grain, as if Zuzu were carved from her own wood. Heart light, he greeted her in the old language.

Her pout was predictably sultry, trees being trees. "I'm American, too, you know."

Melody interjected, "That was a traditional greeting my dear. It's from the lullabies of trees."

"I don't know them." Zuzu backed away.

Juuyu wondered if he'd offended her, but she'd only gone to collect her sister. Tugging Fumiko closer, Zuzu caught his hand and raised it to her sister's face. "Her, too."

For they were two.

He'd *known* their safehouse was under the limbs of an orphan tree. When he'd studied the file, he'd merely been grateful for a convenient location.

Foolish.

Selfish.

Here were two meant for the community of groves. Hemmed in by humans, with no room to sow new seeds.

Used to indulging the whims of trees, Juuyu repeated the greeting for Fumiko, translating it into English. "May the scent of flowers linger in your dreams. May the blessing of trees linger in your embrace."

Fumiko leaned into his touch. "I want to hear the lullabies you sing for this boy."

"Hey! I'm older than I look," Akira grumbled. "I'm twenty-six,

I'll have you know."

A pointless protest, since he made it in Japanese. But before Juuyu could translate, Fumiko pulled Akira into her arms. "Maybe so, but you remind me of Remi. Don't you think so, Zuzu?"

Zuzu shimmied her way into the hug and kissed the top of Akira's head. "Mm-hmm. But Remi had freckles."

Juuyu drummed his fingers against Akira's shoulder, four soft taps.

Immediately, the young man relaxed into the sisters' embrace.

Over the years, Akira and Suuzu had worked out many useful signals. Juuyu suspected that this one had become necessary because Akira had first visited their island as a young teen. In essence, the signal meant, *this is customary*. Perhaps a truer interpretation would be, *do not lend human meanings to Amaranthine affections*.

Akira had always adapted quickly. "I have a sister, too," he shared. "Her name's Tsumiko."

Zuzu giggled. "Rhymes with Fumiko."

"Nice. Do you like words?"

"I like *names*," countered the tree. "We've given so many!"

Akira seemed to be tracking fine with the English. "You give names. Who is named?"

"Babies." Zuzu rested her cheek against Akira's hair. "I love all our babies. Like Remi with freckles. He was always playing on the shore."

"Kids are great." Akira addressed Fumiko. "You're a mom?"

"Sometimes."

Her eyes were old for reasons Juuyu could guess. Tree-kin might share their twin's years, but if they were human, they usually outlived the families they created. This would be especially true of

21

an orphan tree. Fumiko didn't have the option of taking another tree-kin for a husband.

Rechecking his pocket watch, Juuyu realigned his priorities. "Go meet the dragon. He is *also* with me. Akira, perhaps you can explain? I must hurry to my next meeting."

"We're good," promised Akira, as easygoing as ever. "Take care of your stuff. We'll see you after."

"And sing for us," demanded Zuzu.

Juuyu breathed deeply, savored a small burst of anticipation, and repeated, "Yes. I believe I could sing here."

The safehouse was truly convenient to the museum. Hisoka had chosen well. Juuyu only checked his watch twice during the drive because they arrived before he could fret further. His appointment was for five o'clock, closing time.

With two minutes to spare, Candor pulled up in front of the Amory Fine Arts Center. "I'll hang out in that lot over there until you're ready to head back," he said. "Moving forward, it'll probably be simplest to take the trolly. Though rental bikes are also a cinch."

"Understood."

Juuyu strode to the doors, which were not yet locked. He stopped inside and forced himself to focus, to take in all the details he would have otherwise intentionally tuned out. Because *this* was the reason he'd been chosen by Hisoka Twineshaft. This was his task. His contribution to the team.

Three sets of double doors, facing south onto Mainsail Street.

Spacious lobby. Ticket windows straight ahead.

Planters with live trees—predominantly ficus and palm.

Banners advertising current and upcoming displays.

Gift shop. Two clerks. Two customers ringing up.

Plentiful seating. Mostly café tables. Six lingering guests—two couples, two individuals.

Restaurant to the right—Masterpiece Sandwiches. Two workers at the counter. Three people in line, all wearing museum uniforms. Departing staff getting dinner to go?

Coffee shop to the left—Brew & Bubble. Three workers. Four customers waiting to pick up orders. One at the register, chatting with a barista.

Juuyu would post Sinder here for a few days, let him sort out the employees and regulars.

He passed through an archway flanked by mosaic columns. The next room was really more of a courtyard since it was open to the elements. High overhead, a dome of metal mesh and mirrors kept birds at bay. Wards were also in place. Juuyu recognized Argent Mettlebright's handiwork.

Additional seating, umbrellaed tables and memorial benches.

More trees, all palms, these set directly into the soil.

Central fountain topped by bronze statues of four figures.

An emergency exit, facing west onto Neptune Street.

A silver-haired security guard perched on a stool beside the entrance to the museum proper. He was a reaver, battler class, which simplified matters. Juuyu's name was on his clipboard. The man stood and took a respectful posture, signaling welcome before waving him through tinted glass doors.

Another lofty, echoing space, this one with glass elevators, balconies, and display cases on every side. Guests could access every gallery from this central point. Pacing slowly across tile floors—black granite with a multicolored sparkle additive—Juuyu noted every skylight, sprinkler, and the ring of track lighting oriented on a luminous glass installment, all in the shades of a blue-green sea.

To his relief, this portion of the museum was fully enclosed. A controlled climate. A quantifiable, defensible space. Hallow would be pleased.

Now what?

No sign of guests.

No sign of guards.

No sign of a greeting.

Juuyu was checking the time again when he caught a flash of movement in his periphery. An enormous lynx swayed toward him on silent paws. Her green eyes glittered with intelligence ... and authority.

Taking a receptive stance, he declared himself. "Juuyu Farroost. I am expected."

She nosed his forehead, wheeled, and walked away, stubby tail flipping in a *follow me* fashion.

A hushed hall led to offices and conference rooms, one of which had been taken over by the newly appointed security team. Its leader stepped forward, palms up. Juuyu took in every detail.

Battler. Middle-aged. Well-armed. Well-muscled.

Short blonde hair. Wideset blue eyes. Tanned and freckled.

It was unusual to meet a woman who matched his height.

"Mirrim Locket," she said crisply. "I'm your local liaison. Argent Mettlebright placed us here, but we're operating under the assumption that you and your team are in charge."

Juuyu slid his hands into a supportive position before turning to the second woman. She was a handsbreadth shorter than Mirrim. A heavy braid topped her head, the sides of which were shaved in a style reminiscent of the equine clans. Kohl-rimmed eyes. Multiple piercings. Potent crystals.

Her snug sheath and openwork pants bared a lot of brown skin. He realized he was staring, inadvertently attempting to memorize her tattoos, which were unusually complicated. Highly advanced sigilcraft. The dangerous sort.

"Curious?" The woman smiled broadly and crooked a finger. "You can look, but don't touch. They're loaded."

The sigils stood out like lace upon her skin, inked in white, shimmering with power.

"These are what I like to call a competitive edge." She turned, encouraging his perusal. "This set has shields for deflective attacks. Ever been hit by an airbag in a moving car?"

Juuyu's eyes widened.

So did her smile. "Broke my nose once. Gave me the idea. Defensive measures can pack a wallop. So does my partner. I'm Magda Locket, by the way. We're the Lost Harbor Lockets."

As if he should recognize them.

He met her palms and admitted, "I am ... unfamiliar."

"Seriously?" Magda propped a hand on her hip. "We're on the

battler circuit. The games are televised and everything. Ever watch any extreme sports? No?"

"I apologize." He was more interested in the delicate sigils that wheeled around her. Six in all. Expanding her sensory field like the whiskers on a cat.

Mirrim's posture shifted as she took charge again. "We're both partnered. You met Lash."

Juuyu inclined his head toward the lynx.

Magda said, "I belong to Tuft. He's sweeping fourth floor. That's where the Junzi is displayed."

"We can take you there first," Mirrim offered. "There's probably time, since the director is running late. Again."

"A moment." Juuyu signaled for secrecy. "While it is just us."

The battlers subtly came to attention.

"Details have not been released, but I am authorized to tell you—and only you—that there has been a theft in Keishi. Another of the Junzi, a weapon known as the Chrysanthemum Blaze, was taken from Kikusawa Shrine. One of my teammates has diverted to Keishi in order to investigate. We will know more when he rejoins us here."

The battlers exchanged a long look.

"Kikusawa Shrine?" Magda asked incredulously. "The home of Eloquence and Kimiko Starmark? Isn't that place behind a bajillion barriers?"

"The shrine itself is open to the public. They see hundreds of visitors on an average day. Thousands on festival days." Juuyu had visited more than once, so he understood why the theft was such a shock. "Even so, the Blaze was taken from a secure area."

"By the so-called Gentleman Bandit?" asked Magda.

"That is the assumption."

"When?" asked Mirrim.

"The theft was discovered four days ago."

Again, the women exchanged a long look.

Juuyu tasted dread. "What has happened?"

"I guess you'd call it ... tampering," said Magda. "Possibly coincidental, but it has my back up."

"When?" Juuyu demanded.

Mirrim drummed her fingers on the hilt of one of the blades at her belt. "Yesterday."

4

THEY USUALLY SEND HUMANS

Fumiko pushed, and Zuzu pulled Akira, who didn't really need persuading. Only a direction.

They didn't often receive guests, despite their location on a prime sliver of beachfront property. Fumiko had forgotten how much fun it was, drawing back the curtain so blinded eyes could see.

"Whoa! This is ... whoa!" Akira folded his hands behind his head and laughed toward the treetop. "Zuzu, that's you! Right?"

"It is! Do you think I'm pretty?"

"Totally beautiful," he warmly assured.

Fumiko liked the ease with which he bestowed compliments. She asked, "You knew?"

"Not at first. I probably should have figured it out sooner." Looking back the way they'd come, Akira added, "Juuyu didn't say anything, but he's careful like that."

That one. Fumiko had thought he was human until he'd

28

touched her. Betraying the truth of his existence. Bestowing words like a blessing. "He's Amaranthine."

"Avian," revealed Zuzu. "But I don't know which kind."

"He'll definitely share his name properly. Juuyu has good manners." Akira cobbled together his sentences slowly, sometimes mixing in Japanese words before translating to English. "He's from a grove, and I've been there. Those trees are like you."

"A grove," Zuzu breathed wistfully. "Is it far?"

"Across the ocean." He looked toward the water. "Not sure where, though. The whole island's hidden. Like you."

"It's safer that way," murmured Fumiko.

Akira eagerly explained, "So I've met tree-kin before, but the whole time, I thought they were some kind of islander clan who wore flowers in their hair. And that all foreigners were touchy-feely. I didn't catch on at all. But I was just a kid, and everything was new then. Right after the Emergence."

Zuzu tapped his nose. "You are still young."

"Compared to Amaranthine, sure," he agreed amiably. "Some of the kids I hang out with are decades older than me. But they're still growing, and what they need changes over time. That's the same for anyone. Even trees, yeah?"

"What I need is always the same." Zuzu pouted. "But nobody gives it."

Akira looked to Fumiko, who couldn't help laughing. "She wants pollen. They restrict it with barriers to prevent accidental fertilization."

Fumiko was in much the same circumstance, but for different reasons.

"Would that be so bad?" asked Akira.

"Portia could explain it better. Something about cross-pollination ... and population explosion."

"Wish I could visit that grove," Zuzu said wistfully.

"Guess that's not an option. But we can visit you. See? There's the guys!" But he hauled up short and gawked anew. "You live in a *lighthouse*?"

While Akira and Zuzu paused to admire the tower, Fumiko strolled on, hoping for a glimpse of the aforementioned dragon. Beyond the tree and the lighthouse, a thick sea wall forestalled further erosion. Steps led down to a long breakwater, and on the dock at its end, a boat bobbed.

More of their guests were in the process of unloading plain black cases of various sizes. One of the men caught sight of her and turned from the task, a smile on his face. He strolled closer, already presenting his palms. "Hello, there. I'm Ricker Thunderhoof, but everyone calls me Colt."

"Fumiko." His hands were so large. "You're the healer?"

Concern flickered through brown eyes. "Among other things. Do you *need* a healer?"

"Sometimes." This was very confusing. "Usually, they send humans."

"Pardon me, lady." He bent closer and changed his grip to her wrists. But before he could begin any of the healers' rotes, her sister inserted herself between them.

"Horse clan?" Zuzu asked, rubbing her fingertips over the bristling stubble on one side of Colt's head, where the gingery hair had been shaved.

"Yes. I'm Colt." His surprise faded into amusement. "Would you two lovely ladies happen to be sisters?"

Zuzu whirled to wrap her arms around Fumiko. "I *like* him, Sister."

Fumiko did, too. However, she couldn't help holding this newcomer up against Juuyu, who'd made a rather dramatic first impression. "How many are there?"

"Six total. One of our teammates will be coming in later, so it's five for now." Colt shifted into a receptive posture. "If you'll show me the way to our rooms, I'll shift our baggage."

Akira caught up. "I'll help!"

Colt nodded. "Ours are probably too heavy, but your case is in there somewhere."

"Zuzu moves fast!" Akira was all admiration. And acceptance. "Did you ever meet a tree?"

"A few. Enough to understand." Colt offered his palms to Zuzu. "Thank you for allowing us to shelter under your branches."

She was in his arms in an instant, and Fumiko hoped he didn't mind. But he chuckled and went to pat her head, only to hesitate over Zuzu's flowers. Fumiko caught his eye and touched her own shoulder. Colt flashed a grateful smile and gently enfolded Zuzu, who was dwarfed by his larger frame.

"I *like* him," Zuzu repeated with a blissful sigh. "Oh! But where has the dragon gone?"

And just like that, Colt's arms were empty.

Akira jogged after her, calling, "Wait for me! I'll introduce you!"

A slender young man was just pulling himself out of the water and onto the dock. Long green hair and a yellow tunic clinging to pale skin. He waved and called out to Akira in Japanese, but when he spotted Zuzu, he froze.

31

Her embrace only flustered him further.

Akira laughed and said, "English for Fumiko, please."

The green-haired Amaranthine asked, "Tree-twin?"

"Yes." Fumiko thought he might be blushing. "Zuzu is my sister."

"You are very pretty," cooed Zuzu, nuzzling the young male's throat. "And you smell nice."

"Thanks, I guess." And to Fumiko, a tight, "Call her off?"

Fumiko had seen this sort of thing before. "Gently, Zuzu. I think this one is shy about girls."

"I could teach him." Zuzu's smile turned sultry.

"Don't tease," Fumiko scolded. "I think he's your dragon."

She drew back, eyes wide. "Is *that* what this feeling is? Are you a dragon?"

"Sinder Stonecairne of the Icelandic Reach. And yes, I'm from a dragon clan." Rolling his eyes toward Akira, he muttered, "This was easier when the tree was male."

"Oh! Sorry, sorry." Akira gesticulated at Fumiko. "Sinder's a dragon without ... what's the word?"

He tried a few in Japanese, and Sinder looked scandalized. "Did you just call me a gelding?"

Colt's laugh was a friendly sort of nicker. As he passed by, balancing cases, he said, "Celibate is the usual term." He gave it in Japanese, too. "There are no females in the heights, so Sinder isn't used to these small attentions."

Zuzu promised, "I will be gentle."

Sinder wriggled free and dove back into the water, surfacing at a safe distance.

Akira called, "That's perfect! Hey Sinder, Fumiko wanted to see your dragon form."

He ducked under, pulling down a swirl of fanning hair. A moment later, the water swelled, and sparkling scales breeched the surface before vanishing again.

Several yards out, a dragon burst from the water, flipping in midair before diving under again.

"Quite the sight, isn't he?" remarked Colt, who'd returned for more luggage.

Fumiko nodded, then shook her head.

"Is something troubling you?"

There certainly was. This was all so strange. "They really only ever send humans. They *certainly* never send celibates."

"Well ...? I suppose there's a first time for everything," Colt ventured uncertainly. "And look. Here's my good friend. Come along, Hallow. Greet our hostess."

The fifth guest swept up, his cloak rippling just above the weathered boards of the dock. He was easily as pale as Sinder, but his hair was black, and when he bowed over Fumiko's hand, the eyes that lifted to hers were large, thick-lashed, and deeply, darkly red.

"How do you do? My name is Hallow Brunwinger." His aristocratic air was accompanied by a British accent. "Thank you for giving shelter to our little group."

His ears came to points, as did his teeth and nails. All typical of the Amaranthine. But his touch was puzzling. Fumiko remarked, "You feel different."

"I would, I suppose." He passed a long, slender case to Colt, who shouldered it. "Let's have it done, then."

In one smooth motion, he flicked back his cloak and lifted

his arms. A grand gesture that momentarily distracted from the velvety drape of … something. Fumiko dropped to a crouch, her arms around her knees as she tried to understand what she was looking at.

"Wings," he offered blandly. "Or a close approximation. I belong to one of the bat clans, but my father was a reaver. I'm half human."

"I know about crossers," said Zuzu, hand reaching. "Ash Sunfletch is a crosser. He visited us."

"Ah, ah!" Hallow caught her wrist, smiled, and said, "I am *very* ticklish."

Rather than be offput, Zuzu shimmied in delight. "He's good, too, Sister! How will we choose?"

But the matter of choosing was shelved like a book in the Jacaranda Free Library thanks to the arrival of its founder. Fumiko hastily straightened and smoothed at her skirt. Diva wasn't smiling, and that was rare. What had put thunder in her soul?

"Kindred," she called, her deep voice rolling across the water. "If you would gather in, our ward needs to resettle our safeguards."

At that moment, the dragon executed another capering leap.

His splash was met by a low growl. Diva had little tolerance for shenanigans.

"Beg pardon, ladies." Fingers to lips, Colt whistled a piercing note.

Sinder shot to him, changed to speaking form underwater, and accepted Colt's offered hand up. Dripping on the dock, Sinder kept a wary eye on Zuzu. Which was silly. Diva was the one he should be worried about. Her good opinion was more precious than pollen.

"No introductions, no time. I only have a fifteen-minute break, and that's half gone." She gave them each a long, hard look. "Call me Diva. Everyone does. I'm an undisclosed, and I'll be in the library. Portia, they're all yours."

And with that, she stalked away, right past a willowy woman whose tanned face was creased by long life and laughter. Fumiko caught Portia's impish wink and relaxed. Whatever was upsetting Diva, it would pass quickly. Probably as soon as the barriers were reestablished.

Akira sidled up to her. "Is Diva a ... security guard?"

Fumiko replied, "She is our strength. And she is our librarian."

His tone became conspiratorial. "What clan?"

"Bear."

Immediately brightening, Akira said, "Thank goodness! I get along pretty well with bears."

And even though a few of his words were foreign, Fumiko understood. She really must have learned Japanese at some point. She caressed his hair, which was straight and silky.

His gaze turned quizzical. "You act more Amaranthine than human."

"Do you think so?"

"Oh, I *know* so. Do I really remind you of one of your sons?"

"Yes."

"That's kind of cool. I wonder if we're related?"

Fumiko searched his upturned face. "Aren't you from Japan?"

"That's where I grew up. But my family is kinda different. And difficult. You see, my sister and I are orphans." Akira shifted into a receptive posture, accepting her touch, her curiosity. "She remembers our dad, but there's nothing about our mom. And the papers are missing. No pedigree. No genealogy. So who knows? We *could* be distantly related."

"You're an unregistered reaver?"

"Sis is, but not me." His smile turned wistful. "And as far as I know, there's no cure for being ordinary."

This had to be the last straw. An unendowed human? And one who might possibly be her own descendant? Not one of these males was an appropriate candidate for paternity.

But the possibilities they presented were … intriguing.

5

THIS MIGHT BE BAD

Akira had lived with Amaranthine for more than a decade, and he'd long ago adjusted his ideas about personal space and polite distances. Not that it'd been hard. He wasn't especially reserved about touching. But Suuzu craved connections that would have raised eyebrows, especially back in school. Integration had been a new thing, and it was just so hard to explain why Akira let another boy run his fingers through his hair. Or why he was so used to sleeping with Suuzu, it was hard to sleep without him.

So when Fumiko played with Akira's hair, he immediately felt more at ease. This meant good things—acceptance, welcome, even protection. Her familiarity had a familial quality that made it easy to think of her as a big sister. Mentally, he'd already attached that honorific to her name.

Fumiko turned toward the old woman walking their way, and

37

Akira followed her lead. Right down to the respectful posture that promised undivided attention.

"Reaver Portia Groves," the woman declared, including them all with a sweep of sharp green eyes. "I lowered a few of my barriers to let you through. We'll need them back up. Quickly. However, once they are, you'll be in some trouble *unless* the wards are tuned to you."

Juuyu's teammates simply lined up. Like this was standard procedure. One that probably applied to Akira, despite his lack of reaverness.

The woman continued, "I've already swept you and your luggage for foreign particles. All guests need to carry my tuned crystals at all times. I *could* track your every movement, but I won't. If you're concerned about your privacy, pull me aside, and we can chat. On the upside, the crystals satisfy the letter of the law with regard to reaver escorts. While you're here, I'm yours."

Portia distributed bracelets that had been woven with hemp and shells, like those sold in any beachside tourist shop.

"Won't take long," she promised.

Akira knew about tuned crystals. Back in high school, he'd helped pick a pair as a gift for Suuzu. One was knotted into the necklace that Suuzu always wore, and Akira kept its companion on a cord around his ankle. Although the magic of remnant stones was lost on Akira, Suuzu could always tell where he was because the stones were linked.

"You're fast," remarked Colt, admiring his new bracelet.

"Comes with experience," Portia replied blandly.

Sinder said, "You're a ranker. I can tell."

Portia laughed. "I'm long past the age when digits impress. Seventy-five on my last birthday. Semi-retired."

"Go on," the dragon coaxed. "You can tell us."

"May as well have it straight from the horse's mouth. No offense, Colt." Portia calmly revealed, "Once upon a time, I ranked fifth among wards."

"Knew it!" Sinder jerked a thumb at Akira. "He lives with the First of Wards, you know. At Stately House."

"Yes, I recognize Michael's handiwork." When Portia reached Akira, she added, "Michael and I share a branch on ye olde family tree. We're distant cousins, more or less."

"Handiwork? As in sigilcraft?" Sinder was eyeing Akira curiously. "How many ways are you sigiled?"

"Hard to say." Akira laughed and shrugged. "Parting gifts from a protective family."

Everyone at Stately House had invented wishes and blessings, which Argent had then inscribed onto Akira's skin with sigilcraft. They were like *omamori*. As if their words were his armor and their hopes his protection. Some had been serious, some silly.

Make it so people know Uncle Akira is nice.

May your airplane fly good. No crashes.

Don't get lost without Uncle Suuzu to hold your hand.

No mean people. No bad guys.

Akira wasn't sure what Argent actually drew on him, but the kids were impressed, promising that there were glowing patterns decorating his skin.

"They won't last more than a week or two," Michael had later assured. "And Argent was careful with his placement. You shouldn't draw any attention. But we'd like to add something more permanent. If you're willing."

A tattoo.

Jacques was proud to show off his collection. Michael also had three. Ginkgo even had one. And their purposes varied as much as their patterns, acting like keys, alarms, shields, or pathways.

"What would mine do?"

Argent said, "I want to know where you are, and I want to be able to reach your dreams. Also, if you spend enough time in the close company of Amaranthine, you *may* begin to notice things."

Jacques lifted a hand. "Mine let me see Ephemera."

It was such a small, useless benefit, but Akira wanted it. And the connection it promised. "Yes, please."

Which brought them to a discussion of placement, made embarrassing thanks to Jacques' asides. He could be *so* inappropriate.

Ever since Akira met his self-proclaimed uncle, Jacques Smythe had been sauntering into as many private moments as he could find. Probably to tease Suuzu. With excuses in the form of tea trays or messages that could have been texted, Uncle Jackie would interrupt baths, preening sessions, and every attempt to sleep in.

Not because he was being malicious. Far from it.

He thought they were cute.

Which is why Jacques had been able to suggest the perfect spot for Akira to take a mark. How many times had he found them nested together? Akira curled on his side, Suuzu's arms wrapped around him from behind, his nose pressed into the crook of Akira's neck.

"Just here," said Jacques, resting his fingertips on the spot where Suuzu's lips always pressed.

An unobtrusively intimate place.

Akira wondered how Suuzu would react when he found the spot permanently marked with the pattern of a curling phoenix feather.

"Give me a hand?" interrupted Sinder.

Twisting the new bracelet knotted at his wrist, Akira hurried to the small mountain of cases that still needed to be moved. "Are these all yours?"

"Hardly!" Sinder showed him the color-coded tags. "Colt will be setting up a lab in his room. Hallow does the war room thing, with maps and blueprints and case files. My tech does a whole range of things. Information gathering, long-distance monitoring, and team communications."

They lugged baggage toward the lighthouse that was almost lost among Zuzu's leaves. Her tree was easily as big as the ones Akira had first seen at the Farroost colony. All dark bark and teal leaves, with fragrant purple flowers tucked amidst the greenery.

When they caught up to Portia, who was walking with Hallow, she was explaining, "This section is our guesthouse. As you'll soon see, there's a central common area and four bedrooms."

"You don't live here?" asked Colt.

"No, no. My room is over the flower shop. And the interns live above the library. But we all gather for meals at Fumiko's." She indicated the lighthouse's tower. "We expect you to join us, if your schedule allows."

Akira was just going to ask about Fumiko when she came toward them from the direction of the gate, her arms full of packages. "I'll just ... drop these off. Please, make yourselves at home."

Portia excused herself.

41

It was just the team.

Colt went through first and stopped short, which caused Hallow to bang into him.

"What's the deal?" called Sinder.

That got things moving again, and they filed into a room crammed with stuff.

Given their location, Akira wasn't surprised to pick out fishing gear and life preservers, an inflatable raft, surfboard, and a tangled heap of goggles. But there were also innumerable cardboard boxes, their flaps splayed open to display a haphazard jumble of women's shoes, badminton rackets, and whirligigs. Flat things were stacked precariously high: communiques, magazines, boxes of jigsaw puzzles, and canvases.

It was like walking into one of those games where you had to find hidden items. Akira was tempted to snap a picture for Suuzu and include a list—sewing machine, perambulator, trombone, barbershop pole, highchair, croquet mallet. He wouldn't, of course. Suuzu *hated* those kinds of games. They were so messy, they made him tense.

Akira heard Hallow whisper, "Maker have mercy."

They slowly fanned out, cautious as if this were a minefield.

Abandoning his suitcase at the door, Akira skirted an easel and a rocking horse to check behind a door that had been painted lavender. It *was* a bedroom. Technically. "Same in here," he reported. In truth, it was worse.

Sinder muttered, "It's a good thing Juuyu's not with us."

Exactly what Akira had been thinking. "Let me check the others."

Four bedrooms in all. And a fifth door that led to some rather rustic amenities. The toilet was tucked into a niche, but the rest wasn't. "Outdoor shower," he reported.

"What's our plan?" murmured Colt.

Before anyone could formulate an answer, Fumiko returned.

Hallow stepped lightly through the chaos to reach her side. "Would you mind if we … rearranged a bit? To make room for our equipment?"

"I suppose," she said. "If you're careful."

"Nothing will be damaged. I promise." Hallow raised a hand. "Also, I fear we are one room short for our needs. I think, perhaps, we should send Juuyu to a hotel."

Fumiko hesitated. "There are five of you?"

"Six," reminded Colt. "One of our team members is coming later. Hallow and I are used to sharing, but … I agree. Juuyu should find other accommodations."

Sinder quietly pointed out, "He'll insist on keeping Akira with him."

Disappointment flashed through Akira. He liked these sisters. Wanted to explore this neighborhood. But he knew that Juuyu wouldn't be able to relax here.

"I have another room," Fumiko slowly offered. "The one below mine is empty."

Akira thought she looked hesitant. "We don't want to impose."

Popping out of the last of the bedrooms, Sinder briskly said, "If you can make it work, make it work. Hisoka wouldn't approve of us splitting up. We're *meant* to stay here."

"Go on, Akira," said Colt. "Check the additional room. We'll get a start here."

43

So he offered Fumiko his hands. "Show me?"

"Where's Zuzu?" asked Akira.

Fumiko led him to the lighthouse tower's wide front door, but she paused to wave a hand. "Here. All around us."

Which might apply to a sizeable section of the neighborhood, given the spread of root and branch. "I meant her speaking form. Does she live with you?"

"Sometimes."

Fumiko ushered him into a large, circular room ringed by tall, narrow windows. Before them was a long, narrow table flanked by benches and stools. There was a sink, appliances, and some blocky cupboards. Baskets held fresh produce. Canning jars, platters, and crocks lined two long shelves with decorative guard rails.

"Our gathering room. This is where we share meals. And talk." Fumiko wove past an empty birdcage and a stack of coffee table books as tall as she was.

Mismatched furniture had been pulled into a rough circle around a low table dominated by a vase of fresh flowers and several candlestands. Akira thought the space was cheerful. Yes, it was crowded, but it was clean. However, as he bypassed a rolling cart stacked with dozens of coffee cups, he couldn't deny that this didn't bode well for Juuyu.

Fumiko climbed a staircase broken into short flights. "Four floors. Five, if you count the gallery at the top."

Akira paused at each window to check the view, but he had to mind where he put his feet. Things had been stacked along either side of the steps. Mostly books and boxes, but he spied a soup tureen and a gramophone. He couldn't discern any rhyme or reason to the accumulation—roller skates, dog collars, terra cotta figures.

On the third level, past a bamboo screen, which appeared to be the only nod to privacy, was another roughly circular room. "Doors?" he asked, surprised to find double doors set into the thick stone walls.

"A balcony." Pushing aside a box of holiday decorations, she swung the doors wide. "We added it a while ago. It makes things easier for the interns."

He stepped into dappled sunlight. To the right, he could see sunlight on water. "Facing south," he murmured in Japanese.

"I'll tell Antigone you're here." Fumiko indicated another balcony above, half-hidden by the tower's curve. "During your stay, she can use my room for observation."

"Observation," he repeated, peering up into Zuzu's swaying limbs. That was a kind of studying. "What does she watch from here?"

Fumiko gave him a puzzled look that slowly softened into pity. "You're not a reaver," she repeated, nodding to herself. "Antigone is a preservationist, but her specialty is Ephemera."

"Oh! Yeah. I've heard a lot about them. Do you get pretty ones here?"

"They're certainly amusing." She cast a final look into the air, then stepped back inside. "Will this work for you and ...?"

"Juuyu." Akira made a slow turn. Fumiko had called the room

empty. Maybe it was empty of people, but it wasn't empty of stuff. Still, it wasn't nearly as crowded as the guesthouse had been. He was mentally rearranging when Fumiko spoke again.

"We usually only use this room after I choose."

Something in her manner tipped him off that this was embarrassing somehow. He reviewed her words, trying to decide if he'd missed some American euphemism. All the words seemed safe on the surface, so he asked, "What do you choose?"

"There has to be a father for me to fulfill my contract."

Akira glanced around more carefully. "Are you saying this is your husband's room?"

"Sometimes."

She was looking for a husband? Akira slowly raised both hands. "Not me?"

"No." Fumiko smiled and shook her head. "I offer this room in friendship."

"Friends." Hoping his posture would help convey his meaning, he went for a flat-out helpless stance. "Could I ask questions? They might be clumsy or rude, and I don't want to offend you."

"I'll hear you out."

"First. Will it bother you if I'm in this room with Juuyu?" Rearranging his question, he asked, "Is this too close, too private?"

Fumiko crossed to the bed and sat on its velvety green coverlet. "I want you to stay."

When she beckoned, Akira perched next to her on the edge of the mattress, half-turned so he could see her face. "I want to stay. Your home is amazing. But my friend likes things ... simple."

She nodded, but he could tell he wasn't getting through.

46

"For Juuyu to be comfortable, I'll need to move things around. Or … out. He likes an empty room."

"That's sad."

"Not really." Akira fell back on postures to set the tone. "He'll think it's peaceful. Quieter without so many details."

Fumiko didn't make him ask again. "You may move things. I don't want you to go."

He took her hand and squeezed it. "We'll stay. Juuyu and I will be right here."

6

MEMORY LANE

umiko offered to let their guests know about dinner, mostly so she could check on their progress. It wasn't that she didn't trust them. Every Amaranthine she'd ever met had been courteous to a fault, and they never took their promises lightly. But her things were a part of her. They triggered memories and daydreams and long conversations with Zuzu. Having someone else touching them was unsettling.

The guesthouse door stood open, so she walked in ... and wavered.

She couldn't have been absent for more than forty minutes. An hour at most. Yet the central room had been cleared. "Where is everything?" she exclaimed.

Colt immediately set down the black case in his arms and crossed to her side. "We've been moving things. You said we could ...?"

Concern shone in his eyes, and the touch to her shoulder was gentle. "I'll show you."

Fumiko nodded.

To her surprise, Colt took her hand and led her like a child. He would get on well with Antigone—the hippie and the healer. Both prone to coddling.

"Your things are in here. It's not as organized as some might like, but nothing's been harmed." They'd packed the first bedroom on the right with her things, all the way up to the ceiling in the far corner. He promised, "We can put everything back before we go."

She nodded. Then shook her head. Then nodded again.

Colt seemed to think she needed a tour. "We'll use this central area as a meeting room. Hallow and I will share the room at that corner."

The door he indicated was thickly daubed with paint, all in purple hues. Peering around the echoing room, memories flooded back. She'd painted the four doors herself—whelk and wisteria, jade and cerulean. This had been her studio for a while.

Although the memories were fuzzy at the edges, they were sun-drenched and happy ones. From one of those times when the father hadn't immediately left, and she'd known a husband's love. The mares had stayed on, and there had been six children. Every room full to bursting with life and laughter.

Soren.

Yes, she'd loved a man called Soren. Tall and blond and tanned, with sparkling blue eyes and a bristling beard. Zuzu had loved tucking flowers into it, and he'd laughed and let her. How long ago, now? The time before last? Surely no more than three centuries.

49

He hadn't wanted to fade before her eyes, so he'd gone away in order to mentor their grandchildren. Soren, who was an accomplished ward.

But he'd returned, bringing back a trove of stories and souvenirs. And they'd convinced him to stay. She and Zuzu had held him at the end. To his very last breath.

"Fumiko?" Colt touched her face. "Fumiko, you're crying."

"Soren," she whispered. "His years were gone too soon."

He cautiously asked, "Do you have good memories?"

"Sometimes."

"Then you'll be fine, Fumiko." Colt's smile was sad. "You're very brave."

Brushing at her cheeks, she clung to a different fragment of memory. One of Soren's grandchildren—her grandson—had been an artist. If she could find it, there was a portfolio. Full of lovely drawings of Ephemera. Maybe Zuzu would remember where it was? Fumiko wanted to show it to Akira.

Colt drew her across the room to the green door. "Sinder's setting up his equipment in here. We'll ward his generator so the noise doesn't bother anyone."

Fumiko was familiar with computers. Ever since the Emergence, she'd been borrowing those at the library. Mostly for shopping. Sinder's equipment was on a much larger scale. Absorbed in assembling the various boxes and cords spilling from foam-lined cases, he didn't notice them at first. When he did, he pulled off headphones and asked, "Problem?"

"Dinner." She'd almost forgot her reason for coming. "In an hour, more or less."

"Great! I'm starved." He snapped his fingers and added, "If you guys like fish, I can bring in as many as you need."

Promising to pass that along to Antigone, they left him to his work.

Colt continued his tour. "And this last room is reserved for our missing member. He'll be coming in tired, so he'll be needing a den."

Fumiko hoped he didn't mean another bear. Diva wouldn't like that.

Perhaps he read the worry on her face. "Wolf clan. And in desperate need of a long rest. He'll probably sleep a week, if not two."

"I've met wolves before. Many times. They've been kind to us." Fumiko wondered if an old friend might be returning. "Which pack?"

"He's an Ambervelte."

She shook her head and nodded. "The last wolves were Elderboughs."

"Yes, they've been everywhere lately."

They paused to watch Hallow and Sinder maneuver a ping-pong table into the center of the emptied room. Rapping its surface with his knuckle, Sinder said, "Welcome to mission headquarters!"

Hallow surveyed the space. "Juuyu will want a clock. Anyone remember seeing one?"

"I do!" Sinder darted into the room they'd packed tight. He returned moments later with a flat box. "Check it out!"

Lifting the lid, he revealed a whimsical wall clock, all bevels and prisms and mirrors.

"Fancy," murmured Hallow. "No wonder it caught your eye."

Colt chuckled. "Dragons like a bit of shine."

"I've seen clocks like these before. It's like a music box, right Fumiko?"

"Yes." One of Soren's precious souvenirs. "I think the craftsman was a dragon."

"I think so, too." Sinder tinkered with its innerworkings and soon had the clockworks spinning. Nudging the hands to the top of the hour, he grinned widely when the decorations on the clock face unfurled like flowers and danced in time to a chiming tune.

Fumiko had forgotten how charming it was. They'd made a game of guessing which of its many melodies would play.

Soren had considered it an object lesson. Proof that the passage of time could bring pleasant surprises. She'd believed it for as long as he was with her, but after *his* passing, she'd packed the clock away. It's gentle music only reminded her that he was no longer there, humming along.

But the pain had been fresher then.

The memories were welcome, now.

The clock could be something she treasured, even as she'd been treasured.

"Fumiko?" It was Hallow this time, proffering a handkerchief. "Should we put it back where we found it?"

Drawing herself up and trying for a smile, she said, "I like reminders when they're nice. Leave it out. Let it play. Maybe remembering one good choice will lead to another."

7

HAPHAZARD AT BEST

Akira excused himself from dinner early. The people who lived under Zuzu's branches were a cheerful, chatty bunch. With the possible exception of Diva, who spent a lot of time dishing out quelling looks. But Akira was having trouble following the conversations. Probably jet lag setting in. And he'd barely started fixing up his room.

"I need to finish unpacking," he murmured to Sinder.

The dragon leaned close. "Need help?"

"You've got work, yeah?"

"More than usual. But I'm guessing you have your own challenges?"

"Understatement."

"Juuyu won't be happy if either of us slacks off." Sinder glanced furtively around the room. "Do your best. Holler if you need heavy lifting."

With abundant thanks to all assembled, Akira padded stocking-footed up the stairs, mentally rolling up his sleeves. "What would Suuzu do?" he muttered under his breath.

And since he really needed to know, Akira stood back, snapped a picture, and texted it.

What would you do?

Where are you?

This is the room I'll be sharing with Juuyu

The phone rang in his hand.

"Hey," he said wearily.

"Is my brother there?"

"Nope. He's at a meeting. I have two, maybe three hours to save his sanity."

Suuzu warbled worriedly.

"I know, I know. Can't really stop to explain." Akira softly added, "But I'd welcome some advice. Like where to start."

"Show me the room. I will endeavor to help."

Akira sent snapshots, and Suuzu devised a plan of attack.

"I wish I was there."

"No way," retorted Akira. "This would stress you out."

"I do wish it." Suuzu's tone went all stiff and stubborn.

"How long before you can get away?"

"There are many variables. Two weeks. Perhaps three. Argent is back, and he has no patience for quibbling."

"He's back? From where?"

"I could not say. We have done little more than exchange nods across chambers."

"Maybe he's giving you time to cool down," teased Akira. "Since he approved this trip."

Suuzu sighed. *"I am not angry."*

"Yes, you are."

"A little," he conceded.

"I'm sorry."

"You regret the trip?"

"Nooo." Akira laughed weakly. "But I don't like for you to worry."

"You are safe and well, and you have been kind enough to remind me of this at regular intervals." In conciliatory tones, Suuzu added, *"The pictures are welcome."*

"I'll keep sending them. Just like always."

"Good. Now, will you tell me about your day?"

"Can I put you on speaker? We can talk while I start rearranging."

Akira cleared the section of floor nearest the balcony doors, then dragged the mattress off the bed and arranged it in the center. Next, he used boxes—and other easily-stacked items—to make a wall. There was no way he could put everything away. So Suuzu had suggested hiding it. Finding blankets in the closet, Akira draped everything he could and stepped back to survey his handiwork.

Bare floor. Balcony. Bed.

If you didn't look too closely, it might work. Akira snapped pictures and sent them along. "I think it's gonna have to be good enough. For tonight."

"It is much improved," Suuzu said diplomatically.

"There isn't room for him to take truest form."

"Even so, Brother promised to watch over your sleep in my stead."

"He's as good as his word. You know that."

"I seem to need reminding." Melancholy was creeping back into Suuzu's tone.

"Can do. So! Is there anything you can tell me about your day?"

"Very little of interest." Suuzu's tone shifted, and he added, *"Isla seems unhappy."*

"She's there?"

"In Hisoka's place. She often speaks on his behalf, since she is his apprentice."

"What's got her down?"

"She has not confided in me."

"Best guess?" Amaranthine were perceptive in many ways, and Suuzu knew Isla quite well.

"I believe she is frustrated by the current necessity. Isla speaks for Hisoka in order to ease his burden."

Akira knew that much. "It must be a big help, having her fill in for him."

"She is as capable as ever."

"But ...?"

"Perhaps I see it more because I sympathize with her plight. The person Isla most wants to see is always somewhere else."

Night had fallen, and the shops along Mainsail were closed. However, people gathered at restaurants with big screen sportscasts or patios strung with lights. Juuyu noted salt-rimmed margaritas in a whole range of pastels. Buffalo wings and beer. Carne asada and fish tacos.

An ice cream shop had a line half a block long, and in passing, Juuyu inadvertently memorized all twenty-six flavors, as well as the posted specials at a tiny sushi shop that Sinder might like.

Once Juuyu realized he was collecting the names of every beach cottage, he shut his eyes. When working, it could be difficult to stop. And at a time like this, the last thing he needed was extraneous details.

Candor pulled up in front of Jacaranda Circle, which was hushed and seemingly empty. But Sinder stepped out of the shadows, ready to usher him past the barrier.

"Tuned crystals?"

"Only the finest! Here's your temporary pass, since their ward turns in early."

Pocketing a sigil-laced stone, Juuyu grimly relayed, "There has been a development. Where is Hallow set up?"

"Main room of the guesthouse. Which you need to ward, by the way."

"Why?"

Sinder hunched his shoulders and mumbled, "You can ward against trees, right?"

Juuyu simply patted his partner's back. He knew several ways to politely dissuade Zuzu from manifesting inside the guesthouse. "There have been signs of tampering at the museum."

"That was quick."

"I am sending Hallow over tonight."

"And Colt?"

"No. He will take a daylight shift. With you."

Inside the guesthouse, Juuyu peered suspiciously at a door with a handwritten sign taped to it. "Why is that room forbidden."

"Just a storeroom."

Sinder might have been more convincing if Juuyu wasn't immune to a dragon's sway.

His partner added, "You really don't want to know."

Sinder and Hallow gave reports while Juuyu systematically worked his way through the house, warding walls and windows. The task was familiar enough to be relaxing, especially with the steady roll of surf to soothe him.

He checked his pocket watch against the clock on the wall. "That timepiece is twenty seconds slow."

Sinder sighed, but he synchronized them.

Only then did Juuyu register that it was nearly two in the morning. "I have been remiss. Akira will be asleep by now."

"He waited up. Colt's keeping him company," reported Hallow.

"See you for sparring in the morning?" checked Sinder.

"Only if Akira rises early enough." Juuyu would not be stinting in his responsibilities to a nestmate. "He will be travel weary."

"You're looking a little strained yourself." Sinder narrowed his eyes. "How many wards did you have to set up at the museum?"

"Enough to assure that I can rest easy tonight."

"I'll be off." Hallow touched Juuyu's shoulder in passing. "Unless you want tending?"

Juuyu declined.

Sinder scowled.

"I *will* rest," he assured.

The dragon's expression softened. "Umm ... do as Colt says, okay? It's for your own good."

Undoubtedly, Sinder had just said more than he was supposed to—as usual. The tip-off was well-meant but worrisome. Juuyu wondered if he was about to face Colt the healer ... or Colt the swordsman.

8

HOOD THE HAWK

Juuyu found Akira and Colt sitting on the wide steps leading to the lighthouse's front door.

Akira bounced to his feet to deliver his, "Welcome back."

"I have returned," Juuyu offered. "I apologize for the lateness of the hour."

"It's okay. Couldn't sleep. Too tired. Kinda wired. Kinda worried." He always laughed so easily, even at himself. "Pretty sure Colt has been dosing me."

With a low nicker, Colt said, "Herbal tea. Nothing more."

Juuyu plucked the most important element from Akira's list. "What has you worried?"

"You."

That startled him. "This job is not inherently dangerous."

Akira bit his lip. "Do you trust me?"

"I do."

60

"Okay, so ... I did what I could tonight. And I'll do more tomorrow. Maybe the next day, too, to be honest." Ruffling his hair, Akira revealed, "I had a long talk with Suuzu tonight, and Colt agrees it's best if you get into our room through the window."

Juuyu shot a look at Colt, who radiated sympathy.

Nothing seemed to be amiss. Except the young man's hair. Stroking it back into place and touching his cheek, Juuyu quietly asked, "Akira, what is wrong?"

Leaning into his touch, Akira closed his eyes. "Inside is a little ... cluttered."

Was that all?

But the young man's shoulders hunched. "More like *a lot* cluttered."

Colt lifted a strip of cloth and calmly said, "I prescribe a blindfold."

"That bad?" Juuyu managed.

"Trust us." Colt carefully covered Juuyu's eyes, knotting the cloth.

"Meet you upstairs," Akira hastily promised.

The front door shut, and Juuyu murmured, "Is this truly necessary?"

"Yes."

Juuyu warbled a weary note. "You will have to guide me."

"Oh, I'll just carry you." Colt scooped him up and soon chided, "Juuyu, your condition! Why are you so depleted?"

Leaning into the horse clansman's sturdy presence, he admitted, "I have been warding for hours. The thief may already be here."

"Then our trip is not wasted."

Juuyu hummed. "Were there no other volunteers for this room?"

"You were voted least likely to fluster if a voluptuous tree turned up in your bed." More seriously, Colt added, "I think the lady took a liking to Akira. And to you."

They were rising slowly, probably to give Akira time to reach their destination first. Juuyu tipped his head back, listening to the faint rustle of leaves.

"Here we are," said Colt. "There's a small balcony."

"I'm here." Akira was tense, breathless. His hand found Juuyu's before Colt released him.

"Get the boy to relax," ordered Colt. "He needs it more than he realizes."

And then it was just the two of them.

"Suuzu helped me tidy up." Akira rattled on about the phone call longer than necessary.

Finally, Juuyu interrupted. "May I remove my blindfold?"

"Mmm ... maybe not. I didn't do *that* good of a job."

"Then I shall need a valet."

Juuyu listened closely as Akira unpacked the loose pants and short robe he used for night clothes and passed them along. For a while there was only the rustle of cloth. Akira seemed to be changing, too, though he paused to take each article of clothing from Juuyu.

"There should be a hanger."

"I remember how you do it," Akira promised. "Suuzu likes it the same way."

Juuyu supposed there was little choice but to trust his valet.

"There isn't room for you to take truest form."

"Then you shall have to do without feathers." Juuyu submitted to the sort of tucking in one might give a nestling, mostly amused. And more grateful than he liked to admit. As Colt had said, it was too soon for him to be needing sleep. "I will watch over your rest."

"Thanks." Akira wriggled close. "Guess I'm a tiny bit homesick, after all."

"A nestmate is here."

Soft as a sigh, Akira admitted, "I miss him."

"Be sure to tell him."

They'd skipped over the rituals Juuyu knew his younger brother observed—bathing and preening. Patting Akira's head, he repeated, "A nestmate is here."

"Tell me a story?"

He sounded half asleep already. Understandable, given their day and the hour. So instead of embarking upon a traditional tale, Juuyu chose something trivial. "There is an ice cream shop on the main road that appears to be popular."

Slowly, deliberately, Juuyu recited the flavors, but before he could divulge all twenty-six, Akira was asleep. Lapsing into silence, he let his thoughts drift as he stroked the young man's hair.

But then the mattress dipped. Leaves rustled closer, and the fragrance of flowers intensified. Lips brushed his cheek.

"Good evening, Zuzu."

"Why are you blindfolded?"

"Akira thinks it will help me relax." Juuyu suspected it was true, making him little better than a hooded hawk.

Zuzu softly asked, "What else?"

"Hmm?"

"Sister likes ice cream. You stopped before I could hear all the flavors."

"I am certain the shop is within range. She could go and see for herself."

She said, "Sister never goes."

That hardly seemed necessary, but he knew nothing of this enclave's history or traditions. So he asked, "Where did I leave off?"

"Pumpkin mousse."

Calmly, Juuyu completed his recitation. "Lemon Mascarpone. Bubble Gummy Bear. Pretzel Sundae. Almond Amoretto. And Honey Thai, which is their flavor of the month."

Zuzu petted his hair, twining her fingers through long curls. "Your healer said you are depleted."

"I am."

"You need tending."

Juuyu said, "Do not trouble yourself," but she was already gone.

Moments later, the rustle and scuff of slippers came from the opposite direction of the window, as well as the low murmur of sisters in conference.

"Softly, Sister. Do not wake the boy."

This time, when the mattress dipped, Fumiko spoke. "You promised us a song."

"I apologize. Perhaps another night?"

She hesitated, then whispered, "You look different."

"Hmm?"

Fingers tugged at the loose knot, and his blindfold fell away, revealing his hostesses awash in candlelight. Fumiko had a hand pressed to her heart, and her eyes were wide.

Ah. His disguise was gone.

Offering a palm, he greeted her with as much formality as his position allowed. "Juuyu Farroost, phoenix clan."

Fumiko bypassed his hand in order to touch his cheek.

Instinct stirred like appetite. Only natural, given the nearness of so much power when he was at low ebb.

"I'll tend you now."

With practiced restraint, he confined himself to courtesy. "I would be grateful."

But she threw him off by sliding into the bed.

Zuzu whispered, "Is he not beautiful?"

"Very." Fumiko crowded against Juuyu's side, mirroring Akira's position. "They never ask me, you know. So I'm probably not very good."

Juuyu's instincts cried a warning. "You are untrained?"

"Probably."

"I know what to do," said Zuzu. "We'll tend you together."

Before he could protest, the first ripple of power lapped against his soul.

9

SHORING UP

Juuyu had never been tended by a tree-kin before.

His colony was intentionally isolated, and his clan's lives intertwined in intimate ways with those of the trees in their grove. The vast majority of their tree-kin were phoenixes. Only a few of the newest trees—part of a fairly recent scattering—were twinned to humans, and Juuyu hadn't mingled with them. At that time, he'd been preoccupied with his training and with raising Suuzu.

"Too much?" Zuzu checked, sounding far less frivolous than usual.

"Not at all." He cleared his throat and repeated, "You *are* untrained, Fumiko?"

She hummed an affirmative. "It works out, though. Zuzu understands my soul better than I do."

"How can that be?"

"I am hers, and she is mine." Zuzu's tone was decidedly smug. "All I have is hers."

66

"So that is how it is." He'd seen this sort of doting back home. "You add to her luster, year upon year. She is your pearl."

Zuzu's low laugh was pure delight. "I am beautiful. My sister should be beautiful, too."

Juuyu didn't know how long these sisters had been here. That detail hadn't been included in his briefing. How many years had Zuzu been adorning her sister's soul? Long enough for her to rival the stars.

"Not only that," interjected Fumiko. "For a long time, Zuzu hid me."

That piqued his interest. "In what manner?"

"Just ... hiding."

Zuzu solemnly said, "Amaranthine were greedy for her soul, and humans were greedy for mine. This was before the kindness of tending."

Juuyu turned his head in order to meet the tree's gaze. "That long ago?"

With a coy smile, Zuzu allowed a fresh swirl of power to buffet him. More this time.

"Slowly," he warned. "I am not used to so much at once."

Fumiko added a soft, "Behave, Zuzu. He's a guest."

"Duty can be a delight, and delight can be shared." Zuzu's attention switched to her sister. "I *like* this one."

"Then show him the kindness of tending," directed Fumiko. "I don't remember trying this with anyone but you."

That sent a warning note through Juuyu's soul. "You are untrained. Are you also ... untried?"

"I couldn't say for certain," Fumiko said wistfully. "But I think I would remember something like this."

Juuyu tried to calm himself. Tried to remember his first taste. "I will exercise restraint."

"Why?" she asked. "I'm used to it. I have Zuzu."

"While I am certain I cannot overwhelm you, I have no wish to impose."

"He's shy," interjected Zuzu.

"Oh. Like that dragon?" Fumiko patted his chest. "That's okay. There's no hurry. We both have the years to be patient. That's nice, for a change."

Juuyu was no longer certain they were talking about the same thing.

Fumiko softly added, "Portia probably wouldn't approve. Of the tending, I mean. So we should keep this our little secret."

Before Juuyu could formulate an answer, Akira promised, "I won't tell."

Fumiko propped up on an elbow. "We woke you? I'm sorry, Remi."

His expression was soft in the candlelight. "I'm not Remi. I'm your new friend Akira."

"Whoops, I *knew* that. I'm sometimes forgetful." She felt silly, but it was a small mistake.

Juuyu warbled, which was fascinating. Very birdlike. Fumiko wasn't sure exactly what the notes meant, but Akira looked chastised. Were they being scolded?

"Humans need sleep," Juuyu said sternly. "That includes tree-kin."

"True." Fumiko rested her head on his shoulder and murmured, "But this is *interesting*."

Akira asked, "You need tending, Juuyu?"

"I do."

"Why does that have to be a secret?"

"Fumiko is a beacon."

"Oooh, I get it." Akira's expression was so easy to read, and he was concerned now. "You could spoil him for life if you don't take it slow. Plus, he's here to do an important job. So it'd be bad if your tending left him tipsy."

She caught the gist, but he was talking fast in Japanese.

Juuyu interrupted him by threading his fingers into his hair and clicking his tongue. As he offered an English translation, Akira grew increasingly sheepish.

"Sorry, Fumiko. I am sometimes forgetful, too."

"It's fine," she assured. But she wasn't sure that was true. Not when Juuyu continued to toy with Akira's hair, then pressed the boy's head to his shoulder. Welcoming him close, even as he subtly kept Fumiko at a distance.

Was it shyness? Or ... distaste?

Zuzu's low laugh eased most of Fumiko's fears. This wasn't only interesting. It was *fun*. Like bedding down with the children in tapestry tents on the beach. Or stringing hammocks into the treetops. Those had been good times. She missed them. Wanted more like them.

Fingers lightly drummed her shoulder. "Do you understand?" asked Juuyu.

She must have missed something. "I'm sorry?"

"Are you content to stay?"

"I want to," she quickly assured. "I like you."

A faint smile. Another birdish warble.

How did he manage that sound? Fumiko tried shaping her mouth the way he had, but she wasn't sure how to flutter her tongue.

"Fumiko?"

She blinked back to attention.

Juuyu patiently said, "Zuzu will shutter your soul for my sake, but we will still be connected. I will endeavor not to intrude."

"All right," she said. Although she didn't really understand what to expect. They really *didn't* let her tend.

She'd always sort of assumed it was because they had more than enough reavers compared to Amaranthine. Or that nobody wanted to trouble Zuzu, who was protective of their bond. Was it actually that Fumiko's tending would do more harm than good?

"*Will* it be all right?" she asked.

"All will be well." He pressed her head to his shoulder. "Close your eyes and find me."

"You're right here," Fumiko pointed out, amused.

Juuyu's next words came quietly. "I think you will find I am even closer."

She let her eyes fall shut and stiffened in surprise. When touching Juuyu, she was certainly aware of him as an Amaranthine, but all the details were fuzzy. Like a memory that danced just out of reach. But now, everything was crisp and current and unnervingly close.

"Peace, sister to bowers and kindred to stars." Juuyu's voice was pitched to soothe. "You have nothing to fear from me. I am the beggar at your door, asking for crumbs."

"This is tending?"

He hummed. "This is trust. I will take nothing until I first gain yours."

Fumiko tried to make sense of what she was feeling. "It's a little like having another twin."

"Is that so?"

"No one else knows what Zuzu knows. But now you're both here."

Whenever Fumiko closed her eyes, Zuzu was in her periphery. A luminous constant. Her best-loved companion. Juuyu felt entirely different. A billowing darkness. An unknown danger. Her heart was skipping, for on some level, her soul recognized him as a threat.

"Peace," Juuyu repeated, and he seemed to move away.

"Where are you going?" Fumiko caught at his clothes and pulled.

"I have learned to lessen my presence." He lightly touched her shoulder. "You seemed alarmed."

Zuzu interjected, "You are old and vast and hungry."

To Fumiko's surprise, Juuyu chuckled.

He said, "Trees always think people are hungry."

It was so true, Fumiko smiled. And just like that, she calmed. Yes, this Amaranthine was strong enough to cause terrible harm. But Zuzu was just as dangerous, if not more so.

"Don't lessen yourself," she said, tapping his chest. "How can I get used to you if you hide from me?"

"You will trust me?" he checked.

"Yes."

"Then sleep," he urged. "Leave the rest to me and Zuzu."

Her sister giggled. "Rhymes with Juuyu."

"So it does," he said mildly.

Akira mumbled his goodnight and burrowed into his pillow. Zuzu rustled over to his side of the bed and spread another blanket over him, earning a sleepy smile.

"Sleep, Fumiko," Juuyu repeated.

So she tried to relax. This time, she was more prepared for the brooding presence awaiting the crumbs that Zuzu would scatter.

He didn't hide from her, but neither did he reach for her. *Old and vast.* That's what Zuzu had said. "*Are* you old?" she murmured.

"Compared to some."

"Compared to me?"

Juuyu hummed. "I am not sure which of us has the years. Do your people keep records?"

"Sometimes."

"You have no chronicler?"

"Diva might know. She's the librarian."

"If you wish, I will look into the matter."

The phrase tugged at her memory. Something about wishes. Someone who wanted to grant every one of them. Fumiko wasn't sure who it had been. Only that it was a good memory.

Juuyu's quick intake of air preceded a cautious, "Fumiko?"

"I hope you're older."

"It is possible." His tone matched the mood of the soul he'd bared. Polite restraint. Baffled curiosity. "Does it matter?"

"It never mattered before." She peeped up at his profile in the candlelight. "I wonder what changed?"

"Has something changed?"

"Yes. Everything's different this time." She closed her eyes and basked in the secretive thrill of finding another in the darkness. "I might be happy."

10

FIRE TO THE PHOENIX

Juuyu wasn't sure what to make of the woman at his side. Beacon bright, yet not much of a reaver. She clung like a tree, nestled like an Amaranthine, and seemed intrigued by novelties. Her attention often drifted, and her remarks took strange leaps, as if she were carrying on a slightly different conversation. But Fumiko wasn't part of his investigation, and people weren't his expertise. Better to leave her to Akira and Sinder.

After tonight.

Definitely tomorrow.

Because her generosity was more than a match for his unanticipated need.

Regular as the clockworks in his pocket watch, Juuyu submitted to a reaver's tending whenever he was due for a long sleep. It only made sense to optimize the time that would pass while he was deep, so he let Colt arrange the sessions, usually with one of his acquaintances.

Pleasant. Fortifying.

They put him right to sleep.

Not tonight.

Because Fumiko's soul was rare and untamed.

Perilous. Invigorating.

Some might say he was playing with fire. But wasn't he a phoenix?

Easing onto his side so that he and Akira were back-to-back, Juuyu settled Fumiko more comfortably in his arms.

"She is sleeping," murmured Zuzu. "How did you do that?"

"Hmm?"

"I sing for hours. Or tell stories half the night, and still, she cannot find her way into dreams."

He frowned. "That is not typical."

"I wondered." Zuzu's leaves rustled closer. "She doesn't like it when the interns pry, but there's no one else. I was still small when the others fell, so I don't remember how it's supposed to be."

Juuyu's heartstrings plucked, but he hesitated to meddle. *This* wasn't his job. Yet he found himself asking, "Are you concerned? You know your sister better than any."

"Let me show you."

Fox dreams were famous, the mythical trickster's tool for entrapping the unwary. Few recalled that they'd learned their technique from trees, who used a combination of sweet scents and soft dreams to seduce passersby.

As a child, Juuyu had lingered often in the luminous dreamscapes that Letik created. Zuzu's presence was similar, but her style was different. Trusting her to guide him to understanding, Juuyu didn't resist. In his mind's eye, he was in truest form, and Zuzu's branches bent and twined to create a nest.

Flying to it, he found Fumiko's considerable light contained within a protective shell. Had Zuzu wanted him to see an egg, knowing he was avian? It seemed only natural to drop into the hidden nest and cover her with his wing.

"You are her favorite." Zuzu exuded confidence.

Juuyu found he could speak, even in truest form. Likely because Zuzu wished it. "I am glad there can be peace between us."

"You should stay."

"I will be here for as long as it takes my team to complete our mission."

"Sister does not need a team. One will do, and *you* are her favorite."

"I cannot promise this."

Zuzu retreated from words, but her mood drifted against his awareness—piqued, pouting.

"While I am here, I am willing to help." Juuyu asked, "What did you want to show me?"

"Look."

Juuyu considered the egg tucked safe against his side. Tiny fractures formed and faded, evidence of Zuzu's blessing. But should there be so many?

"Is it more difficult to hold back the years than it once was?" he asked.

"I do not know ...?" Zuzu sounded frightened. "Everything is better when she is happy. You make her happy. You should stay."

He spread his wing to cover both the egg and the nest. "Peace, sister tree. I am here."

Zuzu softly repeated, "Stay ...?"

Juuyu calmly changed the subject. "Look."

"Where?"

So he showed her his weariness. How the deep darkness that should be lush and laced with borrowed stars had turned gray at the edges, flaking away like cooling embers.

"You are hungry?" asked Zuzu.

"In a sense." Juuyu really had depleted himself. Perhaps foolishly.

He could feel the tree's curiosity and submitted to her gentle prying. Zuzu was incredibly strong, but it was becoming patently obvious that she was also self-taught. Without the wisdom of a grove to guide her, she'd been forced to figure out on her own what Fumiko needed. Her sister's sadness must be truly unsettling.

"She is hungry." Zuzu sounded uneasy. "Sister is hungry for something I cannot give."

"Perhaps." Juuyu reasoned, "She is human, so her instincts are different."

"There is only me, and I am not enough?"

Juuyu acted immediately to quell the tree's fear. Depleted or not, he threw his entirety around Zuzu, surrounding her from root tendril to twig. It was such a wolvish thing to do, this posturing. But Juuyu needed to startle her out of a downward spiral that could spell the end for both sisters.

Zuzu didn't struggle. She should have.

Instead, she changed the dream. Gone was the tree and the nest, and in their place, the phoenix now sheltered two shining souls. They were of a size, one a shining egg, the other a golden seed. The enormity of Zuzu's trust hinted at the depth of her self-doubt.

She needed someone to lean on.

Someone with his years and his experience.

"Trust tonight to me, and when time allows, I will make a call." He could do this much for them. "I know who to ask for help."

11
FOR THE BEST

Juuyu spent much of the night teaching Zuzu how to be a tree.

Some of it was the lore to which every tribute was privy. Some of it was personal stories from his years growing up in the grove under the protection of the Farroost colony.

Zuzu hung upon his every word, and Juuyu could understand why. Unfortunately, the reason infuriated him. After his promised call, he might just place another. To Estrella Mettlebright.

These sisters might be protected by the In-between, but they were also sadly neglected. Zuzu should have been granted the provisional rights granted to every grove. Had her orphan status been used as a loophole?

It was clear that Zuzu was being studied, but she'd never been mentored. A conundrum he intended to take up with Riindi.

The whole thing made him wistful for home. However, he was

in this place for an entirely different purpose. "Lull your sister and this man if you like, but I cannot sleep," he murmured. "I have a job to do."

Zuzu pinched his arm and softly replied, "I will not let you sleep."

Once the sky began to lighten toward dawn, Juuyu eased away from Fumiko and left the bed. "Take my place," he suggested.

"This has always been my place," countered Zuzu, whose mood was vastly improved. "But I don't mind sharing, if it's you."

"Perhaps. If my duties deplete my reserves again."

"You are *my* favorite." She hadn't given up. "Stay?"

Juuyu bent to touch her leafy crown. "I have a sister who is older and wiser than I, the mother of many tree-kin and the surest voice in our grove. Let me speak to her of you and Fumiko. She will know what to do."

"Will she come to us?"

Riindi could not. He honestly couldn't imagine any of his siblings leaving the colony. He and Suuzu were the only two of their clan to ever do so. "I cannot speak for my kindred, nor choose for them. We must wait to see what Riindi recommends."

She pouted.

Not ideal, given how many tools she had to entangle and entrap him. Zuzu could easily break him, ruining him for all other forms of tending. Yet Juuyu chose to embrace the threat. And to disregard it. He, too, was not without resource.

Juuyu warbled soothingly and stepped back, only to brush against one of the blanket-draped piles. He'd nearly forgotten about Akira's ... project?

Circling around to see what on earth the young man had been

up to, Juuyu was forestalled by a soft grunt from the direction of the bed and the pad of bare feet.

"Wait," Akira whispered urgently. "Juuyu, wait."

"It is early. You should be in bed."

"I know. I'll go back, but ...!" Tugging him insistently, Akira begged, "Don't go that way. Or over there, either. In fact, it'd be best if you just go out the window."

Juuyu turned to face the young man. "In my sleeping attire?"

Akira's posture shifted into that of a supplicant. "Just this once, could you hold off on the usual preening? And ... maybe dress with your eyes closed?"

He trilled softly. "Akira, this is absurd."

"I promise I'll tidy up today. Give me time to get this ready."

Juuyu resisted the urge to look around. Closing his eyes, he pulled Akira close and said, "I will comply."

Having proven—to both Akira and himself—that he *could* dress with his eyes closed, Juuyu strode purposefully along the sand, his gaze upon the surf. When Sinder came up for air, Juuyu warbled a shrill summons, to which his partner fluted an answer.

Moments later, Sinder sloshed onto the beach in speaking form.

"Antigone tells me they don't usually eat fish for breakfast. Thought I'd make a little fire on the beach for these." Holding up the three wriggling fish he'd caught so far, Sinder asked, "How many do you want?"

"You are not sharing the morning meal with our hosts?"

"No. *You* are not sharing the morning meal with our hosts. Colt's orders. We already let the ladies know that you'd just take a tray."

Juuyu raised his hands in surrender. "I need to borrow your phone."

"Sure. It's charging."

He indicated the house, and they strolled that way.

"Is everything set up to your satisfaction?" checked Juuyu.

"All good. So I can start poking around the museum today. Oh! And we heard from Moon. He'll be here by evening."

"Is his room ready?"

"All but the warding."

Juuyu nodded. "I will take care of it after I make a call."

"Checking in with … Argent?"

"I need to call my sister."

Sinder eyed him curiously, but only asked, "Do they even have phones on that island you're from?"

"One."

Lights were on in the guesthouse, and as they neared the door, Hallow stepped through the front gate. Being a crosser, he needed sleep more often than the rest of them. Hallow's wellbeing technically fell under Colt's purview, but Juuyu searched his gait and countenance for signs of weariness. The bat crosser's heritage made him an ideal night watchman, but he wasn't actually nocturnal.

"Anything to report?" asked Juuyu.

"Oh, indeed." Hallow cut a small bow. "Felines like to toy with their prey."

Sinder's grip tightened on the fish hooked over his fingers. "You *saw* the Gentleman Bandit?"

With an apologetic posture and a light laugh, Hallow said, "Allow me to clarify. Felines like to toy with *me*."

"And vice versa?" guessed Juuyu.

Hallow dimpled. "Lash, Tuft, and I passed an otherwise uneventful night pleasantly enough. No signs of mischief."

Juuyu asked, "Colt?"

"Sent me back. Is it true Moon's on his way?"

Sinder said, "Due tonight, but overdue for sleep. He won't be able to pitch in."

Hallow hummed. "Should I spend the next few nights patrolling the vicinity? If our bandit isn't inside, they might be looking for a way in."

"Do that," agreed Juuyu.

"But more importantly…." Gesturing to Sinder's catch, Hallow's tone turned hopeful. "Are any of those for me?"

Juuyu paced slowly on the sand, checking his pocket watch at intervals while waiting for Riindi to take his call. Would a herald have been more efficient? Perhaps life abroad had made him impatient.

Finally, his elder sister's voice carried through the connection. *"Peace, Juuyu. What do you need?"*

Always to the point.

He could only be grateful.

"I am lodging under a tree, and I am concerned for her twin."

"You are?" And after a pause that stirred Juuyu toward impatience again, she said, *"I see. May I know which grove?"*

"There is no grove. She is an orphan tree."

Riindi's trill was filled with sorrow. His sister was tree-kin herself, twinned to one of the largest trees near the center of their grove. *"That is cause enough for concern, but what has she done to stir your heart to sympathy?"*

She sounded surprised he was capable.

Juuyu hesitated. He usually didn't try to gather information unless it was for work, but Fumiko had definitely left an impression. "Her tree is concerned for her."

Another long pause. Riindi suggested, *"Tell me something about the tree's twin."*

"A human female, age uncertain, but this pair has surely surpassed the millennia mark. Her spirits are flagging. She seems thin, fragile. Lost ...?"

"What do you think she needs?"

"I do not know." Juuyu toed the sand. "That is why I am asking you."

"How could I know from here?"

Juuyu was feeling increasingly foolish. "Intuition?"

Riindi's low laugh held no real mockery. *"You are* there, *brother. As is she. Did it not occur to you to ask?"*

He sighed. "I am hesitant to become involved."

"Yet you would involve me?"

"I trust you most."

His sister warbled affectionately. *"Surely her tree has given you some guidance?"*

Juuyu wasn't about to admit that Zuzu thought *he* was the answer to all their problems. "Some. But she does not have our perspective." More softly, he revealed, "Her grove was ravaged before she could learn their songs."

"Songs you could teach." And when he didn't immediately respond, Riindi said, *"You have always been attentive to details, Juuyu. Look, and you will learn all the answers you require."*

Not the answer he had wanted.

But a true answer, nonetheless.

Riindi offered a soothing cascade. *"Next time you call, ask for Father. He is nearer the reaver outpost, so he could bring Letik. I am sure he would be delighted to speak with a distant daughter."*

So simple. Juuyu laughed softly. At himself. "*This* is why I called you Riindi. You always see what I should have."

"Let us speak again. Soon."

"Perhaps."

"I insist. Promise me."

Juuyu was puzzled by the lightness in her tone. It smacked of teasing. "Why do you think that will be necessary?"

Riindi blithely answered, *"Intuition."*

12

TEEMING

umiko picked at her breakfast, too distracted by the guests at their table to eat. Sinder was at the center of everyone's attention, lively and laughing. Colt was nearly as personable, but he took a slower pace and tended to speak to people one-on-one.

"Did the other one make it in last night? The one Melody mentioned?" asked Dru, one of the interns who lived over the library. Though she took her share of shifts shelving books, she was officially apprenticed to Melody Skyflutter. At fifty, Dru was the youngest reaver currently residing under Zuzu's branches.

"Juuyu," supplied Sinder. "He did. Thanks for asking. You'll have to forgive him. He's a bit of a workaholic. Prone to long hours."

"I brought his breakfast tray to the guesthouse earlier," reported Antigone. "But he was already gone."

"Sorry about that!" Sinder explained, "Juuyu's filling in for our leader, so he's kind of doing two jobs right now. Things will balance out once the rest of our team is in action."

"Did I hear someone else is coming?" Dru asked.

"Sure is." Sinder traded a look with his teammate. "You'll probably start seeing him around ... by next week."

"If you're lucky," interjected Colt.

"He *does* make himself scarce. Unlike me." With a winsome smile, Sinder asked, "Is that last muffin spoken for?"

Colt passed it to him. "I fear all of us will be scarce from time to time. Apologies if that makes us poor company."

Fumiko would have to break it to Zuzu later. That these weren't potential husbands. That they had work nearby. Such a silly misunderstanding. She really hoped no one else had noticed her getting her hopes up.

"Where's that lovely bat crosser?" asked Portia.

"He works the night shift, so he's catching a nap," said Sinder.

"Hallow usually stirs by lunchtime, and he has a big appetite." Colt smiled at Antigone. "If you'd be so good ...?"

"Leave it to me!" She flexed and patted her bicep. "I do love cooking for folks who know how to eat."

Fumiko could feel the intern's attention swing her way and pretended not to notice.

"*Gochisousama deshita*," murmured Akira, pushing back from the table, shuttling his dishes to the sink, and bolting upstairs.

With a laugh, Sinder explained, "He's grateful for the meal and on to his next task."

Fumiko abandoned her breakfast to hurry after him. For once, the ladies let her go without argument. Another nice thing about having a house full of guests. She hoped they'd stay for a long, long time.

In his room, Akira had dragged blankets from the pile he'd made the previous night. Turning to her, he asked, "Do you have time to help me? I want to put these things away, but I don't know where they go."

"They're here because this is where I happened to set them down. Nobody else uses this room."

"I get that. Kind of an overflow. Do you mind if I find them a temporary home? It's for Juuyu's sake."

"Because the room needs to be empty?"

Akira crossed to a cabinet and began rearranging its contents, presumably to make room for more things. "I live with a phoenix, so I know. Crowded places make them uneasy. I want to clear this space and clean it up. That way Juuyu can relax."

"You live with Juuyu?"

"I live with Juuyu's brother." Coming to her side, he pulled out his phone and flipped through photos. "Here. This is Suuzu."

It was a selfie taken on a beach. They were posing with a man with windblown curls and laughing eyes. In the background, children in bright swimsuits played in the shallows. But the one Akira gently touched with the tip of his finger looked like a younger, leaner version of Juuyu.

"He's my best friend." Akira's smile was sad. "He'll come if he can. I know he wants to."

"Would he sing for us?"

"Yes! You should hear him and Juuyu sing together. It's the best."

Fumiko asked, "And he'll be happier if this room is empty?"

"Yes."

"And you're happier when he's happy?"

Akira's smile turned shy. "Yes. Please?"

She nodded. "We can find new places for everything."

For the next few hours, they shifted piles. When the closet was full, Akira ferried a box up the spiral staircase to her room. Moments later, his voice carried down. "Is it okay if I go to the top?"

"Go ahead. Yes." Climbing the stairs, she joined him on the gallery with its view of the ocean.

"This is *amazing*," he said. "I want to show Suuzu."

He snapped a picture and sent it to the one he wanted to be with. Fumiko could understand. She often wanted to show things to Zuzu. And her sister was always showing things to her. Because they were part of one another. Lives intertwined.

She noticed him enter another message and send it along. "Did you tell him that we are getting ready?"

"Oh, no. I'll probably tell Suuzu later, when we talk. That one was for my uncle. You saw his picture. Uncle Jackie made me promise to keep in touch. Same goes for Ginkgo and Isla and Quen and ... well, a bunch of friends. See? This one's from Ginkgo."

He showed her the message and its reply, but she couldn't translate the characters. "Read to me?"

"Oh, sorry!" Akira read the exchange even as he added to it.

> **Home away from home is a lighthouse**
> **This is the view from the top**
>
> **Are you imposing on your hostess?**

Maybe a little
She's a patient lady

The kiddos want a turn
I'm foisting you off on them for a bit

Fumiko touched his shoulder. "You haven't imposed on me in the least. I like having you here. It's almost like having a friend of my own."

Akira searched her face. "Are you not allowed to have friends?"

"I have the interns."

"And now you have me. Oh, boy. It's Nonny. He texts in English, so that's better for you."

Nonny here
About time you turned up
Where ARE you?

America

For good?
Better not be for good
Or I'll kick your arse

Fumiko giggled.

A beat later, once he'd worked out the English, Akira mumbled, "Sorry, sorry. Nonny is a little ... blunt. He isn't angry. He's probably been worried about me, since I left in a rush. Akira tapped in a response.

Just visiting
I'll come home again
Who's there with you?

Straight to the point, Nonny sent through a selfie. It showed four children mobbed around the same man from the previous photo, though he was clad in a chartreuse dressing gown this time. There were pillows everywhere, and the man had a baby curled on his chest.

"That's the newest member of the family," said Akira. "Those booties hide her hooves, but you can see how we modified her diaper to make room for her tail."

A tuft of fur was indeed sprouting from her backside. Fumiko whispered, "She's a crosser?"

"Yep. All of them are. Hang on."

How's Ella doing?

> **Been fussing**
> **Mare's milk doesn't sit so good**
> **Won't settle for anyone but Jacques**
> **Now that SOMEBODY skivved off**
> **To America**
> **Without us**

Is Ella sick?

> **Michael thinks she might**
> **be like Gilen was**
> **Shy of reavers**
> **You and Jacques are our only normies**
> **So you better come back quick**

As soon as I can
Hey, I have a friend with me
Want to meet her?

> Someone's there?
> Damn it, Akira
> Say something sooner
> And say hi

"Nonny says *hi*," Akira relayed, albeit unnecessarily, since their heads were bent together.

"Which one is he?"

Scrolling back up to the selfie, he pointed to a blue-eyed teen with a thicket of straight, sandy hair. And horns. "This is Nonny. His father is from a goat clan. And the one with his head on Uncle Jackie's shoulder is Gilen."

A ginger-haired boy of about twelve smiled shyly up at the camera. Fumiko couldn't decide which was more remarkable, his green-gold eyes or the faint stripes that marked his round cheeks. "Is he a tiger?"

"Half. On his mother's side." Akira drew her attention to another child, a little girl this time. "The one holding the baby bottle is Mei. You can kinda almost see her tail. And this is Arnaud. Up past his bedtime again, but he's another of our French-speaking kids, so he clings to Uncle Jackie.

Fumiko was amazed. And frankly, delighted. Striped tail for Mei, whose heart-shaped face made her dark eyes huge. And a spotted tail for Arnaud, who had kitten ears. Or ... cub ears? "Is Arnaud a leopard child?"

"Cheetah, actually. He came to us from Ivory Coast."

"Came to you?" Fumiko tried to remember where Akira was from. Surely, someone had said. "Where is this place?"

"I live at Stately House most of the time. There's a school for crossers, and we also take in mixed-species kids with nowhere else to go."

She'd heard of it and said as much. "You know Argent Mettlebright?"

"Sure do. But he's hyper secretive about home. So this has to stay between us, okay?"

"Zuzu and I are secrets, too," she pointed out.

Akira beamed. "That's part of what makes this safe. Want to send a selfie?"

As she smiled for the camera, it occurred to Fumiko that her sister was being unusually quiet. Not that Zuzu was truly absent. That's the way she was sometimes, though. Because it gave Fumiko something to share when they came together later. Even though Zuzu always knew everything that happened under her branches.

While they'd been talking, Nonny had loaded the chat window.

> **You met an American girl?**
> **Is she my age? Your age?**
> **Does she understand you?**
> **You have a dreadful accent**
> **Wait, Jacques says there's a lighthouse**
> **Show us!**
> **WE WANT TO SEE**
> **Oi! Akira!**
> **Akiraaaaaa!**

That's when Akira shared the picture. Nonny immediately switched gears.

> **Oh, hey, nice pic**
> **Is it just me or did you**
> **find yourself an onee-san?**

"That means 'big sister.' He thinks we look like family." Akira laughed as he tapped. "Not sure if we do or not. I don't think you look like Tsumiko. She's my actual sister."

> She's American. A little older than me
> And my English improves
> I'm getting lots of practice

> Jacques wants to know where she shops
> Not sure if that was a compliment, tho
> Maybe don't ask

> Tell him to behave

> He always behaves
> Just not always nicely

"Sorry about him. Uncle Jackie is a tease. And a flirt. And a snob. It sounds bad when you pick the pieces apart, but all together, he's a really nice guy. Except ... kind of a snob. And a flirt. And a tease."

Fumiko laughed.

More texts pinged through.

> Mei says she's pretty
> Gilen wants to know if she has a name

> My manners are terrible
> Meet Fumiko
> I'm staying at her house

> Oh. Also. Lady says hi

"Who's Lady?" asked Fumiko.

"My sister. Tsumiko." Akira's eyebrows shot up. "You know ... Sis never leaves Stately House, but she has friends from different places. They talk online. Maybe I could introduce you. I'll check. It's up to Argent."

Fumiko was fitting all his little hints together. "Your sister is Lady Mettlebright?"

"Yeah." Akira lowered his voice. "You don't have to say, but is someone in charge of you?"

She frowned. "What?"

He waved his hands, clearly searching for the right words in English. "Do you need permission for the things you want to do? Is there someone in authority over ... this place? And ... and *you*?"

Fumiko honestly admitted, "I don't know."

13

AMARANTHINE INFLUENCERS

Since he was early, Juuyu took the time to stroll around the museum's exterior. Modern lines. Tinted glass. Tasteful banners promoting the Amory's new exhibit, "Art Without Barriers." Ironic, given how many barriers were in place to safeguard the Junzi.

Amory Fine Arts Center was one of an increasing number of much-needed establishments, founded and funded by the public sector, yet wholly in favor of inter-species cooperation. The director and curator had worked together to fill the Amory's galleries with art by humans and by the clans, and Juuyu appreciated their efforts. The search for common ground in this country had found its first, staunchest ambassadors in places like this.

Because art and literature pointed to similar ideals of beauty and tragedy.

Historians clamored for meetings with people who remembered their forebearers.

Musicians delved into the trove of "new" compositions that rivaled their masters.

Educators added Amaranthine to their faculties at every level of learning. Indeed, continuing investments in education had brought the Amaranthine people into the daily lives of American families.

But none could deny that the biggest influencers in the States were the entertainment networks. Broadcast television, streaming media, and blockbuster films fed the fascination and helped to shape public opinion in positive ways.

Documentaries that wrestled old myths into the open.

Talk shows that raised questions everyone should be asking.

Children's programming that fostered inclusion and acceptance.

Openly Amaranthine actors and actresses, models and musicians—they created a buzz the Amaranthine Council couldn't duplicate. *Clannish*, a tabloid that stalked the Amaranthine elite, recently asked the average American citizen to rank the Rivven they admired most. Hisoka Twineshaft barely scraped into the top twenty, usurped by media darlings like Ash Skyfletch, Pim Moonprowl, and Eloquence Starmark.

Granted, Spokesperson Twineshaft did routinely make a better showing on Most Eligible Bachelor lists. Which usually topped by Lapis Mossberne. And in a recent—and amusing—trend, had begun including Suuzu.

Juuyu was grateful that he could carry out his duties largely in secret.

When he rounded the final corner of the building, he spied Colt waiting beside a drab little door, one of the emergency exits.

"Something to report?"

Colt shook his head. "A morning as quiet as the night Hallow passed, but I took a look at today's schedule. School groups. Community groups. Our bandit may try to mingle with the crowds."

Juuyu inclined his head.

They finished his circuit of the building together. Colt remained silent, which was helpful. Juuyu wondered why this teammate understood his need for focus when his own partner would have chattered heedlessly all the while.

Freed to relax any kind of personal guard, Juuyu set his sights on the sigilcraft, singling out each individual pattern in turn. He might not normally have bothered, but he couldn't discount Mirrim's and Magda's certainty that someone had slipped—however briefly—under their guard.

Argent's sigilcraft could only impress. Exquisite. Efficient. Ruthless.

Juuyu's steps slowed as he picked apart the meaning of each interlocking pattern. Colt stood quietly at his side, hand on his sword hilt, gaze roving.

Finally, Juuyu closed his eyes. "It is well made, this trap."

"Glad to hear it." Colt's hand slipped supportively under his elbow. "Orders?"

He breathed deeply, organizing his thoughts. "Until Sinder arrives, watch the guests and customers for anything out of place."

"Openly?"

Like many clansmen, Colt no longer bothered with disguises

because his stature gave him away. Something that didn't usually matter, since he routinely took the night watch with Hallow.

Juuyu hummed. "You would be good for publicity. Provided you stow your weapon."

"I'll just check with the director first, shall I?"

"That would be courteous." As they entered the lobby together, Juuyu added, "I will confer with the reavers."

"Mirrim and Magda are resting in their newly established naproom. Healer's orders." Colt shook his head in a fond way. "They've been skimping on sleep, but we're here now. No need to push their limits."

Checking his pocket watch, Juuyu nodded again. "I will begin with records, then. If you need me, I will be reviewing documents at reception."

Parting ways, Juuyu settled in the chair behind the front counter, which served as the Amory's information desk. While most of the day-to-day business at the museum was computerized, the receptionist who was in charge of scheduling tours and assigning guides adhered to the school of pencils and highlighters. Her master calendar involved dog-eared corners and sticky note supplements. Charming in its way.

Even more endearing was a guest book, where visitors from far and near had been encouraged to leave their name and where they were visiting from. Juuyu flipped through a few pages before trying to find a safe place to set it aside.

More than half the counter had been overtaken by live plants and festive bouquets. One of the cards caught his eye, then his interest.

Congratulations, Trip! Art Without Barriers is a stroke of brilliance and of beauty. You're making a difference. —Kimiko Starmark & Isla Ward, cofounders, ClanRomantics

Kimiko had ties to this museum? Was that significant? Juuyu's mind raced. When Argent selected the Amory to display the Bamboo Stave, they'd had no way of knowing that the Junzi stored at Kikusawa Shrine—Kimiko's home—would be snatched first.

Rising and circling the desk, he checked the other tags. Several local businesses had sent bouquets.

Sending good vibes for the opening of your new exhibit! —your friends at Bohotique

Raising a glass! Here's to peace! —Vic & Trix, The Spume Room

Proud to be running your story on Page 1. You're an inspiration! — Levity Jones-Highwind, *The Emergent*

Several notables in the Amaranthine community had also taken the time to send tokens of support. Usually in the form of potted plants, not cut flowers.

Many thanks. May your efforts touch many hearts. —Hisoka Twineshaft

All the best to everyone at the Amory. Save me a spot on opening night! —Cyril Bellamy, Amaranthine American

Until all is as it should be. —Argent Mettlebright, Stately House

Rather oblique. Then again, Argent wasn't the most ebullient of souls. Juuyu gently touched the leaves of a bonsai that had to be centuries old. Had the fox parted with something from his own conservatory? The dwarf orange tree sent by Harmonious was also in keeping with its sender. Bright and cheerful.

According to the receptionist's calendar, opening night for this exhibit had been the previous weekend. Five days ago. An invitation-only affair, held prior to the tampering Mirrim and Magda had detected. Even so, Juuyu made a mental note to ask Mister Raphael S. Amory III—reportedly known to his friends as Trip—for the guest list. And to have Sinder hunt up any articles and photographs.

You never knew which details would become pertinent.

And Juuyu only knew how to be thorough.

14

MIND THE GAP

Juuyu found the "naproom" easily enough. Colt's handmade sign cheekily announced, DO NOT DISTURB THE WARRIORS. The notice was wholly unnecessary, given the extravagance of the barrier now in place. If there was one thing Hallow was good at, it was warding against light and sound.

With a perfunctory tap, Juuyu slipped through the door and into darkness.

A staff lounge with a sofa and armchairs had been adapted for the reavers' use. The women had borrowed cushions and spread bedrolls, creating an almost avian nest for themselves in one corner.

Mirrim raised an arm, acknowledging him. Easing away from her partner, she softly kissed Magda's temple, adjusted her blankets, and stood to stretch. Silently indicating the door, Mirrim essentially ordered Juuyu out before quietly exiting the room behind him.

"Magda's been monitoring wards for three days straight," she said, traces of pride warming her tone.

"Why so small a security detail?"

"Not my decision." The woman smirked. "My theory is quality over quantity."

Juuyu considered. "You were handpicked, not merely assigned?"

"Some of it's definitely convenience. Lost Harbor is a short flight up the coast, as the condor flies. But we have roundabout ties to Twineshaft and Mettlebright."

"Which are?"

Her brow quirked, as if to say, *you asked for it.* "My daughter's father is currently part of Spokesperson Twineshaft's cortege. And that same daughter's bondmate is apprenticed to Lord Mettlebright's denmate."

It was enough for Juuyu to make the appropriate connection. "Melissa Nightspangle is your daughter. Yes, I see the resemblance. I was introduced to her and to her bondmate during the founding of the Reaverson enclave."

"It's a small world." She pushed at rumpled curls and squared her shoulders. "Did I miss anything?"

"Not at all." He rattled off the date, the time, the Amory's program schedule, and added, "I wish to accompany you on your usual rounds."

"Understood."

After that Mirrim was all business.

Juuyu observed and listened. He searched for and found no gaps in Mirrim's detail. She was both experienced and exacting.

Argent had chosen well.

"Are you aware that many of Spokesperson Mettlebright's wards are targeted?" he asked.

"Magda told me." She ushered him through the door that led onto the roof. "Dragons are understandable. Foxes are ... all kinds of trouble."

The Amory was indeed warded against foxes. "Argent already tuned his wards to accept my partner. Sinder is a dragon."

"Fighting fire with fire?" Mirrim moved from one vantage to the next, scanning the grounds and the streets beyond. "Dragons are impervious to another dragon's sway. As are phoenixes. And Kith, which gives Magda and I another small edge. Are we meant to be on the watch for a fox?"

"That is a reasonable conclusion."

She considered him closely. "I don't think we're dealing with a fox."

Juuyu simply asked, "Why not?"

Mirrim's smile was humorless. "Because if any fox was skilled enough to get past Argent Mettlebright's wards, they wouldn't have left any signs. And they wouldn't have left emptyhanded."

Juuyu quizzed Mirrim on the signs of tampering she'd reported. As it turned out, those signs weren't much, but they weren't nothing.

While on patrol in the galleries, Magda had heard the sound of something drop. Just a small *clack* and patter.

On Mirrim's orders, they'd split up, one to investigate the noise, one to confirm that the Junzi was secure. Mirrim found nothing amiss with the Bamboo Stave's display case. Magda's investigation yielded a lone gray pebble, which she'd secured.

Insignificant. Dismissible. But odd.

Yes, anyone could have dropped it there at any point during regular business hours. But Magda swore she heard it drop. Eight hours *after* the cleaning crew finished their work, which included floor-cleaning. And three full hours *before* the doors opened for employees the next day.

"Someone was here," said Mirrim.

Juuyu weighed her conviction against the available facts. "What makes you so sure?"

She waved a hand. "A feeling. An instinct."

"You sensed a presence?"

Her jaw tightened. "I can't prove it."

"Neither can I dismiss it." Juuyu was a warrior in his own right, and he placed great trust in his own instincts.

They were on their second circuit of the facility when Mirrim stopped to chat with the security guard posted at the gallery entrance. Juuyu indicated the man's clipboard, which he surrendered without protest.

"Colt's been a real hit, especially with the children," he was saying. "We should bring in one of the troupes. Maybe the folk singers?"

Mirrim answered, "It would mean more eyes on the place, but it might also increase the crowds."

Valid points on both sides. Worth considering.

But Juuyu's attention was locked on the guard's record of comings and goings. A four-digit number and a time were listed in tidy columns. As well as a small checkmark. Given the depth of the stack, the notes went back several days, with the most recent page on top.

"What is this, please?" Juuyu asked.

"Oh, that's just me keeping busy." The silver-haired reaver tapped each column. "Ticket number, the time they entered, and I check them off when they leave again."

It was all very orderly. And potentially useful, since they could cross-check ticket numbers in the system. Juuyu could only approve the keeping of such a systematic record. But that was also why he was concerned. "There is a gap."

The man blinked. "Is there?"

Juuyu turned the clipboard. "More than one, actually. It happened yesterday. And the day before."

"Huh." The man's brow furrowed. "I didn't notice."

Mirrim asked, "Why'd you leave a space, Jim?"

"I don't remember." Tapping the empty row, he murmured, "I think it was ... something nice, though."

Juuyu flicked open his watch and glanced around the courtyard. "Note the time."

"Sixteen minutes ago." Mirrim whistled sharply enough to make Juuyu wince, then shoved through the gallery doors. Over her shoulder, she snapped, "They could still be here!"

15

THE FOUR GENTLEMEN

Juuyu swiftly double-checked the clipboard before catching up with Mirrim. "There are currently twelve guests and one school group in this section. We should not cause a stir."

"Won't need to." Mirrim grimly slapped a sigil on the wall. One of Magda's. The trigger set off a cascade of interlocked sigilcraft, scattering secondary sigils through every gallery.

"An interesting adaptation."

"Pretty standard, really. We use these in hunting games. Magda's been hoping to tag our sneak." Mirrim initiated two more sets, then pointed at Juuyu. "I'll confirm the safety of our guests. Make sure the Junzi's secure."

"Agreed."

The whole exchange took no more than eight seconds, and Juuyu was gone before another could pass.

107

He arrowed along the most direct route, closer to the ceiling than the floor. A contingency that was only permissible because of Juuyu's orders to protect the Junzi by any and all means. His own sigils were deploying in their order, diminishing the impact he made on human senses. While not truly invisible, he was difficult to notice. And gone in a blink, even if someone did.

Fingers flicked through familiar forms, and sigils spun out behind him. But Juuyu's gaze was firmly fixed ahead. He, too, was a hunter. Eager for the chase.

It might not be the Rogue, welcome as that would be. Dragons were the natural prey of phoenixes, and he was confident he could bring death to their elusive foe, once cornered.

A fox capable of sidestepping Argent's barriers was a far more frightening prospect. But difficult to imagine. Juuyu was of the opinion that the Gentleman Bandit hailed from one of the other trickster clans. But it was all speculation.

Nobody knew the thief's identity.

When the Plum Cascade vanished from Lord Beckonthrall's trove, polite murmurs and condolences were traded along with pleas of ignorance. However, the subsequent attempt on the Orchid Saddle had raised the proverbial hackles of everyone who understood the significance.

Still, nobody knew the thief's identity.

But their motive had shifted into focus.

The Junzi were ancient dragon-slaying weapons that reavers had nicknamed the Four Gentlemen. Among the dragon clans, they were called the Four Storms. Most believed them to be little more than fable fodder. The stuff of scary stories whispered to younglings in the heights and harems.

Priceless. Dangerous.

Hidden. Found.

Was the Gentleman Bandit looking for a way to lash out against the dragon clans? Or had the Rogue—and the accomplice Argent now believed he'd acquired—acted to remove a potent threat from reavers' hands. Either way, the Amaranthine Council had acted.

The Plum Cascade was lost without recourse.

The Orchid Saddle had been removed to a secure location.

The Chrysanthemum Blaze, believed secure, had been taken.

What of the Bamboo Stave?

Juuyu dropped to the floor beside the display case and surveyed the room, hands still weaving sigils to search, to stagger, to stun.

No barrier had swayed. No alarm had tripped.

All was still. And apparently safe.

Juuyu turned his gaze upon the Bamboo Stave, which had been arranged upon folds of black velvet. Directed lighting sparkled across a slender shaft of green crystal. There were metal joins, enforcing and embellishing, and each segment was bored and etched and tuned to the whole. A masterpiece.

At first glance, few would recognize this as a weapon. Indeed, they might question the name, for this stave wasn't a blade. The term was related to the staff used for musical notation, for *this* stave was a wind instrument. A flute longer than Juuyu's arm. And according to the old tales, capable of turning the tides of war with a tune.

Nothing.

Nothing *creditable*. Yet Juuyu was as sure as Mirrim and Magda that someone was teasing at their security measures, testing limits.

Magda was grim. "I'll be resetting my array. Let me know if you guys think of any ways to finesse it."

"After you eat," directed Colt. "Healer's orders."

She looked ready to argue, but Mirrim touched her arm. "I'll buy you a sandwich."

To Juuyu's mystification, Magda burst out laughing. Mirrim's expression softened, and the two women strode purposefully toward the front of the building. He offered a soft chirrup of puzzlement.

"It doesn't have to make sense." Colt beamed after them. "I'm sure it was just an inside joke. Couples have them."

Juuyu supposed the horse clansman would know.

Jostling him with an elbow, Colt said, "So do families."

"Suuzu and I do not joke."

His teammate chuckled. "I'm sure you're both far too dignified to horse around, but it's still the same. It's about knowing how to coax someone into a better frame of mind, sometimes just by reminding them that you're there."

Juuyu's heart panged, and he averted his face. "I will do another circuit of the gallery."

Colt hooked a finger under his chin and lifted. "Does my past really bother you that much?"

"I apologize."

"I'm not after an apology." Glancing around, Colt urged Juuyu into a quieter corner of the courtyard. "I want to understand. Do we ... have something in common?"

The question was put delicately enough, but Juuyu grasped his meaning. "I have no attachments of a romantic nature."

"Ever?"

Juuyu warbled a frustrated cadence. "I simply do not wish to cause you pain by reminding you that she is no longer here."

Colt's brows drew together, then rose. "This isn't about Fira. This is about Suuzu and Akira, isn't it?"

Perhaps it was. Again, Juuyu murmured, "I apologize."

With a gentle nicker, his teammate said, "It's not easy, being brave. But it's even harder to be brave for someone else. Never really works out."

He hated to think of Suuzu's sorrow. Yet he'd added to it. "I have taken Akira from him even sooner."

"The decision was made before you became involved. And the choice was ultimately Akira's."

Juuyu found no comfort in excuses. "If anything happens to him, I will blame myself."

Colt pulled him into a loose embrace. "Trust me more, Juuyu. Give me a chance to tell you about all the *good* that came from having a human bondmate."

"I would be honored to hear your stories."

"Not a single one's a tragedy," he promised. "Now, do two things for me."

Juuyu searched Colt's smiling face before saying, "I will if I am able."

"You've been brave before, Juuyu. You can be brave again. Don't forget that."

If he'd had feathers to ruffle, he would have. Instead, he borrowed from Sinder and rolled his eyes.

Colt nickered again and took him by the shoulders. "Go back for today. Healer's orders. Hold onto your boy and send me mine."

16

GOODNIGHT MOON

umiko had few escapes, but climbing was a tried and true one. Her fingers and feet knew every path through Zuzu's heights, where they'd created hideaways. Nests of woven branches padded by faded blankets or folded towels. Platforms created by surfboards and driftwood that had washed ashore. A plank swing that was wide enough for two to share.

The things Akira had said were bothering her.

Fumiko didn't know the answer to his question.

Did Zuzu?

She could have called her sister to her side, but there were so many things to say, and up among the leaves was the safest place to say them.

"Where are you?" Fumiko murmured.

"Here."

Arms twined around her from behind, and in an instant, she

was safe in the highest niche. A nest for two that swayed just out of sight from passing birds. Fumiko huddled against Zuzu's side and asked, "Did you hear?"

"Maybe. So much has been happening at once."

Fumiko remembered then, that Zuzu would vanish when their home became crowded. Not because she was shy or trying to hide from their guests, but because it was easier to catch everything when she wasn't looking through a pair of eyes. Zuzu absorbed it all, from the passing of a migrating vert nippet to a stolen kiss between the bookcases in the library, simply by being there.

"Sister?" Zuzu stroked Fumiko's hair and asked, "Do you think we'll have a visitor this evening?"

"What kind?" It was one of their little games, born of hope and fond memories. "Since there's no fog bank, maybe we'll catch the last sunbeam?"

Zuzu giggled. "You don't want a frisky fog?"

"They're so clingy."

"Cold kisses," Zuzu agreed. "A rainbow?"

"Too late in the day." Fumiko hid her face against her sister's shoulder. "Maybe an evening star?"

"They are saying that the moon will visit."

"Who? The stars?"

Zuzu kissed the top of her head. "All these males are watching for the moon. They're saying it will come this evening, even though it's already sinking into the sea."

"I think they mean a person."

"A man named Moon?"

"Not a man. They're not reavers, Zuzu. And they weren't

sent for me." She softly added, "I don't have to worry about choosing yet."

"You chose."

"It doesn't count. I haven't been given a choice." Which reminded Fumiko of the question Akira had raised. "Who's in charge of us?"

Zuzu hesitated. "Is it us?"

"I'm not sure." Had either of them ever lived as if their lives were their own? "I don't think we are. When did we start letting someone else decide?"

"I don't remember." Zuzu cautiously asked, "Does it matter?"

"Probably." Fumiko struggled to put her thoughts in order. "What if I wanted something?"

"What do you want?"

"A phone. Like Akira's. So that we can talk to people we know even after they leave us."

"I like that idea. We definitely need a phone." Zuzu's hug tightened, and she whispered, "But you know, they might not *all* leave us."

"Everyone does eventually."

Zuzu's voice took a dreamy turn. "If we're in charge of ourselves, we can change that."

"We can't keep people from leaving."

Her sister swayed with the breezes, clearly pleased with her idea. "You're right. He won't promise to stay."

"He?"

"Your favorite. He understands about trees. His father is twinned."

Fumiko was curious and pleased and a bunch of other things, all at once. But Zuzu had said it herself. "Juuyu won't promise to stay."

"True. But what if he promised to come back?"

After hours of carting clutter upstairs and down, Akira was finally satisfied. Their room was so empty, it echoed. The bed—neatly made—now stood in a room that boasted nothing more than freshly-mopped floors and a fine view.

Akira took a snapshot and sent it to Suuzu.

> It should be all right now
> If he uses the window to come and go
> And bathes with his team
> And doesn't get curious about cabinets

> Thank you for seeing to
> my brother's comfort

> And yours
> You're coming, right?

> I will try

> Tomorrow I'll explore,
> find all the good places
> That way I can take you around

Suuzu didn't answer, but that was okay. He was always being

interrupted by work. For all Akira knew, he'd been sneak-texting during some important meeting.

Pulling on a hoodie and tossing a beach towel over his shoulder, Akira edged his way downstairs.

Dinner preparations were underway, and Antigone turned from the stove with a smile. "Need anything?"

He pointed to the door. "I will stay close. The beach."

She sent him off with a bottle of water, an apple, and a dense block of something that looked like seeds and peanut butter, which turned out to be quite tasty. Strolling along the dock behind the lighthouse, he found stairs leading onto the sand, which was fine and pale and speckled with pebbles.

Having put in a full day of hauling, Akira was ready to be lazy.

Downing the last of his snack, he chose a good spot, dug a shallow trough in the sand, and lined it with his towel. It was a little lonely. Usually, he had to make these nests wider, to crowd in with a bunch of youngsters. Or Suuzu, if he was home long enough to spend a day or two after a long sleep. But this was nice.

Akira turned his face to the sun, slowed his breathing, and let himself go limp.

He must have still been jetlagged, because the next thing Akira knew, the sun was much closer to the horizon, and voices were carrying across the water. First propping himself on elbows, Akira sat up.

Sinder was strolling down the dock with Portia.

Though they weren't far from his hidey-hole, Akira had trouble distinguishing words. It didn't help that they were speaking in English. He peered around. All he could see of the beach was empty. There had to be crowds of people to either side, and he wanted to see what the view was like on the other side of the barriers.

Tomorrow, he'd explore. Like a proper tourist.

A fluting drew his attention back to Sinder, who'd probably known Akira was there from the start. The dragon waved both hands and pointed skyward. Was something happening?

Even with his new tattoo, Akira was as susceptible as the next guy to the kinds of illusions Betweeners used to keep their secrets. So he wasn't sure what Sinder was gesturing toward. As far as Akira could tell, there was nothing but the deepening blue of a sky that was heading toward sunset.

But then Portia must have dropped some portion of the barrier.

An Amaranthine in truest form burst through the opening. Akira's first impression was wolf, but it could just as easily have been a dog. Not until they took speaking form was it possible to tell which clan they identified with.

This must be Moon, the missing team member. Wolf, then.

Akira sat up a little straighter, because the leaping canine had veered his way. Huge paws settled lightly on the sand, and then there was a moment when it was hard to focus, because the newcomer shifted into speaking form.

Definitely wolf, judging by his tail. But Akira had to do a quick reassessment, because there were still paws on the sand. And a lot more fur than usual. Was Moon a crosser?

Raising a hand, Akira murmured a soft, "Good evening."

"I'll assume that was some kind of *hello*," Moon said. In English.

"Are you Akira?"

"Akira Hajime. Yes." He scrambled to his feet and offered his palms.

Moon's big, furred hand closed around both of Akira's wrists and pulled him off his feet, and Akira found himself tossed over a shoulder. Like most wolves, Moon was tall, so the position put Akira way above the ground, which was being eaten up by long strides.

The only times he'd ever been plucked off his feet by an Amaranthine, it was either for good reason ... or for play. So Akira only squirmed enough to get comfortable.

Sinder was jogging at their side a second later, eyes wide. "Moon! This is incredibly rude!"

"Oh. Right." Patting Akira's leg, the wolf declared himself. "I'm Moon-kin Ambervelte, and I hope you have more English than I have Japanese. Which is likely, since I've got none."

"I understand you," Akira assured.

"Well, I don't!" Sinder was taking two strides for every one of Moon's. "Why are you manhandling Akira?"

"Orders."

"From whom?"

Moon stopped—and swayed—at the foot of the stairs onto the dock. "Sinder, which way's bed. Or do you want to carry my furry carcass when I drop?"

"Are you okay? Dunce and double dunce. Colt's on patrol." Sinder pointed the way, then met Akira's gaze. In Japanese, he relayed, "Sorry about Moon. He's overdue for a long sleep."

"I get it. I've seen it before." Akira couldn't help laughing. "You're like a bunch of toddlers trying to put off bedtime."

Sinder poked Moon's shoulder. "He just called you a toddler!"

Moon turned his head, giving Akira an up-close view of copper eyes under shaggy white eyebrows. "Not a speck of fear. Bodes well for the future."

The wolf pushed down Akira's head as he ducked through the guesthouse door, sparing both of them from knocking the lintel. Sinder threw open one of the bedroom doors. "All yours. Juuyu warded it, and I'm right next door. It's safe to let your guard down."

Akira was swung into a cradle hold, giving him his first really good look at Moon. Something about his grin reminded him of Harmonious Starmark. But before he could check anyone's pedigree, he was tossed onto the bed.

The wolf collapsed next to him with a grateful groan. "Wasn't sure I'd make it."

Sinder knelt beside the bed, looking worried. "Is this okay? Anything need to change?"

Moon buried his face in a pillow, which muffled his answer. "Peace, Sinder. I'm past caring."

"Food?"

"Can't be bothered."

"Drink?" tried Sinder.

Stirring a little, Moon answered, "Star wine, if you have it."

"*Of course* we don't have it." Sinder's smile turned sly. "Though I know where the ladies keep their kombucha."

Moon made a face.

"I'll bring water." And switching back to Japanese, Sinder said, "Don't worry. I'll be right back."

As soon as they were alone, Moon said, "Akira. I can barely keep my eyes open, so let's keep this short."

Idioms were tricky, so Akira was only clear on the obvious. "You need sleep."

"I do. But I promised a bunch of people to pass along messages." Moon's smile was a weary thing. "Scold me later if I fall asleep somewhere in the middle."

That's right. Moon had come from Japan. From Keishi, in fact. Akira had so many friends there. "A message?" he prompted.

"More than one. You are missed by a whole bunch of good people." Rolling onto his side, Moon revealed the Junzi Chocolates logo on his T-shirt. "Best first?"

Akira wasn't sure what to expect, but Moon didn't leave him guessing for long. Pulling Akira into his arms the wolf cradled him close.

Any number of his friends could have sent a hug. And Akira would gladly have hugged them back. "Do I need to guess?"

Moon huffed. "You are loved with a wholeheartedness that is sure to inspire many a song."

Which might mean any number of things.

Akira realized that Moon wasn't going to say anything more. "Did you fall asleep?"

"Still here." A hint of copper showed between white lashes. "That wasn't the actual message. It's more of an aside. Or meddling."

"Is there a message?"

"There really is. Or was." Moon yawned hugely, then sighed. "Okay if I paraphrase? Kind of ... put it more simply."

"Yes, please?"

Moon placed a gentle kiss on Akira's forehead.

"Suuzu asked you to kiss me?"

"No. He sent words. But there was a kiss at their heart, and I thought you'd want to know."

17
LAYING GROUNDWORK

When Sinder flagged down Juuyu from the guest-house door, he turned aside. "Did something happen?"

"Moon's arrived. And I've never seen him this bad. Akira took the brunt of it on the chin." Sinder smiled lopsidedly. "You're just in time to rescue him."

Juuyu knew his partner had to be exaggerating. Though Moon was a powerful combatant, more than a match for the eldermost and ancients, he was a gentle soul. Perhaps the gentlest. Akira was in no danger.

Juuyu halted on the threshold to Moon's den and exhaled on a fluttering note.

Akira left off humming and raised a hand, wiggling his fingers in greeting. Keeping his voice low, he exclaimed, "I met Moon!"

He hadn't just *met* their team's best tracker. Moon was curled

123

around Akira from behind, cradling him to his chest, nose in his hair, long tail draped along the young man's flank. Sound asleep.

Akira was entirely at ease and flush with happiness. He understood better than most humans that Moon was paying him a high compliment.

Sleep was virtually sacred to wolves, something shared with trusted friends. After Moon's long rest, he would forever consider Akira as a part of his pack. Indeed, the wolf's protection would undoubtedly also be extended to Zuzu and Fumiko as a courtesy for sheltering him at his most vulnerable.

"You were singing?"

"A crosser lullaby. Ginkgo made it up." Akira stroked the back of Moon's hand. "He looks like a crosser."

Juuyu came to sit on the edge of the bed. He offered a trill of approval, pleased by Akira's assessment. Most humans would say that Moon looked like a werewolf. Marking him as a monster. "Moon is Kith-kin."

"What's that?"

"One of his parents is Amaranthine, and the other was Kith."

From the doorway, Sinder eagerly volunteered, "Moon was born in truest form, but he found his way into this speaking form. Only one in four with the same kind of parentage ever manage it, so it's pretty rare."

Akira kept right on petting the fur-backed hand. "So he *is* a crosser."

"Of a sort," Juuyu agreed.

"He reminds me a little of Harmonious Starmark. His smile."

"Moon is brother to Harmonious' mother."

Akira looked pleased by this revelation. "And he's Boon's partner?"

"He is." Juuyu supposed it was as good a time as any to lay some groundwork. "Although Moon has more years, Boon is our leader. Our strength is currently divided. Moon seeks the bandit, while Boon seeks the Rogue. If they are one and the same, then our paths may converge. Here."

Eyes widening, Akira whispered, "Does Suuzu know the Rogue might be here?"

"Nobody knows *where* the Rogue is. Everything is speculation." Juuyu looked to Sinder. "Although I do not think the Gentleman Bandit is a dragon."

Sinder's eyebrows shot up.

Juuyu signaled for patience. They would have to talk later. "Do you require rescue?"

Akira tentatively suggested, "We could sleep here tonight, couldn't we?"

"What about dinner?" interjected Sinder. "They're expecting us, and we can't be rude. Switch with Juuyu. Since Colt and Hallow are at work, it's up to you and me to entertain the ladies. We'll bring back a tray and tuck you in with Moon after that. Yeah?"

"You're right. Yes, okay."

Sinder lifted, and Juuyu pulled.

Before Akira left, he caught Juuyu's sleeve. "You'll stay right here, won't you?"

Eyeing the confines of the room and the available floor space, Juuyu bowed to the wishes of his brother's nestmate. Grown or not, Akira would always be a chick in his nest.

With a flick of his fingers, Juuyu silently urged Sinder and Akira to give way. Once they were both hovering on the threshold, Juuyu took truest form. It was a close fit, but he managed with only a minor crush of feathers.

Akira was clearly used to this sort of thing, for he was quick to help adjust the curve of Juuyu's trailing tail feathers.

Fanning a wing over his sleeping teammate, Juuyu took a deep breath and trilled the opening notes of a nestling song. The same one that Father had sung over him. Much as he'd sung it over Suuzu.

Colt had spoken of shared jokes, but for Juuyu, family was more about shared songs. And because Juuyu's team shared bonds as strong as those of family, he transitioned into a song of love and trust. Because Moon was where he belonged. And a phoenix's song could enter dreams and guide a slumbering soul into peace.

Juuyu gave himself up to a song for the first time in far too long. Though he knew his music couldn't reach beyond the barriers protecting this room, he sang for the sea, for the stars, for the fragrant flowers in the branches overhead.

Hours passed, and he dimly registered Akira's return. Juuyu preened and tucked, fluffing his softest feathers over Akira, who was quickly reclaimed by Moon.

Even after both were deeply asleep, Juuyu continued softly tuning. This was restful for all of them, and it allowed Juuyu to review the facts of their mission. At this stage, it was impossible to say which details were important, so he assumed each held value.

Without focusing too hard on any one thing, he rearranged the pieces, searching for patterns.

Sometime later, Sinder tapped on the door and entered, an uncharacteristic interruption. By now, the dragon knew Juuyu's habits. And left him to them.

"Hallow came back."

It felt early. Shifting into speaking form, Juuyu checked his watch. It *was* early.

"He needs a word." Pleasant smile. Pleading gaze. Sinder was clearly trying his utmost not to let his tension bleed into Moon's haven.

Pausing long enough to make sure Akira was properly covered, Juuyu whisked out, closed the door, added a sigil to alert him if anyone stirred, and pivoted to face Hallow.

The bat crosser was doubled over. Not injured, but winded.

"Colt wants you there. Now." Hallow shook his head. "The Stave is safe, but there's been an attempt."

18

RETURN

Juuyu straightened his tie as he strode along the gallery to the room with the Bamboo Stave's display case. Nothing seemed amiss. All of his sigils were intact. Every trap untriggered. "What happened?"

Colt turned, his expression grim. "Something small. And troubling. Look here."

Drawing his finger across the top of the case, he called attention to a sparse dusting of granules. Juuyu's focus narrowed, and he mimicked Colt, sliding one fingertip across glass. The residue was slightly sticky. And very familiar.

Seeing Colt touch it to his tongue, Juuyu followed suit. There was no doubt.

"Pollen?"

"It is," confirmed Juuyu.

"Can you tell what kind?"

"Hardly. I would like to know what Moon thinks." Juuyu thought to ask, "What do the Kith make of it?"

"That would be easier to show than tell." Colt beckoned

In the next room, Mirrim scowled at the two lynxes. Tuft sprawled on his back, purring loudly while his forepaws kneaded the air. By his side, Lash lay limp, so deeply asleep that her ears and whiskers didn't so much as twitch at their arrival.

Colt crouched beside the big male and scratched his speckled fur. "It is this healer's opinion that these good cats have been thoroughly pollinated."

"They used pollen to get past our Kith," growled Mirrim.

"So it seems," acknowledged Juuyu. It was the natural assumption, given the outcome.

"In the lobby, even the courtyard, I might understand." Mirrim looked furious. "But they shouldn't have gotten this far."

"Could they have been among the guests?"

Colt nodded. "It will help to bring Sinder in."

"First thing," Juuyu promised. "But Moon was beyond weary. He will sleep at least four days. Seven would be better for him."

Mirrim said, "So all we have to do, for now, is hold our ground for a week."

Juuyu inclined his head.

Colt rubbed his fingertips together. "Preservationists specialize in pollen. Should I bring a sample to ...?"

"No!" Juuyu cut in. "There is a *reason* they filter ... ah."

His teammate's expression cleared when he caught on, as well. "We can ward against pollen!"

"Bring Portia here." Addressing Mirrim, he explained, "She is a ward who works with preservationists, so she specializes. Have her work with Magda to incorporate a blocker into your personal wards. For you and for your Kith partners."

Mirrim rolled her eyes at Tuft and Lash. "Can we ward the entire museum?"

Again, Juuyu inclined his head. After a moment's thought, he looked to Colt. "Who has access to the kinds of pollen that can do this?"

"Healers. Scholars. Brewers. Perfumers. Collectors. Recreational users."

"And friends of," added Mirrim.

Colt quietly conceded, "Or a friend of a friend."

That cut a wide swath through the In-between, but Juuyu couldn't help feeling optimistic. Pollen was a known entity. They could refine their alarms. Find its source.

Rubbing a thumb across his fingertips, Juuyu forced himself to face this problem one step at a time. "Bring in the janitorial crews. The air ducts will have to be cleansed. I also want air filtration devices in every wing."

Colt said, "I'll inform the director and make those arrangements."

Juuyu turned to Mirrim. "Induced sneezing can help with the pollination. Baths and a thorough brushing. Once Tuft and Lash are coherent, I would like their version of events."

Mirrim said, "A Kindred from our enclave can be here in an hour at most to confer with them. Would you like to be there?"

"I would. In the meantime, clean up."

"On it."

As soon as she was gone, Colt touched his elbow. "Addendum, acting leader."

In response to the sudden formality, Juuyu withdrew a slim rod of crystal from his pocket and proffered it on his palm. Their handclasp triggered a simple ward that would keep their words between them.

"There are two other possibilities, assuming the pollen belongs to an Amaranthine tree."

Juuyu appreciated Colt's discretion. While Mirrim and Magda knew details about the Rogue and the Gentleman Bandit, they probably weren't aware of Zuzu's presence in Beacon. More than likely, they weren't even aware that the most valued pollens in the In-between came from Amaranthine trees.

"Anyone who lives in a grove could have access." Colt smiled wryly. "Or anyone who finds an orphan tree."

Akira was already awake and texting friends when Sinder opened the door and quietly asked, "Want to come to work with me?"

"The museum?"

"The Amory Fine Arts center qualifies as touristy. There's a trolly ride involved, and I hear the gift shop is nice. Plus, you'll get to see an elite taskforce in action. And I'll buy you lunch."

"What about Moon?" Akira was all wrapped up in the wolf's embrace.

"Hallow will take the next shift." Sinder trilled soothingly as he lifted Moon's arm, giving Akira room to scoot free. "Don't worry. We've been taking care of each other for a while now. The trust is real."

"I'd like to see the museum. Will it be safe?"

"Should be." Sinder steered Akira into the main room. "We're dealing with a sneakthief. They're not likely to cause trouble in the middle of a busy day. I got the grand tour yesterday, so my main job today is people-watching."

Akira checked his phone. "How much time do I have."

"Plenty. An hour, more or less. We'll have breakfast with the ladies, then catch our ride into Beacon."

Hallow was just coming in from the shower out back and offered a drowsy smile. Their palms met in passing, and the bat crosser murmured, "Enjoy your day, Akira."

"Rest well."

"I always do when Moon's here." Hallow arched his brows at Sinder. "Remind Portia that she *doesn't* know you when Colt brings her around later."

"I will," promised Sinder. Though once they were out the door and aiming for breakfast, he smugly added, "Not that she'll see me."

"Is this a covert operation?"

"You bet. Are you up for it?"

"Wouldn't miss it."

Akira was halfway up the stairs to his room before it occurred to him to wonder where Juuyu was. Probably already at the museum. Akira was halfway out of his clothes before he realized that he wasn't alone in the bathroom. "Zuzu?"

"You didn't come to bed last night." She folded her arms and pouted. "Fumiko waited and waited."

"I slept in the guesthouse. We told everyone about it at dinnertime. Remember?"

The tree clearly wasn't satisfied. "Juuyu didn't come to bed."

"He did." Feeling bad for leaving the ladies out, Akira tried to explain. "He made a promise to watch over me when I sleep. So he was with me."

"There was a barrier."

"Yes. Sorry."

Zuzu demanded, "You will sleep here tonight. And every night."

Akira answered carefully. "From now on, while I'm staying here, I'll use my room."

"*And* Juuyu."

"I can't promise for him."

She huffed. "But he made a promise to watch over you."

"Yes, but ... well. Sometimes there are emergencies, so don't be mad if he can't always be right here. Actually, sometimes, he might ask *you* to watch over my sleep."

Zuzu blinked. "Really?"

"Next time I see him, I'll remind him that he owes you and Fumiko a lullaby."

She beamed at him. "I'll go tell her!"

And in a twinkling, Akira was alone again. Or as alone as anyone *could* be while in reach of a tree.

After breakfast, when Akira came down from one last quick trip to his room, Fumiko was waiting at the foot of the stairs. She barred his way, even as she pointed to the door. "Sinder says he'll be waiting in the farmer's market. Antigone thought he should meet the people who run it."

"Are they Amaranthine?"

"Usually."

"Only sometimes?" Akira couldn't help smiling. Fumiko seemed to want to say something, and it wasn't about fruits and vegetables.

"Different people come. Sometimes they're reavers." She edged closer. "Akira?"

He took a receptive posture. "What's up, Fumiko?"

"Zuzu says you'll stay with us tonight?"

"Yes. I will."

"You *and* Juuyu?"

"That's the plan. I'll talk to him about it." Nodding toward the door, he added, "I'm going to where he is now. Say, do you want anything from the gift shop?"

Her expression softened. "I like things. They last longer."

"Hey, it's too soon to be looking for stuff to remember me by. I'm right here."

Fumiko touched his hair and stepped out of his way. "Go, then. But don't forget to return."

"I'll be back," Akira promised. "And I'll bring something to share."

19

BUZZ

Outside was a little chilly since the entire beach was draped in fog. Slipping through the secret gate, Akira took the alley between the library and the flower shop. Sounds were muffled, but people were getting an early start. Women in red aprons were unloading crates of produce from the back of the red truck he'd noticed before, the one with a rooster logo on the door.

He spied Sinder, who was deep in conversation with a man with spiky brown hair and Melody from the flower shop. Antigone wasn't far away, chatting with two ladies who wore the aprons.

Akira moved to join Sinder, but a man stepped into his path. "Haven't seen you around here before. How goes it, friend?"

"Good morning. Hello," Akira answered, trying not to stare. And probably failing.

The guy was deeply tanned, which made his eyes really stand

out. They were such a light blue, they were almost colorless. But even more striking was his hair. Thick blond dreadlocks had been knotted with colored thread, wooden beads, and tiny seashells. His shirt hung open, and the wireless speaker clipped to the waistband of his board shorts softly played surf rock.

"You're Japanese?"

"*Hai.*" And laughing at himself, Akira added, "Yes. I am visiting from Japan."

"Thought so! I'm American. Do you speak American?"

"I understand you, but I have a lot to learn. My words are clumsy."

"I'm reading you loud and clear." Smile lines fanned out from the corners of his eyes. "What should I call you?"

"My name is Akira. You can call me Akira."

"Nice! I'm Rafter." He turned to display the surfboard-shaped sign he held to his side. It was painted with purple daisies, with big blue letters spelling out RAFTER'S RENTALS. "Have you had much of a chance to look around?"

"This is my first day."

"You'll have a good day for it." With an assessing look at the sky, Rafter said, "This'll burn off in a couple of hours. Clear skies and a feisty breeze all day long."

"Good." Akira indicated the sign. "Do you rent surf boards?"

"No, but I know who can set you up if you're interested. These are mine." He pointed to a long line of sky-blue bicycles in a rack under the jacaranda trees. "They're good for touring. I also have maps, and I can tell you where to get the good stuff."

"What kind of stuff?"

"Glad you asked!" Rafter gestured broadly to the neighborhood.

"Best ice cream. Best tacos. Best hamburgers. Best doughnuts. Best pizza."

Akira laughed. "You like to eat?"

"Come to think of it, I do!" Rafter laughed in a good-natured way. "But more to the point, do you? International tourists always seem to be interested in American food."

Based on the last few meals Akira had been served, he had to wonder if Fumiko ever got to eat pizza ... or the kinds of crazy snacks Kimiko loved. Maybe he could smuggle in some junk food?

"I can also point the way to souvenir shops, dog parks, kite rentals, live bands, and bus tours. Anything you need."

It was almost as if Rafter had set himself up as Wind-and-Tide's concierge. Akira offered a grateful bow. "I will rely on your advice for as long as I am here."

"Awesome." The man pointed between them. "Can I hear you talk in Japanese?"

Akira didn't mind. "If I'm late, Juuyu will worry, but I'm glad you introduced yourself. I wonder if you'd let me take a picture?"

Rafter asked, "Do I get the translation?"

He paraphrased, pulling out his phone and giving it a small shake. "For my friends back home," he explained.

"Your friends are my friends!" Wrapping an arm around Akira's shoulders, Rafter cheesed for a selfie. After, he presented his fist. "You know this one?"

They bumped fists.

But when Rafter drew his hand back, he wiggled his fingers and whispered, "Yeaaah!"

Akira offered a re-do, but his new friend shook a finger. "Next time. And I'm sorry to keep you." Cocking his thumb over his forefinger, Rafter pointed at Sinder, who waved. "He's your buddy?"

"My friend, yes."

"Good guy. I met him earlier." Stepping back, Rafter added, "Come see me anytime, Akira. I mean it. For anything."

"I will. Thank you, Rafter."

When Akira caught up to Sinder, the dragon was reaching for his phone.

"How late are we?" Checking the display, he grimaced. "Okay. Work with me on this. We're blaming the fog."

"You can't tell time by the sun if you can't see it?"

"Exactly." Sinder lifted his chin toward the man he'd been talking to. "At this point, what's ten more minutes? Akira, meet Buzz."

Though the introductions were brief—by clan standards—Buzz knew how to posture. Either he was an enclave-bred reaver or an Amaranthine who wasn't living openly. Akira leaned toward the latter. "Where is Red Rooster Farm?" he asked.

"An easy drive up the coast." Buzz was soft-spoken, and his gaze had a dreamy quality. "We're part of a big co-op. Orchards. Vineyards. And all this market fare."

Akira glanced around. Fresh produce was being displayed alongside cartons of eggs, homemade jellies, and jars of honey. "Maybe we can visit?"

Buzz smiled. "You'd be welcome."

"Permission, though?" Sinder shook his head. "We can *ask*. That never hurts. I'll get back to you on it, Buzz. Now, we *really* need to catch the next trolly."

Hooking Akira's arm, Sinder set off at a brisk pace.

"Is Red Rooster Farm an enclave?" Akira asked in an undertone.

"It is, but it's undisclosed."

"Do they know about Zuzu?"

"Buzz certainly does. Buuut, it's best to assume the rest are only there to sell heirloom tomatoes and sun-ripened guacamole fixings." Pointing to a TROLLY sign at the end of the block, Sinder urged, "Pay attention to the route. You'll have to return on your own."

"I can handle it."

"Oh, I know." Sinder spared him a sympathetic look. "But I'm under orders. And all of them have threats attached. So feel free to tune me out, but I want to be able to report back with a clear conscience. Yes, I showed him the way. Yes, I explained about currency. Yes, his manners are excellent. Yes, he's eating his vegetables."

Akira snorted his way into laughter.

Sinder grinned and rolled his eyes. "I might even earn extra points if we hold hands while crossing the street."

Without hesitation, Akira offered his hand.

"You're really a good sport."

"They worry about me because they care. How can I complain?"

"*I'd* complain."

Akira gave his hand a squeeze. "Wouldn't that just worry them more?"

With a resigned shrug, Sinder admitted, "You're totally right. It would."

139

The trolly let them off on the same block as the Amory Fine Arts Center.

"Think you can handle that?" Sinder asked innocently.

Akira blandly pointed out, "It's a straight line."

"You were paying attention!" With exaggerated patience, the dragon asked, "Did you notice the name of this street?"

"Mainsail."

"And the name of the street where we're staying?"

"Jacaranda Court."

Raising both hands, Sinder said, "And don't hate me, but ... how's your battery life?"

Akira checked. "Ninety-three percent. Is that it?"

"With that, we're both in the clear. And there's our way in."

Colt lifted a hand in greeting, and they jogged to meet up.

"You're late."

"Would you believe fog?" Sinder mumbled. "So, where does he want me?"

"There's a table ready," said Colt.

Sinder grimaced. "Did Juuyu have to do it?"

"I took care of it for you."

He fluted softly. "Thanks for covering my ass."

Colt rested his hand atop Sinder's head for a moment, then moved on. "Once you're settled, I'll go back, let Antigone feed me, and escort Portia to the conference room where the Lockets are set up. Do you happen to know if she requires any special equipment?"

While Sinder answered, Akira drifted apart. It wasn't that they seemed to be discussing top secret stuff. He just wanted to look around a little. The museum lobby was huge and high, and it echoed with the voices of people wearing different uniforms.

Two restaurants anchored either side. But most of the noise was coming from the direction of an information desk, where a group of children milled together. Akira ambled closer, surprised by how much he missed the sound of kids. He'd have to send a bunch of pictures today for the crossers back home.

This looked like a school group.

He wished they could take Stately House's crossers out like this. Maybe someday it would be safe to do so. But Argent was really good at indulging the many children who wore his crest. Over the summer, they'd laid tracks for a private railroad, and plans were in the works for a small theater that would double as a lecture hall.

All of the sudden, Akira realized that one of the adults escorting the children wore the traditional capelet of a snake clan. This school must be part of Sensei's integration program.

Akira formed his hands into one of the more subtle greetings. The kind that allowed you to quietly declare yourself as a Betweener.

She noticed the courtesy and returned it, adding a blessing.

He probably had a silly grin on his face.

Now that he was closer, he could see what had the children so excited. This was also something familiar, because Stately House was home to several large felines. A huge lynx sprawled in front of the information desk, and a handwritten sign with bold lettering announced:

My name is Tuft.
I am Kith.
Yes, you may touch.
Please, be gentle.

Akira repeated his greeting for Tuft's benefit, and the big cat's ears angled his way.

Once the teachers and tour guide led the school group away, Akira could see that other signs had been taped to the front of the information desk. Presumably, they said the same thing, but in Spanish, French, Korean, and … a language he didn't recognize.

Stepping up to the desk, Akira asked, "Do you know this language?"

The woman came around and clapped her hands together. "This is Hawaiian! One of the workers at Brew & Bubble is originally from there. Lovely, isn't it?"

"I think so, too."

"All of these were contributed by members of the staff. May I ask where you're from?"

"Japan."

"Will you add to our collection?"

"Sure! I would be pleased."

"You should also sign our guest book," she urged as she rummaged through things on the desk.

Akira scanned the open page of a fat ledger, making a note of the different places people called home. Suuzu would have known which states the two-letter abbreviations represented, but after a few pages, Akira saw enough variety to tell that visitors came from all over America.

International guests stood out.

A recent message was in Japanese. He knew a little Russian, so he could make out parts of messages in blocky Cyrillic. One visitor left their message in Greek. To his surprise, there were even some famous names. Cyril Sunfletch. Kimiko Starmark. Tenna Silverprong.

The museum worker held up a fresh sheet of paper and a thick marker. "Will these work for you?"

"Just right," he promised. And since there wasn't much room on the plant-strewn counter, he knelt. His calligraphy wasn't nearly as polished as his sister's or Isla's, but the characters would be legible.

While he worked, a familiar *clack* sounded on the stone floor. Even without looking up, Akira knew the sound of geta. All of the crane clansmen at Stately House favored the traditional wooden sandals. It was a safe sound. Homey.

Finishing his sign, Akira sat back on his heels and smiled up at the man who was studying him curiously. He wore a kind of linen short coat that was commonplace in Japan, with full sleeves that tapered to points. His was black with a scattering of tiny red flowers. Perhaps quince?

Akira angled his sign for the man to see. His features had a vaguely Asian cast. Perhaps mixed heritage? But Akira had the strongest impression that he'd be able to read the Japanese characters.

The man *did* scan the paper. Then he winked and walked on

20

LUNCH DATE

A couple hours passed before Akira wandered back into the lobby and scanned the tables.

"Look here," Sinder softly commanded.

Akira was essentially immune to a dragon's words, but he could still feel their pull. Which gave him a bearing. He'd actually walked right past Sinder's table. The chunk of blue crystal at its center was probably anchoring some minor illusion, making it difficult for the average citizen to notice both the table and its occupant.

"Hungry yet?" asked Sinder, whose fingers were idling over his laptop keyboard.

"Sure. If I'm not interrupting."

"We're good. I've already interviewed everyone on the morning shift. And they've pointed out which of the current customers are regulars ... and therefore above suspicion."

"How did they react to being interviewed by a dragon?" Sinder hadn't done anything to disguise the fact that he was Amaranthine.

"Oh, they don't remember." Sinder slouched a little in is chair. "Not me. Not my questions."

"Very stealthy. And kind of cool." Akira might not be a starry-eyed teen anymore, but he still thought Juuyu and Sinder made a convincing pair of international spies. "What are you looking for?"

"Anomalies. People who don't fit into this place's version of normal." Sinder lightly asked, "See anything strange while you were roaming?"

"Nope."

"Enjoy your tour of the galleries?"

"Guess so."

Going through the museum would have been more fun with Suuzu. His best friend would have read every plaque and paused to discuss the finer points of each piece. Always asking for Akira's own impressions. Because Suuzu liked to learn more about Akira. Stuff Akira didn't even know about himself. Sure, touring the galleries had been very nice, but it could have been so much nicer.

Shaking his head to redirect his thoughts, Akira said, "I didn't see Juuyu."

"He's probably lurking." Sinder's brows drew together. "How do you feel?"

"Fine?"

"Humor me. How would you describe your current mood?"

"Nice?"

Sinder slouched further in his chair. "Yeah, that's what I thought."

"Is that bad?"

"It's damned weird." Sinder closed his laptop. "When I'm on

a job, I'm *always* keyed up. Focused. Quick to make connections. Hang on. I'm going to check something. Sit tight."

Akira answered texts while the dragon made a circuit of the lobby. Sinder ordered something from Masterpiece Sandwiches, chatting with the workers while he waited. After that, he moved on to Brew & Bubble. Having added two brightly colored drinks to his collection, he strolled back.

Sliding the heaped tray onto the table, Sinder indicated one of the plates. "Behold, the Harmonious!"

Layers of toasted bread and cold cuts had been stacked high and held together with long, copper-fringed skewers. "What?"

"They call this sandwich a Harmonious. It's right there on the menu board." Sinder set two more sandwiches on the table between them. "According to the owner, they used to have artist names—the Picasso, the Monet, the Raphael—but they're showing their support for peace by honoring its founders."

"With sandwiches?" Akira pulled out his camera. "I wonder if they know?"

"They have framed thank you notes on the wall beside the pick-up counter. Even Argent is represented, although his note is in Jacques' handwriting. This here is the Double Dare."

Akira gently lifted the bun from what appeared to be a hamburger topped with thinly sliced pastrami.

"And here we have the American Crosser, which appears to be an homage to Ash Sunfletch."

The portions were beyond generous. "I can't possibly eat this much food."

"Figured as much." Sinder proffered a plastic knife. "Carve a slice of whatever interests you. I'll have no trouble finishing the rest."

Akira snapped pictures of each sandwich before claiming a reasonable portion. Meanwhile Sinder snagged the yellow boba smoothie, leaving an orange one for Akira. "Pineapple for me. Peach for you."

"Thanks. So, did you learn anything?"

Sinder blinked. "About what?"

"Weren't you asking questions or something?"

Sitting up straight, Sinder pulled out his phone and swore softly under his breath while he tapped furiously at his screen.

"Is something wrong?"

"I. Forgot."

"How do you mean?" Akira glanced warily about. "Is it some kind of … fox dream?"

"Something is influencing people. And I'm affected. Colt probably didn't notice because he's always so chill. But there's a difference between relaxed and relaxing your guard."

Taking a bite of the first sandwich, Akira nodded. But there wasn't much he could contribute. He was susceptible to everything *except* dragon sway. And that wasn't the problem here.

"What's nice?" Sinder demanded.

"Hmm?" Akira looked down at his wedge of burger. "This pastrami is nice."

Sinder waved a hand. "Think about why you said what you did. Because it's what everyone else is saying, too. What makes you think today's nice? Or that this place is nice? Or that you feel nice?"

That was easy. "Home is nice."

"You mean Stately House?"

"No. Japan. I like things from Japan."

"Yeah?" Sinder leaned forward. "Anything else?"

It took longer for the thought to form, but Akira finally said, "Red flowers are nice."

"Where did you see them? In the courtyard? In the gallery?"

The answer was on the tip of his tongue. "I'm not sure."

Sinder peered around, sucking moodily at his drink. "After lunch, we'll retrace your steps, see if we can't figure out what brought red flowers to mind. It could be important."

"Sure. We can do that."

But after lunch, Akira washed up, thanked Sinder, and left.

While strolling toward the corner where he'd board the trolly, Akira sent a series of texts. He showed Quen a picture of his father's namesake sandwich. A selfie with Sinder for Tenma, who'd apparently become friends with the dragon over the summer. He also sent it to Jacques, mostly to see if his message would show up as read.

It did. So Akira sent a bunch more snapshots. Jacques texted back as soon as there was a lull.

**Since when did this become
a culinary tour?**

Food is culture

> **Sandwiches, though?**
> **Is that the best you can do?**

The shop is in the museum
where Juuyu is working
Masterpiece Sandwiches

> **How droll**

Akira was feeling better the longer the exchange went on.

Is Sis there?

> **Saints forbid**
> **Twould be awkward**
> **This is the grooming hour**

Jacques sent through a selfie that might have been indecent, if not for the abundance of foam. Bubble baths weren't very Japanese, but neither was Uncle Jackie. Deece and Gilen smiled shyly at the camera. And a beat later, Akira realized that none of them were holding the phone.

Who snapped that pic?

> **Me!**

A selfie came through, too close and cross-eyed, of Nonny. In the next one, the goat crosser was so busy flexing, he hadn't yet noticed that Deece was about to pounce.

Jacques must have reclaimed his phone, because the next selfie showed the teen in a casual headlock while Gilen huddled next to Jacques. If the tiger crosser's flattened ears were anything to go by, Nonny was swearing up a storm.

I miss you guys

All is as it should be
But are you having fun?

Some
Today was nice

His gaze lingered on that word. Wait a minute. Wasn't he supposed to be looking around the museum with Sinder? Why hadn't the dragon reminded him?

How had they forgotten?

Akira stopped in the middle of the sidewalk, then stepped to the side. Switching to Sinder's messages, he sent a quick text.

Sorry I left

Miss me already?

We were going to look
for red flowers in the gallery
Remember?

Sinder sent through a string of furious emotes. Then Akira's phone rang.

"Do me a favor, since I might forget." His words were thick with urgency. And sway. *"Tell Argent it's no good."*

There was a long pause, so Akira asked, "Is that all?"

"No. We're under the influence of something insidious. And it's so danged pleasant, we forget about looking for the source."

"Got it. I'll call him right away. As soon as you hang up."

"That's great. Wait. One other thing." Sinder asked, *"How far*

were you from the museum before you remembered what we were supposed to be doing?"

Akira turned to look back at the building. "Not far. I'm on the sidewalk along Mainsail. Almost to the trolly stop."

"I'm making a note. Why is this so ...? Is this what Dickon meant ...?" Another pause, and Sinder hissed. *"I need to find Juuyu."*

"Be careful."

"Same to you." And Sinder ended the call.

The trolly was coming along the street, so Akira hurried toward the stop while he backtracked to Jacques' messages. Because the only direct line to Argent Mettlebright went through Uncle Jackie.

You still there?

While he waited for a response, Akira glanced up and froze. On the bench sat the man with vaguely Asian features. He smiled pleasantly and beckoned. And spoke in flawless Japanese. "Good afternoon, young man. Could you spare me a few minutes?"

He pointed to the trolly. Others were boarding. "I'm supposed to ..."

"Akira?" With a searching look, he asserted, "It *is* you. Naoki's son."

151

21

UNFORGETTABLE

When the man beckoned again, Akira joined him on the bench. "You know my name?"

Dark eyes grew sad. "You do not remember me."

"I'm sorry. And also confused. How do you know me?"

"Akira Hajime," he said, caressing each syllable. "How could I *not* know you? You look so much like Naoki."

This was so strange. "That's my father's name. You knew my parents?"

"Rather well."

"I don't remember much. Sis is older, so she has clearer memories."

"Is Tsumiko safe?"

"Tsumiko's good. Busy. Happy. She's always surrounded by kids, and they love her as much as she loves them."

"She is like Naoki in that way. He loves his children." The man rubbed his fingertips together. "I knew Saint Midori's would be a good place."

Akira hesitated. "She's not there anymore. Stuff happened right around the time of the Emergence. She's Lady Mettlebright now. Argent is her bondmate."

Color drained from the man's face. "Someone *took* her?"

"Hey, now. It's not like she was kidnapped or anything." Akira placed a steadying hand on the man's arm. "Argent *cherishes* her."

He was trembling.

"I did not know. I have been away. It was necessary." Covering Akira's hand with his own, he asked, "And you? Are you happy, Akira?"

"Sure. I mean, usually. Hey. What should I call you?"

The man looked away, and when he looked back, he had his emotions more in control. "You could call me Tabigarasu."

"All right." It was obviously a nickname, not any kind of given name. "So you're a wanderer?"

"I love to travel." His expression turned shy. "National parks. Preserves. Wild places, where beauty remains a secret to all but the wind and the stars. And me."

"But you're originally from Japan?"

"As it happens, yes, we share a homeland. But *this* happenstance is confusing. What brings you so far from home?"

"It started out as a favor to a friend, but really, this part's a vacation. I'll go back home eventually. Did I mention I live with Tsumiko?"

"That is well. Families *should* be together."

The man's gaze softened in a way that surprised Akira. And tugged at his memory. "Did you used to visit?"

"I did linger about." Leaning closer, Tabigarasu asked, "Do you remember?"

"Maybe." Akira studied the man before him. Slender and not very tall. Which was to say Akira's height. Glossy black hair was long enough to have been gathered into a knot, which was held in place by a pair of sticks. A kanzashi was a quirky touch, since the hair decorations were usually worn by women. This one had a knot of woven cords, tiny bells, glittering crystals, and a spray of red flowers.

"You do seem familiar."

"I should."

It occurred to Akira that this man wasn't old. While he radiated maturity, his skin was free of wrinkles. His features were delicate, almost feminine, and there was an impish quality to his growing smile. How old would his parents have been now? Fifty, at least. Older than this man appeared to be. Unless ... was it possible that this person was Amaranthine?

"I feel like I *should* know you," Akira admitted. And very carefully, he formed a hand sign that declared him a Betweener.

If Tabigarasu noticed, he didn't let on.

Akira asked, "May I call you Tabi-ojisan? Tabi-oji!" Surely a friend of his father's was owed uncle status.

"Please do."

"And ... may I send a picture of us to Sis?"

His smile faded. "She may not remember me. We lost ties after ... what happened to your parents."

"Understood, but I show her all the nice people I meet. That way she knows I'm okay." Akira flipped through his recent photos, showing off the one of him with Rafter. "Maybe she won't recognize you, but maybe she will. Want to find out?"

"I must confess I do."

"Can I come closer?" He held up his phone, miming a selfie.

Tabi-oji stretched an arm behind Akira, and they slid together. He took a few snapshots, and they sat, heads bent together while choosing one to keep.

"Do you have a picture of Tsumiko?" he asked.

"No. They're not allowed." Rolling his eyes, he said, "Argent's *very* protective. So if you want to see Sis, you'll have to go to Stately House."

"I see. Yes. I will consider it."

Akira asked, "How long are you staying in Beacon?"

"Until I move along," he said vaguely. "A little while longer."

"While you're here, do you want to meet again? I'd like to hear stuff about my parents."

Tabi-oji bowed his head. "That would be an unparalleled pleasure."

"Great! How can I contact you? A text?"

"Here." With a graceful sweep of his hand that included the museum, he said, "I would gladly meet with you here."

"Easy enough." Akira offered, "Want to have lunch with me tomorrow?"

Tabi-oji drew in a long breath, then exhaled on a low chuckle. "Yes, Akira. Tomorrow, I will be here for you."

Akira closed the crystal gate firmly behind him before softly calling, "Zuzu? Zuzu!"

The tree winked into existence before him, all clasped hands and wide eyes. "You need me?"

"I do!" Lifting a flat box that was still hot from the ovens of a nearby pizzeria, he asked, "Can you smuggle this into Fumiko's room? I thought she might enjoy a feast."

Zuzu's lashes fluttered. "Pizza?"

"Yep! Ever have it?"

"Twice before." The tree's gaze bounced between the box and the lighthouse behind her. "She likes gifts. This will make her smile."

"Do you like pizza?"

"Me? I wonder."

"Do you eat?"

"I can, but I don't need to. My roots delve deep." She waved a hand between them. "I would rather feed you. Are you hungry? Because dinner might be late tonight."

"Is something wrong?"

"I think so." Zuzu whispered, "Fumiko is unhappy, and Juuyu is unhappy. But I don't understand why, and that makes me unhappy."

Akira was astonished. "Juuyu is here?"

"Since a little past midday. He asked if you were here, and then he went in the front door."

"Oh, no."

"And he stopped. And he stares." Zuzu fidgeted. "He seems displeased, and Fumiko has been crying."

Pushing the pizza box into her hands, Akira said, "I understand. I can help."

"Is he angry? Sister thinks he's angry."

"No. Far from it." Akira was already backing toward the lighthouse. "In a weird way, Juuyu is hugely, ridiculously happy."

And that was bad.

22

FEAST FOR THE SENSES

Juuyu took one step to the side and fixed his full attention on a rolling rack of coffee cups. No two were alike, so he needed longer than usual to memorize each pattern and its placement.

"Did you need a cup?" asked Fumiko. "You can borrow one. These are for everyone to use. I keep the special ones upstairs."

So there were more? Why would anyone scatter a collection of like items?

"Ooo!" Fumiko reached past him, plucking a small cup from the shelf. "I was looking for this one."

Juuyu spared her a glance as she disappeared up the clogged stairway, moderately frustrated by the sudden removal. He knew he'd be searching for it later, and who knew where she might have hidden it. Still, he made a mental note of the small, white cup with its pink interior, a single strawberry decorating its front. The size suggested that it was intended for a child's use.

Although there were some interesting items strewn in that direction, Juuyu forced himself to focus on the cart again. An organized approach was required. One section at a time.

Fumiko returned, slightly breathless, to hover at his elbow.

Juuyu asked, "May I move things?"

"Do you think it's necessary?"

"Increasingly so." His fingers twitched to sort these piles.

"As long as you're careful."

His attention leapt to a freestanding cabinet with glass doors. Unlike the collection of cups, the contents of these shelves were randomized. Yet pertinent to the function of the room, where the enclave members clearly gathered for meals and for conversation.

Board games. Cookbooks. Jigsaw puzzles.

There was also evidence of postal deliveries, both from the public sector and the In-between. Communiques. Grocery fliers. Takeout menus. Mail order catalogs. Back issues of magazines addressed to the library. Volumes of a journal called *The Perambulating Preservationist*.

Juuyu glanced at dates and began culling.

He stacked decades old phone directories. Beside them, he began a pile of mail order catalogs for everything from gourmet cheese to telescopes. He slowed when he realized there were potentially important documents in the mix.

Alumni newsletters from top reaver academies. Invitations to Parent's Day events at Wardenclave. Promotional literature addressed to no less than seven reavers. Had they been interns? Or did these represent children in Fumiko's line?

Excitement sharpened his senses.

While he couldn't imagine living like this, he liked flirting along the edges of chaos. Like a young phoenix on a dare, skimming low over water that could swamp feathers and quench flames, Juuyu challenged himself. The mess put him on edge, but at that edge, he found clarity.

It was like battle, yet he didn't face an opponent.

This room represented a mystery. A case.

Every little thing was clamoring for his attention, begging to be noticed and considered and remembered. There were valuable clues amidst the mess.

He shouldn't.

Really, this was absurd.

In some distant part of Juuyu's mind, reason battled against instinct.

"What's this pile?" Fumiko tapped his arm, pointed urgently. "Why is this pile so far from the rest?"

"These print materials are outdated and should be recycled." Juuyu lifted a finger and teased a dainty cup squirreled away in one corner. "You might consider discarding damaged goods. This is chipped."

With a soft noise of dismay, she snatched it from his hand and darted upstairs again. So he was doomed to another game of seek and find. This time, the cup was opaque blue, with carnival glaze giving it an iridescent sheen. Probably part of a larger set. The sort that included a punch bowl.

It might be a meaningless detail.

It might be a defining moment.

Juuyu usually couldn't tell which was which until he'd absorbed all the available information. Gathering it up was a painstaking process. One for which he was uniquely suited.

But he shouldn't. Others were meant to do this work. Why hadn't they?

"Fumiko."

"Yes, I'm here." Her breathing was uneven. Her tone wavering. "Yes?"

"Why have you not been provided with a chronicler?"

Then Akira was suddenly in front of Juuyu, pulling him down until they were eye-to-eye. Serious and stern, Akira said, "You're making Fumiko nervous."

Juuyu's gaze flicked to the woman. Were her lashes wet? He bowed his head. "Entirely unintentional."

"Tell her you're not angry," Akira ordered in Japanese.

"I am not."

"Tell *her*."

Though he warbled a low protest, Juuyu raised his voice. "Fumiko, I am not angry."

"Okay," she said, sounding uncertain.

Akira tugged on Juuyu's tie. "Can you stop?"

Loath as he was to admit the truth, Juuyu said, "No."

"Right. Then we go forward, but like gentlemen." Akira turned to face their hostess. "It's true. He really isn't angry. This is his focus face. When he's working, Juuyu can be pretty scary."

Juuyu eased into a more neutral posture. How many times had this young man taken charge of Suuzu in this manner? Juuyu knew full well that his younger brother was maturing into a skilled

161

diplomat, a true spokesperson. Very likely in direct proportion to the time he spent with Akira.

"Are you sure you don't mind?" Akira was asking.

"As long as he doesn't throw anything away," Fumiko answered.

"Right. Thanks ever so. I'll make sure of it." And then Akira was back in Juuyu's personal space, hands framing his face. "You may have six hours, from the hour after I fall asleep until the hour before I wake. That should work, right?"

Juuyu didn't break eye contact. "I promised Suuzu ...."

"I'll be asleep whether you're staring right at me or sorting bottlecaps in the next room." Akira turned to address Fumiko again. "This is going to be just fine. He'll be more at ease if you let him do his thing. Juuyu will work at night, while we're asleep. So it won't really be a problem."

"Only at night?" Fumiko looked between them. "All night?"

"You'll still get the lullabies I promised." Akira's posture shifted into a pleading pose. "I promised."

Juuyu was in no position to refuse.

Akira went right on. "He'll still be gone all day, though. He was sent here to do a job, and it's important, too."

Fumiko smiled tentatively.

"Can you do it this way?" Akira searched Juuyu's face. "You won't get in trouble with Boon if you spend time on a personal project?"

Juuyu shook his head. Boon wasn't the issue. Argent represented a far more devastating threat if the bait was plucked from his trap.

Everything sank in then. Akira had brokered a deal that allowed Juuyu to neaten this nest. He could gather and sort and study ...

and fit together the jumbled pieces of Fumiko's life. Once he fully understood her position, he might be able to help her and Zuzu. Improve their way of life. All while attending to his duties as a member of Hisoka's team.

"You're secretly pleased," Akira accused in an undertone.

"The timing is terrible."

Akira sighed. "Sorry, Juuyu. I tried to keep you safe. Why didn't you use the window like we agreed?"

With a frown, Juuyu tried to think back. "I do not remember."

"What's done is done. And it's temporary, right?"

"In what sense?"

"You're acting leader," Akira reasoned. "So you're only in charge until Boon gets back."

Already tallying the collection of ramekins on a sideboard, Juuyu distractedly answered, "Boon is not coming. You are going to him."

"Wh-what?"

Akira's stunned expression brought Juuyu back into stark focus. Too soon. Far too soon. All of the arrangements were not yet complete. And if Akira told Suuzu, everything would become ... difficult.

23

ROCKABYE

umiko wanted Juuyu to stay. That part was simple.

But Akira had explained enough for her to understand that the only way that was happening was if Juuyu was *comfortable* here. So why did letting him rearrange things to his liking make her *un*comfortable?

When Juuyu studied the contents of a cupboard or a drawer, what did he see? Did he think her foolish to cling to reminders? Was it pitiful that she needed them? And where was Zuzu?

She eyed the stairway, ready to run, anxious to climb.

Had it ever been like this before? She couldn't remember.

Akira called her name, and Juuyu came over, presenting his palms.

"Trade with me in the manner of friends. Let us find a peaceable balance. Songs for sorting. Advocacy for indulgence." Juuyu's manner was solemn. "I will extend every consideration to you and your belongings if you can make allowances for this ... quirk of instinct."

His restraint had a pained quality.

Was that her fault?

"Fumiko?" He changed the way he stood. "Are you willing?"

She asked, "You want to be my chronicler?"

Juuyu angled his head to the side, and something in his gaze brightened. But then he shook his head. "I cannot take that role. Others would be more suited."

"But I trust *you*."

"Are you certain?" Juuyu tucked his chin and lowered his voice. "You are hiding things from me."

She had. She might again. "You'll want to see *everything*?"

"I will. *If* you will allow it." He took one of her hands in both of his and asked, "Is this intimacy so different from that of tending?"

Fumiko thought the difference vast. "It's one thing if it's just me. I can't lose myself. But everything else is completely different!"

He peered around, his attention catching on different items before returning to her face. "In what way?"

"I'll show you." And since he already had her hand, Fumiko used it to tug him after her. As she crossed the room, she touched items. A pale yellow soup tureen. A hummingbird feeder still in its package. An old brass compass, sigil-etched but scratched. Fumiko explained, "This was Akemi's. Margaret would have loved this. And this was a favorite of ... of ... Zuzu?"

Her twin appeared.

Fumiko touched the compass. "Zuzu, who loved this one?"

"Carl," said her sister. "Carl loved boats and tried to sail away on a raft when he was nine. What a furor that caused. But Soren jumped in after him and towed him back to shore. He wouldn't let me help at all."

Fumiko remembered now, and she laughed, though at the time, she'd been so afraid that she'd lose a child to the sea. "Yes, Carl. I miss Carl."

"Is that how it is?" Juuyu looked between them and asked, "You have been compiling your own chronicle."

"I am?"

"By longstanding custom, tree-kin of human descent are afforded a chronicler. Every grove and every familial copse employs one or more, yet you have done without. An egregious oversight." Juuyu offered one of his hands to Zuzu, who snuggled right up to him. "You found your own way to honor your line."

Fumiko's lip trembled.

Nobody thought well of her growing accumulation. The interns let her have her way, since this was her home, but her choices confused them and concerned them by turns. They'd shake their heads and dust her piles. But some disapproved, and others whispered.

Greedy.

Wasteful.

Clingy.

Touchy.

Yet Juuyu not only seemed to understand, he approved. And lent words to her longing, giving it a certain dignity. She was a chronicler. Not a very good one, so she probably wasn't suited to the role either.

"It's a chronicle?" she whispered. "Truly?"

"Far from traditional. But I have little doubt that the facts are all here."

Akira raised a hand. "Are you talking about Fumiko's family tree?"

"That's me." Zuzu pulled the young man into their huddle. "I'm the tree."

"Do you receive progeny reports?" Juuyu asked. "Official documents regarding your children's children, throughout their generations."

"Diva might know."

Zuzu backed her up. "We love people, not papers."

"Do your people ever visit?"

Fumiko looked away, looked back, looked down. "Sometimes. At the end."

With a soft trill, he gathered them closer. "That is the way of things in groves. At such a time, it is only natural to seek comfort from the one who carried and kept them close."

"They want their mother," agreed Zuzu.

Juuyu inclined his head. "Or the one who raised them."

Akira wriggled his way more firmly into the hug. "Hey, Juuyu? For Suuzu, that person is you. But who's your person?"

Juuyu's expression softened. "Do you remember Letik?"

"Sure. He hung around a lot while I was visiting."

"Naturally, since he is the tree among whose branches my small house is hidden. Letik is the one I clung to when I was small."

Fumiko let herself relax against Juuyu's side. He *did* understand. Not only had he been raised in a grove, he'd lived in a tree.

Akira's eyes widened. "Hang on a sec. Your dad was a tree? Does that mean Suuzu's dad is a tree?"

"Our father is twinned to a tree," Juuyu corrected. "Did Suuzu not tell you?"

"I had no idea."

"Perhaps it is my place to tell. Our father Liiri was born with Letik's seed in his hand. Our mother is Baala, and many do say that Suuzu and I resemble her."

Akira shook his head. "I didn't meet your mom. Both times."

"Female phoenixes are somewhat rare and therefore precious to the colony. Baala was in seclusion. She will not leave an egg for any reason."

"Your mom was expecting a baby?"

"In a sense. *Chick* would be somewhat more accurate. Mother is very traditional when it comes to ...."

Fumiko watched them with a growing sense of relief. Juuyu was overly serious, but he was patient. The hand at her back kept her close, and he gave Zuzu the same courtesy. Someone who could welcome both of them? That was beyond rare in Fumiko's experience. If only he would stay.

Wait. Sorting her things would take a while.

If she let him, didn't that mean he'd stay longer?

"... because during your first visit, Viiri's egg was newly laid. And your second visit was three years later, just before he cracked shell."

"It takes three years for a phoenix egg to hatch?"

"That is the usual duration of an Amaranthine pregnancy." Juuyu hummed and added, "Crosser pregnancies, as well."

"Yes," she blurted. "That's what I want."

Juuyu blinked.

Akira laughed. "Maybe you should explain, Fumiko-onee-san. What are *you* talking about?"

"I want Juuyu to help with my chronicle." She looked up into orange eyes. "I'm willing. I'll trust. I won't hide anything."

Juuyu closed his eyes and sighed a soft, "Thank you."

"But first!" interjected Akira. "I promised these ladies a lullaby. Tonight. Will you sing for them?"

"I will. Is there someplace where I can see the sky, and you can see me?"

Zuzu giggled, and Fumiko asked, "Do you like to climb trees?"

After dinner that evening, which was only slightly spoiled by cold pizza, Akira received a lesson in tree-climbing.

Suuzu probably would have protested such precarious exercise, but Juuyu left him to his own devices, undoubtedly confident in his ability to catch anything that might fall. With Fumiko's guidance, Akira made it into Zuzu's branches, where chimes and seashells twirled.

"Is that a hammock?" he asked.

"We've added many different seats and swings." Fumiko pointed into the maze of branches. "Sometimes I nap up here."

"Is that safe?" Akira worked his way along, trying not to think about how far above the lighthouse they were. Wait. "Are we over the farmer's market here?"

"Yes." Fumiko pointed to a different branch. "Let's go this way. You can pick a hammock."

She hurried ahead, much faster than Akira was willing to follow.

"Tired?" asked Juuyu.

Akira laughed at himself. "I *really* shouldn't have looked down."

"May I take you the rest of the way."

"Please."

Juuyu came alongside the limb so Akira could clamber onto his back.

With both arms wrapped around the phoenix's shoulders, Akira closed his eyes and took deep breaths. "I'm not usually afraid of heights."

"You are not usually without Suuzu."

Juuyu was right. Somewhere in the back of his mind, Akira had been worrying about how Suuzu would take the news if he slipped and fell. The very idea had locked his knees. "Guess I'm not so brave without him."

"My brother is also braver when you are near." Juuyu sauntered forward, sometimes putting his foot upon a branch, sometimes placing it in midair.

"Then why are you sending me away?"

"Boon needs you." Pausing, he quietly added, "Please, do not tell Suuzu."

"I can't promise that until I know what's been planned and why."

Juuyu turned his head just enough to meet Akira's eye. "I can tell you two things. First, this is Argent's plan."

That was reassuring. But baffling. "And ...?"

"We need your help in order to rescue Inti."

Juuyu tucked Akira under a faded quilt in the center of a double-wide hammock that rocked slightly in the evening breezes. Rising higher, he transformed into truest form, his wings fanned wide, his tailfeathers trailing, his throat swelling as he piped through the avian equivalent of scales.

From a similar hammock, a little to one side and even higher up, Fumiko and Zuzu were giggling and swaying. Akira could understand their excitement. His heart still raced whenever a phoenix sang. Nothing compared.

As Juuyu began a traditional lullaby, Akira placed a call.

Suuzu picked up, but he didn't immediately speak. There was a soft rustling and a low grunt.

"Your brother is singing us to sleep. Can you hear?"

"I miss this song." Faint snatches of humming came through.

"Are you busy?"

"Akira ...?" Suuzu sounded especially bleary.

"Right here. Hey," he whispered. "You okay?"

"Better now."

From somewhere close by, another voice drawled, *"Give it over, lover boy."*

Akira was surprised. "Uncle Jackie?"

"Your timing is beautiful. Lord. Is that Juuyu? I'm putting you on speaker." Jacques went right on. *"Somber as a gray sea and twice as restless, but the sound of your voice, and he remembers how to smile."*

171

"Don't tease."

"I'm not teasing. If anything, I'm relieved. Suuzu is rather drunk and thoroughly worn out. He needs sleep, and he's having trouble finding it. Your voice and Juuyu's song seem to be doing the trick though."

"Are you overseeing his long sleep this month?"

"Yes. Argent has us stashed in one of the towers. Suuzu's here in a highly unofficial capacity."

"Is something the matter?"

"Usually." With a husky chuckle, Jacques said, *"You didn't hear it from me, but Hisoka and Argent cleared your boy's schedule. He'll sleep a week, whether he wants to or not. And when he wakes, he'll be on his way."*

Akira's heart leapt. "To where?"

"To you."

24
MEET UP

Akira woke beside Juuyu, whose loose embrace was a guard against falling, at least partially. One of his hands rested over Akira's tattoo. The promised tending. Easing onto his back, Akira gazed peacefully at the play of light and leaves overhead. The shush of lazy waves came from far below.

"I could see living in a tree," he murmured.

"Suuzu will be delighted to know it."

"Are any of those Ephemera?"

Juuyu opened his eyes long enough to follow his gaze. "The small green birds."

"Cute."

For a while, it remained silent. Juuyu was probably working on the sigil. Not that Akira could tell. Then again, it was early days. Michael had warned that it might take time for him to gain anything from the connection. Assuming it worked at all. It

173

might not. Argent hadn't exactly been optimistic on that score. Cautionary words. Slim chances.

"Does the sigil work?" he whispered.

Juuyu hummed. "I am not entirely clear on its intended purpose. It is ... complex."

"I'm pretty sure it's meant to do a few things."

"I can activate the outer two rings, and I can infuse them with power. You are traceable. And you can see nippets. That is something."

Akira knew he should be glad of *anything*. But it was hard not to hope for everything. For his own sake, sure, but mostly for Suuzu.

"He's coming here." Akira backed up to provide more context. "I called Suuzu last night, and Uncle Jackie was there. Suuzu's started his long sleep, and as soon as he wakes, he's coming here."

Juuyu opened his eyes, held his gaze. "Did you mention ...?"

"No."

"Thank you."

Akira changed the subject. "Did you clean things all night?"

"I did not exceed the agreed upon six hours. Also, it is too soon to rearrange things. I am still making an initial assessment."

"You spent all night looking?"

"I did. I cannot decide upon a sensible course without first gaining a sense of the task's scope."

"Do you need help with anything?"

"No. You will be asleep."

Akira cautiously asked, "Will this cause you trouble? With your main job, I mean?"

"I cannot imagine it will. Since this obligation overlaps with my prior obligation to you, the team was already prepared to carry on without me."

"Until Suuzu gets here."

Juuyu's eyes widened ever so slightly. "Until Suuzu gets here."

Since he was early, Akira took his time making his way to the trolly stop. There were so many tiny shops and restaurants along both sides of the street. The Bohotique. Seascape Art Supply. The Spume Room, which appeared to be a microbrewery.

He joined the queue in front of a long, narrow building with a take-out window at the front. A paper tray of hot cinnamon-and-sugar doughnut holes left him feeling amply rewarded for his curiosity.

Breezing through a couple of souvenir shops, he collected ideas for small gifts he could bring home. Only... picking would be more fun with Suuzu along. He snapped pictures of American snacks in a convenience store and sent them to Kimi. But there were no pork buns and no one to split them with.

Only a week.

Ten days at most.

He could hold out.

Akira snapped a selfie in front of a tumble of vibrant pink flowers that was growing over a fence. He wasn't used to seeing so many flowers blooming in October. The woods around Stately

House had been showing autumn colors, yet this city seemed caught in an endless summer.

Boarding the trolly, he tried to guess who was local and who was a tourist. Several wore what he suspected were restaurant uniforms, so they were on their way to work. Others had messenger bags or backpacks. Perhaps there was a university nearby? They seemed the right age to be students.

Passengers came from a wide range of people groups, but Akira couldn't help wishing there had been an Amaranthine in the mix. Or someone in reaver colors. He guessed he was searching for someone who'd understand a friendly gesture or two. Smiles and nods had to suffice.

Not that there were *no* signs of Amaranthine. Because they were on all kinds of signs.

They passed a bus that had been plastered with a campaign poster, reminding folks that there was an Amaranthine candidate running for president. Argent and Michael often discussed how much the United States would change if Cyril Sunfletch won his way into the White House.

A billboard promoted the final season of *Pure Instinct*, the crime-fighting drama whose popularity had skyrocketed thanks to an openly Amaranthine actress. Another channel was hyping a lineup that included *Dare Together* and *Crossing America*. Alongside *Between Friends*, a new daytime talk show hosted by a beaming Amaranthine duo.

It was progress. But Juuyu would probably insist that Suuzu disguise himself as a human before he'd let them tour around.

The trolly poked along, stopping at every corner, but they

finally reached the Amory, and Akira stepped off. He and Tabi-oji hadn't set an exact time or place, but Akira decided to wait inside.

If Sinder was stationed at a table, he was out of sight. Or maybe he was in some kind of team meeting. Colt should be around, too, but the only Amaranthine in the lobby was Tuft, who was doing his ambassadorial part for the In-between. Akira drifted close enough to confirm that his sign was still in place … and to offer the lynx a silent greeting.

The slight inclination of his head cheered Akira immensely.

He wandered over toward the lunch counter and scanned the names of sandwiches on the menu board. One of the workers smiled and waved him over. "Any questions?"

"Umm … no. I like the names."

"Great, huh? We have nutritional information for all of them. Say, would you like the menu in another language?"

Akira asked, "Do you have Japanese?"

"Of course!" She passed him a menu card with the shop's logo on it. "You can have this. We do catering, so if you're throwing a party, keep us in mind!"

"May I have two?" Akira wanted to bring one home to share with the family. "Thank you very much. I'm waiting for a friend before I order."

"No rush. Whenever you're ready."

While he'd gotten the gist of most of the English descriptions, it was nice to have the assorted toppings and sauces demystified. He could kind of see how they'd tried to match up the sandwiches to their namesakes.

The Elderbough was piled high with sliced meat, served au jus with a side of fries. Plausible. By contrast, the Mossberne involved falafel in a pita with cucumber relish and tahini sauce. Akira had to wonder if people were more comfortable thinking that dragons were vegetarian. Because he'd *seen* the trays of food Jacques brought upstairs when Lapis first woke from his long sleeps, and rare steaks figured prominently on his menu.

But the real kicker was the Mettlebright. Argent's name had been added to the kind of katsu sandwiches that were typical at lunch counters back home. Thin pork cutlets, shaved cabbage, and tonkotsu sauce on white bread with the crusts removed. Served in a box with a side of pickled vegetables. They were *Jacques'* favorite. A guilty pleasure, he called them.

To be fair, they were a family favorite, as well. Argent, Ginkgo, and Michael would make platters of them, enough to feed the whole enclave, whenever they decided that Sansa and Sonnet needed the evening off.

Akira wanted one. Or maybe he just wanted *them*.

He couldn't ever remember being homesick before.

Pulling out his phone, he sent texts until the telltale clack of wood on stone alerted him to Tabi-oji's approach. The man was dressed in the same manner, and it hit Akira that it was the first time they'd been standing next to each other. If not for the centimeters he gained by his geta, Tabi-oji and Akira would have been about the same height.

"You made it!"

The man offered a slight bow, then considered the menu board. "Is this what you would like to eat?"

"Sure. The food's good. I tried three of these sandwiches yesterday."

Tabi-oji's eyebrows shot up. "I am surprised by your appetite."

Akira laughed. "I shared with a friend."

The man hummed, and his attention strayed back to the menu. "I am not used to these kinds of things. Choose something and share with me?"

"That works. Do you have a preference?"

"You would like to try something new, yes?"

That *was* appealing. "It'd be fun to work through the whole menu. Will you be here long enough?"

"I could be."

Akira handed him the menu in Japanese. "Maybe if you help me, we can make it through all of them."

"In exchange for stories of your father?"

He jammed his hands into his pockets. "I'm sorry. That was presumptuous of me."

"It is all right to be greedy sometimes." Tabi-oji tucked the folded paper into his sleeve. "Share with me, and I will share with you. Please, order our meal."

So Akira stepped up and ordered the Mettlebright, adding two bottles of tea to the tray.

While he chatted with the cashier, Tabi-oji lingered at his side, a serene expression on his face as he gazed out over the lobby.

"Ready?" Akira peered around. "Do you want to sit in here? Or try for a spot outside?"

"The day is pleasant."

So they found a round table in the courtyard, where the sun was bright, but not too warm, and a light breeze ruffled the scalloped edges of their umbrella.

Once the sandwich was divided, Tabi-oji asked, "What do you know about Naoki?"

"Not much. I was still in diapers when we were bundled off to Saint Midori's. The sisters let Sis and I stay together, but Midori's is an all-girls school once you get past elementary classes. So I moved to a boys' school nearby."

"You were both alone?"

"Not really. I made friends. And our uncle arranged for visits." Akira chewed thoughtfully. "That part's a little strange. Argent looked into our family tree. I guess there's something unique about our bloodline or something. But there's no papers. Nothing. Anyhow, the man I always thought of as Uncle Saburo is actually just a lawyer. Sis called him uncle out of respect, but he's not a blood relation."

"You were not ... neglected?"

"No, no. I had Sis, and she had her job at Midori's. And then Suuzu and Argent happened." Akira pulled threads of cabbage from his sandwich. "All that to say ... the only real record we have of our parents is Tsumiko's memory."

"And what did she have to say?"

"Umm ... Dad was patient and kind, and he loved plants. She says she used to play with the stones in the trays that held his bonsai collection." Akira thought back. "Other than that, he seemed to be a scientist or something. Maybe? I mean, he had to be a reaver. Or an unregistered reaver. There's almost no other way Sis could be a beacon, otherwise."

"Almost," agreed Tabi-oji. "What kinds of things did you want to know?"

Akira shrugged. "Was he as kind as Sis remembers?"

"He has always been unfailingly kind where his children are concerned, but with the rest of us ...?" Tabi-oji laughed. "I would call Naoki stubborn. Very sure of what he believes is the right course. And something of a rebel."

"Was he a reaver?"

"He is a reaver, yes. Though he essentially vowed out."

Akira couldn't imagine leaving the In-between once he was a part of it, but he wanted to hear Tabi-oji out before plaguing him with questions he might be about to answer.

"The home into which you were born was indeed filled with plants, but there were far more books. Naoki is the studious type. A scientist, yes, but also a researcher."

"Tsumiko is that way, too!" Akira was ridiculously excited by this hint of a family resemblance. "She's been studying all kinds of old books lately, scriptures and prophecies and legends and things. Anything, really, so long as there are dragons involved."

Tabi-oji's jaw worked. "Dragons?"

"Yeah, umm ... it's a long story." He took a big bite of sandwich.

Unfortunately, Tabi-oji simply waited for him to chew and swallow. "Why is Tsumiko interested in dragons?"

"Mostly on account of Kyrie. Her son. I mean, he's adopted, but he's hers. She's a good mom." With a small smile, he shared, "All the kids, the crossers who live at Stately House, they call her Lady."

"Dragons are dangerous," Tabi-oji whispered.

"They can be," Akira agreed. "That doesn't mean they all are."

"Naoki listened to a dragon and nearly lost everything he holds dear."

Akira had noticed it before. He was doing it again. Maybe it was nothing, but ... maybe it was important. "Why do you speak of him in the present tense? Is ... is it because my dad's alive in your memories?"

"No, my dear boy." And with a sad smile, Tabi-oji said, "It is because Naoki is alive."

"I'm sorry?"

"So am I." He looked away and asked, "What did your sister have to say about the photo you took of us? The selfie."

"Umm ... come to think of it." Akira flicked to his messages and frowned in confusion. "I guess I forgot to send it."

"A small oversight. No harm done." With a reassuring smile, Tabi-oji said, "It is not important."

But it was. Akira had been excited to tell Sis about meeting one of their father's friends.

"It is for the best. Some memories should fade."

Akira looked away, and his attention snared on a scattering of small red flower petals on the pavers. The puff of a breeze sent them tumbling away. Red? Akira glanced around. None of the flowering plants in the courtyard were red. He rubbed at the tattoo on his shoulder, trying to force his thoughts into order. It almost felt like ... dragon sway.

"You're not a dragon," Akira said, sure of that.

Tabi-oji quietly answered, "No."

"But you *are* Amaranthine."

"What gives you that impression?"

Akira frowned. "You are. It's okay, you know. I don't mind. Which clan do you belong to?"

"I am alone. No clan." With a small shake of his head that sent the bells in his kanzashi jingling, he said, "As my name implies, I am simply a wanderer."

"Were you part of my family somehow?"

Tabi-oji's expression gentled. "What makes you think so?"

Akira didn't realize the reason was so true until he spoke it aloud. "You smell like home."

25

MOONLIGHTING

Nothing out of the ordinary happened all that day at the Amory, and Akira spent the evening in high spirits. One hour after the young man fell asleep, Juuyu eased from the bed, satisfied that his duties to his brother and to his team were done.

He warded the bed against sound, set up a folding screen he'd located the evening before, lofted a handful of softly glowing crystals, and set to work extracting a tall, boxy cabinet from amidst the clutter on the landing below their room. Juuyu placed it against the wall. The cabinet front swung open, revealing a close-set series of wide sliding trays. Perhaps it had been designed for map storage. Or geological samples. He'd even seen something similar used to preserve musical scores. Any important papers Juuyu found would be sorted here.

Easing carefully downstairs, he selected a small pile of

documents and photographs he'd set aside earlier. School papers. Newspaper clippings. A black-and-white photograph of Fumiko seated in a rocking chair, nursing an infant. A more recent one in which Fumiko led a little girl by the hand along the beach.

Presumably, the things he located at the tops of piles or in the fronts of storerooms were more recent. As he worked his way toward the bottom and toward the back, he'd uncover older and older items. Like an archeological excavation.

But one thing was bothering him. "Zuzu?"

Arms slid around his waist from behind, and the tree asked, "Yes?"

"You are in complete seclusion here."

"Except for the interns, yes."

"All comings and goings are strictly controlled."

"Barriers keep us safe from every direction."

Juuyu hummed. "Thus far, I have found a reference to three different reavers, and each appears to have fathered a child with Fumiko. How does she meet these men?"

"They send them. It's in the contract."

"What contract?"

"We are kept secret and kept safe, and in exchange, Sister gives the reavers children."

Juuyu tried to hide his anger. "How many?"

"All of them." Zuzu sidled around to face Juuyu, clearly puzzled by his response. "Sister's children are always strong. This pleases the reavers."

"How many times ...?" He was too upset to finish his own sentence and hissed.

"The contract is for one child per century."

"And she accepts this? Do they give her any choice?"

Zuzu giggled. "Our interns are always females. We know when it is time for a child because they send a group of males. Sister chooses a favorite."

"I see," he said stiffly.

Zuzu touched the photographs he held, smiling softly. "Look closer, Juuyu. Look at my sister. Once a century, Fumiko is allowed to be happy for a little while. Or longer. Some stayed, and we had nice big families. We're a dynasty, you know."

"I was unaware." Juuyu grappled with a sense of injustice, but calmly replied, "All the more reason to set her house in order."

"Will you let me help?"

Juuyu warbled softly. "I will be relying on you."

"I know!" Zuzu vanished. Moments later, she was back and pushing a small sheaf of papers into his hands. "You will need these."

They were portraits—pencil, charcoal, ink—on aged paper. Each depicted a smiling child of about ten years. There were names, but not in English. Three languages were represented, and he couldn't fathom the additional notations.

Half Marrow, gold as honey mead
7th of Honeysuckle, low and heavy
Tinder and 18, biting night, stars bright
Fullness of Maiden, auspicious pink

"Do you recall the year each of these were done?"

"Hmm?" Zuzu nodded and shook her head. "The dates are right there. Before the reavers came, we used the moons. A lone wolf taught us. We could not have survived without her protection."

Details like this enriched a chronicle. Excitement stirred, and Juuyu made up his mind. One drawer per century. He asked, "Who brokered the contract?"

"Linlu Dimityblest, on behalf of Glint Starmark."

Juuyu blinked. "So there *will* be a record."

"We're a dynasty," she repeated softly. "Our children were so good."

"What name was given to the dynasty?"

"Mine."

He cocked his head to one side. "I must confess, I have never heard of the Zuzu dynasty."

She dimpled and said, "My given name is Kazuki."

Juuyu riffled to the last picture she'd brought out, which was certainly Zuzu as a child. Her name was spelled with the kanji for "one tree." Something that belatedly brought a fresh detail into focus. "Fumiko is an artist?"

"Sometimes." Zuzu's expression turned wistful. "She put away her paints when Soren died."

Birds were stirring even before the sky began to lighten, which hastened Juuyu's steps toward the guesthouse. "Sinder, I need some things."

Turning from his computer, Sinder beamed at him. "Thank all four winds. Work! Does this mean we have a lead?"

Juuyu eased into an apologetic posture. "Can you find a listing of the moon calendar used by the packs?"

"The Seven Score Moons? Easy. Want me to print it out for you?"

"Please."

"Is this relevant to the case?" Sinder's look was knowing.

"I need it in regards to a side project."

"Fumiko's chronicle?"

Juuyu cautiously inclined his head. He probably shouldn't be using their resources for what amounted to a personal matter.

Swiveling to face his computer screen, Sinder typed and clicked as he said, "Zuzu's beyond excited. It's all she could talk about this morning."

"She was with you?"

"For a while. She likes to watch me fish." The printer whirred to life. "Seems they don't get many dragons in these parts. Mostly seals. And the odd comet."

"Comet?"

"So she says." Sinder folded his hands behind his neck. "Sashimi for breakfast? Or Colt and Hallow are conspiring to do a fry-up on the beach after the changing of the guard."

"Who will be with Moon?"

"My turn. At least until Hallow is sated and sleepy." Hopping up to pull a short stack from the printer tray, Sinder said, "Speaking of which ... you're going to be late. Akira's an early riser now that he's no longer jetlagged."

"Thank you." Juuyu skimmed the listing. "Seven score. The packs *actually* mark time via 140 unique moons?"

"It's actually 144 if you add in the migrating moons. But who's counting?" Sinder made a face and pointed to the door.

Akira stood there, barefoot and wearing a hoodie over his pajama pants. His hair was a mess. Juuyu was already preening away his bedhead before murmuring, "I apologize. I am late."

"It's no big deal. I'm early. And Zuzu knew where you'd be. Everything okay?"

"Nothing to worry about," Sinder promised. "Juuyu was just giving me some things to do."

Juuyu inclined his head. "There was one other thing. It has come to my attention that Fumiko is an artist of some talent. However, the only supplies I found during my review of the contents of her home were unusable. Creative occupation might improve her mood. Find out if she would like new paints and canvases?"

Akira raised his hand. "I know where there's an art store. It's close. I passed it on my way to the museum yesterday."

Sinder raised *his* hand. "You were at the Amory yesterday?"

"Sure. I had lunch at Masterpiece Sandwiches."

"That's so weird." Sinder looked to Juuyu. "I swear, I never saw him."

26
SEASCAPE

nce Juuyu excused himself for work, Antigone chased Akira out of her kitchen, adamant that she needed no help with dishes. So he faced the stairway's obstacle course and formulated a different plan. Fumiko hadn't come downstairs for breakfast. Maybe she'd be up for a walk to that little doughnut place he'd found.

Quickly changing into street clothes, he stole up the spiral staircase to her room, softly calling, "Fumiko-nee? Am I intruding?"

"Akira? It's fine."

From his position on the staircase, he spied her propped in bed, reading. She looked so much like Tsumiko in that moment, he grinned. "Did you sleep at all last night?" he teased.

Zuzu was suddenly sitting on the top step, blocking his view. "She did! Juuyu should sing her lullabies every night!"

"I know, right? Suuzu spoils me with songs." Now that he knew

Suuzu was coming soon, the days ahead felt long and empty. Filling the time was part of what motivated him to ask, "You liked the pizza, yeah?"

Fumiko sat up in bed. "It was *good*."

"Want to try something else?"

"Did you smuggle another treat past Antigone?"

Akira laughed. "I was hoping to sneak you past her."

She slid from bed, padding over in her nightgown, to kneel beside Zuzu. "What do you mean?"

"Will you go for a walk with me? I found this little place that sells doughnuts right out of the fryer. It's not far."

"I can't leave Zuzu."

"You could," countered her sister. "You *could*."

Akira looked between them. "Is two blocks too far? I feel like we would still be under Zuzu's branches."

Zuzu touched her sister's face. "Akira will hold your hand."

"I'm a very good hand-holder," he promised. "I even hold Sinder's hand when we cross the street."

Fumiko's expression gentled. "You won't let go?"

"Not until you're ready," he promised, feeling uncommonly gallant. "Come down to my room when you're ready."

"I'll be quick," she whispered.

Minutes later, Zuzu hugged them both close. Akira blinked, and he was in a different location. It took a moment to orient himself. They were next to the flower shop, which hadn't yet opened for business.

"We skipped the gate?" he asked. "What about the barrier?"

Zuzu simply smiled ... and vanished.

Fumiko said, "She can come and go as she pleases. The barriers mostly hide her existence. And filter out pollen."

"So that's how it is!" Akira offered his hand. "Hungry?"

She slipped her hand into his, which is how he knew she was shaking.

"Do you like cinnamon and sugar? Or glazed?"

Fumiko frowned. "I don't remember."

"Shall we get one order of each?" Akira got her moving.

"Can we do that?"

"I'm feeling extravagant. Why not?" He waved to Rafter, who tipped an imaginary hat.

Much as he'd been doing for Suuzu since middle school, Akira coaxed Fumiko to the fringes of her comfort zone. And gave her the courage to step beyond them.

Akira distracted Fumiko with doughnuts, then the displays in shop windows. They took selfies wherever they found a setting, and he told her stories about the crossers at Stately House. She let him distract her, but he knew she was conscious of every step. Fumiko never once let go of his arm.

"Can you see it?" he asked, pointing to their actual destination. "Juuyu thought you might like this place."

She looked between him and the sign. "Seascape?"

"He didn't mention anything to you?" Akira was used to acting as a phoenix's personal liaison. "Juuyu is both really good and really bad with details. They can overwhelm him. But he can overwhelm them, too. I mean … once he looks closely, he sees everything. And knows stuff, because he puts the pieces together."

"Is Juuyu a detective?"

"Kind of, yeah. A really good one." He checked the time on his phone and beamed. "And I have good timing. They just opened. Want to go inside?"

The art shop smelled of paint and paper and wood, and it was nice to see Fumiko get lost in her delight. Her hand slipped from his, so he trailed after her, keeping watch, just in case. It was a little like bringing crossers to the convenience store.

When she finally looked for him, he stepped closer. "What do you need?"

"I'm not sure what I still have."

"Probably best to assume your old things are worn out or used up. What kind of art do you do?"

"Paint." Her whole face was aglow. "I paint."

So they found a long aisle of paints—tubes, pots, jars. One of the shopkeepers came over, and Fumiko's conversation veered straight into artist jargon. Akira's grasp on English wasn't this specialized, so he meandered away. He translated color names, sometimes relying on the smattering of French he'd picked up from Uncle Jackie. He took a picture of the rainbow display for Suuzu, then turned and took a picture of Fumiko wavering over too many choices.

Why had she given up something she clearly loved?

A painting kit with smiling children on the box caught his eye. He picked it up and deciphered the directions. This might be just what she needed. Different enough. And fun.

"Fumiko?" He offered the set. "Could we get this?"

She studied the box of body paints—water soluble, non-toxic, easy-wash, and in a range of sixteen vibrant colors.

Akira explained, "You wouldn't need a canvas if you're painting on skin."

"You want me to paint on you?" She seemed a little confused, but a little intrigued.

"I'll volunteer. Zuzu would, too."

The shopkeeper produced a book on fantasy face painting for all ages, and the longer Fumiko flipped through it, the more excited she became. "Yes. This would be fun. Do you think anyone else would let me?"

"Sinder for sure." More softly, he added, "Dragons like to be pretty."

"And ... Juuyu?"

That was harder to answer. "I'm not sure. He doesn't like messy things, but I know he likes beautiful things. And we'd have to wait until after work. I need to wait, too. Can we start in the afternoon? I promised to meet a friend for lunch."

"I'll show Zuzu first. And when you get back, we'll play with you."

"I'm not a child. Remember?"

"Do you have to be a child in order to love to play?" she countered.

"Nope!" Akira quietly admitted, "Playing with kids is pretty much my only job."

"You're a teacher?"

"Not really. I'm more like everyone's big brother."

He didn't usually worry about his lack of a degree or a career. A job would take him from Suuzu's side, and he didn't want that more than he wanted anything else. But Akira lived at a school. He wasn't a scholar like Sis, but nothing was stopping him from learning a trade. Maybe Michael would have some ideas about a more official role.

"I wouldn't mind being a teacher, I guess."

Fumiko squeezed his hand and spoke with conviction. "You can teach them how to be brave."

Akira was running a little behind when he skipped up the front steps to the Amory. He slowed to cross the lobby, and he veered toward the information desk. Tabi-oji was already waiting.

"You came," he said, sounding surprised.

"Did you think I wouldn't?" Akira countered.

"I am not accustomed to being remembered."

"I don't exactly remember you. From before, I mean. But you feel familiar. It's hard to explain, especially when you won't explain."

"Ply me with sandwiches, and we can talk some more."

So Akira went to the counter and ordered the "Best Ever" Starmark, a fancy grilled cheese sandwich, so he could sent snapshots to Ever and his favorite people.

Out in the courtyard, Tabi-oji invited Akira's questions.

"How did you know my dad?"

"Naoki and I met at work."

Akira tried not to be frustrated. It would have been so much simpler for Tabi-oji to simply tell him everything. Akira would have sat through the whole story, no matter how long. Instead,

195

Tabi-oji volunteered nothing. And though he willingly answered Akira's questions, he was brief about it. It made Akira feel as if he wasn't asking the right questions. Yet.

"Are you a scientist, too?"

"No. Nothing like that."

"Do I need to guess?"

Tabi-oji was pleating his paper napkin. "I do not think you could. Naoki and I met under unusual circumstances."

"Did you work somewhere in Keishi?"

"No."

"Where is the place you met?"

"An island."

"One of Japan's islands?"

"No."

"Where, then?"

Tabi-oji softly said, "I could not say. It is uncharted."

That rang a bell. Living at Stately House meant Akira was privy to random secrets. "You mean like the Eldermost Islands? A protected place in an undisclosed location?"

His brows lifted. "How would you know about such things?"

"I've visited a place like that. Suuzu's home is on a hidden island."

"Suuzu?"

Akira was a tiny bit mortified. He'd been so eager for Tabi-oji's stories, he'd skimped on those he could have been sharing. "My best friend. We're nestmates."

"An avian?"

"A phoenix."

"Can this be true?" Astonishment had overtaken Tabi-oji's

features. "You have ties to a phoenix clan?"

"Close enough that I can wear Suuzu's colors and crest. At least, when I'm not wearing Argent's. I guess it kind of depends on the event. Sometimes, I fill in for Sis. Kind of … represent the family. You know?"

Tabi-oji slouched back in his chair, one hand covering his eyes. "How are you here? And why now? I cannot decide if this is a blessing or a curse."

Akira asked, "Was there a dragon in the lobby when I arrived?"

"Him? Yes."

"Did he see me?"

Tabi-oji dropped his hand to consider Akira. "Why would a dragon be looking for you?"

"He's a friend."

"Dragons are *dangerous*." He sounded genuinely concerned.

And the pieces fell into place. This could actually be really bad.

Heart drumming, Akira asked, "Are you having dragon problems?"

Tabi-oji seemed to have made the same connection. "You are with these sigilcasters and sentinels."

"Yeah." And because he didn't know if things were about to go from bad to worse, Akira asked, "Are you going to try to use me against them?"

He shook his head, looked away, muttered something in Old Amaranthine, and sighed. Finally, Tabi-oji said, "Naoki saved me once. We ran away together. Made a home. But in time, they found us and took him back." He pulled his kimono coat close and hugged himself. "He saved me once. I will do *anything* to save him."

197

27

UNSUSPECTING PREY

For the second day in a row, nothing untoward had happened at the Amory. No signs of tampering or trouble. As much as Juuyu appreciated the reprieve, since it put them another day closer to Moon's waking, he didn't understand why the Gentleman Bandit had left off.

Had their sneakthief given up?

Juuyu thought it more likely that it was a strategic retreat—withdraw and watch. So they were varying the patterns of their patrols, and Juuyu had spent much of the day adding additional layers of protection to every corner of the museum. The expenditure had taken its toll. One look and Colt banished him from the premises, prescribing food, rest, and tending.

He'd given in. Partly because the change-up in routine would keep their quarry guessing. But mostly because Colt was right. Juuyu's focus was flagging. He should go to Portia.

Though he'd rather spend another night with Fumiko in his arms.

The unguarded honesty of that thought was flustering. Juuyu really needed to pull himself together.

As he passed through the crystal gate, Hallow signaled from the guesthouse doorway. "Come and see what your darling nestmate has wrought!"

"Akira?"

"Who else?" Hallow's eyes glittered. "They've been at it for hours, now."

In the cool sand that sloped from the back of the guesthouse to the shore, Akira stood with arms outstretched while Fumiko bent to some task at his back.

"Juuyu! You're early!" Akira spoke to Fumiko. "May I show him?"

She straightened and waved a paintbrush in greeting. Then pushed windblown hair out of her eyes, leaving a pale orange streak across one cheekbone.

Akira took a few steps and pivoted, showing off Fumiko's handiwork. Daubs of paint swept from his shoulder blades right past his hips, curving along his buttocks and thighs, which his fundoshi exposed. The impression was that of multicolored feathers.

"She gave me wings!"

"So I see," Juuyu managed.

Zuzu darted over and twirled before him. She was similarly dressed for the beach, her short skirt and crocheted top barely containing her curves. But the ensemble was effective, since it had bared every possible inch of skin to her sister's brushwork. Dark leaves and purple flowers. Tiny birds and shining motes of fogskimmers. Fumiko had even added a delicate windchime to Zuzu's face, its silvery strand sliding down her cheek like the track of a tear.

"Am I transformed?" Zuzu asked hopefully.

"I am amazed," he admitted softly. "Both by your transformation and by hers. Your sister sparkles."

"She is *so* happy." Zuzu's triumphant smile faded somewhat. "You are tired."

"Perhaps."

"Will you let us come to you tonight?" she whispered.

Juuyu didn't even try to resist. "I would be grateful."

She gave a little bounce and kissed his cheek.

Akira called, "Hallow! Take another picture?"

"Happy to oblige."

While Akira was posing, Zuzu frisked over to Hallow. "Your turn?" she suggested.

"Alas, I cannot." Hallow spared her a smile. "I have work. Perhaps Juuyu ...?"

Just then, Sinder jogged up, and Juuyu warbled his disbelief. His partner was covered in rainbow scales, each rimmed in pale yellow. His step faltered and he awkwardly said, "Oh. Hey, Juuyu. You're off early."

"As are you." Scanning the elaborate paint job, he asked, "Did you spend *any* time at your post today?"

"Oh, umm. I was there for a little while, but Akira suggested I come home early."

"He called you away?"

"He was there."

Juuyu hadn't realized this had been Akira's plan. "He spent

the morning with you?"

"Nooo, he spent the morning with Fumiko. Then found me ... after lunch, I guess?" Sinder's gaze slipped out of focus. "More importantly, Akira took Fumiko to an art store. Isn't she amazing? This is body paint."

"So I see," Juuyu agreed mildly.

Striking a pose, Sinder urged, "Tell me I'm pretty."

His partner could be *such* a dragon. Juuyu said, "You know you are pretty."

Entirely smug, Sinder stepped back to make room for Fumiko. Now that she was closer, Juuyu could see the miniscule flecking of paint on her skin. More smears decorated her arms and the tips of the fingers that reached for him.

Sinder looked worried.

Juuyu shifted into a receptive posture to ease his mind.

"Will you?" Fumiko asked, trailing a finger along his jawline. "You would make a very nice canvas. I want to try."

"He might not like it." Sinder's gaze jumped between them. "Too messy ...?"

"I would hardly call Fumiko's handiwork messy. Also, body paint is a part of certain phoenix traditions."

"You will? Oh, thank you!" She tugged at his suit coat. "Undress for me."

Juuyu simply inclined his head and retreated toward the guesthouse.

Sinder hurried after him. "I packed our swimming stuff. Jacques insisted."

"Why?"

"Are you kidding? There's a beach at our back door."

While Juuyu changed into an orange fundoshi, he asked, "How is Moon."

"Still completely conked. You know, you're next on the docket for some downtime. How are you holding up?"

"Well enough."

"Portia's good about tending. Want me to talk to her about giving you a session."

"No, thank you."

Sinder frowned. "You've been expending like crazy. There's no way you're not dragging."

Juuyu sighed. "Zuzu will look after me."

"Trees don't tend." Eyes widening, Sinder whispered, "Fumiko?"

He merely hummed.

"Is that ... safe?"

Juuyu didn't have an answer for that. He carefully gathered and twisted the length of his hair, and Sinder scrambled to locate hair sticks.

"You may be a bird of prey, but that doesn't mean you can't become prey." The dragon fussed and fidgeted and finally asked, "How far gone are you?"

"I have not gone anywhere," Juuyu assured. "I am right here."

"Cut the crap. You know what I mean." Sinder's tone took on an edge. "Do you know how much I miss Zisa and Waaseyaa? It's been what ...? Six weeks? And there are nights when I just want to get back to where they are. Because it was *good* there."

Juuyu understood all too well.

"And I miss *him*." He looked away. "I miss Timur."

"That is only natural."

"They were *careful* with me. Excruciatingly careful, and I'm still in withdrawal." Sinder's posture turned pleading. "Is Fumiko a beacon?"

His voice nearly failed him. "Yes. She is."

"Juuyu!" It was almost a whine. "She's barely holding *herself* together. She could break you."

"I do not believe it will come to that."

Sinder muttered, "Since when are you so optimistic?"

It really was very unlike him.

When Juuyu presented his body as a canvas, Fumiko tapped her paintbrush against her chin and circled him. Akira looked on with a thoughtful expression.

"Are you well?" Juuyu inquired in Japanese.

"I am." Akira asked, "Did anything happen today?"

"Nothing of consequence."

"Guess that makes sense," he said with a sigh.

Fumiko startled Juuyu when her fingers danced up his arm and grazed his shoulder, stopping just shy of his blaze. He was used to the familiarity of trees and Fumiko often behaved like one, so he simply arched an inquiring brow.

"What should we do?" she asked.

"Please yourself." It hardly mattered. In a few hours, he'd wash it away.

Akira suggested. "Red flowers. Lots and lots of tiny red flowers."

Fumiko's gaze was both intent and impersonal as she studied Juuyu's torso and limbs. "Yes, all right. Good choice, Remi."

"I'm Akira," he gently corrected.

"I *knew* that. I was distracted." Then she painted a tiny red flower on Akira's cheek and two more alongside his eyes. "Like these?"

Akira reclaimed his phone from Hallow and used it to check. "Can you add a dark yellow center? Or maybe it was more orange?"

With a smaller brush she added tiny speckles, giving the impression that the flowers were thick with pollen. Juuyu had a sudden sense of déjà vu, but he couldn't put his finger on why.

"Like so?" she asked.

"Perfect!" Akira snapped a selfie and moved to Juuyu's side. "Let me show you where we started. Portia went first."

Juuyu appreciated the distraction from Fumiko's brushstrokes, which trailed and twirled in ticklish ways. Akira had taken pictures of Portia, whose green eyes sparkled from amidst a swarm of tiny butterflies.

"I needed to ask Portia some stuff," Akira continued. "And while we talked, Fumiko painted. Did you know that she has a pollen sample from the museum?"

"Portia does?" Juuyu frowned in concentration. "What for?"

Akira was unusually calm. "I did some asking. Colt remembers escorting her there, and he says that a lady named Magda remembers meeting her."

Juuyu was having trouble aligning this detail with the other facts from the case. "When was this?"

"The day before yesterday. I found the pollen sample in a fancy locker thing in Portia's workroom. It's labeled and dated, but she doesn't remember how it got there."

Akira's eyes were shimmering. What had made him sad?

He flicked to another picture. Melody's face wreathed in flowers.

"Did you know that some kinds of pollen have lingering effects? Especially if it's from an Amaranthine tree. According to Melody, after it gets into your system, it'll keep working for two or three days."

The next photo was of Antigone, who flexed an arm decorated by dainty seashells.

"Antigone says that the fresher the pollen, the more potent it is."

"True enough."

"This batch must be *really* fresh, because I already explained all this to Colt. And Sinder. And Hallow. You'll forget, too."

Akira's expression made Juuyu's heart sink.

"Antigone says that the only reason everyone here isn't loopy on Zuzu's pollen is because of Portia's barriers. Filters and dampeners and things. Plus, if you're around one type of pollen for long enough, you can build up a resistance to its effects."

Juuyu knew these things. It was one of the reasons he felt so at home here. "Zuzu's pollen should not affect the memory."

"I know. It's not her pollen."

"Was there pollen?"

"Oh, man." Akira ruffled his hair, then gave it a frustrated tug. "Look, I promise I'll call for help. But first, I'm going to hear him out."

"Have you told me this before?"

"Yeah. Parts, at least. But it's no good." He took a pleading posture. "I'm sorry for being selfish."

Juuyu's attention jumped to Fumiko, who hummed tunelessly to herself as she embellished his forearm with dainty clues. He remembered now. Red flowers. A mysterious Amaranthine tree. Kikusawa shrine.

But even as he made the connection, his focus strayed to Fumiko. The wind kept stealing strands of hair from her braid. His fingers twitched to put them back where they belonged. To preen.

He could justify the adorning. She hadn't singled him out, and her artistry wasn't any sort of claim. But preening would be taking matters a step too far.

All at once, he realized that Akira was watching him with a thoughtful expression. Cocking his head to one side, Juuyu asked, "Are you well?"

"I am. Don't worry." Akira caught his hand and held it. "Thanks for bringing me along. Turns out, I'm really glad I came."

28
LITTLE BY LITTLE

Fumiko caught parts of what Akira was saying. The unfamiliar words mixed up with familiar ones. The concern in his tone. The respect in his attitude. She let their words flow by, enjoying Juuyu's richly accented responses, which were pitched to soothe. At least at first. He'd descended into vague hums and warbles by the time Akira gave up.

He sounded distracted. By what?

She glanced up, only to find his gaze on her.

"Are you quite comfortable?" he asked.

"I'm fine," she assured, and went back to adorning his kneecap with dainty red flowers. She recalled red flowers. Not well, but enough to know these were correct. But hers smelled of paint instead of a beckoning sweetness she could *almost* remember.

Sinder came over then, trading words in yet another language. The dragon and the phoenix. If she hadn't seen for herself, she might not have believed that these two were a fabled bird and a legendary beast. Each beautiful in their own way. Both patient beneath her brush.

They *could* have spoken freely. Even if she overheard, who would she tell? Secrets stayed safe in this place. Or maybe they became trapped. Some days, Fumiko thought the sands in which she knelt were actually a graveyard for secrets.

A hand touched the top of her head.

Sinder had wandered off, and Juuyu now seemed the concerned one. "You need not continue," he murmured.

She wrapped her hand around his ankle. "I was not finished. Unless … you want to go?"

"I will stay." He frowned and clarified, "For this. You may finish your painting."

"You make a good canvas." She smoothed her hand up the back of his calf to demonstrate.

The muscle twitched. "What are you doing?"

"No hair. Sinder, either."

Zuzu was suddenly crouched beside her, scrutinizing Juuyu's thigh. "You're right! What lovely skin. Makes me want to touch."

"You'll smear the paint," Fumiko chided, adding more red petals.

"What if I only touch the unpainted spots?" Zuzu asked sweetly.

Juuyu patted Zuzu's leafy crown and said, "Have a care for your own paint."

She shot to her feet and turned this way and that. "Did I smear? Is it spoiled?"

"No, leafling," he soothed. "But this kind of art is ephemeral."

"Like nippets?" Zuzu pointed to a tiny painted bird perched

near her navel. "Aren't they sweet?"

"The smallest of avians. They are sweetness itself," he agreed.

Fumiko took extra care, admiring the way red looked against Juuyu's skin. He was perfect for reds. And oranges. And golds. Was it silly to admire someone for something they'd been born with? Maybe he wouldn't have minded. After all, Sinder said dragons craved compliments. Did avians like to be admired?

Again, a touch on her head made her pause.

"Mammalian Amaranthine tend to have more body hair than those of us from other lineages." Juuyu angled his head and calmly added, "You seemed curious."

She was. Enough to ask, "What tradition does your clan have that involves body painting?"

"Many of our clan's stories are not so much told as *performed*. Those reenacting our histories and legends are first painted, to indicate their role in the story."

"Like theater?" She'd watched so many plays in the library's audio-visual room, back when Diva first added video cassettes to their collection.

"Perhaps *dance* would be more accurate."

"You like to dance?"

Juuyu hummed. "Under appropriate circumstances. And in accordance with the customs of my people."

She would have loved to see that. But she wouldn't ask for it. Juuyu's tone suggested that these weren't appropriate circumstances. And she wasn't his people.

"This is fine. This is more than I ever expected," she murmured, struggling to rise in the soft sand.

Juuyu caught her hand and supported her other arm, steadying her to her feet.

Red flowers next bloomed along his collarbone, across his chest. Juuyu was so much more approachable when he wasn't buttoned into a suit.

His breaths were coming deep and slow, and when she stole another peek at his face, he blinked placidly at her. He was as mellow as a tourist drunk on summer pollen.

She painted a cluster of red flowers beside his eye so that he'd match Akira.

He let her.

More gathered over his eyebrow, across his cheekbone.

In her imagination, every petal was a kiss.

Juuyu's pupils widened, and his lips parted. She wondered what kind of story Juuyu would tell, wreathed as he was in flowers. If it were up to her, it would be a love story, like those of the noble wolves who somehow managed to win the hearts of elusive moon maidens. There would be kisses and a promise to keep. One that wouldn't fade.

Fumiko looked away long enough to load her brush, then slowly, carefully painted a red flower onto the fullness of Juuyu's lower lip.

And he let her.

Juuyu watched the sun skim along a distant bank of clouds, lighting them in hues that presaged a far-off storm. "Are you finished?" he asked.

"Not yet." Sinder's phone clicked off to the right.

"Just a few more?" pleaded Akira, who'd been crouching and craning for the last five minutes, trying to frame the perfect photo.

Juuyu spared his partner a look.

Sinder fluted insistently. "When the light changed, it did really nice things to your ...."

He trailed off, leaving Juuyu's curiosity unsatisfied. But he wouldn't ask. Sinder might accuse him of fishing for compliments.

"Could you let your hair down?" asked Akira. "It'd be more *you*."

Juuyu hummed. "Is the paint dry enough?"

Fumiko came forward. She had a light touch and a serious expression. "Should be safe," she murmured. "Need help?"

"No, thank you." Zuzu had been letting slip a little of her sister's brightness. He couldn't tell if the tree was teasing him, whetting his appetite, or simply worried about him. Juuyu probably should have protested. This wasn't setting a good precedent, though she was well within safe bounds. Far from harming him, Fumiko was shoring up his flagging strength. However, he dared not allow anything akin to preening.

Plucking Sinder's hair sticks, he hesitated. His current attire didn't allow for much in the way of storage, and he couldn't very well drop them on the ground.

"Here," Fumiko said softly. "I'll take them."

Her hand came under his, and another tiny burst of awareness seeped into his soul.

Admiration. He could deal with admiration, since he was essentially a painting. Artists were allowed to step back and admire their work.

Interest. Easily accounted for by both her isolation and his clan affiliation. People rarely met a phoenix in person, so curiosity was only natural.

But there was a wistfulness lurking under it all. A pining that she kept to herself most of the time. Until his touch stirred it up ... and caused his hand to linger.

"No?" she asked.

What? Oh. The hair sticks. Before she could withdraw, he caught her wrist and pressed them against her palm. "Once the sun sets, I will need to wash."

She understood the implied question and nodded. "I know. It's fine."

"Nearly time," called Sinder, who snapped a picture of the sinking sun before stowing his camera. "Who else wants to dive in?"

"I will!" Akira set aside his own phone and lined up beside Sinder.

Eyes on the thin scrap of light remaining above the horizon, the dragon counted down. "Three ... two ... one ... GO!"

He and Akira took off with a graceless, high-stepping run that turned into two shallow dives. They disappeared for a matter of seconds, but then the water churned, and Sinder surfaced in dragon form, Akira on his back.

Applause pattered from the direction of the dock, where the interns looked on, all lined up in folding chairs, with blankets on their laps.

"They have been waiting dinner for us." Juuyu waded into the water, but he stopped when he realized Fumiko had followed.

"I can help," she offered.

Juuyu hesitated. To nest safely was a bond of sorts. Perhaps ... under the circumstances. With a low trill, he backed up a few steps and sat in the shallows. "What you have made, you may unmake."

She kilted up her skirt and bent to slosh water on his arm.

"Like so," he urged, scooping wet sand and using it to scrub at the back of his hand.

"Good idea. I'll get your back. Oh! Your hair!"

And then she was lifting and twisting and pinning with the sticks she'd pocketed earlier.

He told himself it was a practical necessity. Because that's all this was. To her.

"Fumiko ...?" he tried.

"Hmm?" Her hum was light and bright, and her hands moved in careful circles over his back and shoulders.

When her fingers briefly grazed his blaze, he tensed.

"I left this part bare," she said, moving along to his other shoulder. "Something so beautiful doesn't need embellishment."

Unintentional intimacies, every one of them.

Yet they were devastatingly effective.

How did one find the strength to refuse a beacon?

Juuyu made up his mind to ask Argent. Because Juuyu was increasingly certain that he could not—would not—unless ordered to do so.

Fumiko asked, "Why do you like empty rooms?" She couldn't understand why anyone would find emptiness appealing.

Juuyu, who had remained seated on the beach even after the light faded, glanced her way. "Why do you fill rooms?"

"Vacant spaces are lonely."

He hummed. "Is that how it is for you? I see."

"How else could it be?" she ventured, because he must have disagreed. Akira had worked so hard to clear a place for him. Like Juuyu would be traumatized by her accumulated belongings. Yet ... as far as she could tell, her things fascinated him. It was contradictory enough to be confusing.

"There is a beauty in vastness." Juuyu leaned back on his hands, his face tipped toward the sky. "Look at where the stars have perched."

Is that how he saw it? The stars were roosting? Then again, Zuzu liked to say that the stars bloomed in the sky each night. As if the sky were a bower under which she took shelter.

Fumiko was used to looking at stars. Or *for* stars. She was far less accustomed to considering the spaces between them. The shift in perspective momentarily took her aback.

Light illuminating the darkness.

Darkness strengthening the light.

"Consider the sea, a fathomless expanse." Juuyu breathed deeply, blinked slowly. "You live on the verge of so much vastness. Is it not peaceful?"

She could hardly believe it. "You *like* it here?"

"You are startled?"

"Well, *yes*. I thought you liked empty rooms." She was back where they'd started. "Akira was anxious."

"He is considerate, and he is correct. But he knows my brother's ways better than he knows mine." Juuyu dipped his hand into the sand. "In my place, Boon would look to the moon and sing his devotion. Similarly, Sinder would frisk in the surf and dive after fishes. But I see more than the sky and the sea. Though the vastness beckons, I am caught up in minutia. I sit upon the shore, counting every grain of sand."

Fumiko was horrified. "Should I bring help?"

Juuyu chuckled. "That was an analogy. But it *is* in my nature to notice, and I am easily caught up. Sometimes by the wrong things. My teammates know to watch for signs of distraction or compulsion."

"I'm a distraction?"

"A formidable one."

Fumiko forced a laugh. "That makes me sound scary."

"Anyone in my place might well tremble." Juuyu still breathed deeply, still blinked slowly. Utterly calm despite his words. "You are a beacon."

She sat a little straighter. "What does that have to do with anything?"

Juuyu's low whistle was as impossible to interpret as his analogies. But then he said, "You are a vastness, Fumiko."

And she was almost positive that he was calling her beautiful.

29

BANDIT

After breakfast the next morning, Akira bought a pile of postcards, brought them to a coffee shop, and spent a couple of hours composing silly messages. Wind-and-Tide had its own tiny post office, and once he had the pile safely sent, Akira texted Uncle Jackie.

Do me a favor?

> **Within reason**
> **I'm feeling rather favored out**
> **Actually, nevermind**
> **Favor away**
> **This will help me slip into character**

What?

> **Favoritism**
> **I'm embracing it**
> **I will be so good to you**

Akira had always thought he and Tsumiko were alone in the world. So when Jacques Smythe had sashayed into their lives and demanded favorite uncle status, Akira had wholeheartedly embraced the novelty of an extended family.

They had real ties. Sort of. Jacques was related to the husband of the previous owner of Stately House, the lady who'd left everything to Sis. Also, Jacques was cousin to the husband of the woman who'd given birth to Kyrie. That lady had given Kyrie to Sis. For keeps. And somehow or other, they'd also inherited Jacques. Definitely also for keeps.

I love you, Uncle Jackie

> **You say that now**
> **How do you feel about pastels?**

I have no strong feelings

> **You say that now**

About that favor?
I'm meeting a friend for lunch
At the sandwich shop in the museum
Just in case something strange happens
I wanted someone to know where I went

> **Why are you telling ME?**
> **Aren't you currently hemmed in**
> **on every side by Hisoka's finest?**

He was. And he wasn't. But explaining why would have to keep for a tiny bit longer. Akira sent through the selfie he'd taken.

This is my friend Tabi-oji

Lord
Yes
He'll do
Why on earth do you
call him Uncle Socks?

Just do me a favor.
If I don't call within the next 6 hours,
tell Argent where I went
That should be plenty of time

For?

Lunch

On a scale of velveteen
to studded leather,
how worried should I be?

Maybe a little

Give me a reason not to
summon Argent now

I don't think I'm wrong
to trust Tabi-oji

Why?

I think he's part of my family
He knows stuff about my dad

Is he a relative?
There is some resemblance

I don't know about that, but
it's an amazing coincidence

A little too amazing
Lord. What are the chances?
Do you know how long
Argent has searched?

Yeah

Why do you need me to back you up?

I don't think Tabi-oji is human

In a bad way?

I can't explain now
Give me 6 hours

Fine. But bear in mind,
you'll break more than *my* heart
if something untoward happens

I know

I am counting the minutes

Thanks
Talk soon

When Akira stepped off the trolly, Tabi-oji was waiting for him on the bench. In a way, Akira was grateful, because his stomach was in knots. He didn't think he could have eaten a bite. Juuyu, Sinder, and Colt had no idea he was out here. That made him uneasy. Not because he thought Tabi-oji would do something to him. Akira was on edge because Tabi-oji had done something to *them*.

Even so, he took a seat at Tabi-oji's side. "Hey. Good morning. Guess we're both a little early."

Tabi-oji clasped and unclasped his hands. "You came alone."

"My friends are more forgetful than usual." Akira asked, "What kind of pollen did you use?"

"Something obscure. From a variety of tree that is all but extinct and always forgotten." He chuckled and showed his palms. "Imagine a grove that was safe simply because nobody ever remembered seeing it."

"The scent of their flowers makes you forget?" Akira frowned. "Couldn't that be dangerous?"

"Not at all. It is too specific. Think of it as a grove's defense mechanism. Completely natural. Quite harmless. Always effective ... or nearly so."

"I'm immune."

Tabi-oji's smile was fond. "I had noticed."

"Why?"

"Early exposure. Or perhaps a quirk of heritage."

"My dad was immune?"

"Naoki? Yes."

"So he had this rare pollen?"

Tabi-oji nodded, shook his head, and turned his body to face Akira more fully. "Did you know that phoenixes are the natural enemy of dragons?"

"Yeah. I know about that."

"Will you help me? You and your phoenix?"

Akira firmed his resolve. "Are you the one who's been stealing the Junzi?"

Tabi-oji looked away, toward the Amory. "I must arm myself against the ones who took Naoki."

So it was true. Tabi-oji really was the Gentleman Bandit.

"I don't get it. What would the Rogue want with a man? He only takes females."

"Rogue?"

Akira knew a lot of things in an unofficial way. "Isn't that why you want the Junzi? They're some kind of crazy anti-dragon weapons. Oooh, wait. Are we talking about two different dragons?"

"There is no way you could know anything about the monster who holds Naoki captive."

"Okay. But ... does he have purple hair and red eyes?"

Tabi-oji flinched. "It is not possible. How could you know?"

"So you *are* connected to this whole mess?" Akira grabbed Tabi-oji's wrist. "There are so many people trying to find that dragon. To *stop* him."

"People know about Kodoku and his experiments?"

"I don't know all the details, but I know there's a dragon that's been rampaging across the world, murdering and kidnapping and raping."

"No. Kodoku-sama never leaves the island. Unless ...."

Akira slid his hand into Tabi-oji's. "Anything you know could save so many lives. Please?"

"Kodoku never leaves. Futari *cannot* leave. But there is a third, and he is a devil."

"His name? His clan?"

Tabi-oji pressed his lips together. "I *need* the Bamboo Stave. Help me secure it."

"I can't do that."

"Our meeting here cannot be a coincidence. Impossible things never are."

Akira couldn't betray all the trust that had been placed in him. *That* was the impossible part of this situation. "Listen. If we go to my friends and explain ...."

An upraised hand cut him off. Tabi-oji said, "There are things I know. Things you should know. Things that will change your mind."

"I'm the last person you need right now. Trust me, I have friends who'll consider you an answer to every prayer."

With a stubborn expression Tabi-oji said, "You would have no way of knowing. How could you, since you are the youngest?"

He wasn't listening.

"And you have it all backwards. About Naoki and me."

Was he pouting?

Akira adjusted his posture, willing to listen. Any detail could help. "What don't I know?"

"You have siblings."

"I have Tsumiko."

"She is nearest to you, but she is not your only sister. There have been brothers as well."

"We have family?"

Tabi-oji nodded urgently.

"Where?"

"Here and there. Siblings and half-siblings." He quietly offered, "Come with me, and I could show you all the roads I have traveled."

"Come with me," Akira countered. "I can introduce you to two phoenixes. And the trackers who've been training to take on a dragon. And ... and Sis. Tsumiko will want to know about you and about Dad and about a family we've never met."

"Almost, you persuade me." Tabi-oji gently withdrew his hand. "I am sorry that we cannot share any more sandwiches."

"I want to help!"

Tabi-oji stood and solemnly shook his head. "You would need to walk away. You would need to become a wanderer like your true father."

"Wait!" Akira leapt to his feet, desperate to hold the man back. "Wait ... *what*?"

Without warning, Tabi-oji stepped forward, pulling Akira into a firm embrace. The bells in his kanzashi tinkled lightly, and the scent of home grew stronger.

"You are *my* boy." He patted Akira's hair. "But I must put my Naoki first. Just as you must put your nestmate first."

Akira grabbed hold. "Are you trying to say that *you're* my father?"

Tabi-oji leaned back and beamed. "Naoki even gave you my name."

"Your name is Akira, too?"

"No, leafling." He glanced along the street. Another trolly was coming. With a quick kiss and a quicker wink, Tabi-oji said, "My name is Hajime."

And he vanished.

30

LINK

Akira was so rattled, he almost forgot his promise to Jacques. Back in Jacaranda Circle, he sat on the library porch, feet dangling, arms over a rail, while he tapped a quick message.

I'm fine
But I need Argent

> **My lord and master is currently away**

Without you?

> **Simple escort mission**
> **K&L have a playdate with Ever**
> **No public appearances, so he can**
> **be as slovenly as he pleases**

How long will they be gone?

> Returning in a day and a half
> Now spill about lunch

Later, I swear
Right now, I need to
talk to Argent

> Use your sigil, my dear nephew
> It's not just for looks, you know

Oh
I forgot

> You remember how to call for him?

Think so
Let me see who's around

> I want ALL the juicy details later

I promise

Everything was quiet in the guesthouse, but Akira had expected that. Juuyu, Sinder, and Colt would still be at the museum. Which left Hallow. The assorted sigils and barriers on the door to Moon's den let him through.

Hallow glanced up from the book he was reading and frowned. "Something wrong, Akira?"

"Can you do the thing with my sigil?" He rubbed his shoulder. "I want to reach Argent."

"Well, I *was* briefed. In case of emergencies." Hallow eased out from under Moon's arm and sat on the edge of the bed. "I know the theory, but ... I'm not exactly full-fledged."

225

"I practiced with Ginkgo. It worked with him."

"Right, then." Hallow offered his palms. "May I touch?"

"Yeah. And it's best if I lie down."

Patting the space beside Moon, the bat crosser cheerfully said, "We happen to have an opening."

Akira scooted into place and hid his face against Moon's chest. Michael had explained everything in excruciating detail, and Akira had practiced with Argent, Deece, and Ginkgo until he'd learned to properly direct his thoughts. But even if he got that part right, he needed someone with Amaranthine blood to jumpstart the sigil.

Michael had compared it to placing a call. Argent would know someone was messing with his sigilcraft, and he would take care of everything from there.

It wasn't difficult. Neither was it easy.

Especially with his thoughts skittering every which direction.

"Settled?" checked Hallow.

"Sorry," he whispered.

"Hold still, yeah? I don't want your blood on my fangs." Clearing his throat, Hallow blandly added, "Feel free to overlook the vampiric overtures."

Akira chuckled.

Hallow tugged down the neckline on Akira's T-shirt and lightly pressed his teeth to the sigil.

"Some of the guys growl."

Withdrawing, Hallow asked, "Whatever for?"

"Not sure. Juuyu doesn't, of course. He can't. He does make bossy bird noises. Triggering a fight-or-flight instinct ... I guess."

"Understood. I hope."

This time, Hallow slid his hand across Akira's throat. The teeth returned, and he carefully firmed his grip.

Trapped and partially draped by a bat's wings, Akira tried to relax, but a sibilant hiss kicked his heart into a higher gear. Even knowing there was nothing to fear, he was very aware that if he moved, Hallow's claws or fangs could draw blood.

Jacques had been through this before, so he'd given Akira his perspective, which had been a lot more helpful than Michael's descriptions of anchor nodes and soul bonds.

"You won't feel a thing but the fear. So embrace your inner masochist and trust your dom. And Argent. He really is very good."

Hallow adjusted his grip, using his other hand to cover Akira's eyes.

It was a helpless feeling. Nothing magical about it. Falling back on his many rehearsals, Akira focused on his desperate need to reach Argent. Was he too far away? It was like flailing blindly in the dark, keenly aware of all that he lacked.

But then a pair of hands slipped out of nowhere, caught his forearms, and pulled him into a vivid dreamscape. Definitely one of Argent's fox dreams, which were capable of capturing any person, even a dullard like Akira.

He was in the sunlit conservatory back home. Argent's special haven. The place he'd insisted on bringing Akira for the application of the sigil that linked them now.

"What is wrong? You are distraught." Argent gripped his shoulders, touched his face. "Akira, are you safe?"

"I'm between Moon and Hallow. Safe behind wards."

"But you *are* distraught." Cupping his cheek, Argent searched his eyes and offered a soft, "*Tsk.* What is the most important thing?"

"I'm not even sure."

A silvery brow quirked. "Pell-mell, then. Have it all out."

Akira laughed weakly, closed his eyes, and messily unburdened himself. "The team is forgetting things. Even me, at first. I was supposed to relay a message. Sinder says, 'It's no good,' and Tabi-oji says my dad is alive. The pollen makes people forget, and he's the Gentleman Bandit. And there's more than one dragon, plus an island. I tried to tell everyone what I found out, but I'm the only one who's immune. Because he's our dad. And I know why the barriers aren't working."

"Is that all?"

"Umm ... red flowers. I think they're important."

Argent patted his cheek and drew him aside to a bench. He made Akira start over, asking questions until he was sure of the order of events.

"Don't be too hard on the guys," Akira begged. "Tabi-oji is using some kind of pollen on them. It makes them forget."

"I have never heard of a grove with such an effect," he muttered.

"Pretty sure that's the point."

Argent huffed.

Akira dredged up a wan smile.

"I will come immediately. Expect us tomorrow. Until then, stay with Fumiko and Zuzu."

"You'll come? Just ... just like that?" It sounded too good to be true.

"I am already making the necessary arrangements."

"You are?" Akira's eyes stung.

"Hush, little brother. You have done well."

In the dream, Argent held Akira, letting him sniffle and shudder on the verge of tears, but when he opened his eyes, it was Hallow's shirt with a damp patch.

"All right, there?" the bat crosser asked softly.

Akira shook his head. Then because he knew Hallow wouldn't remember a word and Zuzu couldn't overhear him in this well-warded haven, Akira tried out the words he'd eventually have to say to Suuzu. "My parents might be alive. And I think my dad's a tree."

31

INTERVENTION

Juuyu was on his third circuit of the building when Mirrim signaled to him from a stairwell. He whisked to her side, silent and attentive, but her report was more of a command. "Magda needs you in the conference room."

She escorted him there.

That should have been his first clue. Normally, Mirrim would have finished his rounds for him so there were no gaps in their perimeter. But the fleeting thought was fuzzy at the edges. And it was hard to remember why that should worry him.

Mirrim opened the door and gestured for him to precede her.

That's when he registered a strange pressure and balked on the threshold.

"Excuse me," she said, planting a hand between his shoulder blades and shoving.

Magda was waiting on the other side of a new barrier. Catching his wrist and elbow, she hauled backward, saying, "Thank you for your trust!"

Juuyu stumbled forward, passing through a shimmering curtain that buzzed and snapped with enough power to have ended him, if that had been the intent. Hissing, he tore free and leapt high, putting his back to one corner of the ceiling as he triggered defensive sigils and drew a blade.

"Oh, very nice!" Magda gave him two thumbs up. "You can stand down, though. We're not attacking-attacking."

"Not that we wouldn't enjoy the challenge." Mirrim had empty hands upraised. "Within the bounds of the games, of course."

"That *would* be fun." Magda's shields wheeled slowly around her, and her stance remained neutral. "I love a bit of limit-testing."

Without taking her eyes from Juuyu's, Mirrim crisply asked, "Did it work?"

Bringing Juuyu's attention to the least threatening—and most stunning—soul in the room. "What are *you* doing here, Reaver Foster?"

"At the moment, I'm testing the efficacy of a variation on my flea flicker barrier." With a bright smile, he added, "Just call me Jiminy. Everyone does. Oh, and this next bit might sting a little."

Juuyu's eyes widened as the fourth strongest ward in the world swirled a finger through the sigil he'd been finessing. A breeze seemed to blow straight through Juuyu, chiming faintly with the crystals in Jiminy's hand.

"Any pain?" he asked solicitously.

Rolling his shoulders and sheathing his blade, Juuyu said, "More of a tingle."

"That's promising." Shifting into a posture that subtly asserted command, Jiminy said, "Come here, friend. Tuning time."

Juuyu dropped to the floor.

Mirrim maintained her passive stance, but Magda swaggered to Jiminy's side. "Well, son-in-law? Did it work?"

"That's really more of a question for Juuyu." Jiminy exuded a confidence that was confusing. "How are you feeling?"

Juuyu could only repeat, "What are you doing here?"

"Argent asked nicely. And I begged for the chance." Jiminy's eyes sparkled, and his voice dropped conspiratorially. "One of the Four Gentlemen is upstairs. How could I *not* come?"

Juuyu supposed that would be a draw. Especially for a ward with another of the Junzi in his care. But he was still confused by this sudden turn of events.

Mirrim looked and felt frustrated. Her ire was barely under control.

Magda was all triumphant smiles. Having Jiminy here pleased her.

"May I touch?" Jiminy inquired.

With a weary warble, Juuyu took a receptive stance. And tried to wrest an answer out of Jiminy. "When did Argent contact the Nightspangle pack."

"Wee hours in our time zone." Jiminy added, "I had breakfast here in the lobby."

"How did you get across the country so swiftly?"

"Uncle Denny brought me."

Juuyu's gaze slanted to Mirrim. "There is a squirrel lurking about the place?"

She rolled her eyes.

232

"He's clearing the ducts for us," said Magda. "Jiminy already warded him against pollen, so he'll be fine."

"Pollen," Juuyu echoed. Why did that sound familiar?

Jiminy's smile was sympathetic. "Essentially, you've been pollinated. All of you were. Though Magda's personal wards were partially effective at stemming the tide."

"I knew something was wrong." She slyly added, "When are you going to get around to calling me Mom? Hmm?"

"When I have fewer mothers?" Jiminy cut a glance in Mirrim's direction, reset his feet, and cautiously asked, "Or ... maybe we could switch things up? How does Grandma grab you?"

Jiminy was in a headlock so fast, Juuyu was impressed.

Mirrim growled, "Our grandchildren call me MayMay. Clear?"

Her son-in-law chuckled. "Really? That's so cute."

Hands on hips, Magda bent at the waist and angled her head to beam at him. "And I'm DahDah. From Magda. Get it?"

"Got it," he wheezed. Mirrim must have been adding pressure.

"Good." Magda tugged his ear, kissed his forehead, and announced, "I'll be in the next room, calling Melissa. Smack a sigil if you need me."

When he was free, Jiminy's smile faded as he refocused on Juuyu. "Sorry. This must be disorienting. I can talk and tune, though I don't know much."

Juuyu presented his palms and waited.

The man's sigilcraft was so potent, the air between them practically sizzled, but Jiminy's mood was as light as his touch. "Argent trusts me, so I'm here. Uncle Denny and I are the first wave. To extract your team. Medical support is on the way, to deal with the pollen and its influence. Should arrive anytime now. And sometime tomorrow, Argent will be here."

So they had failed. "Who alerted Argent to our ... situation?"

"Akira Hajime went over your head. Called in the cavalry." Jiminy slowly closed Juuyu's fingers over a small amber stone that now sang in unison with his soul. With an almost apologetic pat, Jiminy added, "I hear he's immune."

Juuyu wished the facts made more sense. "Why not tell *me*?"

"I'm sure he did. Now! I've made sure you aren't taking in any more pollen, but there's plenty still in your system. The healer might have some ideas about countermeasures, but you and your teammates are still affected."

With a soft rap, a lanky redhead let himself into the room. Linden Woodacre, one of the most influential Amaranthine in the United States. Normally, he'd be at home in Fletching, baking cookies for college students.

"Spokesperson," Juuyu greeted respectfully.

"Denny, if you can. Linden if you must." He scanned the room before asking, "In your experience, what kind of range does a tree have? How far from their roots can they manifest?"

Juuyu hesitated. "A tree?"

"Your young friend is under the impression that the Gentleman Bandit is a tree." Denny shook his head. "It would explain a few things, but it raises a whole crop of questions. Shouldn't be possible, but I thought I'd take a scamper through the neighborhood. So ... range?"

"It varies, depending on the age and inclinations of the individual." Juuyu tried to come up with a satisfactory estimate.

"Three kilometers at most. And that would be a strain."

Denny tapped at his phone. "Less than two miles. Got it. What about the ocean? Any chance we're dealing with a tree aboard a boat?"

Juuyu frowned. "I cannot imagine. Surely not?"

"Oh, it's farfetched," conceded the spokesperson for the squirrel clans. "But it would be a nice trick. Which reminds me! I have a suggestion with regards to that pretty little flute upstairs."

Jiminy snapped to attention as only a wolf could.

Denny smoothly signaled for patience as he went on. "I agree with Argent. It's as good as gone. So there's really only one thing we can do."

Juuyu swiftly reached the same conclusion. "As you say," he conceded.

Mirrim took a step forward. "Orders?"

"Cooperate with the extraction order," said Juuyu. "You and Magda find Sinder and Colt. Bring Lash and Tuft. Walk out."

She nodded once and strode away.

Jiminy was bouncing on the balls of his feet. "And us?"

"Just a bit of mischief." With a bright smile, Denny said, "To keep the Junzi safe, we'll have to steal it first."

32

SECOND WAVE

Akira had been zoning out for a while when he registered that someone was petting his hair. Had he drifted off? Had Hallow returned? But when he lifted his head from Moon's shoulder, the wolf ran furred knuckles over Akira's cheek. "You've been crying."

"You're supposed to be asleep."

"Again, in English?"

"Oh. Sorry." Akira translated.

Moon's smile was sleepy. "Tears will do that to a guy. Especially this guy. What's the matter?"

He didn't know quite where to start. "I'm sorry. They said you needed to sleep a week, at least."

"Don't change the subject. Wolf on a scent, and all that."

Akira grumbled, "There's too much to explain. And you wouldn't believe me if I told you."

Rolling toward him, Moon propped his head on his fist. "This gets more interesting by the moment. Unbelievable things are a specialty of mine."

The wolf's tail draped over Akira's legs. A companionable gesture he recognized from mingling with the Elderbough pack. It welcomed trust. It invited confidences.

Most of what needed saying should probably come from Argent. Or Hisoka-sensei. But Akira was invested in this mess, too. And on a personal level.

"You've been around, right?"

"Is this about my age or my territory?" Moon flashed a hint of fang. "Both are impressive."

Akira asked, "Do you know any trees with red flowers?"

"Sure, I do. So do you." Moon's ears went all cockeyed. "Everyone does, really. It's famous. Don't tell me you've forgotten about Kusunoki."

The enormous tree in the courtyard of Kikusawa Shrine. Akira had been introduced back in high school. Kimiko had jokingly referred to Kusunoki as her best friend, and it had been in bloom for the first time in centuries during Quen's and Kimi's first televised kiss. He could remember all those tiny red flower petals drifting through the air.

They were the same.

Weren't they?

Just then, Hallow opened the door. He closed his mouth on whatever he'd intended to say.

Moon waggled his fingers.

"Right, then. Shake a leg." Angling his head toward the room behind him, Hallow grimly announced, "We have company."

Akira let himself out the gate and beyond Zuzu's barrier, cutting between the library and flower shop at a jog. It didn't take long to spot the one he needed. "Rafter!"

With a final toss and twirl of his sign, Rafter propped it against the bike rack and turned to beam at him. "Akira, my dude! What brings you out here?"

"A list. From Antigone." He passed along two folded slips of paper. "And a message from Diva. Plus, I'm supposed to tell you that Moon woke early."

Rafter scanned the list and whistled softly. "Antigone is going all out."

Akira wasn't sure how to ask, so he went for a simple stance, identifying himself as a Betweener. "You shop for them?"

"Now and then. When they need something extra." Rafter tucked the papers into the front pocket of his Hawaiian shirt and smoothly matched Akira's posture. "Diva likes more in the way of meat than Antigone generally provides."

"So you watch out for them?"

"I'm their man on the outside, so to speak." With an arm around Akira's shoulders, Rafter guided him through the farmer's market. "I stick to the fringes, finetune the ambiance, if you catch my drift."

Akira followed his gaze to the clear blue sky overhead.

"Want a peek?" The corners of Rafter's eyes crinkled. "It's

something most tourists never see. Mind you, it's not something you can write home about."

With a touch, Akira promised secrecy.

Rafter's smile widened. "You speak my language just fine."

The change was so swift, it startled Akira into ducking and crowding against Rafter's side. One second, the blue sky went on for days. In the next, a ceiling dropped over the whole market, casting it in shadow.

"Peace, friend. She's been here all along. Since waaay back." Rafter stood proud, face tipped to the sky. "Give yourself a second. Take it in."

Though his heart was still jumping, Akira uncurled and peered around.

He'd seen Zuzu, touched her, been up among her branches, but that had been Zuzu out of context. Here, towering dramatically over the surrounding neighborhood, it was so much more obvious that she existed on the grandest scale.

The noontime sun was gone. Or rather, it filtered through her leaves, lending sparkle to the many doo-dads she and Fumiko had added to each branch. Chimes. Mirrors. Pretty rocks that were probably wardstones.

Akira offered a palm. "What clan?" he whispered.

"Ohhh, one of the trickier ones. Ever met a Glimspinnet?"

"No. Or at least, not to know it."

Rafter flicked his fingers and the sky cleared. "That *is* how we roll."

Akira shook his head. "Which animal …?"

With a sly smile, Rafter got him moving again, aiming for a food truck parked along the street. "Are you afraid of spiders?"

"Not much."

"Then you may think of me as an *eensy*, *weensy* friend. Like in the song." Rafter wriggled his fingers and asked, "Know it?"

"No ...?"

"Hang on." Stepping up to the window, Rafter held up four fingers on each hand. "Eight doubles with everything. In fact, double the meat, too."

The lady at the window laughed. "Diva on a tear?"

Rafter rapped twice on the counter. "We have a woke wolf on our hands, Lola. Don't skimp."

She laughed again. "I'll hold the jalapenos. Give me ten minutes."

While they waited, Rafter taught Akira a children's song about a spider that would probably be a hit back home. But it was hard to stay distracted for long. Things were happening, and they were happening fast.

Rafter finally asked, "What's on your mind, friend?"

"Wolves have big appetites. This won't be enough."

"Nooo doubt. This is for starters. By the time he downs the lot and licks his chops, we'll have fresh meat on the grill."

"Can I help you with the shopping?"

"Between me and Buzz, we've got it handled. Besides, you aren't supposed to leave ... am I right?"

Akira had sort of forgotten. "I did promise."

"Then this is as far as you go." Going up on tiptoe, he peered down the road and hummed. "Looks like you'll head back in style. Check out your escort."

Sinder was quickstepping along the sidewalk.

Akira raised a hand in an *all's-well*. To his surprise, the two women close on Sinder's heels answered with upraised fists. Colt was bringing up the rear.

Oh.

Nope.

As the tight-knit group drew closer, Akira realized that two Kith sauntered along behind. They were causing a stir among the people they passed, who turned to follow, cameras out.

Rafter snorted. "Subtle much?"

Sinder stalked up, radiating annoyance. "Could be worse. Could be tickertape. Fix it."

Akira cuffed the dragon's shoulder. "That was *rude*. Mind your words."

"He's not susceptible," Sinder grumbled. "And we are supposed to be avoiding attention. Though whose, I couldn't say."

Rafter took charge. "Lynxes, up. I'll meet you on the roof of the flower shop within the hour. Ladies, into the library, please. Portia will be with you shortly. Sinder, you're with Akira." He slid a cardboard box out the pick-up window and presented it to Colt. "Your Moon has risen. Stoke some coals while I run to the butcher."

And just like that, it was Akira, Sinder, and Colt.

"Moon woke up?" Colt asked, his gaze roving. "Odd, that."

"What is going *on*?" muttered Sinder, pulling Akira toward the gate. "If anybody said, I don't remember. And I hate orders that don't make sense. Did you know *Argent* is coming? *Himself*?"

"Yeah. He mentioned that," whispered Akira.

Sinder's gaze sharpened. "You talked to him? When?"

Akira simply hurried to the guesthouse. Not much had changed since he left.

Hallow perched on the edge of the table while a big, blond healer did things with swabs.

Moon lounged in the door to his room, casually gnawing on a strip of what looked like rawhide. Though when Colt entered, wafting the scent of beef, Moon's tail took to wagging.

The healer turned. "Sit here," he said to Sinder, pointing to a spot on the other end of the table from Hallow. And withdrawing an aspirator from the pouch at his waist, he strode to Colt. "Open. Inhale. *Deeply*. Again."

Eyes wide, Colt obeyed. But once he was able, he weakly asked, "Bavol?"

With a faint and fleeting smile, the healer replied, "Hello, little brother."

33

UNDER THE INFLUENCE

Juuyu escorted Jiminy out of the Amory and toward the trolly stop. At least, that's what Juuyu thought he was doing. Until Jiminy took his arm, deployed a sigil, and pressed a crystal between their palms. Juuyu had been subject to enough wolfish handling to know that *he* was now being escorted.

Jiminy calmly ordered, "Keep walking, please."

"Why?"

"Keep walking," he repeated.

They strolled along at an easy pace for two blocks, and Juuyu remained alert for the source of the alteration in Jiminy's manner. Nothing stood out. His bafflement must have shown.

"Let's continue like this for a little while longer."

"Why?"

"Back at the corner. By the trolly stop." Jiminy studied his face with open interest. "How many people were sitting on the bench?"

243

Juuyu barely resisted the urge to turn his head. With frank dismay, he asked, "There was a bench?"

"Don't worry," Jiminy soothed. "He had as much chance of seeing me as you had of seeing him."

"Are you saying that we just walked past the Gentleman Bandit?"

"We did."

"You saw him?" He couldn't believe their quarry was so close.

"Sure did. I recognized him from Akira's photo."

Juuyu pulled on Jiminy's arm. "I am supposed to apprehend him."

"That's certainly the goal. But now's not the time."

"Why not?"

"*He* has a goal, as well." Jiminy patted the strap that crossed his chest. "Or have you forgotten what I'm carrying?"

Juuyu followed the line of the strap to the slender case riding on Jiminy's back. He vaguely remembered appropriating one of Mirrim's weapons cases. "I do not remember."

"Interesting! You know, I think this was a very near thing." Jiminy cheerfully asked, "Do you remember the way home?"

Too unsettled to be offended, Juuyu answered, "The safehouse is in this direction."

"About this Junzi. The Bamboo Stave. Do you know anyone who can play it?"

Juuyu cast a startled glance at the carrying case. He remembered now. This absurd. No wonder Argent had handed down the order to extract. Shaking his head, he focused on older, clearer memories. "According to legend, a furious storm descends and blows a devastating tune. It may be one reason why dragons call the Junzi the Four Storms. Although I've heard some call this flute an instrument of angels."

"Sounds like the kinds of stories Lady Mettlebright likes."

The world was full of draconophiles these days, but Tsumiko's interest was more personal. Her fascination was founded in her love for Kyrie. "I am aware of her interest."

"According to First-sensei, she's been researching ancient writings. He thinks she knows more about dragons than most dragons."

Juuyu doubted that. "An exaggeration, surely."

"I don't think so." Jiminy's gaze was drawn to the ocean as it came into view. "Jacques says she made a favorable impression on Lord Beckonthrall's brides, so she gets whatever she wants. Including access to Lord Yonkeep's trove."

Although Juuyu knew Argent had found the Bamboo Stave in a private collection, nobody had mentioned *whose* collection.

To think, they had nearly lost it.

They reached Jacaranda Circle and the farmer's market without incident. "Were we followed?"

"We're in the clear," Jiminy assured, though he was understandably distracted. "This is it, isn't it?"

Juuyu barely had time to wonder how he'd get Jiminy through the barrier when he spied Fumiko sitting on an overturned bucket outside the gate. He asked, "Can you bring this man through?"

She nodded. "I was waiting for you."

After the briefest of introductions, Fumiko drew Jiminy past the crystal gate. Although it was entirely unnecessary, she then took Juuyu's hand and pulled him through. And didn't let go.

She was unhappy.

This was concerning.

He folded his hands around hers. "I would like to temporarily add something to your collection. A rare treasure."

"May I see?"

Juuyu signaled for Jiminy to relinquish the carrying case. Placing it in Fumiko's hands, Juuyu said, "Hold onto this for me. You and Zuzu keep it safe. No peeking."

"You'll show me later?"

"As soon as I am able."

"You won't forget?"

Juuyu warbled softly, partly in resignation. "If I do, will you remind me?"

"I promise." She kissed his cheek, hugged the case to her chest, and hurried away.

Jiminy was giving him the strangest look. "Should you have done that?"

"It will be safe with her," Juuyu stiffly assured.

"But … she was waiting for you. And the way she looked at you." Jiminy cleared his throat. "She kissed you."

Juuyu waved that aside. "She is tree-kin."

"And you're avian." Jiminy's posture shifted into something more apologetic, but there was a stubborn tilt to his chin. "Maybe pheasants are different than phoenixes, but where I come from, gifts and promises mean courting."

More than a little aghast, Juuyu said, "The Bamboo Stave is hardly a courting gift."

"Not your average one," Jiminy agreed. "But as you say … she's tree-kin."

The pervasive scent of grilling meat made more sense to Juuyu as soon as Moon strode into view. He hustled them into the guesthouse, trading packish pleasantries with Jiminy all the while. So Juuyu had no idea that Hallow's war room had been turned into a clinic until an enormous male in healer's colors pressed an aspirator between his lips and ordered, "Inhale."

"My brother." Colt sat meek and shirtless in a row with Hallow and Sinder. "He has five distinct masteries in the healing arts. Bavol, the pride of the Thunderhoof herd."

Bavol prodded, kneaded, and scrutinized Juuyu without remark. Only after he'd finished his examination did his gaze come into a friendlier focus, "Well met, Kindred. Ricker always mentions you with fondness. Thank you for looking after him."

Juuyu inclined his head. "We rely upon Colt for reasons I have no difficulty remembering."

"Feeling forgetful?"

"Selectively," Juuyu confirmed.

"An effect of pollen, I am told. Which is one of the reasons Hisoka Twineshaft called upon me." With a fond look in his brother's direction, Bavol explained, "It is one of my five masteries. Though your symptoms are a mystery to me."

Sinder raised his hand. "I get that we have a bunch of preservationist expertise to pull from here, but I was coming to a point earlier."

Bavol straightened. "I will hear you out."

"You want to know wind lore, you ask a dragon. You want moon lore, grab a wolf." Sinder met Juuyu's gaze with palpable urgency. "If we need to know about pollen, I think it's pretty obvious where we need to go."

"To the trees?" asked Hallow.

Sinder rolled his eyes. "To the bees!"

Everyone exchanged puzzled glances. Finally, Juuyu said, "Hypothetically speaking ...."

"I'm not talking about hypotheticals!" Swearing under his breath, his partner jumped from his perch and pointed out the door. "He's probably still here. Let me bring him in."

Juuyu caught on first. "Buzz."

34

WHILE AWAY THE HOURS

Juuyu left the interrogation of bees to Sinder and went in search of Akira. The young man was sitting on the beach near a long, low grill, where Moon and Diva presided over sizzling meat. But Akira's attention wasn't on the excitement surrounding the wolf or his meal. He was curled over his phone, tapping messages.

Heedless of his attire, Juuyu sank to a seat in the sand at his side.

Akira's attention bounced up, and he leaned in.

"I apologize." Juuyu eased closer and pulled Akira snugly against his side. "I was presumptuous enough to believe I could keep you safe. Yet it is *you* who have protected us."

"How much do you remember?"

Juuyu hesitated. "Less than I should. But my duty to you remains clear."

Akira turned into Juuyu and whispered, "I don't know whether to be happy or scared."

"Tell me." Juuyu might not be able to remember, but he could listen. "Tell me all the things that happened to you."

Akira searched his face. "You'll just forget."

"The telling will not be for my sake. It is for yours." Juuyu urged, "Let me bear witness to your struggle, even if you will need to remind me in a few days, when I am rid of the pollen's effects."

So Akira began to talk.

Juuyu had never experienced the like. He struggled to fit the facts into a framework, to commit every detail to memory. But too many slipped from his grasp, leaving him with a piecemeal account.

For the first time in his life, Juuyu gave up trying.

He listened, but not to Akira's words. Rubbing his thumb back and forth across the young man's tattoo, Juuyu searched for his soul. He let the facts slide past and clung to the feelings they'd inspired. This chick in his nest—grown though he was—radiated urgency and confusion and fear. Yet deep under Akira's restless uncertainty, Juuyu found something unforeseen.

A soft gleam. A subtle ... *something*.

"What are you hiding?" Juuyu murmured.

Akira stopped talking. "Huh?"

Uncertain what to say, Juuyu placed his hand low over Akira's abdomen.

"Oh. Is it more noticeable now?" Akira rested his hand over Juuyu's. "We showed Michael, and Argent knows. Before that, Suuzu was the only one who ever looked close enough."

"What is it?"

"Nobody knows. Yet." Akira smiled crookedly. "You know how

Argent gets when he's interested in something. He'll figure it out."

Juuyu hummed.

Looking at him slightly cross-eyed because of their closeness, Akira asked, "How much of what I said do you remember?"

With a wry warble, Juuyu said, "You enjoyed sandwiches with ties to notable Amaranthine."

"That's all you got?"

"No." Juuyu quietly listed, "Something surprised you. Something frightened you. Something worries you. And … you are impatient, but I interrupted before you could explain why."

"Oh! I was about to show you this." Akira held his phone so they could both see the screen. "Argent had to take the slow way. And he's not alone."

The messages were from Jacques Smythe, who'd sent through a series of photos, interspersed with snappy asides and nonsensical hashtags.

In the first selfie, Jacques posed on a steamer trunk surrounded by a small mountain of luggage in a rainbow of glossy pastels.

**Fortunately for all parties,
I started packing *weeks ago*
#AllPraisePosey**

"He knew he would be coming?" Akira asked.

Juuyu hummed noncommittally. It wasn't his place to say.

Akira scrolled to the next picture, and Juuyu's focus tightened on the scene Jacques had captured. They were inside an airplane now, likely a private jet.

Suuzu almost looked small, curled as he was against the

broad chest of Merit Starmark. Argent bent over Suuzu, knuckles brushing dark curls from his forehead.

Special delivery <3
#HandleWithCare

"They're moving him while he's asleep?" Akira searched Juuyu's face. "Is that safe?"

"His rest is imperiled, but he is likely lost in a fox dream."

Akira frowned. "Suuzu doesn't usually like anyone but us with him when he sleeps. And he can't have given permission first."

"I believe my brother would have counted it a greater betrayal to be left behind."

"He'll be here sometime tomorrow." Akira looked out toward the ocean.

Juuyu did some quick calculations. Even with customs, courtesies, and traffic delays, they should arrive here by mid-high tomorrow.

Another text came through along with another selfie. Jacques had switched into one of his innumerable dressing gowns, and he and Suuzu were tucked into an onboard bed. Jacques pouted up at the camera over a pair of tinted glasses with heart-shaped lenses. Suuzu had nestled into him, relaxed and softly smiling.

Rest while you can, lover boy
#HeDreamsOfYou

Denny Woodacre arrived a few hours behind everyone else and cheerfully informed the enclave residents that they were buttoning down. All of them. Indefinitely.

Or at least until Argent Mettlebright said otherwise.

Diva posted a notice on the library door, and a similar sign went up at Flutterbys to say that the proprietresses were out of town. Buzz was conscripted as a consultant. Rafter would stand sentinel. As far as their team was concerned, Juuyu was only too glad to defer to Moon, who decided that they were in the ideal location for a short holiday.

For dinner, Antigone pulled out all the stops ... and several corks. Diva tapped a small keg of honey mead. Dru had enough beach music to play through the night, and Sinder rigged speakers into Zuzu's branches. As sunset neared, Jiminy and Portia lofted crystals to serve as party lights, and the Thunderhoof brothers contrived to build a bonfire.

Jiminy wanted a dip in the ocean, so Akira introduced him to the delights of swimming with dragons. Moon, finally sated, had stationed himself at the end of the dock in truest form, either life-guarding or dozing. It was hard to tell. Zuzu had taken a liking to Magda and was helping her and Mirrim brush the lynxes, who sprawled well away from the gentle wash of waves.

Juuyu had to wonder how long it had been since this small patch of beach was so crowded. And if that was the reason why Fumiko had disappeared.

He knew where she was. How could he not?

Waiting until everyone was thoroughly distracted, he slipped inside and climbed the stairs, which he intended to clear tonight.

There was more than one way to enjoy a holiday.

Juuyu was catching hints of Fumiko's mood now, and it worried him. Once he realized he could taste tears on the air, he lunged up the remaining stairs without actually touching them.

Fumiko sprawled in bed, reading, a box of tissues close at hand. Blinking up at him, she offered a tremulous smile. "You remembered."

"You are crying."

"It's okay." Fumiko sat up, grabbed a tissue, and dabbed. "This part always makes me cry."

He eyed the book's glossy cover warily. She was reading what appeared to be a romance novel, authored by Chastity Landis. The name meant nothing to him, but the stickers on the spine indicated that the book was a new release and had been shelved in the Amaranthine Romance section at the Jacaranda Free Library.

"You have read it before?"

"Three times." Fumiko sat up and smiled. "It's *wonderful*."

Juuyu knew that the guest suites at Stately House were provided with romantic literature, but he'd never done more than centralize and alphabetize the accumulation. For which Jacques had scolded him. Apparently, each suite had been provisioned according to the taste of its usual occupants. Which suggested some surprising things about the interests of certain guests.

Since then, Juuyu had avoided all but Michael's abundant research materials.

Scanning the cover illustration on Fumiko's book, Juuyu ventured, "What is it about?"

"It's a love story." She offered it to him.

Juuyu took it cautiously and scanned the summary on the inside flap. It claimed to be an account of a love triangle involving a dragon, a phoenix, and a young woman whose ordinary life is overturned when she discovers that she is an unregistered reaver.

He offered it back. "The scenario is *highly* implausible."

Fumiko looked injured. "But … why?"

"Dragons amass harems."

"Well, *this* one is searching for his soulmate."

Juuyu could think of nothing to say to that, so he stuck to facts. "Phoenixes rarely leave their colonies. The likelihood of meeting one in the public sector is miniscule."

"Really?" Fumiko hugged the book to her heart. "Why did *you* leave your colony?"

Deflection was automatic. He countered, "Why did *he*?"

She smiled softly. "To protect his sister, who'd been elected to the Amaranthine Council."

He didn't quite stifle a soft chirp. Clearing his throat, he asked, "What is the dragon's excuse?"

"That's where things get really interesting!" Fumiko scooted forward on the bed. "She knows the dragon's greatest secret. Or *thinks* she does."

Juuyu shook his head. Too few facts. Too much drama. Still, he found himself asking, "Which one does she choose?"

Fumiko's eyes sparkled. "Who says she does?"

"Is that not the point of such fiction?"

Holding out the book again, she said, "If you're curious, I'll let you borrow it."

Juuyu fended off the offer with a firm palm. Yet he asked, "Why did you cry?"

"Because she's so close to happiness." Fumiko wouldn't meet his gaze.

"Is that not a reason to be glad?"

"No," she whispered. And with more confidence, "No. It is terrible and terrifying."

The strength of her conviction rocked through him, and he found he needed to sit. Perched on the edge of her mattress, Juuyu asked, "Yet you enjoy love stories?"

"Not exactly." She traced her fingers over the cover of her book, her expression gentling for the characters depicted there. "I think I only enjoy other people's love stories."

Juuyu found it difficult to breathe.

Or to look away.

And in that moment, his downtime plans took an unforeseen turn. Hand outstretched, he gravely said, "I have changed my mind. May I read your book?"

Fumiko relinquished it with a smile, but she was trembling.

It made Juuyu feel terrible … and terrifying.

35

FARFETCHED HAPPENSTANCE

When Fumiko's head popped up, Juuyu sighed and said, "You need sleep."

"Which part are you at?"

"Another farfetched happenstance in which there is much fluttering and a complete lack of resolution."

Fumiko's brows drew together. "That could be anywhere."

"Hence my growing suspicion that such tales are better suited to others."

"But you're still reading," she pointed out. "Doesn't that mean you like it a little?"

"I will see this through." Lowering the book, he added, "I have not forgotten my promise to show you the contents of this case."

He'd placed the Junzi between them in the softly swaying hammock, high among Zuzu's branches.

Juuyu wasn't sure if he could recall it because of his promise to Fumiko or because Bavol's treatment was having some effect. Either way, the Bamboo Stave was safe. And that put him at ease.

"Don't you need more light to read by?" Fumiko asked.

"There is enough."

"Can't you illuminate crystals?"

"I can." Juuyu once more lowered the book. "Darkness is more conducive to sleep."

"But I can't see your expressions."

With a low trill that was more amused than anything, Juuyu asked, "Why are you so resolute in avoiding those things you need most?"

Fumiko gravely said, "Some stories are more important than sleep."

Juuyu raised the book to hide the smile that was threatening. "Shush, or the author's words will never invoke their intended response."

For a few minutes longer, he was able to continue his investigation of the book. If pressed, he would have to confess himself surprised. The phoenix character behaved as an avian should, and the dragon's predicament was not only plausible, it was poignant.

Juuyu was quite sure the author was a Betweener. And given the unsettling parallels between his own situation and that of the main character, Juuyu grew increasingly certain that he must know the author. Or at the very least, they knew of him.

"Sing me to sleep?" Fumiko asked.

"I cannot sing *and* read. Choose one."

"Then I guess you should read," she sighed.

Interesting priorities.

He asked, "Would humming suffice?"

"That would be nice. Yes, please."

When he was alone, Juuyu sometimes hummed under his breath. Not a proper song, just disjointed snatches. The habit drove Sinder crazy, which is why he usually curbed the impulse, but Fumiko seemed to take comfort from his vocalizations. Enough that she was soon asleep.

Able to focus once more, Juuyu reread two sections before pressing onward, intent on collecting clues. Allusions to lore. Turns of phrase. Setting details. He was still working up his profile—and the *very* short list of people who fit it—when Sinder clambered onto a nearby tree branch.

"You look comfortable."

Juuyu supposed he was. "Try not to wake her."

Sinder tutted sympathetically. "Good that someone reminded her that she needs more than sun and soil to live."

It was an odd thing to say.

"She thinks like a tree." Sinder gestured below. "The interns have a hard time getting her to eat and sleep. You're a good influence."

Juuyu hummed. Perhaps he should speak with Riindi again. Which reminded him, "Fumiko needs a phone. To connect with my grove. And others. Perhaps the orphan tree at Reaverson Farm?"

"Can do."

On impulse, Juuyu held up the book. "Can you find out who wrote this?"

"Even easier." Pointing to the cover, Sinder said, "It's right there in print. Chastity Landis."

"That is a penname."

"You sure?" His partner hummed. "I suppose it does sound doggish."

Juuyu knew Sinder well enough to reach a startling conclusion. "You already know."

"I'm sworn to secrecy." Sinder innocently added, "Didn't know you were a fan. Want me to get ahold of the next book in the series for you?"

"Hardly necessary."

"Who do you want to win?" Sinder asked. "Dragon or phoenix?"

"I have no influence over the outcome of the story," Juuyu said stiffly. "What has been written will be accomplished."

If they'd leave off long enough to let him find out.

Sinder brushed at his shoulder and relayed, "Moon is offering to sleep with Akira tonight, assuming the kid can sleep at all. He's keyed up."

Juuyu supposed it was only natural. "Suuzu."

"Yeah. Suuzu." Sinder gestured with his chin to the activity below. "Colt has the fire banked. There's going to be singing. Want a part in the proceedings?"

"I am otherwise occupied."

"Yeah, I figured. Make sure we don't wake her?"

"She will sleep." Juuyu was vaguely disconcerted to realize that he'd been stroking Fumiko's hair. When had that started?

Sinder cautiously suggested, "If she wakes, make her eat."

Juuyu realized something important. "You are worried about her."

"I mean, she's a beacon, right? And tree-kin. Everyone's doing everything they can to keep her safe. But it's like … they mean well with all their measures, but she's a caged bird. Or more like a caged star. With no one to shine for." Sinder shrugged uncomfortably. "It'd be sad to see a soul as lovely as hers burn out because there was no one to tend it. Kinda?"

"She has been neglected," Juuyu agreed.

Sinder quietly admitted, "I keep thinking of Waaseyaa and Zisa. Sure, there's a grove nearby—and you did *not* hear that from me—but those guys are isolated, too. Think I could sneak them a phone?"

He still missed them.

"I believe it is a good idea." Juuyu suggested, "Broach the subject with Glint?"

"Yeah, I will. As soon as I get Mikoto on my side." With a brighter smile, Sinder asked, "Anything else you want me to handle on my one day off?"

Juuyu warbled and waved him away.

Sinder saluted and dropped from view.

The book had taken a surprising turn when Zuzu popped into existence on the opposite end of the hammock. Her smile was soft. "You make Sister happy."

He was aware. How could he not be?

Juuyu simply said, "You are happy, too."

"Tonight is good, and I am grateful." Zuzu pointed to herself. "Will you let me share? I can be careful."

"What did you have in mind?"

"I can make it rain. Like a shower of petals. Like a drift of pollen."

He was catching a sense of her intent. "Are you talking about tending?"

"Yes. Soren showed me how." She softly added, "He was a good teacher."

261

Juuyu inclined his head. "I have seen his name in the lineages. Soren Reaver was a ward of considerable talent."

"He was kind."

Perhaps that *was* of greater import.

"Fumiko is asleep," he pointed out. "And she needs the rest more than any of us need tending."

Zuzu shrugged. "I am the one who makes it rain."

"Who do you intend to favor?" Zuzu flitted from one to another of them, so it was difficult to tell if she had a favorite.

"*Everyone*. I can reach anyone inside Portia's wards."

Affecting an entire zone was a service sometimes performed by cossets. Diffusion kept the influence within the realm of safety. Some clans employed reavers specifically to lend a pleasing ambiance to special gatherings. Or they were brought in to soothe crochety babes, convalescents, or expectant mothers. No matter their role, cosseting took exceptional control.

"You will be careful?"

Zuzu's smile was coy. "You might never have noticed if you were not already so close to Sister."

Juuyu got the distinct impression that Zuzu approved of the casual nest he currently shared with her twin. Which was *immeasurably* better than any tree's disapproval. Still, he chose not to acknowledge her remark. "Perhaps you should share your plan with Portia. Or Jiminy. They can guide your efforts and provide safeguards."

"I will." And with a knowing look at the book in his hands, she breezily added, "So that you can read."

He wanted to protest that his interest in the novel was

academic, but she was already gone.

Minutes later, Juuyu sighed as the first blissful hint of power touched him. Delicate as down, it brushed against his awareness, lifting his spirits. He read on, though he shifted several times, slouching lower, adjusting his long limbs, getting comfortable.

The book concluded well, and Juuyu closed it with a giddy sense of rightness.

Folding his arms around Fumiko, he whispered against her hair. "You are right. This is terrible and terrifying."

36

BROUGHT TOGETHER

T he smell of cinnamon pulled Akira from sleep, and it took a moment to remember why he was in Moon's room. He'd been too keyed up to relax, and his stomach lurched when he remembered why. "Am I late?" he croaked.

Denny Woodacre, who'd been waving a cardboard tray from Dinky's Doughnuts in the vicinity of Akira's nose, grinned. "It's early, but gaining. These are from Rafter with his compliments. And a request."

"What does he need?" Akira sat up and reached for a doughnut hole.

"Cooperation." Denny nicked one for himself. "Don't so much as poke your nose through the gate, young sir. You need something, you holler for me or Buzz. Got it?"

Akira nodded, though he couldn't help wondering at the squirrel clansman's solemnity. "Why?"

"Here's the thing." He dipped into his shirt pocket and urged, "Hold out your hands."

When he did, Denny spilled a skimpy pile of red petals into them. They were fresh, and they smelled like home.

Akira asked, "Where did you find them?"

"A little here, a little there. Someone's been looking for us. Or *you*."

"How close did he get?"

"A fair few were in Rafter's sweepings." Denny searched his face. "Did you ever tell your mysterious friend where you're staying?"

Akira started to shake his head, but he hesitated. "I mentioned places I visited on the way over to the Amory or on my way back here. Like Dinky's. Oh! I showed him a picture of me with Rafter."

"Got it!" Denny held out his hands for the petals. "I'll just turn these over to Bavol, then give Rafter a heads up."

"I'm sorry."

"What for? You shared some things with a friend. Perfectly natural."

"But … he turned out to be the thief."

Denny's expression softened. "He's more than that, isn't he?"

"He's not after me. He wants the Junzi. And my dad, who might actually be my mom."

With a low chuckle, Denny said, "Every family has its quirks, and he's a grand one. I'd love to know how he's pulling this off. But it's clear he can't find you behind our barriers, so stay put."

"Tabi-oji wouldn't hurt me."

"Agreed. But he'll figure out soon enough that he's outmatched, and that can change a fellow's priorities." Denny backed toward the door. "Argent wants you safe, so that's my priority. Keep in mind, there's someone else who's eager to reach your side. For their sake, keep to quarters."

He meant Suuzu.

Though Akira was still confused about what to do with what he'd learned about Tabi-oji, he was as sure as anyone could be about Suuzu. "I promise."

While he munched his way through the rest of the doughnut holes, Akira texted Tsumiko.

> **Argent told you why he's on his way here?**

> **I was shocked to see you with Uncle.**

> **Is Tabi-oji really part of our family?**

> **When I was little, I called him Haji-oji. He was always around, All times of the day or night, Like he belonged. He *did* belong. To us.**

> **How was he connected to Dad? Naoki**

Best friends or maybe lifelong friends.
They fit together in a comfortable way.

What about our mother?

I really don't remember her.

There are no pictures of her?

None.
I don't know her name
or her family name.
We never visited her grave
at Oban, either.

Sis, what if we didn't have a mother?
Not the lady kind

There was a long pause on Tsumiko's end. Hadn't Argent told her this part? Maybe not. He was touchy about personal things. If Argent had decided this was a family matter, he'd definitely leave it to Akira to break the news.

Tabi-oji, Haji-oji, whatever we call him
I think maybe he loves Dad
At least, he's risking
everything to save him

Our father is gone, Akira.

Here's the thing
Naoki *is* gone, but not dead and gone
Tabi-oji says he was kidnapped
When we were little
That's what broke up our family

Akira's phone rang. He picked up.

"My hands are shaking too much to text," Tsumiko softly confessed.

"This is probably better anyhow. Sorry about the time. It must be the middle of the night."

"Don't worry about it." His sister sounded subdued. *"I'm up rocking a baby anyhow."*

She often was. Every crosser at Stately House adored their Lady.

"I'm sorry if this comes out in a jumble, but ... Tabi-oji says we're his kids. And Naoki, the one we call dad, carried us. I think we might be tree-kin."

Tsumiko took her time responding. *"I'm familiar with tree lore. I had no idea it might be personally relevant. Argent knows?"*

"Yeah."

"We can probably trust this to him, then. I asked Argent to invite Haji-oji home. He vanished from our lives, and I was so happy to know we might have him back." With a low laugh, she added, *"I wanted to introduce him to you."*

"He's something else." Akira sighed. "I like him a lot, Sis. But I think he's mixed up in something bad."

Tsumiko sounded like she was smiling. *"Then he found you when he needed us most. Trust Argent. He'll find a way to bring our family together. All of us."*

Akira wished he had half his sister's faith.

He said, "I'm sorry I didn't tell you right away. I guess I was so caught up in finding out everything I could about our dad—our dads—that I ... I left you out."

"You aren't the only one who's been treasuring up something

good. Argent has discovered that there are more children fathered by the Rogue than were initially reported. He intends to bring them home, too."

"How many are we talking about?"

"Oh, he was evasive. I think he doesn't want me to get my hopes up. But he did say that Inti went to find them, and he met with more success than expected. It seems they're being kept in a lab somewhere."

"Inti?"

Akira tried to hide his concern as Juuyu's words came back to him—*We need your help to rescue Inti.*

"About the same time you arrived in California, Argent brought home a tiny foretaste of the future. Kyrie is beside himself with delight. Here. I can show you. I took pictures earlier today."

One came through. It showed Kyrie seated on the sofa in the kitchen, cradling a small child to his chest. The baby was gazing up at him with large red eyes. Their pale skin was freckled with lavender, and there was a familiar frizz of purple hair.

"A half-sibling," Akira whispered.

"She's in my arms now," Tsumiko said gently. *"We let Kyrie name her."*

Another snapshot came through. In this one, Ginkgo held the little girl. He was trying to get her to look at the camera, but she was far more interested in Kyrie ... and the fistful of his hair that she'd captured.

"Uncle Akira, meet Mercy."

37

RESTLESS

After a quick shower and change of clothes, Akira hurried downstairs, marveling at how wide the stairway felt. Juuyu must have worked through the night for all the steps and ledges to be cleared. Where had he put the excess?

In the main room, where neatly labeled boxes now lined one wall, Akira found Juuyu deep in a meeting with Buzz. Not about trees or pollen. Nope. They were discussing carpentry and shelves with Fumiko, who had a sketchbook in hand.

"My skills are at your disposal, Lady of Trees." Buzz seemed a little smitten with Fumiko and Zuzu. Or maybe he was understandably in awe.

Juuyu gestured to one stretch of wall. "I will need at least eighty niches, more if space allows, floor to ceiling. But the primary work will be in the guest bedroom at the fourth turning."

"I can show you," Fumiko offered.

Buzz indicated her sketchbook. "May I make a suggestion?"

All three of them crowded together as the pencil scratched, and Akira crept closer for a peek.

"Oh, my!" Fumiko giggled and turned to Juuyu. "Do you like it?"

Somewhat sheepishly, Buzz said, "If you'll indulge me, I can turn Zuzu into a honey tree. Figuratively speaking, of course."

Juuyu angled his head toward Fumiko, indicating that the decision was hers.

"I love your idea!" she exclaimed. "Zuzu will, too. I'll go tell her."

She kissed Buzz's cheek and hurried out, leaving an abashed bee clansman behind.

Akira smiled at the proposed design, which involved shelves of varying depths sprawling artistically across the interior wall. The lighthouse would soon have honeycomb storage.

"How soon can you begin?" asked Juuyu.

"Almost immediately. I'll just work up some numbers and pass a supply list to Rafter."

Juuyu inclined his head, then turned to Akira. In the next moment, the phoenix's hands were in Akira's hair, preening. Honestly, this was why he no longer owned a comb. Zero need.

"Are you well?" Juuyu inquired.

"All fidgets and nerves."

"If my brother was not asleep, he would be similarly fraught." Juuyu patted his cheek and promised, "Soon."

"*How* soon?"

"May I see the stone at your ankle?"

Akira dropped onto the closest chair and lifted the leg on which he wore a crystal suspended on braided hair.

The ankle bracelet was part of the reason he was beholden to Boonmar-fen Elderbough. Back when Akira was still in high school, he'd traded favors with Boon. The wolf had created the necklace that Akira had given to Suuzu. One of the items on that necklace was an especially fine remnant stone, which Michael had tuned to this one Akira wore. No matter where Suuzu was in the world, he knew which direction Akira was in.

"It works both ways?" Akira asked.

"Not in equal measure. Suuzu's stone is meant to find yours, not the other way around, but there is a faint echo." Juuyu hummed and huffed. "They are near. Ahead of schedule."

"What's that in minutes?"

Juuyu checked his pocket watch. "Twenty-eight. As an estimate."

Akira's jitters redoubled. "I think I'll go down by the water."

With a soft warble of sympathy—and one last fuss over his hair—Juuyu let him go.

Although he'd been hoping the beach would calm him down, Akira found something even better. Distractions.

At the water's edge, Mirrim was sparring with Colt, both armed with swords. It looked dangerous, but they were clearly professionals.

Meanwhile, Zuzu had gotten into her sister's things and was painting tiny white daisies between the sigils on Magda's body. Magda clearly didn't mind a bit. She was pretty cool. Scary, too, but no worse than Sansa. Akira had a feeling that the crossers back home would've adored her. Maybe he should check with Timur, see if they could stream the battler games she'd talked about. Akira could show off his new friends, and the crossers could root for the Lost Harbor Lockets.

Diva sat on the end of the dock with Antigone and Dru, cheering on—or possibly heckling—Sinder, who'd adopted truest form to fish. That must be the plan for lunch. They'd have an even bigger crew than usual to feed.

Fumiko was sitting with Jiminy, who'd also been decorated with daisies. Akira caught a little of what he was saying and slowed to listen.

"... wouldn't say avian instincts are *complicated*. And to be fair, I know more about pheasants than phoenixes."

"That's what Zuzu said," Fumiko replied.

Jiminy turned to look at Zuzu. "She heard that?"

Suddenly Zuzu was kneeling at his side. "I hear *everything*."

"I see! Anything said or done under a tree is known to the tree?"

With a laugh, Zuzu returned to Magda.

"Surely there are similarities," pleaded Fumiko. "Please, tell me anything you know about avians and their romantic ideals."

Akira edged closer.

Jiminy noticed and beckoned him over. "Akira may be some help. He's close to a phoenix."

"I remember. Your best friend is Juuyu's brother." Fumiko patted the sand at her side and murmured, "Thank you both."

"Now, Miss Fumiko, have you, perhaps, taken a shine to a certain phoenix?" Jiminy asked lightly.

"I didn't *mean* to choose. I didn't need to." Fumiko pushed hair behind her ear. "Usually, they send people like you. Strong reavers. And I fulfill my contract with their child."

Akira shifted uneasily. Reaver contracts were unnerving. He received his fair share of offers, thanks to his connection to the illustrious Lady Mettlebright. Not that he'd ever looked at one. Argent simply passed them along to Sansa, who'd taken to building monthly bonfires ever since their family achieved dynasty status.

Jiminy didn't bat an eye. "*Thank you* for your contribution to our community. According to the pack that adopted me, my birth family lives in similar circumstances. But it's not *my* story you're interested in. Let's see. Generalities first?"

"Yes, please."

He included Akira. "And you can tell us if they apply to our phoenix friend. You probably know more than anyone about this sort of thing."

Akira murmured, "Not really."

Because it was true. He and Suuzu had simply grappled with issues of instinct and preference as they came up. There'd never been anything like a lesson plan. Just … life.

Jiminy spoke a little slower than usual and in simple terms. Akira appreciated the consideration.

"Avians are prone to love at first sight."

Fumiko asked, "They can't be persuaded?"

"Anyone can be persuaded, given the right circumstances," Jiminy said with a laugh. "But with avians, a strong first impression can be all it takes. One look, and they know."

She shook her head. "It's too late for that. We already met."

Jiminy turned to Akira. "When did you and Suuzu first meet?"

"In school. We were part of an early integration program. Suuzu was visiting my class, and he singled me out."

Fumiko leaned forward. "Love at first sight?"

"More like *roommates* at first sight. We've been living together since I was fourteen."

"Nestmates?" Jiminy inquired.

"Yes. Both Juuyu and Suuzu consider me a nestmate."

"And his colony approved the choice?"

"Yes. I can even wear his colors and crest for official stuff."

Even seated, Jiminy's posture was as nuanced as Kimiko's, though nearly all of his non-verbal inflections were wolvish. They helped Akira process Jiminy's meaning. Which is how Akira could tell this detail surprised him.

But Jiminy focused on Fumiko and said, "Gifts are the ultimate classic. They're widely considered the best way to catch an avian's interest. Birds love to receive little presents, especially if you tell them why each gift made you think of them."

"Little presents," Fumiko mused. "Like what?"

"Anything will do. Items made from eggshell are traditional. Crystals are favored, especially if the color has significance. Feather motifs are common. Or imagery from a family crest. But anything with a bit of sheen or shine is sure to appeal."

Fumiko seemed pleased. "What else?"

"Feeding an avian would count as courting behavior."

Akira blurted, "Sharing a meal is courting?"

"More like handfeeding," he corrected. "Also, clothing is actually really important to avians, especially the males. I think it's an instinctual carry-over. Avians like eye-catching plumage and are fastidious to a fault. Giving a gift that an avian can wear is doubling down."

Fumiko asked, "Is it romantic?"

"Not necessarily. But it's personal." Jiminy considered the matter. "If you're looking for romantic gestures, how they touch you matters."

"Like kissing?"

"No, actually. Which I believe is another carry-over from truest form. Birds don't have lips, so kissing is ... an acquired taste. For avians, *preening* is the thing. The rearranging of hair denotes trust, affection, belonging. Right, Akira?"

"R-right." He didn't mean to sound defensive when he said, "It's not just Suuzu. Juuyu preens me all the time."

"Certainly," said Jiminy. "He considers you kin."

Fumiko was patting at her own hair. "So it isn't love?"

"Like most things, it depends on the context. But attention is *always* a good thing with avians. They like receiving it, so it always means something when they give it." Jiminy went right on. "The most famous contemporary example of avian romance is Ash Sunfletch's courtship of Tamiko Reaverson. Did you follow that?"

"A little," said Fumiko. "After we met him, Diva set up one of the library computers so I could watch *Crossing America*."

Akira shook his head. "I know about it, but nope. Never watched any of it."

Which was strange, really. He might have been interested, since there was an avian crosser involved. Plus, Akira knew for a fact that Argent had acted as Ash's and Tami's go-between.

"Gifts were part of the show's schtick, right from the start. At every enclave Ash visited, they'd present him with a gift, usually something of local significance. Always something small. Just a trinket, really. And Ash would bring it home to Tami as a courting gift."

"That's a lot of gifts," said Fumiko. "Aren't there six full seasons already?"

"Are they still courting?" asked Akira.

"No, but Tami still receives tokens of affection from Ash's travels. It's tradition now, after so many years."

As Jiminy went on to describe the initial courting gift, to be followed by smaller tokens, Akira tried not to think about how much it sounded like his gift to Suuzu. Had he accidentally proposed to his best friend? Surely, Suuzu would have mentioned something. Set him straight. Turned him down. Explained.

When Fumiko ran off, presumably in search of an appropriate gift for Juuyu, Akira latched onto Jiminy's wrist and all but groveled in the sand. "What if I gave a gift that was definitely a big deal?"

"Did Suuzu accept it?"

"Well, yeah." He didn't really want to explain the circumstances, so he mumbled, "It was a really good gift."

"And he was happy to receive it?"

"He definitely was." Thinking back, Akira admitted, "He seemed ... surprised? But glad."

Jiminy adjusted his hands so they were grasping each other's wrists. "And you've continued to give him things?"

"Small stuff. Things he'd like." Akira was embarrassed to admit, "I mostly just buy snacks at the convenience store, and we share. But we have this ... I guess you'd call it a collection. When we find something really nice that fits, we add it."

"Does he reciprocate? Does he give you presents?"

"Nope. Never." Akira slowly shifted his posture into one of dominance. "I've always been more outgoing, so I almost always take the initiative. Oh. I *did* get a set of traditional clothes to wear for events. I'd borrowed things before, but these were tailored to me. I think Juuyu arranged for them."

"Okay. I think Suuzu accepted your present in the spirit it was intended, and he doesn't think you're courting. That's why he's careful not to reciprocate. That would give the wrong impression. However, the gift of clothes is significant."

"It is?" Akira asked faintly.

"Not to pry, but was your initial gift costly or intimate or ... something he could wear?"

"Yes. All those things." Really, that was an understatement. Suuzu wore his necklace obsessively, and Akira was only beginning to understand the cost he'd incurred by trading favors with Boon.

"Chances are that's why Juuyu responded with such a lavish gift—the crest and clothes." Jiminy bobbled his hands back and forth. "Amaranthine often strive for balance. It also means that your gift was formally accepted by his clan."

Akira cleared his throat. "My name was added to the family registry."

Jiminy's eyebrows shot up, and he fished a crystal from a pocket. With a sign for secrecy, he waited until it was clasped between their palms before quipping, "The trees have ears. May I be blunt?"

"That would be helpful."

"If you're happy, be happy. You have a good friend." Despite the privacy he'd secured, Jiminy lowered his voice. "But if you're inclined to bond and build, be sure your next gift includes a bit of eggshell. Your phoenix will understand."

38

ENTOURAGE

Akira had attended enough official functions—including Kimi's courting of Quen—to understand how his foxish brother-in-law operated. Argent could stroll calmly through a crowd, clasping hands and accepting greetings with as much serenity as Hisoka Twineshaft. *If* he wanted to be seen. But if he was minding the time or protecting a companion, there was a ruthless glint in Argent's eye, and people simply didn't notice him.

Foxes made excellent allies. And frightening enemies.

And then there was Merit, Harmonious Starmark's eldest son. And Boon's best friend. Any canine's protective streak was wider than oceans and could run several generations deep. Merit was a serious-minded guy who considered everyone at Stately House to be under Starmark protection. He'd see to Suuzu's comfort with the same care he'd give to any of his own pups. Or grandpups.

Without a doubt, Suuzu was safe. But weren't they running a little late?

He was just about to text Uncle Jackie when Diva bellowed, "Incoming!"

Akira had already been loitering near the crystal gate, so he was there when it swung open. He caught and held it, figuring he had sufficient skill to be a doorstop.

Portia hurried forward, as did Jiminy, who caught Jacques' hand as Argent ushered him through the barrier.

"Lord." Jacques removed sunglasses with peach-tinted lenses and muttered, "Watch for a tree, he said. You can't miss it, he said. *Lord.*"

"Gawk later," Argent ordered with token annoyance. "Lend Candor a hand with your considerable baggage."

Akira probably should have offered to help, but he was trying to catch a glimpse of Suuzu. However, the next person through the gate wasn't Merit. Rafter backed in, wrestling a small mountain of luggage. Candor followed, toting a fancy trunk with a crest emblazoned in gold on its top and sides. It wasn't the Stately House crest. Actually, it wasn't a clan crest at all.

"Impressed by the family heraldry?" Jacques beamed at him. "Been in the family for ages. Had it shipped from Uppington. Needed to look authentic."

But Akira's attention was already straying back to the gate, where Merit Starmark paused on the threshold. Argent took hold of Suuzu's limp hand, and Rafter wrapped an arm around Merit's back, guiding them safely through the barrier.

Portia and Jiminy were already tuning crystals.

Diva was talking, and so was Jacques.

But Akira wasn't focusing very well. He was too busy standing in Merit's way.

The dog clansman took a receptive posture and suggested, "Show me where to go?"

"Where do you want to go?"

"To whatever nest you've made in this tree." Merit may have been smiling.

Akira fled toward the lighthouse without a word, figuring a tracker of Merit's skill wouldn't have any trouble following.

The dog clansman had to duck in order to ease through Fumiko's front door. Only then did it occur to Akira that Juuyu's most recent cleaning frenzy hadn't been all about compulsion. He'd cleared a path for Merit, who'd never have made it through otherwise.

It was hushed inside, all distant chimes and lazy waves, shaded from the midday sun, though bits of light danced in the dimness, just out of focus. Was he imagining things? Or was he catching glimpses of Ephemera? Akira's fidgets and nerves were multiplying.

"Here," he whispered, backing into the guest room.

Merit lowered Suuzu onto the bed, gently smudged his thumb across the phoenix's brow, and grunted in satisfaction. "Stay with him. I'll bring what's needed in a little while."

"Thank you."

With a faint smile, Merit gave him a nudge toward the bed and left.

Akira crawled onto the mattress and sat beside Suuzu. He'd been helping oversee Suuzu's long sleeps since his first visit to the Farroost colony when he was fourteen. At that time, Juuyu had explained his brother's requirements so thoroughly, Akira had gotten the idea that Suuzu needed looking after.

It had seemed silly at the time, but Akira's perspective had been subtly shifting. Unlike Suuzu, Akira was getting older. He'd shared his teen years with his best friend, but a decade and more later, Akira felt like an adult. However, Suuzu was the same. Or nearly so.

He *did* look older in his Western suits than he had back when he'd worn a school uniform. And he'd been letting his hair grow. It wasn't nearly as long as Juuyu's, but the loose curls that just brushed his shoulders had changed him somewhat.

Still, Juuyu sometimes said things that embarrassed Suuzu. Stuff about his years.

Akira carefully brushed back Suuzu's hair and searched his sleeping face. His best friend—Spokesperson Farroost—might be a world-renowned and well-respected member of the Amaranthine Council, but he was *young*. Younger than Akira, and the age gap could only widen.

He didn't like to think about it.

But it was getting harder not to.

Akira reached for Suuzu's hand and focused on the phoenix's breathing. Was he breathing in time with the waves? It didn't take long to confirm it, which meant that on some level, Suuzu was aware of his surroundings. A sure sign that he was coming around.

Counting back, Akira knew for certain that it was too soon.

But Suuzu's fingers twitched and curled around his.

Should he warn Suuzu that he'd been smuggled overseas? Probably. But Akira couldn't get the words out as his friend took a deep breath, turned his head, and opened his eyes.

Suuzu murmured, "This is unexpected."

"Yeah." Akira released his hand. "Sorry."

"Do not apologize." Suuzu reached up to touch Akira's face. "There are risks when entrusting one's rest to foxes."

"Welcome to California."

Suuzu hummed, and his gaze drifted around the room. But his attention soon returned to Akira. "You are still too far away."

Akira slid into his usual spot. His ... because he'd made a strong first impression?

Rolling onto his side and hiding his face against Akira's chest, Suuzu said, "I do not like you so far from me."

He sounded so sulky. Not at all the illustrious world leader.

"I missed you, too." Akira fussed with Suuzu's hair to soften the blow of his next admission. "But I'm glad I came. So many interesting things have happened."

Suuzu hummed in a distracted way. Maybe he was still half asleep?

"There's so much to tell, I hardly know where to start."

Propping himself up on one elbow and looking very much awake, Suuzu said, "Begin here."

He pulled and pushed, pinning Akira face-down on the bed as he tugged at the collar of his T-shirt. The tattoo. Akira went limp and let his friend explore.

"What has been done here?" Suuzu grumbled.

"You don't like it?"

"This is permanent?" A note of distress colored his warble. "It must have hurt."

"Some. Not anymore, though." Akira craned his neck. "Michael designed it, and Argent applied it. They used what they learned from Uncle Jackie's tattoos."

284

Suuzu's fingers traced lightly over the pattern.

"It works," Akira reported. "Or so they tell me."

"I know." Tipping his head to one side, Suuzu whispered, "It is calling to me."

39

PRIVATE WORD

At the first opportunity, Juuyu addressed Argent. "May I have a private word?"

The fox arched a brow. "I doubt there is anything of significance you can tell me about the case while you are pollinated."

"This is a private matter."

"*Tsk*. Will the wolf's den do?"

Juuyu followed him into the small room and managed not to flinch when Argent flung a fresh round of sigils past him. He did glare though.

Trust was trust, and Juuyu *did* trust Argent. But foxes were foxes, and Argent was as sly as they came.

Argent's gaze was cool, almost clinical. "How do you feel?"

While he did need to broach the subject of feelings, Juuyu decided to bide his time. "Physically, I detect no changes, but I appear to have lapses in both observation and memory."

"Sit."

Juuyu lowered himself to the edge of the bed.

Argent didn't need the switch-up in height advantage to dominate a room. The fox loomed large in Juuyu's eyes, a daunting figure. But Juuyu appreciated power, especially when it was wielded with skill. Without hesitation, he angled his head and waited respectfully.

"I am aware of your Old Grove upbringing. Are you unable to proceed against our culprit now that you know he may be a tree?"

Juuyu warbled a plaintive note. How could the Gentleman Bandit be a tree? It made so little sense. Trees could not travel the world, snatching up rare treasures.

"You have forgotten that part?" Argent grumbled. "Very well. What other personal matter could you wish to discuss with me? Most people entrust their secrets to Twineshaft."

"Hisoka has never been in love."

Argent went very still, disbelief plain on his face. Then one by one, he began unfurling tails. "Are you accusing me of love?"

"Certainly." Juuyu had seen the fox demonstrate his affection on multiple occasions. "You are in love with a beacon."

More tails slipped into view. "And this is related to your situation ... how?"

Juuyu spread his hands.

Argent's tails puffed. "What—*precisely*—are you attempting to confide?"

"There is a beacon here."

"A fact. One long-established." Argent blandly added, "You do not normally dither your way through your reports."

287

"I permitted a tending session." Juuyu's gaze slid sideways. "And there has been a certain amount of cosseting."

"You *know* trees and their temptations. You understand tree-kin. I believed you capable of resisting ... ah!" Argent's eyes widened slightly. "You sympathize."

"How could I not?"

"And what is her opinion of you?"

Juuyu sighed and admitted, "Fumiko is becoming attached."

Argent's hum was decidedly more interested. "And ...?"

"I have become a liability. I will understand if you order me away."

"Why would I do that?"

"She is a beacon," Juuyu reminded. "How do I even begin to resist such a soul?"

"You find her interest ... inconvenient? Has she imposed upon you?"

Juuyu waved his hand in urgent denial.

Argent's lips twitched in the direction of a real smile, which was unsettling in a new way. He sweetly asked, "You were hoping I would provide a means of escape? Do you believe your interest is somehow inappropriate?"

"I have responsibilities."

The fox snorted. "You will not be the first person to face balancing official obligations with the needs of their bonding. Allowances can be made. They were for me."

Juuyu gaped.

Argent smoothly asked, "Do you dislike the woman?"

"No."

"Is the attachment mutual?"

He thought that might be going too far. "I am hardly free to ...."

"Does Zuzu approve?"

Juuyu could only stare at his hands. "Trees usually do."

"Higgledy-piggledy?"

"Zuzu is no sapling. Years have a way of adding discernment."

Argent sighed. "Why are you being evasive?"

Juuyu opened his mouth, closed it again, and weighed his words. "Because I could sing here."

"Then sing."

"It is not that simple. I am in an awkward position where courtship is concerned."

Argent hummed. "You are a tribute."

"I am a tribute."

The fox's hand settled on his shoulder. "Do you need a go-between?"

None of this was going as he'd expected. Juuyu fidgeted unhappily. "Are you contemplating the strategic value of a beacon-bound phoenix in the conflict to come?"

"No." Argent's tails drifted closer, surrounding Juuyu in silver. "I was contemplating the unique challenges presented by youngsters with wings."

Juuyu wondered if such a thing would please Fumiko.

Argent's tone turned thoughtful. "I think you are wrong, by the way."

"About ...?"

"Twineshaft." With the hint of a smile, Argent said, "It is my private opinion that love marked him deeply. And compels him, still."

40
DOWN TO BUSINESS

Akira tried to explain the various methods his friends had used to trigger the sigil. "Michael described it as 'getting in touch with basic instincts,' which would probably scare most people. But Argent and Sensei and Ginkgo and ... uhh. What are you doing?"

Instead of pulling the collar down, Suuzu had switched to pushing the T-shirt up.

"Access," he grumbled.

"Sure. No problem." Akira pulled the shirt over his head and twisted it in both hands.

He'd known Suuzu would be interested. But he hadn't expected feather-light touches and soft notes crooned against his skin.

Akira tried for a casual tone. "You know, usually there's fangs and growling. Or hissing."

"There is no need." Suuzu actually sounded amused. "I am the one this was meant for, and I am accepted."

That hadn't been in the user's manual. "What do you mean?"

Suuzu said, "Your soul sings for mine."

"Even though I'm not a reaver?"

"Somehow. Let me study the intricacies a little longer."

Akira was almost positive that Suuzu kissed his shoulder. Which was fine. Except that Jiminy's words were circling through his mind. If avians weren't into kissing, when had Suuzu acquired a taste for it? Come to think of it, Suuzu spent a lot of time with other clans. Way more than the other phoenixes, who lived in isolation. Maybe he'd borrowed some new behaviors, like how Kimi picked up all her assorted non-verbals.

The internal pep talk wasn't working too well.

His case of fidgets and nerves intensified.

"Calm yourself, Akira."

"You're so close." He pulled over a pillow and hid his face against it.

Suuzu sounded genuinely puzzled. "Have we not always been this close?"

"Yeah." With a weakish laugh, he admitted, "Guess I hadn't noticed before now."

"That is a good sign." Suuzu switched to gentle warbling, and he stroked Akira's hair. "Your soul sings for mine."

"Not on purpose. I mean, if you're trying to tend me, I can't tell. I'm not a reaver. But … umm … turns out I *might* be tree-kin."

Suuzu inhaled sharply. With extreme care, he rolled Akira onto his back and knelt over him, speechless.

Akira hugged himself and said, "There really is a lot to tell."

They were interrupted then by Merit's return. He carried a flat box lined with a couple dozen street tacos. "Specialty of the area, according to Rafter. It'll take the edge off until the next meal, which promises to be a feast worthy of waking."

Suuzu sat back on his heels, and Akira slipped away to take the food, thanking Merit, whose expression was studiously neutral.

"A lot has happened," Akira mumbled.

"But has anything truly changed?" Merit asked before exiting.

Akira was stumped. Because he was sure something had.

Suuzu called his attention back, asking, "When did this matter come to light?"

"While you were asleep. Or I would have told you right away."

"Come." Suuzu had moved to the floor and beckoned. "Share this meal and tell me everything."

Which felt so much more normal that Akira relaxed. He pulled his shirt back on and claimed a seat. Suuzu ate steadily, his gaze hardly wavering, while Akira started at the beginning.

The chance meeting with Tabi-oji, who recognized him and knew his name.

How much easier it had been to chat in Japanese, and their standing lunch dates.

The strange turn of events, because Juuyu's team kept missing or forgetting things.

Akira's growing certainty that Tabi-oji was the Gentleman Bandit.

All the reasons why being with him had felt like going home.

Suuzu took it in without comment, his expression increasingly grave. Finally, he asked, "May I meet this person who may have sprigged you?"

"I want to find him again," Akira admitted. "So much."

"We will look together," promised Suuzu.

"You know a lot about tree-kin, right?" He clasped his hands tightly in his lap. "Is it possible for Sis and me to be like that, even though neither of us has a tree?"

Suuzu warbled sadly. "A child born with a golden seed in their hand cannot prevent another from taking it. This is one of the ways the ancient groves were exploited. In times past, tree-kin were bred in order to harvest their seeds."

Akira had been hoping and praying for a golden seed. Knowing he'd probably been born with one was tragic. In a small voice, he asked, "Do I have a twin somewhere?"

"I do not know."

"And Sis, too?"

Suuzu solemnly repeated, "I do not know."

Everything was suddenly awful. "I lost all the things I wanted to give you."

With a low trill, Suuzu claimed his usual spot, seated behind Akira. Pulling him back into his chest, Suuzu began preening. Akira leaned into the familiarity, even though a small voice—Jiminy's voice—whispered that for birds, preening was an intimacy on par with kissing.

"Suuzu?"

"Yes?"

"Are you happy?"

"Yes."

Akira knew they had to have this out. "Could you be happier?"

"Perhaps. New reasons can arise, even in the unlikeliest of places."

"Suuzu?"

"Yes?"

"Am I meant to be courting you?"

Suuzu's fingers stopped their sifting.

Akira determinedly continued. "The necklace. It was exactly the right kind of thing to initiate an avian courtship."

"Was that your intention?"

"No. I had no idea."

Suuzu sighed and wrapped his arms around Akira's shoulders. "That day, when you offered to build with me, I knew you did not understand the significance of your words or your gifts. But that did not diminish their import. I cherish my nest as a sign of the pact between us."

"Oh."

"Akira?"

"Yeah?"

Suuzu asked, "Are you happy?"

"I can't decide." Akira mumbled, "I don't think I'm *un*happy."

The preening resumed, slow and gentle. Normal.

Except for the questions it stirred up in Akira.

"We will not stop searching," Suuzu quietly promised. A renewal of the pact they'd made to find a way for Akira to stay with him. To find a golden seed.

But knowing that every stray seed in the world had been stolen from their twin's hand made Akira's heart ache. Was happiness real if it was laced with regret?

Suuzu crooned a tentative note.

"I'm okay." Akira let himself go limp, grateful for the little tugs and nudges that meant he was back with Suuzu. "I missed you."

Steps sounded on the stairway. Firm, intentional steps that were a warning. Neither of them moved, though.

Sinder's smile was sympathetic as he went through the motions of rapping on the wall at the top of the stairs. "Akira, you're needed in the guesthouse. Just you."

"Suuzu can't come?"

"Not until he's eaten more. And changed out of his pajamas."

Suuzu brushed his thumb over Akira's tattoo. "I will return to you as quickly as I can."

"Get a move on." Sinder's tone was casual, but his posture made it a command. "I'll show your greedy chick where more foodstuffs can be found. You answer to Argent."

41

SEEING RED

Juuyu chose one of the stools arrayed along the edges of the guesthouse's central room. Argent had summoned the taskforce for what promised to be a lengthy debriefing. Bavol arrived with a tray that steamed and stank. More dosing. Buzz was also making the rounds, checking pupils and *auras*. Juuyu wasn't sure if this was bee clan lingo or a California thing.

When Buzz reached him, his touch was light and his gaze was kind. "How are you feeling?"

"No different."

"No?" The bee clansman kneaded Juuyu's throat and remarked, "You've brightened up beautifully. Glad to have your brother here, maybe?"

"I suppose."

Buzz peered closely into Juuyu's eyes and casually asked, "What color are the flowers that affected you?"

"Red."

"And you remember this?"

"No." Juuyu smiled thinly. "You asked Colt and Hallow the same question when it was their turn."

Buzz flashed an easy smile. "Humor me. Do you see anything red in this room?"

"Five paperclips. The lines denoting highways on the city map. Your right sock. The text on one of the mugs Bavol brought. And Moon has a spot of catsup at the corner of his mouth."

"Are you always this thorough?"

"It is my job."

Buzz briefly gripped Juuyu's elbow, murmuring, "Thank you for your patience."

Juuyu caught his sleeve. "Why did you ask?"

"Oh, it's just a simple test. To see if the effects of the pollen have diminished."

"Did I miss something?"

With a small smile, Buzz said, "If you want to amend your answer at any point, speak up. Okay?"

Buzz went to help Bavol distribute tea, leaving Juuyu to scan the room anew. Had he missed something? Surely not. Why was *red* so significant to the case?

The tea tasted as bad as it smelled.

Moon and Merit filed into the room, closely followed by Jacques, who wheeled a small mint-colored suitcase behind him. The man caught Juuyu looking and slipped into a respectful posture before blowing him a kiss.

Juuyu had long since decided to treat Jacques like a tree.

That way, his flirtatious tendencies fit into a framework. Lord Mettlebright's righthand man was similarly self-assured and self-absorbed. And keenly aware of everything that happened within his sphere of influence.

One might question the appropriateness of Argent's choice in confidants ... until you saw Jacques Smythe steer a press conference, greet foreign ambassadors at galas, or insert himself fearlessly into situations that would intimidate a lesser man.

Situations like this.

Akira tapped on the door and stepped inside, wavering uncertainly on the threshold. Jacques laid claim, and Akira brightened to see him. They were still whispering together when Argent began the meeting in his usual systematic manner.

Questions and answers.

More significant were all the questions that had no answers.

For each gap and inconsistency, Argent made a note on the map of the Amory that Hallow had pinned to the wall. A pattern was emerging, but Juuyu was having trouble focusing on it. So he averted his gaze to consider the scene obliquely—as if their quarry were a particularly elusive Ephemera—only to be distracted by the *click* of latches on Jacques' travel case.

What was the man up to?

Juuyu wasn't the only one whose attention kept darting to the corner, where Jacques was playing valet to Akira. Argent went right on talking, as if he was unaware of his man's antics. Dividing his focus, Juuyu followed Akira's progress out of the corner of his eye.

Was that a wig?

Darting a look around the room, he realized that Bavol, Moon, Buzz, and Merit were watching them watch Akira. So this was a test? Of what?

Akira looked strange with long, dark hair. His resemblance to his sister was more pronounced, but then Jacques made his honorary nephew sit. Gathering, twisting, and pinning, he arranged the wig into a loose knot. And added a yellow kanzashi.

The dainty jingle of its bells stirred something in Juuyu's memory.

Where had he heard that sound lately?

Argent called on him, then. Mundane questions about the parking garage and the grounds crew. When he was able to steal another look in Akira's direction, Jacques had him stripped to his boxers. He warbled his concern, and Akira's attention snapped to him.

Signaling an *all's well*, he stepped into a pair of loose pants.

The next layer confirmed that this was traditional Japanese attire. Jacques folded and tucked the long shirt, knotting its belt like a professional dresser. Perhaps he qualified, having been in charge of Argent's wardrobe for more than a decade.

Sinder slipped through the door and slid onto a chair. "Did I miss anything important?"

"Undoubtedly," said Argent.

The dragon warbled a sassy note, his attention drifting to Jacques and Akira. "Are you up to something?"

"I usually am." Argent went right back to describing Mirrim's and Magda's patrol route.

Meanwhile, Jacques shook out a short kimono coat with full sleeves—black with golden ginkgo leaves strewn along the hem.

This was left hanging open while Jacques knelt to help Akira into a pair of tabi, followed by a pair of geta.

The wooden sandals clicked faintly on the wood planking.

They'd been so much louder on the museum's stone floors.

Juuyu blinked hard, cocked his head to the side. But before he could pin down the elusive impression, the door burst open and Jiminy exclaimed, "I figured it out! I think. Pretty sure, anyhow. I need a volunteer!"

Rather than being perturbed by the interruption, Argent beckoned Jiminy closer. "Show me your sigilwork."

Jiminy held what looked to be a crossbow bolt, one tipped with crystal. While Jiminy eagerly explained his adaptations to Argent, Juuyu noticed his partner. An uneasy Sinder was slowly wheeling his chair backward. He'd never been entirely comfortable with red crystals, and he scowled at this one with as much wariness as if facing off against the Chrysanthemum Blaze.

Juuyu curled his fingers in invitation.

Sinder was behind him in a twinkling, not exactly cowering, but definitely unhappy. "I've been hit with one of those before. It went badly."

"I remember." Juuyu squared his shoulders, making himself a barrier.

Argent finished his inspection with a single word. "Creative."

"Thanks!" Jiminy beamed at the room at large. "So who's first?"

"I volunteer." Colt stood. "It wouldn't be the first time I've given a crystal adept free rein."

Bavol nickered.

Jiminy had Colt pull his stool into the center of the room. "Hold this in front of your face. Just so. Mouth slightly open. Yes, good."

The man gracefully pulled sigils from thin air with both hands until four wheeled around Colt. They were reminiscent of Magda's handiwork, but Jiminy had definitely tweaked them. The red crystal on the bolt glinted, and Colt's expression grew increasingly confused.

Bavol took a stance behind his brother, steadying and supporting him.

Buzz gasped and covered his mouth.

"You seeing that?" whispered Sinder.

Juuyu's focus narrowed on the bolt. Historically, wards had used red crystals to attract Amaranthine. In the right hands, they could become an irresistible lure. Somehow, Jiminy was using this one to attract and collect the pollen. Patches of the stuff clung to the stone's surface.

"Try. Not. To. Sneeze," Jiminy said urgently.

Colt nodded slightly.

"Where's it coming from?" asked Hallow.

Jiminy shrugged. "Oh, you know. Here and there. Wherever it's lodged."

"Portia's barrier strips away pollen that's hitched a ride on skin or hair or clothing, but if the particles are internalized, they aren't affected." Bavol placed a hand against his brother's forehead. "Nasal passages, bronchial tubes, mucus membranes. That sort of thing."

Colt's nose wrinkled. "Jiminy, I'm going to sneeze."

"Hold it for juuust a sec. Induced sneezing is on our short list of remedies." Carefully taking the bolt from his hand, Jiminy backed up several paces. "Go for it."

He sneezed twice into a handkerchief. "Beg pardon," Colt murmured, only to sneeze again.

Jiminy kept his sigils wheeling for several seconds, then asked, "Is there anything I can put this in?"

Bavol was ready with a slender tube used for specimens, and Jiminy gently slid the entire bolt inside. Once it was capped, everyone breathed a little easier.

Colt blew his nose, then rolled his eyes when his brother held open a hazmat bag for the hanky's disposal. When Bavol thrust a tepid mug of tea under his nose, Colt grimaced but choked it down.

"Well?" Argent drummed his fingers. "How long before we know if we should give any credence to Jiminy's razzle-dazzle?"

Buzz performed a cursory inspection and declared, "Clear as a spring morning."

Which wasn't especially helpful. Juuyu crisply asked, "Has anything changed?"

Colt scanned the room, his attention snagging briefly on Akira, but his whole expression changed a moment later. Pointing to the center of their war room's table, he asked, "Has that always been there?"

Radiating satisfaction, Argent said, "Eureka."

42

EYES TO SEE

Juuyu strode forward. "Me next."

"Sure thing!" Jiminy reached into the quiver strapped to his thigh and twirled another crystal-tipped bolt. "This may be the first time I've ever been glad that MayMay and DahDah are always so well-armed."

He repeated the whole process with a confidence that snapped through his sigilcraft.

Juuyu watched closely, trying to follow the patterns.

"I'll show you later, if you want." Jiminy's posture shifted in a way that granted equal standing. "Should be a cinch for you, judging by the finesse in your patterns."

"Thank you."

"Feel anything?"

After a moment's consideration, Juuyu admitted, "The beginnings of the urge to sneeze."

"Good sign. Hold off for as long as you can." Jiminy asked, "What about your memories?"

Juuyu closed his eyes and reviewed the case, looking for discrepancies. "I cannot say for certain."

Jiminy hummed. "Good chance what's gone is gone. This stuff's potent."

He signaled for Bavol, who stood ready with another glass tube. The healer said, "If not for the fact that all those present are already warded against pollen, this method would *not* be advisable."

"Cross contamination," agreed Jiminy.

"Cross pollination," countered Buzz, who smiled into Juuyu's eyes and decreed, "That's more like it. Sharpened up something beautiful."

Argent ordered, "Do you now have eyes that can see?"

At the center of the table, under the dome of what looked to be a cheese board, a splash of red demanded attention. Flower petals. They tugged at his memory, mocked him when he couldn't account for them.

"These are from the Amory?" he asked.

"They are from Denny," said Argent. "The Gentleman Bandit would be on our very doorstep if he could find it."

"Why did he follow us here?" asked Sinder. "Wait. Is that the right question?"

"*How* could he follow us here?" asked Moon. "Trees don't travel."

"Trees? Who said anything about trees?" asked Hallow.

Argent mildly said, "All in due course. Carry on."

Bavol pressed a second dose of tea on Juuyu. It was still awful, but it must have done some good. He was thinking more clearly now. "Sinder, have you lost sight of Akira?"

His partner's expression was blank.

Colt said, "He's there," and pointed.

"Who's where?" asked Hallow.

Jacques shook his head. "Lord. I can't decide if this is a comedy or a tragedy."

Juuyu tugged Sinder forward, sat the dragon on the stool, and commanded, "Him next."

Sinder swore, but he submitted.

Once the process was repeated with Hallow and Jiminy did a final sweep of the entire room, Argent took charge. "Shall we take another run at the facts of the case?"

The recap exposed more memory gaps, which Argent plotted on a timeline.

Juuyu grasped at each new detail, slotting it into the missing moments from his days. Most were small, unobtrusive details, but those were his specialty. His recollection gained clarity, and his questions grew increasingly precise.

Perhaps his subconscious had been at work, accumulating details.

Perhaps his Old Grove upbringing made him less susceptible to pollination.

Colt raised his hand. "I'm missing something big. If we're all here, who's guarding the Junzi?"

"Denny Woodacre is managing things at the Amory," said Argent. "As far as the general populace and the museum management are concerned, nothing has changed."

"And the Bamboo Stave?" prompted Sinder, who wasn't what anyone would call a fan of the Four Storms.

"Someone else already absconded with it." Argent flicked his fingers in Juuyu's direction. "A bold move that gives us a second chance to catch our thief."

"Who is a *tree* ...?" Hallow asked skeptically.

Argent smiled thinly. "Akira thinks so, and I am inclined to believe him."

He beckoned, and Akira stepped into the middle of the room, geta clacking, smile tentative. Juuyu frowned, knowing something was off. Intentionally off. Because everything that was yellow was meant to be red.

"Try to move as he did," said Argent.

Akira wavered for a moment, then straightened his spine, rested his forearm along the small of his back, angled his head differently, and strolled across the room. Pivoting for another pass, he caught Juuyu's eye ... and winked.

Suddenly, Juuyu remembered red flowers on dark cloth. The flutter of falling petals. A figure wearing flowers in his hair. No, they *grew* there. Perfume filled the air, and Juuyu gazed into eyes as brilliant as sunlight through rubies—ancient in the manner of trees and soft with apology.

Juuyu whispered, "I saw him."

"You did?" Akira's expression was so fragile. "You remember him?"

Crossing to Akira, Juuyu touched his face. "You resemble the one who sprigged you."

"I didn't think you remembered my telling you that."

"That part is still hazy. This memory is clearer." Juuyu weighed whether he should say the rest in front of the team, but the information was important to all of them. "Our paths crossed during my patrol. This morning. He told me not to worry if you went away. But to follow if I could."

Argent sharply asked, "He planned to take Akira?"

"I believe so."

Akira shook his head. "Tabi-oji *did* invite me, but I turned him down."

"Should you be expecting a known thief to respect your wishes?" asked Merit.

"Hold up." Sinder raised a hand. "Sprigged? As in ... the highly euphemistic *sprigging* in the lullabies of trees?"

Juuyu rested his hands on Akira's shoulders. "Yes."

Argent offered a succinct report, during which Akira studied the floor.

"Let me get this straight," said Sinder. "The Gentleman Bandit is your father-in-law?"

Argent's brows arched. "In your estimation, *that* is the most salient point?"

"What can I say? I like the human-interest angle."

Hallow stepped forward. "So we have *two* things our thief wants."

"We do," agreed Argent.

"Either—or both—would allow us to reset our trap."

Juuyu silently agreed. If they wanted to reclaim the two Junzi that had already been stolen, they needed to catch their thief.

"Then the thing I need to know is ...." Hallow's gaze flitted briefly to Akira before he asked, "Which of them are you willing to risk?"

From the direction of the door, a softly dismayed warble alerted Juuyu to a fresh complication.

Suuzu was here. Suuzu had heard.

And Suuzu wouldn't understand.

43

PRIORITIZING CLAIMS

The stricken look on Suuzu's face had Akira stumbling over encumbered feet in his hurry to get to his best friend. Geta were a pain. But Argent caught Akira's arm. It saved him from hitting the floor, but it also prevented him from reaching Suuzu.

"Juuyu, *this* would be a good time," Argent said smoothly.

And then Suuzu was caught. Juuyu steered his brother back out the door, though Suuzu was trying to pull away and the last look he cast over his shoulder was desperate.

Akira tried to follow, but fanning tails surrounded them. He was mad enough to bat through them, manners be damned, but Argent startled him by pulling him into an embrace.

"Before you go to him, we must come to an understanding." Argent's voice was frustratingly calm.

"Suuzu needs me."

"He does. But he is not the only one."

Akira confined his protest to a small twist and a grumbled, "Suuzu comes first."

"An understandable sentiment. Until you consider the urgency with which you are needed by several others."

"Others?" Akira looked down at his costume and asked, "Do you mean Tabi-oji?"

Argent inclined his head, but he had his own list. "Juuyu's team needs you. Boon needs you. Inti needs you. Kyrie's and Mercy's siblings need you. For that matter, *I* need you, since my plan hinges upon your participation."

"But Suuzu's here *now*."

"And in the least danger." Argent leaned back to look him in the eye. "I am not diminishing his need for you. He is here because I cannot ignore his claim. But with your help, we could end all of this."

Akira pulled off the wig. "The thefts?"

"There is far more at stake than the Junzi. If you cooperate with my small scheme, you will help Boon out of a difficult position. You will provide Inti with a way of escape. You will make rescue possible for a large number of missing crossers. You will fulfill Tsumiko's wish to bring home more of Kyrie's half-siblings. And you may be able to locate Naoki Hajime."

"We can rescue my dad?"

"There are too many uncertainties for me to make promises, but I will do my best." Argent grimly added, "There is also a chance that we will finally stop the Rogue."

"He's part of this?"

Argent sighed. "I am not sure. But Hisoka *is*, and that is ... promising."

Akira tried to think clearly.

Boon was in a difficult position? That was hard to imagine. Then again, Merit was here, and he was Boon's best friend. Akira glanced to where the Starmark dog stood with Moon. Both had to have heard Argent's words, because both had eased into pleading postures.

"Me, though?" he asked. "How come you think *I* can do anything?"

"There are a handful of small reasons, hardly worth mentioning," hedged Argent. "However, three things make you ideal for what lies ahead. First, you are an unendowed human ... and therefore beneath notice."

Hardly flattering. Or rare.

"Second, I trust you to do everything you can, even if the only ones who will thank you are Kyrie, Tsumiko, and myself."

Akira's irritation faded. "The dragon-crossers?"

Argent nodded. "They may need an advocate until I can bring them under my protection. Speak on their behalf. As their uncle."

"Oh." Akira knew Argent was good at getting what he wanted. On the international stage, he had his share of detractors. Words were bandied about: strategic, manipulative, cunning. Sure, Argent was cornering him, and whatever was about to happen was going to make Suuzu unhappy. But Argent was asking nicely. For him.

Akira knew he was going to hear Argent out.

And then he was going to do whatever Argent asked.

But not until everything was in the open.

"You trust me, and I'm not a reaver," Akira said. "What's the third thing that makes me ideal?"

Before Argent could answer, Jacques sidled into their embrace, looking injured. "*Really*, my lord. Are you trying to break hearts? Here, I thought I was special!"

"*Tsk*. I was not finished."

"*Mon dieu*. You had him at *uncle*." Jacques slid an arm around Akira's shoulders and said, "Don't drag this out. Tell him the other reason we're perfect for the job."

Argent looked annoyed, but his swaying tails looped around Jacques, wordlessly including him in ... whatever this was.

"Nobody will expect unendowed humans to be immune to a dragon's sway." Argent studied their faces and quietly added, "You may be the only ones, which makes you rarer than remnants."

Jacques happily said, "We're in the same boat, my dear nephew, which I promise will be *divine*. I haven't been on a cruise in ages!"

"I am not sending you on holiday," muttered Argent.

"Yet I aim to be convincing!" Jacques held up a finger and quietly said, "My turn."

Argent's eyes flashed, but his tails swept back and away, and he bowed. Then vanished.

Jacques rolled his eyes. "Poor old sot. This is harder on him than anyone."

"Tell that to Suuzu."

"Oh, I will." Jacques patted Akira's cheek. "Argent had the easy job—convincing you. It is my unenviable duty to bring Suuzu around to our way of thinking."

"So ... when they send me to wherever Boon is, you're going with me?"

"All the way." Jacques herded him to their corner and went into valet mode again.

Akira confessed, "I'm glad."

Jacques wryly replied, "You say that now."

Juuyu had been given charge of Suuzu almost from the start, and he'd never once understood what he'd done to deserve such an earnest, sweet-natured chick. It had been hard to maintain a warrior's edge in the presence of so much innocent adoration.

Father had always smiled to watch them together.

Letik had always laughed outright. And doted.

A chick changed things, and Suuzu had changed Juuyu. For the better. Maybe even for the best.

But his sweet chick was gone, replaced by a hissing, quaking bundle of fury.

"Peace, Brother mine," Juuyu begged.

"You would use Akira for bait? Without regard for my claim? He is mine!"

What would Father and Letik say if they could see them? Their warrior begging for peace, and their peacemaker ready for war.

"He is safe."

"I will ensure it! You cannot do this thing!"

With a frustrated warble, Juuyu signaled for Suuzu to follow, and he made for the guest room. He needed to calm his brother, or he'd never listen. And there was so much to tell.

"Akira must help us. There is no other way." Juuyu sidestepped his brother's lunge.

"There is always another way, if you look. Akira is only human." Suuzu took another clumsy swipe, easily dodged. "You *took* him from me! He is all I ...! Why would you even ...? *Why*, brother?"

As the fight left him, Juuyu warbled softly and gathered up his gentle chick.

"My plans are rarely my own." Juuyu didn't intend to deflect, though. "I do think Argent's scheme will work. Yes, it will send Akira even farther from your side, but the risks are minimal. And he will not be alone."

Suuzu was more pliant now, so Juuyu made him to sit on the bed. While he preened his younger brother, Juuyu laid out the essentials of Argent's plan.

Suuzu drooped further. "I do not like it."

Juuyu hummed an acknowledgment.

"Could I go with him?"

"Without you, he is unremarkable. And that is his greatest safety." Suuzu asked, "Do I have the right to protest?"

"He is listed in our colony's registry as your nestmate, but Argent can—and would—argue that his claim as denmate is stronger. Especially since Akira makes his home at Stately House." More gently, Juuyu added, "Even if you were bondmates, you would have to abide by Akira's decision."

"And he will choose to leave," Suuzu said bitterly.

314

"He is not the sort of man to withhold help from a friend in need." Let alone two friends. And perhaps even a father.

"I know."

"Will you stand in his way?" Juuyu pressed.

Suuzu offered a flat note of abject misery.

This wasn't cooperation. This was resignation. But it would suffice.

"I wish I could do more," Juuyu admitted.

Eventually, Suuzu broke the silence. "There is one thing I want."

"Hmm?"

"I have the years. Teach me to dance."

Of all things. Juuyu reminded, "We are tributes."

"You did not learn?" Suuzu's tone sang with challenge.

"I watched the others. I know the steps."

Suuzu half-turned to search his face. "Will you dance for this tree's sister?"

Juuyu averted his gaze and stubbornly repeated, "We are tributes. We do not have the luxury of choosing."

"She confided in Akira. Everyone does." Just like that, Juuyu's earnest, sweet-natured chick was back. Suuzu asked, "You are her choice, are you not?"

"I did not come here to be courted."

Suuzu tilted his head appraisingly. "The song of your soul has changed. It used to sing for me."

Juuyu sank to a seat at his brother's side. "She is human."

"She is tree-kin."

Juuyu resisted the urge to point out that Akira was, too. Because sprigged though he might have been, someone had stolen his birthright. Instead, Juuyu gave his chick the acknowledgement he craved. "Your song has changed, as well. I am sure it will reach him."

ᕴᕴ

STEPPING ON EGGSHELLS

Over the years, Fumiko had collected so many different things—hand mirrors, ornamental hairpins, glass floats, teaspoons, netsuke, sand dollars. "Why did we never collect eggs?" she mumbled.

"How could we know they were so important?" Zuzu wrapped a comforting arm around her waist. "We can begin now."

"Diva closed up the library. I can't get online to order anything."

"I could sneak you in."

Fumiko was tempted. But before she made up her mind, they were found out.

"No." Juuyu topped the stairs and firmly reminded, "We must remain hidden for a little while longer."

Zuzu pouted. "Why?"

Fumiko edged sideways and hoped she was blocking his view of the bed.

Juuyu hesitated. "It has something to do with our current mission. I apologize for the inconvenience."

"You keep too many secrets," accused Zuzu.

"Perhaps."

Fumiko knew that her sister didn't like what Juuyu and his team had done to the guesthouse. Zuzu couldn't pass through its barrier or eavesdrop on anything that happened inside. Exclusion always made her moody.

"Secrets must be kept." Juuyu quietly pointed out, "I have been entrusted with yours."

"You could be *our* secret," Zuzu suggested. "Entrusted and kept."

Fumiko knew it wouldn't be that easy. Nothing ever was. People came and went like the tides, and the only difference was in how long they lingered on their shore. A few weeks. A few decades. Was it so terrible for her to want a husband who could match her, century for century, millennia for millennia?

"Trees are forever generous," he murmured.

"Sister!" Zuzu's eyes had gone round. "Try one. It might work!"

"I don't think they're good enough."

"It might be," she insisted. "It will be if he *wants* one."

Juuyu's attention snagged on something in the vicinity of her bedside table, and Fumiko thought he might be memorizing things again. Although the rest of the house was being quickly and quietly set in order, Juuyu hadn't trespassed here. Until now.

He stood very still.

She waited quietly.

The silence wasn't the empty sort; it was the purposeful sort. Maybe silence wasn't lonesome when it was shared?

Juuyu blinked and looked her way.

Was he there for a reason? Had he forgotten it? She did that often enough that it no longer bothered her. Reasons seemed to come and go, along with everything else. If only she had a good enough one for him to stay.

"Try one," Zuzu repeated in an urgent undertone.

Juuyu overheard. Of course he did, being Amaranthine.

"Try what?" he asked, inviting more.

Fumiko edged sideways and waved at the collection on her coverlet. "Are any of these right?"

He came to stand at her side, and he exhaled on a pretty little trill. Was that a good sign? She and Zuzu had searched high and low, but nothing seemed good enough for the enormity of what Fumiko was asking.

A brown hen's egg, still cold from the refrigerator.

A lavender plastic egg, leftover from a springtime library event.

A coffee cup with a hatching chick and text that read, GET CRACKING!

An oval plate with shallow depressions, intended for devilled eggs.

The prettiest piece was a netsuke that looked to be carved from pale green jade. It was shaped like a nest with three eggs inside.

Jiminy had also mentioned shiny things appealing to some avians, so she and Zuzu had begun adding them to make up for their lack of eggshell.

Sea glass was pretty, but did it shine enough?

A rhinestone-topped hairpin had plenty of sparkle, but it didn't seem very personal. Not when they came in a box of twenty-some.

The sequined Christmas ornament was probably all wrong. Yes, it was avian, but she'd seen Juuyu in truest form, and a phoenix bore no resemblance to a pink flamingo. Except perhaps in dignity.

"I can keep looking," she whispered.

"Fumiko?" Juuyu picked up the lavender egg and asked, "What is this for?"

"Candy, I suppose. You fill it with sweets and hide it for children to find."

"I am familiar with the custom, but I was referring to *your* purpose." Juuyu replaced the plastic egg and selected the hen's egg. "And this?"

Zuzu chimed in. "Free range. Farm fresh. Certified organic."

Juuyu accepted that with a nod and exchanged it for the jade carving, which looked very small and insignificant resting on his palm. "I am detecting a theme."

"Yes. We tried." Fumiko set her fingertips in his hand, right next to the little nest. "Does it count if the eggshells aren't actually from eggs?"

"Fumiko?" His fingers curled over hers. "You should listen to your sister."

She looked expectantly at Zuzu, who was swaying from side to side, hands clasped over her heart. "He wants you to try."

"Yes, I do." Juuyu stood straight, stance expectant, gaze averted. "Questions should be asked. Otherwise, how can they be answered?"

Fumiko had been meaning to ask. "Did you like the book?"

Juuyu's eyes closed, then opened. He calmly answered, "It

held my attention to the finish."

"Is that good?"

He hummed. "It began, and it ended. I prefer things that go on."

"Vast things?" she asked.

"Yes. I have always been attracted to vastness."

Fumiko had so many questions. She was probably asking them out of order, but she wanted to know. "Do you like kisses?"

"I am frequently subjected to them. Usually by trees. Since ancient times, trees have used kisses to entice, but they are a common greeting in the groves."

Which wasn't what she'd meant at all. "I'm not a tree."

"I am aware." With a soft sigh, Juuyu said, "If you need a go-between, Argent has volunteered."

"Why would he do that?"

"He is good at arranging things."

Fumiko wasn't impressed. "*You* are my chronicler. I don't want anyone but you arranging my things."

Juuyu inclined his head. "Will you ask your question if I first promise that my answer will be *yes*?"

She clung more tightly to his hand. "You'll agree?"

"I do not think I could refuse you anything."

"Even if I want kisses?"

He inclined his head graciously. "I will not object."

"Even if I want forever?"

"I would insist."

Fumiko could hardly believe it. "You'd stay?"

Juuyu hesitated. "My duties take me to many places, but I would know my way home."

"Does that mostly mean *yes*?" Fumiko asked.

"It does." Juuyu lifted her hand and gazed at her over it. "If I am invited."

"Is that a rule? Jiminy mentioned Ash and Tami, but ... do you need to be courted? Is this like Kimiko and Eloquence?"

"You must ask for me if you want me. But I do not require a lengthy courtship with much pageantry. All I require is an appropriately direct question."

All the other questions Fumiko wanted to ask faded in importance. There would be time to ask them. They would each get their turn. Juuyu was waiting for the question to his answer. So she asked, "Are you mine?"

Zuzu bit her lip.

Fumiko held her breath.

Juuyu bowed so that his forehead touched the back of the hand he still held.

Had she done it wrong? Even Zuzu looked uncertain.

But then Juuyu lifted his face, brushed his lips across her knuckles, and promised, "I am."

"For all my years?" she pressed.

Zuzu edged closer. "And mine?"

"If not longer."

As if the future was another vastness. One they would share.

45

BREAKING GENTLY

Where will he be?" asked Jacques.

Akira didn't exactly have a homing instinct where Suuzu was concerned. "Nearby."

"Are you being coy? I'm too jetlagged to handle coy."

"Well, I'm not going to call out. That'd just worry him more." Akira aimed for the lighthouse. "He'll be nesting somewhere."

Uncle Jackie pointed out, "There could be a hundred nests in a tree this size."

A valid consideration. Akira stopped and quietly called, "Zuzu?"

He was in her arms an instant later. And sprinkled with carefree kisses.

"Zuzu," he groaned.

Jacques backed up a step. And another. "The tree herself?"

"Y-yeah. Hey, now. Whoa!" Akira tried clumsily to keep up when she twirled with him along the walkway. "Zuzu, what's gotten into you?"

"Sister *kissed* him!"

"No kidding?" Akira obligingly asked, "How did that go?"

"He *let* her!"

"That's good. She must be happy. And you're happy." All her spinning was making him dizzy. "And I'm happy for you, but ... umm. Hey, have you met Uncle Jackie?"

Akira found himself summarily abandoned and immediately felt bad. How would Uncle Jackie deal with a beautiful, clingy female?

He shouldn't have worried.

Jacques twirled Zuzu along the walkway with an unforeseen level of expertise. "My nephew is somewhat lacking in several of the social graces, but I can hold my own in any cotillion. Now ... I *must* know! Who is kissing whom?"

"Do you like kisses?" asked Zuzu.

"*Naturellement!*"

Jacques kept Zuzu talking all the way to the front step, then bowed over her hand, begging a prior engagement. "Where might we find Suuzu Farroost?"

She looked to Akira. "Your room."

"Thank you, Zuzu."

Swooping in for another hug, she quietly asked, "Are you going to kiss him?"

"Err ... no?"

She rubbed her cheek against his and whispered, "Too bad."

Jacques held the door for Akira. The main floor was hushed, and the quiet suddenly felt awkward. Akira cleared his throat, "You dance?"

"All part of the posh and polish. Maman did insist."

"Even though you don't like girls?"

Uncle Jackie caught his wrist and held tight, but his posture was carefully neutral. "I liked them enough not to foster any false hopes. Or to step on their toes. The only woman's heart I ever broke was Maman's."

"Oh. I didn't know." Akira adjusted his posture, uncertain why Jacques was suddenly so serious.

"You are hardly the first to ask a question simply because it popped into your head."

"Sorry. I didn't mean anything …!"

"I know. Lord, don't look so tragic. This isn't about *me*. It's the mission. I love transparency in a pair of harem pants, but where we're going, one word thoughtlessly spoken could imperil everything."

Akira frowned. "I can be careful."

Jacques took his hand and squeezed. "I promised Argent that nothing terrible would happen to you. Aside from the obvious and unavoidable."

"Which parts are those?" Really, they needed to tell him everything, and in the right order.

With a glance toward the stairs, Uncle Jackie sighed. "All the ones Suuzu is going to hate. Come on. I only want to have to break it gently *once*."

They found Suuzu huddled disconsolately at the center of the bed. However, the moment they entered, he scrambled onto his knees and bowed his head. "I apologize for my outburst."

Jacques was back to his usual breezy flippancy. "Was there an outburst? And it's over already? Too bad. I've never seen you in the throes of passion. It must be a sight."

Suuzu blinked.

Slapping Uncle Jackie's shoulder on his way past, Akira went to sit on the edge of the bed. "Are you okay?"

"No."

"Can I make it better?"

"Don't bother trying." Jacques dropped into a picturesque sprawl between them. "I'm about to make things ten times worse. Shall we agree to make the best of what we have to work with?"

"Err … I guess?"

Suuzu simply averted his gaze and waited.

Which worried Akira. He felt oddly out of step with his best friend. They needed to talk. But it seemed that Uncle Jackie would be doing all the talking for now.

"Right. First. You absolutely cannot be angry with Argent. He isn't asking anything of you that he's not risking himself."

Akira traded a look with Suuzu, who shrugged.

Jacques reasoned, "Suuzu, you may have to give up Akira, but Argent is giving up *me*."

"It is *not* the same," Suuzu said stiffly.

"Don't underestimate Argent's possessiveness. Nor his precautions." Jacques arranged himself more comfortably and said, "We need privacy for this next bit."

He took a ring of solid crystal from the first finger of his left hand. It had to be a remnant stone. Probably *really* rare.

Akira asked, "Can you use that?"

"No, but if Suuzu is feeling generous, we can all benefit from Michael's gift." Jacques reached for a pillow and propped himself up. "Come along, me boyos. Pretend we're in the naproom. Nestle down with Uncle Jackie. He has a harrowing tale to tell."

Jacques wasn't satisfied until their heads rested on his shoulders. Pulling them snug against his sides, he grumbled, "Lord. This doesn't have to be difficult. Now, unbutton me."

Akira sighed. "Uncle Jackie ...."

"It's not as if I'm asking you to unbutton my fly. Shirt buttons. Two should suffice."

Suuzu murmured, "There is a sigil there."

"Oh. Why didn't you say so?" Akira lent a hand.

"You both need to be touching the stone, which needs to be resting over this sigil. Interlace your fingers and cover it." Jacques waited patiently for their obedience. "Such good, compliant boys. Makes me want to hand down increasingly interesting orders."

Akira snorted. "Is it any use asking you to stop?"

"Not a bit." Jacques gave them both a small squeeze. "Did it work, Suuzu?"

"Yes."

"Suuzu, you have exactly five days to get used to the idea of my running away with your boy. We'll be incommunicado, so you won't be able to keep tabs or check in. We'll also be undercover. Or he will be." With a haughty tilt to his chin, Jacques said, "I will be Jacques Smythe of the Uppington

Smythes, a highly entitled lordling with expensive—and somewhat dubious—tastes."

Akira chuckled. "It's a good disguise."

"True enough to be convincing." Jacques' smile faded a little. "Following so far, Suuzu?"

"Yes."

"Akira and I will take a lovely little cruise to a highly exclusive resort where anything can be had for a price. Including discretion. It's the sort of place where the rich-and-famous can indulge their fantasies with the world none the wiser."

"I thought Inti was in some kind of lab," said Akira.

Suuzu's eyes widened. He hadn't known.

Jacques said, "Same island. Different section. Argent thinks that whatever goes on in the lab is funded by the exorbitant fees charged by the adjacent resort."

"So we're pretending to be on vacation," said Akira. "That doesn't sound dangerous."

"Not in the least, provided we can maintain our cover." Jacques looked to Suuzu. "You need to know that Akira will be playing the part of my *paramour*."

Suuzu goggled at Akira.

"Hey, this is the first I've heard!"

Jacques calmly went on. "You also need to know that I'm going to do everything in my power to make anyone who sees us think I'm madly in love with him."

"Ehhh?" Akira protested weakly.

"Which will be convincingly inappropriate, since my boy-toy is barely legal."

"I don't look *that* young."

"You can. You will." Jacques addressed Suuzu again. "I'm a very good actor, but I want to assure you that it *will* be an act. So there's no need for jealously." To Akira's dismay, Jacques next gave him a sultry smile. "And *you* must not fall for me."

"That's … not happening."

"You say that now," he teased.

Suuzu warbled a warning note.

Jacques patted the phoenix's head. "See? Marvelous actor."

Akira shook his head. "I can't believe Argent would come up with a scheme like this."

"I believe he took inspiration from that first trip to England with Tsumiko." Jacques' smile turned fond. "As you may recall, they had us Smythes convinced that your sister was twelve."

"I'd never pass for twelve."

"And I'd never make a pass at a twelve-year-old." Jacques' gaze was troubled. "But people *will* assume you're half my age. If we strike the right balance, I'll stay on the right side of the creeper line. More sugar daddy than shoutacon."

Akira shook his head. "Argent *actually* asked you to do this?"

"Terrifying, isn't it? But I can make it plausible, and that works to our advantage." Again, he searched Suuzu's face. "Our part is small, but essential. The risks are low. My tawdry little holiday is little more than a diversion. The others are taking much bigger risks."

"Who are these others?"

"Boon, for one." Jacques softly asked, "Is the privacy ward still working?"

"Yes."

"Right. Not a peep out of either of you, but we'll have ready access to the Cat himself. Hisoka is already en route."

Akira searched Suuzu's face. "That's reassuring, right?"

"I do not like it," Suuzu said softly.

Uncle Jackie kept his voice similarly soft. "But you like *me* …?"

It took a moment for Suuzu to relax against Jacques' side. "I do not dislike you."

"Because you trust me."

Suuzu grudgingly whispered, "I do not distrust you."

"No? Because I have planned a whole array of trust-building exercises. 'Twould be a shame if they went to waste."

Akira bit. "Like what?"

"Walking together, shopping together, dining together. I'm told cycling and snorkeling are popular activities for tourists. And did I mention shopping? Because boutiques are on my agenda. And Rafter passed me Wind-and-Tide's food truck bingo board."

"That … actually sounds kind of fun," ventured Akira.

"*Fun* is one of the perks of traveling with the well-heeled, somewhat dubious second son of Smythe Manor. My tastes are expensive, my pockets are deep, and our time is short. Let's frivol away the next five days in extravagant ways … because this, too, is part of Argent's plan."

Akira frowned, "Doesn't he want us to stay hidden?"

"*Non, mes amours*. He wants us to lure out a gentleman thief."

46
SO MUCH TO GAIN

Fumiko was almost certain that kissing had something to do with claims. But maybe that had been a wolf custom? Or was it dogs? Kimiko Miyabe had certainly gone to a lot of trouble to kiss Eloquence Starmark enough times to keep him.

Up on tiptoe, Fumiko placed kisses everywhere she'd once painted flower petals. Juuyu bent enough that she could reach, but then, with a low warble, he sank to a seat on the edge of her bed.

"Wait a moment, Fumiko."

She did. He seemed flustered, but not necessarily in a bad way. Fumiko hadn't forgotten this part of pairing off. Weak-kneed was good. Breathless was good.

"Zuzu is distracted," he said. "And you are so much."

Fumiko's happiness faltered. "Too much?"

"I am not yet a match for your vastness, but I *will* gain." Juuyu asked, "May I place a sigil on you?"

331

That sounded like a claim, too. And since she'd been thinking about it, she asked, "May I paint something on you?"

"An exchange?" He angled his head to one side. "I am willing."

So she cast about for her paint set. It was here. Somewhere.

Juuyu gestured to the things atop her bedside table. "Is that what you are looking for?"

She murmured her thanks, mind already racing through possible designs. The set rested on the puzzle box, which momentarily distracted her. Something like this would probably be no problem for a detective like Juuyu. Maybe she should invite him to try?

But when she turned to Juuyu, he stood tall, already coaxing threads of power from thin air. They shone as he spun them into a sigil no bigger than the palm of his hand. It shimmered between them, and he nudged it into alignment before lightly touching Fumiko's breastbone. The design vanished through her top. A quick peek showed that Juuyu's mark had molded to her skin.

Juuyu's gaze was carefully averted. "A simple ward to dampen your presence."

She touched the spot. "Is that all it takes? You hid me?"

"Hardly." With a low trill that made it seem like he was laughing at himself, Juuyu said, "I am the one who is hiding. Defensive sigilcraft is a specialty of mine."

Fumiko didn't really understand the difference, but maybe that didn't matter. "Sometimes Zuzu wants to give a mark."

Juuyu's posture slowly shifted, becoming taut, attentive. "Oh?"

"Sometimes," she repeated. Although it wasn't very often.

"Under what circumstances?"

"When someone decided to stay with me. When all of us were happy together—Zuzu, too." Twice for a husband. Once for a friend. Once for a child who came back for keeps. Fumiko touched her forehead and explained, "If Zuzu trusts someone all the way, she wants to put a kind of mark here."

"I am familiar with the custom."

"You are?"

"They were commonplace in the grove where I grew up." Juuyu rolled his wrist. "In the oldest tales, an Impression would show favor by placing such a mark. However, it would not always take; it would not always linger."

Fumiko whispered, "Why not?"

"Such things are said to rely upon a compatibility of souls. And mutual devotion." He quietly added, "Few ever see one. Fewer still display one."

"You like the idea?"

Resuming his seat, Juuyu folded his hands in a manner that fanned his fingers over his heart. Head bowed, he murmured, "I would never presume. Perhaps *you* would favor me?"

Fumiko hesitated. "Is it silly? Since this will only wash away?"

"Having seen Zuzu in full bloom once, would you cease to look up in summertime?"

"Never!" The very idea was an absurdity approaching sacrilege. "Every summer is different. And *rapturous*!"

Juuyu crooked his fingers, encouraging her to come closer. "If I kissed you once, would you be satisfied for all time?"

"I would want more." Truth be told, she wanted more now.

"While some things can be done once and for all, many more things are meant to be renewed. You may mark me as you see fit and as often as you desire."

Fumiko was pleased that he'd compared flowers to kisses. In little ways, they were beginning the give-and-take of union. Popping open the plastic egg, she dribbled white paint into its hollow. So stark. She asked, "What color are phoenix eggs?"

"Coloration varies by clan."

"Your clan?"

Juuyu inclined his head. "Pale gold. With white and orange flecking."

She could almost see it in her mind's eye. A drop of yellow. A dab of orange. Then she eyed her phoenix thoughtfully. "Wrist, I think. So you can see."

He rolled up his sleeve.

She circled a fingertip at the spot.

His pulse leapt, but his voice remained calm. "Should I hold the paint?"

"Good idea," she murmured.

Her brush twirled.

His breathing slowed.

She added shade and shine. Mixed half a dozen flavors of orange. Dabbed and dotted. Her painting was small as a nippet and certain to fade, but it was an eggshell. "Will it count?"

"Mmm. Admirably." Juuyu angled his head in a manner she was beginning to recognize. "Your favor rests upon me. May I beg a favor in return?"

Fumiko painted a tiny heart over his eyebrow. "What would you like?"

"I want to introduce you to my brother."

47

BALANCING ACT

Akira was only half-listening to Uncle Jackie, who'd reverted to English in his enthusiasm for California street fashion. Or something. Akira was more interested in Suuzu's reaction to all this. Their gazes met over Jacques' chest, and Suuzu's fingers tightened around his.

His gaze was the pleading sort, as if he were trying to send private messages.

Akira wished that they really did have that sort of connection. Michael could wax eloquent about the brush of souls. Apparently, tending let you see someone's private self. Or ... *sense* it. You'd catch onto their moods and emotions. Understand truths they might not even know about themselves.

It's not that Akira didn't know a lot about Suuzu. He *did*, but they'd needed time and togetherness and words. They could talk this out, as well. They *needed* to. But as Jacques' plans piled up,

336

Akira was beginning to wonder if they'd be given the chance.

Right now, he was sure of a few things. Suuzu was bewildered. Suuzu wanted to be alone together, but he was too polite to say so. And Suuzu wasn't letting go anytime soon. For the next five days, his best friend would be at his clingiest. Someone would probably have to pry them apart when it was time to say goodbye.

Akira tried for a smile.

Suuzu made his own attempt.

Neither of them was terribly convincing.

That's when Jacques lifted an arm to wave.

Juuyu and Fumiko were descending the spiral stairs. Something was up. Juuyu had not only abandoned his suit coat, his shirtsleeves were rolled up. He seemed to be favoring one arm. And Fumiko had been using him as a canvas again. A sprinkling of peach and gold hearts—or maybe they were flower petals— decorated one side of Juuyu's face.

Suuzu released Akira's hand and pushed away from Jacques, warbling a weak note.

Juuyu's answering trill was definitely pitched to soothe, and he beckoned. "Come, and greet Fumiko."

However, when Suuzu went to present himself to Fumiko, she gasped. "Wait one second! I know just the thing! It'll be perfect!" Fumiko clattered upstairs again, calling, "Be right back!"

Silence reigned for several seconds. But then Suuzu shuffled forward, reaching up to cautiously touch Juuyu's embellishments. "Brother?"

"Mmm." With an expression he rarely showed any but his nestmates, Juuyu said, "I am her choice."

An awestruck trill.

A fraternal embrace.

Foreheads touching.

Akira was fairly sure that the brothers were trading secrets in the manner of close kin, which left him feeling out of the loop. But Suuzu never withheld anything from him. Akira would hear all about it later. *If* they were allowed some time alone. Maybe he could coax Suuzu into sharing a hammock with him tonight?

Jacques patted his shoulder and murmured, "They're both tributes, you know."

"Yeah, I know." They were privy to quite a few things that weren't general knowledge. "Same as Quen."

"Unable to choose. Glad to be chosen." Jacques stroked Akira's hair. "I've been thinking. You're in an awkward position."

Akira hummed to let Uncle Jackie know he was listening. Even though he didn't need yet another person weighing in about him and Suuzu.

"Argent wants to catch a thief, and when he does, you intend to keep him. But if you think about it the right way, he's already caught."

Oh. *Not* about Suuzu. But before Akira could ask what Uncle Jackie meant, Fumiko was back, carrying a fancy wooden box, shiny with inlaid tiles.

Juuyu skipped every formality, only saying, "This is Suuzu, who is a chick in my nest."

"My brother raised me," Suuzu said, his courtesy a little stiff. "But I am no longer a child."

"For you." Fumiko extended the box even as she looked to

Juuyu. "May I give this? Is it all right?"

"Gifts are often exchanged when welcoming a new nestmate. Suuzu is one. Akira is another."

Fumiko looked for and found Akira curled against Uncle Jackie's side. She pointed and said, "I already know what I want to give you, but I haven't found it yet. I'll have to ask Zuzu."

"Thanks, Fumiko-nee." Tapping Jacques' chest, Akira asked, "Have you met Uncle Jackie?"

But then Zuzu was there, demanding her share of the welcome.

Juuyu caught and spun her before lightly inquiring, "Will you call me Brother? Will you be my home?"

"*Mon dieu*," murmured Jacques. "I wasn't aware that Juuyu knew how to smile."

Akira toyed with the ring that probably wasn't working, now that Suuzu had let go. "You saw how Zuzu came in, right? Tabioji's the same. Popping in and out. I'm not sure why you say he's caught. Any tree would be nearly impossible to catch."

"Your Uncle Socks—or perhaps we should call him Papa Socks— is a tree, isn't he?" Jacques slid the ring onto Akira's finger and covered his hand. "What does he need?"

What was he supposed to say? Regular watering and plenty of sunshine? "He wants Naoki." That much was sure. The rest was harder to guess at.

"And he wants you."

Akira shook his head. "He wants me to help him get to Naoki."

"So you're a means to an end?"

"Nooo. I think he cares about me and Sis." His gaze slid sideways to where Suuzu stood listening to Fumiko, the wooden box now cradled in his hands. "But he cares about Naoki first ... and most."

"Because Naoki is his twin?"

"I don't think so. No, he can't be. Tabi-oji mentioned running away together. And he uses Naoki's given name instead of calling him 'Brother.'"

Jacques asked, "So they're together by choice? Like a couple?"

"I don't know exactly. I didn't have the chance to ask much of anything."

Uncle Jackie said, "Well, one thing's easily sorted. Zuzu?"

She was on the bed in an enthusiastic instant. "There has been a lot of kissing," she reported.

"I can only approve." Jacques immediately changed the subject. "Do you love Fumiko's children?"

"Yes. Always." Zuzu's expression gentled. "They are ours."

"And have you ever had a child of your own?"

Her smile tipped to a sultry angle. "If you find me good pollen, I could give you a child."

"Very generous, I'm sure." Jacques asked, "What about Akira, here? If he was one of Fumiko's children, what would you do?"

Zuzu scooted closer and practically crooned, "Keep him safe. Keep him close. Keep him happy."

"Could you find him, no matter where he was?" pressed Jacques.

"Not if he's in the guesthouse," she admitted. "Not if he takes the trolly."

Wards. Barriers. Distance.

"But if I was nearby, you'd know?" Akira asked.

"Yes. Always."

And then she was gone, wreathing herself around Suuzu, who

seemed right at home with this sort of attention.

Jacques hummed in a satisfied way. "I'm quite sure Argent's plan will work, but it lacks a certain ... balance. I'll speak with him before the night is out. Plenty of time to adapt before the shops open tomorrow."

"You want to change Argent's plan?"

Lips pressed to Akira's forehead. "He *does* listen to me, you know."

Only then did it occur to Akira that this whole time, he'd been cuddling with Uncle Jackie, just like a crosser in the naproom. They were pressed closer than humans usually got ... unless they were lovers.

"Umm ...?"

"You finally noticed?" Uncle Jackie smiled lazily. "We'll get on, I think. People see Amaranthine courtesies and interpret them as romantic overtures. Leads to every kind of trouble. Clanfolk are forever breaking hearts."

Akira darted a look at Suuzu and whispered, "He's not happy, but he's not angry anymore."

"Your nestmate is a reasonable fellow."

This time, when Uncle Jackie played with his hair, Akira was thinking about how it might look. He tensed.

"None of that," Jacques chided. "Or they'll think I mishandle you."

Akira felt bad.

Judging by his sad eyes, Uncle Jackie felt worse. "If it helps, pretend I'm utterly harmless. Like Deece or Sonnet."

"Okay, yeah. That actually helps a lot." Akira relaxed under Jacques' hand and asked, "Are you doing this for Suuzu's sake or for mine?"

"Yours. And mine."

"You want to practice?"

"We need to. Here, we still have the luxury of discussion. So if you don't like something, speak now, or forever hold your peace."

Akira wasn't sure he *liked* any of this. But it wasn't Uncle Jackie's fault.

"As I was saying," Jacques murmured, picking up his former thread. "Argent *does* listen to me. Especially when I'm correct. Because, the way I see it, this is no longer a matter of seizing custody of a thief. You want to make peace with Papa Socks. And peace talks require balance."

48

INTERESTED PARTIES

After they returned to her room, Fumiko urgently asked, "Have you seen a portfolio?

"Several." Juuyu's posture shifted, and he tipped his head in an attentive way. "Can you describe the one you have in mind?"

"This big." She held her hands out to show the length. "Blue. With a flap that's tied with a thick string, like a shoelace. And it's full of lovely drawings of Ephemera. It was a gift from one of Soren's grandchildren, an artist."

"I have not seen the item you have described."

Could it be gone? Things did get lost. "I wanted to show it to Akira. But now I think it would make a nice present. He was wishing to see more Ephemera, and I thought ...."

Juuyu slid his hand under hers and said, "It may yet be found. This is the only room I have not undertaken."

"Would you?"

343

"Gladly." And without further explanation, he stood gazing at an overflowing curio cabinet.

Fumiko eased away from him, found a book, and curled up under a crocheted coverlet. It was nice, having him close. When he began softly humming, it was even nicer.

He only distracted her a few times. Once, when he trilled over finding a small cup with a strawberry on it. Another, when he offered a similar greeting, having located a dainty blue punch glass in the bottommost drawer of a man's chest. And again, when an excess of grumbling brought it to her attention that he was halfway under her bed.

The sun was well set before he said, "Fumiko."

She glanced up, then fumbled for a bookmark. Using a seahorse sock to save her place, she hurried to join Juuyu at the edge of the bed. In his hands was a blue portfolio, somewhat faded by age.

"You found it."

"I did."

"May I give it to Akira?"

"Perhaps in the morning." Showing her his pocket watch, he murmured, "He is asleep. And you should be, as well."

"Will you stay with me?"

Juuyu hesitated. "I made a promise to Suuzu and planned to keep it tonight. But first ... would you like to see the treasure you have been protecting?"

It had entirely slipped her mind, but she was eager to have her share in this secret. "Please?"

344

With quiet deliberation, Juuyu undid the fastenings on the long carrying case that she'd been keeping close. It was difficult to believe that he'd forgotten about the Junzi, even for a moment. The weapon's import was staggering, and its loss would have been mortifying.

Fumiko made a soft noise as he eased the Bamboo Stave into the open. Her eyes shone with obvious delight, making it a pleasure to be able to present it to her on both palms.

As she turned toward the faint light of her few candles, he gently lofted a handful of crystals to increase the illumination. "This is one of four legendary pieces, each a work of art."

"Is this stone? It's cold." She ran her fingertips along the length, which caught the light and sparkled, translucent as green water and flowing with power.

"Remnant crystal." Juuyu quietly added, "This instrument is part of an ancient set named for the Junzi, the famed Four Gentlemen."

"I know them—plum, orchid, bamboo, and chrysanthemum."

He wasn't surprised. She was an artist, after all, and most of the coffee table books in the gathering area were art-related.

"This represents the bamboo of summertime?" she asked. And without waiting for an answer, she raised the long flute to her lips and blew experimentally.

The resulting notes rippled up Juuyu's spine and raised the hairs on the back of his neck. He swiftly deployed an additional barrier, not wanting the sound to travel.

"No?" she checked.

"Please," he encouraged.

He'd found several instruments while sorting the contents of the extra room in the guesthouse—predominantly wind and string. There had also been an upright piano and an ancient set of taiko drums. Juuyu had assumed them to be cast-offs of her many children. Only now did a simpler truth resonate. Fumiko had pursued many interests over the years—art, music, and now ... him.

The notes weren't so much a song as a mood. Wistful and hopeful, both at once, they made him long to tune his voice to the flute's. Why not?

"Keep playing," he urged.

Stepping back, he shifted into truest form, fanned his wings in an overt display, and echoed her notes. She played on, and he spun off into harmony, though his voice was not at its best. She made him jittery and urgent and clumsy, but he sang anyhow. Sincere and unstinting. Eager to weave his life with hers—like a song, like a nest, like a lover.

Eventually, Fumiko lowered the instrument, though not her gaze. She approached him slowly, awe in her appraisal. He arched his neck and arranged his wings decoratively.

Her fingers grazed his crest and slid along the underside of his beak.

Using one wing, he pulled her against his breast. She laughed shyly, and with a trill, he returned to speaking form, his arms enfolding her.

"You're beautiful," she whispered.

"I am pleased you find me so." Boldly winding his fingers into her hair, he said, "I did not know you could play."

She hummed and said, "I'd forgotten, but what else could I do? The stone asked to sing."

"Are you sure I cannot carry you?" Zuzu offered again. "I'm stronger than I look."

"I can manage," Akira assured.

"It would be faster," she wheedled.

"I have my pride." He stifled a yawn. "Just be sure to catch me if I happen to slip."

"You are safe. And you are nearly there."

He rummaged up a smile. "What is it you wanted me to see?"

"A surprise. You will like it. Sister does." And raising her voice a little, she called, "It *is* good, isn't it, Sister?"

From one of the bigger hammocks, suspended way out over the water, though well above it, Fumiko hushed them and beckoned.

Moments later, Akira clambered awkwardly into the relative safety of the nest, where Fumiko made sure he had a quilt and a pillow. He flopped onto his back, gazing up at the sky between the branches. "Is there a meteor shower or something?" he guessed.

Fumiko giggled. "You are looking in the wrong direction."

"Not up. *Down*," said Zuzu.

"They're on the beach. The view from here is perfect." Fumiko scooted a little closer to the edge and pointed. "I don't think they've noticed us."

Akira rolled and wriggled into a spot alongside hers. No surprise, Zuzu nestled right in. He couldn't complain. It felt safer, being surrounded. They were a long way up, but a gap in the branches gave a seaside view of the beach.

Colt, Bavol, Argent, and Hallow lounged in the light of a bonfire, which Sinder was still feeding from a tidy stack of cordwood. Those absent were likely patrolling. But their informal meeting wasn't the reason Akira had been summoned from his bed.

Fumiko whispered, "This is a little for me, but I think it's also a little for you."

On the smooth sand of the beach, Juuyu and Suuzu stood a short distance apart, arms moving in measured patterns. It was pretty clear that Juuyu was leading and Suuzu was learning. After another repetition, they added footwork. Pacing, pivots, springing steps and swirling turns that brought flight to mind.

"Do you understand?" asked Fumiko.

"Juuyu is teaching Suuzu the steps to a dance." Hardly surprising, since Juuyu had fostered his younger brother. In all the ways that mattered, he was Suuzu's parent.

The movements didn't look too difficult, but the combinations grew increasingly complicated. And there was no way a human could have achieved some of their leaps. Juuyu paused to speak, and Suuzu retried a sequence. Then Juuyu stepped in, standing behind his brother in order to correct the placement of his arms. Precision was tantamount for a people who communicated with every nuance of posture.

Both moved this time, and there was more assurance to the steps, to the sweep of their arms. They'd even matched the angle of their heads, which made Akira even more sure that there was a message to this dance.

"Can you hear them?" asked Zuzu.

Akira strained to listen, and little by little, he caught sounds. "Are they humming?"

It was suddenly easier to tell because those around the bonfire added their voices. So maybe it was a traditional song? Or maybe they'd been practicing long enough for the others to pick up the melody line. In Akira's experience, Amaranthine loved to sing, and many of the clans had folk songs in common.

Argent's voice carried confidently, but that didn't help Akira. All of their most important songs were in Old Amaranthine.

"Do you understand?" Fumiko asked again.

"Not exactly. I mean, it's a dance."

"It's a *courting* dance. Juuyu told me he's keeping a promise to his brother tonight."

Suuzu was learning a courting dance?

"Phoenixes have all sorts of traditional dances," Akira whispered. "Why are you so sure this is for courting?"

"I know because I heard." Zuzu pointed to Juuyu and Suuzu in turn. "He dances for Sister. And he dances for you, Brother."

"Brother?" he echoed weakly.

"Is that not how it works?" Zuzu's gaze was soft and serious. "Sister is Juuyu's nestmate, and you are Suuzu's nestmate."

Was he brother-in-law to a tree? Akira supposed so, but he brought out his usual protest. "Suuzu is my best friend."

"Yes," agreed Fumiko. "And he dances for you, so watch."

Akira did not look away. Thanks to Uncle Jackie, they hadn't had a moment alone. No chance to talk. But here was a message without words, carrying loud and clear across the water.

Akira asked, "Is it terrible, outliving someone you love?"

"Sometimes." Fumiko patted around until she found his hand and fitted her fingers between his. "I think love is a vastness. The more you give, the less you lose. Because your love returns to you in a thousand shining remembrances."

49

TRINKETS

After spending so many days wishing Suuzu was at his side, Akira felt incredibly awkward asking for ten minutes alone. And maybe even a little foolish over summoning Zuzu to help. But Suuzu had asked no questions, and Zuzu was eager to please. Which put Akira past the crystal gate in a twinkling.

"Rafter?" he called, keeping his back to the wall behind the library. "Rafter? Do you have a minute?"

Wind-and-Tide's concierge strolled into the alley, tugging at his dreadlocks with a troubled expression. "As glad as I am to see you this fine morning, you *have* to know you're on the wrong side of all our safeguards."

"I know. I'm sorry." Akira took a pleading posture. "Rafter, I need something."

With a grin that suggested all was forgiven, he said, "Anything you need, friend. What have you set your heart on?"

351

Akira turned the English phrase around in his mind. Was his heart set? Maybe so.

Rafter gently poked his chest. "What I mean to say is ... what do you want so much, you'd ask old Rafter to make it happen? Because I can. Make things happen, that is."

"Yeah. But this might be hard." Akira took a steadying breath. "I heard there's something special about gifts that include an eggshell. Or ... a piece of eggshell. For avians."

"What can I say? It's true. Even counts as common knowledge in these parts." Rafter's smile was sympathetic as he fished a ring of keys out of his pocket. "I'll show you."

Rafter led the way to the back of Melody's shop, which was still closed for business. An alley door led into a narrow back room with a long counter, deep sinks, and dozens of vases. But Rafter didn't stop until they were in the front of the dim shop, standing before a spinner.

"Because Flutterbys appeared on *Crossing America*, they have a special license to sell these. They're very popular with tourists. All the rage at Valentine's Day. And lately, folks have taken to giving them as engagement gifts."

Akira gaped at the spinner, which held at least thirty avian courting gifts.

Rafter continued in a businesslike tone. "These here in this section are made from crow eggs, which are considered authentic, since Ash's first gift to Tami was a locket on this order. But as you can see, quail, pheasant, and robin eggs are just as popular."

Lifting one down, Akira fiddled with its latch and peered into a tiny, silver-lined compartment. It was hardly bigger than a reliquary. And just as empty as the one he'd given Suuzu. So this sort of thing was commonplace? He was disappointed.

"Avian courtship is fashionable in the States."

Akira dipped his head. "These are nice."

"But ...?"

"They are not ... unique?" He replaced the necklace.

Rafter's eyes sparkled. "Mass-produced not good enough for a one-of-a-kind feeling?"

"Yes." That was exactly it. "Isn't there something else?"

"Just so I'm not assuming, is this gift intended for a certain young phoenix?"

"Suuzu," Akira confirmed. "I mean ... if he wanted. I think he's been waiting ...?"

Hands upraised, Rafter gently said, "Say no more. Unless you want to say it. In which case, I'm all ears."

A funny phrase, but Akira couldn't bring himself to smile. "I do love him. I know I do. I've always assumed we'd be together. I just didn't think about ... *being* together."

Rafter nodded. "Not every web is cluttered with flies, for some still spin for dewdrops."

"Which means ...?"

"I'll be the first to admit that spiders have strange ideals when it comes to romance. Let's go with ... not everyone wants the same thing, but everyone wants something."

Akira wasn't sure that was helpful.

"Not everyone has a big appetite ...?" Rafter tried.

That just translated to confusing.

Rafter sighed and bluntly said, "Love isn't always about sex."

"Oh." Akira studied his feet. "Yeah."

Patting his shoulder, Rafter said, "Give me until moonrise. I'll slip you something. What would you prefer? In your pocket? Under your pillow?"

"You'd actually sneak it to me?"

"I can be subtle." Rafter nodded significantly.

When he checked his pockets, Akira came up with a business card for Rafter's Rentals. A phone number was neatly printed on the back. Along with a handwritten note—JUST IN CASE.

"Trust me, friend. I won't soon let you down."

It was mid-high when Akira lined up for a final inspection.

"Smythe," drawled Argent.

"Yes, my lord?"

"What possessed you?"

Akira wasn't sure if Argent was protesting the people Jacques had included in his entourage ... or the way they were dressed. For his part, Akira felt ridiculous. Not all of Uncle Jackie's luggage had been packed with his own clothes. He'd already been shopping for Akira, and today's trust-building exercise involved breaking in a pair of pale peach jeans. Akira's new sandals were more comfortable than the tight pants, but he wasn't sure how he felt about the pedicure Uncle Jackie had insisted upon.

"Why them?" asked Argent.

Jacques looked pleased to be asked. "This is my own handpicked team, all perfectly suited to the ideal shopping spree."

"*Tsk.* I seriously doubt they are looking forward to the gauntlet of boutiques you will drag them through."

"Doesn't matter. *I'm* looking forward to shopping with *them*." And pointing to Sinder, Hallow, and Suuzu in turn, he said, "Him for his hipbones. Him for his collarbones. Him for his complexion."

Magda and Akira exchanged a look, and Akira asked, "What about us?"

"Your job is compliments," decreed Jacques. "The more extravagant, the better."

"*Or*," countered Argent. "You might consider drawing out our intended prey without losing hold of his."

"I'm not *prey*," protested Akira.

Argent's gaze coolly swept him from head to toe. "Bait, then." And to Jacques, "Do not forget yourself. Or the part I still need you to play."

"We can be integral and still manage a bit of fun. Let me do this my way."

Waving them off, Argent reminded, "We will be at the Amory. Try to draw him there."

And so they filed past Moon and Mirrim, each offering an upraised hand to slap. Like the crystal gate was the entrance to an arena, and the game timers were already ticking. As they slipped through the farmer's market, it certainly felt as if all eyes were on them.

Jacques in the lead, all traipse and sashay. Sinder at this side, quibbling over color theory, which apparently mattered to dragons.

Hallow with his regal air stood beside Magda and gestured for Akira and Suuzu to precede them, since they'd act as rear guard.

Within ten minutes, it was abundantly clear that Magda was out to have fun, and she seemed intent on dragging Hallow and Suuzu straight into more. Barely a block along their way, and Hallow sported a new pair of sunglasses, and she'd wrapped Suuzu's head in a fancy turban.

Jacques approved. And snapped pictures. And found some shimmery gloss that he applied to Akira's lower lip.

"Where's your usual sparkle?" he asked softly. "Are you actually intimidated by pastels?"

"I feel like a one-man boy band."

Uncle Jackie took his hand. "Rather the goal. But I need you to relax into this role. If not for my sake, then for his." He angled his head toward Suuzu, who was undergoing similar indignities.

Suuzu barely resembled Spokesperson Farroost anymore. The lavish headcloth might count as a disguise, and the freshly-applied shimmer of gold on his bottom lip was sort of pretty. But the concern in his best friend's gaze snapped Akira to attention.

"Better," murmured Uncle Jackie. "Now stop trying to decide how to act."

"I can't act."

"That is painfully obvious. So how about this? You drag him about like you usually do, and we'll improvise around you." After a beat, he leaned close to whisper, "And avoid mirrors."

Akira glanced around, wary of reflective surfaces. "Why?"

"Pastels." With a teasing smile, he said, "We need more time to build up your resistance."

"You have barely eaten anything," murmured Suuzu. "Are you nervous?"

This was their third tiny restaurant, since Uncle Jackie showed as much dedication to culinary exploration as he did to adventurous hosiery. They'd foregone the trolly in order to nibble and sip their way along Mainsail.

"Nervous? Mmm ... not about seeing Tabi-oji again. I'm more nervous that I might miss my chance to see him again." Akira wasn't sure how to explain. "I was so close to something really important. But he didn't say a thing until the instant before he was gone."

"We will find him."

"You sound sure."

Suuzu only smiled and looked up as Jacques—predictably—barged in. "You must try this. It's too addicting."

So far, at least once per shop, Uncle Jackie had found some small way to fuss over Akira. It was harmless stuff, but it was all very intentional. He seemed to understand where their comfort zones were and insisted on fiddling about the edges.

"Say *aaah*," Jacques patiently ordered.

Akira obediently opened his mouth to accept a spoonful of something that was creamy, melty, and rich enough to coat his tongue. He hummed appreciatively, but he cast a sidelong look at Suuzu.

His friend only said, "He has not been eating."

"Have another then." Jacques made good on his threat, then looked to Suuzu. "I'll be twice as attentive tomorrow. Bearing up all right?"

"I will … manage."

Uncle Jackie swooped in to kiss Suuzu's forehead. "Good lad."

The phoenix's lips quirked.

Akira held out some hope that everything was going to be okay.

Jacques said, "Right. So … I'm going on ahead. Magda will mind things here."

The battler was at one of the café tables outside the door, smiling as she texted someone. She looked absorbed, but Akira knew that she was the farthest thing from inattentive.

"We're fine." Akira took notice of his untouched food and awkwardly added, "I'll finish soon."

"Take your time." Blowing him a kiss, Uncle Jackie breezed out.

Under the table, Suuzu's hand bumped his. Akira grabbed hold and found a crystal there. A promise of a private moment. Practically their first since yesterday's arrival.

The plastic seat of their booth wasn't particularly comfortable, but it was plenty slippery. So when Suuzu pulled, Akira slid into contact. Picking right up where he'd left off, Suuzu said, "I am certain that you will find your Tabi-oji. Or rather, that he will find you. Trees are devoted. He will want to reach you."

Akira tightened his hold on Suuzu's hand. "I didn't know about any of this."

"Hisoka-sensei and Argent would not keep secrets without good reason."

Which wasn't really what Akira had meant. But it was a safe avenue forward. He admitted, "I'm a little scared."

"I know."

That was comforting. Akira quietly said, "I'm even more scared for Inti."

"As am I."

"And there are kids. A bunch of them." Risking a look into Suuzu's eyes, he said, "They're probably scared, too."

Suuzu's expression softened. "Because they do not know that help is on the way."

"I'm sorry for being so ...." Akira didn't have a word for himself. Only knew he might be missing something Suuzu needed. So he cleared his throat and pushed back his plate. "We should probably make the most of the next few days."

"Hmm," his friend calmly agreed.

"Hey, Suuzu?"

"Hmm?"

Akira mumbled, "I'm not sure how to do that."

"Yes, you do." Suuzu's eyes held a smile. "This will do."

"I'm not doing anything."

"You are."

He slumped into his best friend and prompted, "What am I doing?"

"Leaning into my side. Waiting for my words. Calming as I speak them."

"If that's the *most* I'm capable of, I feel kind of pitiful."

Suuzu warbled softly. "Did you know that an Amaranthine tree may need seventy or eighty years before they are ready for their first bloom?"

"Okaaay." Akira frowned. "Is that a crack about my possibly being tree-kin?"

"No."

"I'm not sure I get most Amaranthine proverbs." Akira shook his head. "I might only live another seventy or eighty years."

"I have not given up." Suuzu angled his head to indicate his tattoo. "Neither have you."

"Today, nippets. Tomorrow, a treehouse of our own?"

"If you like."

Akira mumbled. "It wouldn't have to be anything fancy. Even a hammock would do."

"I know how to build," said Suuzu.

"Umm ... sure. If you like."

Suuzu toyed with his fingers before softly adding, "And your father is a tree."

"Probably. Yeah."

"That is another reason to hope."

Akira shook his head. "Because ...?"

"A doting uncle adorns you with pretty clothes and pink gloss." Suuzu's gaze dropped briefly to Akira's mouth. "A doting tree-father might bequeath you finer, more lasting gifts."

"Tabi-oji might have a seed?"

"Trees bear fruit." Suuzu's gaze skittered sideways. "Tell him you are hungry."

50

MAKING CONNECTIONS

our shops and two food trucks later, Uncle Jackie once again intruded upon Akira and Suuzu, who'd retreated to a quiet bench in a previously quiet corner.

"Sinder found a glassblower's shop!" Down on one knee, Jacques held up an entire handful of glass rings, all different sizes, all in soft-bright hues. "I want to make a proposal. To both of you."

Akira warily asked, "Why do you have so many? You didn't buy them all, did you?"

"Or steal them?" Suuzu countered.

"Don't be gauche. I merely *borrowed* these. To show you." Jacques shrugged. "Sinder convinced the artisan-in-residence that I'm a trustworthy bloke. So? Help each other choose!"

"What is your intention?" Suuzu asked softly.

Uncle Jackie took a more serious tone. "My intentions are entirely honorable, *mes amours*. Pact with me."

"Us?" Akira tried to gauge Suuzu's reaction. Would he want to share a pact with another human?

Suuzu frowned, but his posture remained receptive. "What terms?"

"Suitable ones. Peaceable ones." Searching their faces, Jacques added, "Ones that will protect the trust we're building."

Uncle Jackie's trust-building exercises felt like nonsense. You couldn't build a bond on lip gloss and churros, let alone rings made of glass. Then again, Suuzu was avian, so maybe body paint, hand-feeding, and the exchange of gifts meant that Jacques was currying favor.

Akira asked, "Is there such a thing as a three-way pact?"

"*Naturellement*." Jacques lifted his hands insistently. "Clan colors for our phoenix, do you think?"

Suuzu produced a handkerchief from an inside pocket and spread it across his knees. With a soft tinkling, Jacques spilled the rings onto it and joined them on the bench. He made suggestions as they poked through, looking for a good fit.

"This!" Jacques exclaimed, holding out one that was the rosy orange of red grapefruit. "Try this on him."

Akira was sure his uncle was pushing boundaries again, but when Suuzu quietly offered his hand, there was nothing else to do but check the fit. It was too small for his ring finger, but it fit his little finger just fine.

"Pretty in pink for Akira?" Uncle Jackie suggested, holding up a bit of glass.

Suuzu hummed in a dismissive way.

Akira was honestly relieved.

For a moment, his best friend considered a ring that was a match to his own, but he let it slip back into the pile. With the tip of his claw, he teased a honey-gold ring from the muddle and beckoned for Akira's hand. It proved a good fit for his middle finger.

Suuzu wasn't done.

With a deft flick, he extracted a lime green ring. "You favor this color," he said to Uncle Jackie.

"Usually. It's good of you to notice."

"I pay attention to what is important to Akira."

"Aren't you dashing?" Jacques offered his hand.

The ring made it past his knuckle with only a little coaxing. Still holding on, Suuzu repeated, "What terms?"

"I will cherish him as my own, and I will protect him with my life. He will become so dear to me that returning him to you will break my heart. Again."

Suuzu warbled a soft cadence. "Are you offering your devotion?"

Uncle Jackie's smile was a trifle forced. "Argent may have suggested something of the sort."

"But ... you're *his* man," Akira protested.

"And I will be again," countered Jacques. "But for the foreseeable future, I am *your* man."

Akira waited for Suuzu to protest, to argue. But their sacrifices were similar, and some semblance of balance was met. Reaching for Akira's hand, as well, Suuzu said, "Agreed."

Juuyu paced through the gallery with Argent at his side. The fox said nothing, leaving Juuyu to his task.

Nothing had changed. Of course, there was no reason to expect any alteration. What scanty evidence they'd collected suggested that the Gentleman Bandit had abandoned the Amory the same time they did. "Nothing," said Juuyu.

"I concur." Argent's fingers tapped his thigh. "Let us not be stinting. According to Akira, they ate their meals in the courtyard."

So Juuyu searched for any hint of Akira's Tabi-oji while Argent quizzed the reaver guarding the gallery entrance. Although Juuyu cataloged every red item in sight, not a single flower petal remained.

"He is not here," Argent said.

"Nor has he been here," agreed Juuyu. "Not recently."

They moved into the lobby, and Argent began spinning small sigils. Juuyu watched long enough to guess that they were for pollen detection. They drifted toward the high ceiling, half-lost in sunlight, as sly as their crafter.

Wanting to be just as thorough, Juuyu stopped and slowly turned in place, searching for any variation. Again, his attention snagged on all things red—exit signs above each door, logos at the beverage refill station, poppy-themed reusable bags at the gift shop, baseball caps on the children in a school group.

Had anything been added since the team's extraction? And then a more important question clamored for attention—hadn't something been *removed*?

Juuyu strode to the information desk and placed his hand on its nearly empty ledge. The woman on duty glanced up with a smile.

"May I help you?"

"Can you tell me what became of the botanical gifts that were here two days ago?"

"All of those bouquets were dropping so many petals, we had the cleaning crew clear them out. We did keep the cards, of course." She indicated the few remaining potted plants. "And these."

Juuyu could see it. He could even understand it, but he was having difficulty fathoming it. "It should not be possible," he whispered, awash with a horrible certainty.

Argent drifted over, checked the tag on an overflowing philodendron, then on the dwarf orange tree. "Something amiss?" he inquired lightly.

"Yes. No. Yes." Juuyu spread his hands in a plea for help. "I know how he is doing it."

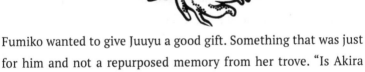

Fumiko wanted to give Juuyu a good gift. Something that was just for him and not a repurposed memory from her trove. "Is Akira back?" she asked.

Zuzu shook her head and handed her a fat purse. "Will you wait?"

"No. I want to do this quickly." Fumiko smiled a little. "But it would have been nice to hold his hand."

"I can go farther than I let on, but ...." Zuzu shook her head. "I *do* know better, even if they think I don't."

Fumiko quietly asserted, "We're in charge of ourselves. And I want to do my own choosing."

"You'll make *another* good choice." Zuzu sounded so confident. "Find something pretty for our bird. That way, he will stay and stay and stay."

"We don't need to bribe Juuyu to stay. He already calls you his home."

Zuzu hugged herself and gave a little shimmy. "He is ours, and we are his."

"You're happy." Fumiko might have been most pleased by that one thing. That Juuyu understood Zuzu and included her in his affections.

"He deserves something *vast*."

"I think so, too." Fumiko was sure that the nearby shops must have nice things. She wanted to look and to touch. To make sure that her gift was just the right color and that it had just the right weight and feel. Something important and beautiful. "I want to spoil him."

"That's a good plan." Zuzu hugged her close, whisking her past boundaries. "If you need me, I will know."

And then Fumiko was on her own.

Walking along the street felt strange, even precarious. But there had been a time when she wasn't locked away behind barriers. Yes, things had changed, but so had she. Akira had shown her how to be brave. She could explore on her own.

The doughnut shop. The art store. Familiar territory.

Farther along, new possibilities opened up. A souvenir shop. Little restaurants. A used bookstore. Each business welcomed her with a smile, and Fumiko relaxed enough to enjoy herself. Many trinkets appealed to her, but they weren't quite right for Juuyu.

She wasn't ready to give up, though.

Fumiko stepped out of a quaint store that specialized in garden ornaments and found herself facing a man who tugged at her memory.

He smiled up at her.

She smiled back.

"Fumiko?" he asked. "Yes, surely it is you. Do you still call yourself Fumiko?"

The man was speaking Japanese, and Fumiko was suddenly, dazzlingly sure that he was the reason she knew the language.

"I have not been here in so long. Everything is different." He uncurled his fingers, showing her a handful of purple flower petals. "But some things cannot change, so they do not. How are you and Kazuki faring?"

"I remember you!"

"That is gratifying."

"I know your voice." She touched his face, searching her memory. "But you've changed."

"Simple tricks. I do not like to call attention to myself." Taking her arm, he drew her a little way along the sidewalk. "Is it safe?"

"We're safe." Fumiko patted his arm reassuringly. "Good people are protecting us."

He shook his head. Tucking her arm through his, he steered her toward home. "I am glad you and your sister are well, but that is not what I meant. Fumiko, child, do you still have my box?"

51

CHANGING WINDS

Akira kept to his place in the middle of their small pack, knowing the rest were flanking him for his safety, but also for Suuzu's comfort. Though the phoenix had released his arm, a hand rested lightly on Akira's back. Probably because Suuzu knew what trees could do. And how fast.

As soon as they were through the Amory doors, Sinder and Jacques made a beeline for Brew & Bubble. Mirrim signaled from her post beside the courtyard entrance, and Magda double-timed it to her side. When Argent strolled over, Hallow quietly receded.

"No sign of our tree," Argent announced. "But I am holding out hope."

"*Our* tree?" Akira quietly echoed.

"As Sinder was cheeky enough to point out, Tabigarasu may well be my father-in-law. I can hardly ignore the connection."

Akira couldn't help smiling. "Jacques talked to you?"

Argent sniffed. "He talks incessantly. I occasionally listen."

"Sis would like his idea."

"She does indeed."

Akira was kind of surprised. "You talked to her?"

That earned him a flat look. "Formidable though her faith may be, it need not be blind."

"I just meant ... well, you don't have a phone."

"While I am quite willing to foster her hopes, I find greater satisfaction in fulfilling them." Argent's expression could be so much more difficult to read away from home. "Tsumiko dreams of me."

"Oh. Right. Fox dreams," Akira murmured.

Suuzu quietly added, "Fulfilling hopes by fostering children."

"Well said." Argent shooed them away. "Go. Wander about in plain sight. It does not matter what you do, so long as you remain inside my wards."

Indicating the restaurants, Akira asked, "Need anything?"

"I am content," replied Suuzu.

"Want to see the sights?"

With a faint smile, Suuzu said, "Show me the things you have seen."

The security guard waved them through without a ticket, and Suuzu's soft trill echoed in the cool, dark central hub. Time slowed as Suuzu moved from one exhibit to the next, and it was just how Akira knew it would be. Suuzu read every plaque. He asked innocuous questions. And he never once let go of Akira.

On the fourth floor, they reached the eerily exact replica of the Bamboo Stave. Akira asked, "Can you tell it's an illusion?"

"No."

As they stood gazing, Suuzu's hand slid to Akira's shoulder. His thumb kneaded lightly against the tattoo hidden under Akira's shirt. "Are you still figuring out the sigil?"

"It is unusually complicated."

"Argent and Michael worked on it together. Maybe Lapis, too."

"Their sigilcraft is beyond me."

"But it's also *for* you." Akira searched Suuzu's face. "You said it called to you? What was that like?"

"It is *un*like anything." Suuzu's gaze turned inward for several long moments. "I need more time with you. Preferably alone."

Uncle Jackie hadn't given them any privacy the previous night. Akira suspected that Argent was limiting how much information Suuzu could gather before they'd be parted. What little conversation they'd managed had been confined to texting, which wasn't ideal for soul-searching.

"Maybe we can get Zuzu on our side? She'd definitely smuggle us into one of her hammocks."

Suuzu's chin dipped to his chest, and he peeped at Akira out of the corner of his eye. "A good idea."

Akira slid a half-step closer, casually bumping into him. According to Kimi, in bird code, he was essentially inviting Suuzu to take him under his wing. Which was really more like giving his friend permission to indulge a nagging instinct. Some of the things Suuzu wanted were so simple, it was silly to withhold them.

Suuzu's smile was shy. That was kind of new.

Akira shrugged and nodded. "We'll figure it out," he promised.

Hooking a finger through a peach denim beltloop, Suuzu tugged him toward the door, moving past the moment. At least, Akira was pretty sure they'd been having a moment.

"Did you notice the fountain?"

"In the courtyard?" Akira matched Suuzu's stride. "I saw it, but I didn't study it or anything."

"I believe it is Amaranthine in origin."

"Yeah? How can you tell?"

"The subject matter." Suuzu led the way out of the gallery, and they circled the fountain, peering up at the bronze figures. "Are you familiar with the story of Lord Beckonthrall?"

"Sure. They put on a play about him during the Dichotomy Day festivities this past June. He was the dragon who accidentally proposed to four ladies at once."

"Four winds—north, south, east, and west." Suuzu studied the statues. "Traditionally, they are associated with the seasons, but that is a literary contrivance."

"So not every north wind brings a blizzard?"

"Correct." Suuzu waved to the four figures. "These are the Changing Winds. As in Bethiel of the Changing Winds."

"Different from Beckonthrall's brides?"

"Entirely different."

"Okay. Because I think this one is a male."

"Yes. The sagas most often applaud the efforts of lusty males in pursuit of elusive females, but not every imp is a maiden. And not every connection made was romantic in nature."

"Are these four from a story?"

"Bethiel is said to have found favor with four winds. Some say they aided him in his duties. Others suggest they caused him much inadvertent mischief, since winds can be fickle."

"And this is them?" Akira didn't see a plaque anywhere.

"I believe so. According to the legend, Bethiel was given the unenviable task of shepherding the winds through their courses. Many mishaps befell him, and along the way, he managed to tame a thunderstorm, a whirlwind, a summer breeze, and a typhoon. They became his companions."

"They're called the Changing Winds because he changed them?"

"Mmm." Suuzu offered a small shrug. "Or because they brought change. As winds do."

The museum director learned of their arrival, which led to a lengthy round of greetings and introductions for both Spokesperson Mettlebright and Spokesperson Farroost. Juuyu was able to avoid Trip Amory's enthusiasm thanks to Magda's quick thinking. She obscured his team's presence with a casually tossed barrier.

Sinder eased to Juuyu's side and asked, "What's put you on edge?"

"Am I?"

"Are you seriously trying to deflect? After all these years with Hisoka, I'm basically immune."

"Are you?" Juuyu had no idea what had inspired Twineshaft to entrust his secrets to someone who seemed incapable of keeping one.

Rolling his eyes, Sinder jostled into his side. It was a familiar demand. Juuyu looped his arm around the young dragon's waist, encouraging him to lean in and triggering a sigil they regularly used to confer.

"I am blaming my recent pollination for being so slow on the uptake." Sinder was definitely sulking. "I demand enlightenment. What did I miss?"

"Hmm. I am Fumiko's choice."

"Knew that *ages* ago." Sinder prodded Juuyu's ribs. "Did I mention I'm immune to deflection? I'm sure I did."

It wasn't a very good impression, but Juuyu smiled anyhow. "What do you think you missed?"

"I'm talking about Hajime, a.k.a. Tabigarasu, a.k.a. the Gentleman Bandit. You said you know how he's been pulling this off."

Juuyu hummed an affirmative.

"And ... I'm guessing that's what's bothering you."

"Yes."

Sinder searched his face. "Care to share?"

"Once sprigged, Amaranthine trees have an endless existence. Year upon year, they increase in height, depth, and breadth. Anchored by mountains, beloved by breezes, staunch in storms, serenaded by stars."

"I can see that." Eyes alight, he amended, "I *have* seen that."

Juuyu hoped Sinder could return to Wardenclave sometime soon. He mentioned Zisa more often than he should, given that the tree's existence was undisclosed. But Sinder's obvious fondness made it difficult to scold. For a single, pivotal summer, Zisa had been his home.

"The old groves were devastated. Their trees culled. Their secrets harvested. Their innocence destroyed."

Pain reflected in Sinder's eyes. "I never liked those ballads *before*. Now, I hate them."

"I do not know if Hajime was salvaged or subjugated, but the truth of his existence pains me deeply." A low note. A long sigh. "He was here before we ever arrived, and I saw him the first time I entered the lobby. Do you recall the display of congratulatory flowers on the information desk?"

"Sure. In passing. But I was more focused on *who* was in the lobby, not *what*."

"Understandable. That was my task." Juuyu winced against a memory involving gnarled roots and stunted limbs. Clipped. Dwarfed. Fragile. *Wrong.* "There was a bonsai among the gifts."

Sinder stared. It took a few beats before he swore and softly asked, "Who would *do* something like that?"

Juuyu tightened his hold and grimly invited, "Help me find out."

At that moment, Argent raised a hand, and his attention snapped toward the front of the building. Mirrim and Magda immediately moved toward the lobby, and Juuyu's own sigils rattled against his senses.

"He's here?" whispered Sinder.

"No." Juuyu glanced to Argent for direction.

Jacques took one look at his boss's face and smoothly inserted himself between Argent and Trip Amory, raising a question that caused the museum director to brighten. And allowed the fox to vanish.

"Lobby," Juuyu ordered.

Hallow and Sinder winked away. Juuyu beckoned to Suuzu, who walked as briskly as Akira could manage. The young man asked, "Is

Tabi-oji here?"

"No, but something must have happened." Ushering them both in the direction the others had gone, Juuyu quietly added, "Someone tripped Argent's alarm, then set off Magda's sigil array."

In the lobby, they found a tense and rumpled Jiminy in conference with Argent.

The fox's expression betrayed nothing, but Juuyu didn't like the steel in his gaze.

Akira ran to Argent, and Suuzu naturally followed. Silver tails spooled outward, whipping and fanning in an ominous flourish.

Still, his voice remained entirely calm. "We are being ... summoned."

Juuyu impatiently flicked his fingers, demanding answers.

"It would seem that the Gentleman Bandit is at Jacaranda Circle." Argent looked to Jiminy. "You could have called ...?"

"Uncle Denny had me out of there faster than I could think. Dumped me out front and headed straight back." Jiminy looked down at shaking hands. "Said you'd still need me."

Juuyu stepped forward, barely clinging to calm. "Tabigarasu found the enclave?"

"I'm not sure *found* is the right word," said Jiminy, whose posture wobbled into something vaguely apologetic. "Fumiko let him in."

52

TAKING SIDES

Juuyu was a mess. He must have looked it, too, because when they reached Jacaranda Circle, Argent signaled for assistance. "Do not let him inside until he calms."

Argent went on ahead, icy calm and perfectly poised.

Buzz and Rafter pulled Juuyu aside.

"Hey, now. Hey, now," Rafter soothed. "Take a few deep breaths and chill. Nobody expected this, but nobody's come to harm."

"He is here?"

"The tree guy? Can confirm."

Juuyu wanted to barge past, find Fumiko, and reassure himself. "She let him in?"

"To the library," clarified Rafter. "They've been catching up. Seems they're old friends from way back. Before my time, so that's a looong ways. This'll be something to add to the ladies' chronicle."

As far as Juuyu knew, nothing in Fumiko's collection had

pointed to a connection with any other tree, let alone this one.

Buzz took to kneading Juuyu's palm. "How are your personal wards? Up to the task? There's fresh pollen in the air."

Juuyu swiftly inventoried his personal wards and bolstered his defenses, well aware that these two were trying to distract him. And that it had worked. For the first time, it occurred to Juuyu that whenever duty called him away from Fumiko, these two would be part of the reason she and Zuzu remained safe and happy.

Adjusting his posture, Juuyu asked, "What do you know?"

"He wants to talk," said Rafter. "Time for some dialogue, you know?"

Buzz countered, "*Fumiko* wants to talk. And your lady has the leverage."

"What do you mean?"

Rafter and Buzz traded a long look. "Couldn't really say," said Rafter. "Be a shame to spoil the surprise."

"Peace," said Buzz. "The sisters have things well in hand."

"Calm enough to check it out?" asked Rafter.

Juuyu signaled a sharp affirmative and conferred with his pocket watch.

Buzz touched his cheek, searched his eyes, and smiled. "Cleared up something beautiful."

"You got this," agreed Rafter, who didn't let him go until they'd bumped fists.

In the reading area at the center of the library's main floor, couches and chairs stood in clusters. Juuyu's attention immediately soared to Fumiko, who sat beside the Gentleman Bandit, her hands around one of his. They were relaxed. She was safe.

Forcing himself to take in the rest of the room, Juuyu inclined his head toward Diva, the only other seated person. From a deep leather chair, she seemed to preside over the gathering. An understandable attitude since they were in her territory.

The she-bear acknowledged him with a sedate smile.

Juuyu had to wonder why she was so pleased.

Both Thunderhoof brothers had taken a traditional stance, kneeling on either side of the sofa Fumiko shared with the elusive tree. At first, he thought they were poised to intervene, which would have been futile, given the nature of trees. But a distant memory from a long-ago Song Circle surfaced, and Juuyu was able to interpret their intent.

Bavol and Colt were bearing witness to whatever unfolded. They were taking a neutral position in order to ensure that a proper balance was maintained.

However, Argent dominated the scene, his body half-turned as if he'd been waiting for Juuyu in order to begin. It looked as if his outflung tails were an attempt to hold back the tides, but Akira's restraint was at an end.

Barreling past proprieties, he blurted, "Tabi-oji!" And then more softly, "Tabi-otosan?"

Changing *uncle* to *father*.

Putting astonishment on the tree's face.

Giving him a reason to reach out.

Without hesitation, Akira hurled himself onto the couch and into the tree's side. Heedless of the fact that he could be snatched away in a twinkling. And since Fumiko had the tree's other hand in both of hers, she'd be gone with them.

Juuyu tensed.

Akira clung anyhow, mumbling, "I was afraid you'd gone away."

"I am here. Do not cry, leafling."

Jacques breezed into the room then, a loaded tray held high, Antigone close on his heels, carrying two pitchers of something iced.

While they distributed refreshments, Diva asked, "Shall we continue introductions?"

Juuyu fidgeted through the courtesies. He understood that this was an official meeting. Introductions were necessary to set a tone and ensure balance, but he would have preferred to extricate his nestmates from the bandit's clutches.

Finally, Argent announced, "If you are willing to enter into peace talks with those gathered, I will take your side and ensure your interests are protected."

"Me?" The tree pursed his lips. "You would take my side?"

"Him and me, both," said Akira. "You're family."

Argent showed his palms. "I am Tsumiko Hajime's bondmate. She has taken my name and is now known as Lady Mettlebright."

"I told you about Argent. He loves Sis." Akira held out his hand. "And this is Suuzu. He wanted to meet you. And I wanted you to meet him. We're nestmates."

Suuzu glided to the increasingly crowded couch, and after a moment's hesitation, perched on the arm.

Hajime breathed, "The phoenix?"

"One of them," confirmed Akira, before pointing his way. "Juuyu is here, too."

"He's mine," said Fumiko, sounding pleased.

Juuyu warbled softly, but Argent raised a hand to hold him back. "Hajime, will you accept Jacques Smythe as a moderator? His devotion to me could be considered an advantage. As could his short attention span."

Jacques bowed. "I am *quite* capable of dedicating hours to worthier pursuits, but I find little pleasure in meetings."

Akira whispered, "Say yes. Uncle Jackie is the best at this sort of thing."

The tree glanced from face to face and quietly answered, "Yes."

"Right, then! Shall we choose up sides? Lord Argent Mettlebright will speak for Hajime, who is joined by Akira Hajime and his plus one." Pointing to the couch opposite theirs, Jacques said, "Jiminy you'll be here."

The ward dropped to a seat and was quickly flanked by Mirrim and Magda.

Indicating a chair to one side, Jacques said, "Sinder, be a dear?"

"Why me?"

"Because I need you to represent Hisoka's interests. You'll speak for the Amaranthine Council."

Sinder dropped to his assigned seat. Moon and Hallow circled the room to stand behind him. Lending balance.

Jacques looked ready to move on, but Diva said, "I am here to support Fumiko, who speaks for this enclave."

"Pardon me, ladies. I wasn't aware you had a stake in the proceedings." Jacques offered his hand to Fumiko, who let go of

Hajime in order to be helped to her feet. Ushering her to Diva's side of the square, Jacques hummed. "Would it be too much trouble to ask Zuzu to join us? For balance."

"Zuzu?" Fumiko called. "They are ready to negotiate."

Her twin winked into existence, smiling slyly.

Juuyu gasped, and his gaze jumped to Hajime, who somehow managed to look calm, though he now clung to Akira's arm with both hands. Because he was at the sisters' mercy.

Zuzu cradled the bonsai in both arms.

Clipped. Dwarfed. Fragile. *Defeated.*

Fumiko hadn't known what to give Juuyu until Hajime found her. In that moment, it was as if the pieces of a puzzle slid into place. It made her feel like she was part of Juuyu's mission. Putting the clues together. Figuring out what had happened. And why.

It wasn't that she was smarter than Juuyu. She'd simply had more of the facts. And remembered what all the others forgot.

"I remember Hajime," she announced. "Long ago, he would trade with Zuzu."

"Trade what?" asked Akira.

"Pollen," said Zuzu. "His is *good.*"

Bavol spoke up. "Although Hajime represents an unregistered variety, there's no reason to doubt that he and Zuzu are compatible for cross-pollination."

"Oh, they're compatible, all right," interjected Diva. "Zuzu has been a very naughty tree."

Fumiko did feel a little bad about that part. Once Zuzu found out that Portia had an entire vial of Hajime's pollen, Zuzu couldn't resist.

"You did not forget him?" asked Argent.

She could have answered, but she looked to Hajime.

"There was once a grove here. Trees of my sort were among the others. Leaflings now lost."

"*Your* leaflings?" asked Suuzu.

Hajime's chin lifted toward the bonsai. "Even a tree in my state can blossom and bear."

Akira asked, "If Fumiko grew up with red flowers nearby, does that mean she's immune like me?"

The tree simply looked to Fumiko and smiled faintly. "So it would seem."

It was time.

Fumiko wished she could make Hajime hear her thoughts— *trust me, trust me, trust me.* And maybe he understood, because his gaze softened, and he gave the tiniest nod. She was being selfish, but so was Hajime. This way, they could both get the things they needed.

Jacques Smythe softly clapped his hands together and took charge. "Let's go for the abridged edition, shall we? Papa Socks has two of the Junzi, yes?"

Hajime blinked, probably at the nickname. Akira murmured something in his ear, looking embarrassed and apologetic, and the tree laughed quietly. It was good to see him smile.

Hajime answered, "I do."

Gesturing to Jiminy, Jacques said, "He has the other two and would like the full set. This is one of the exchanges currently on the table."

Fumiko hadn't realized that. "Which two?"

Jiminy rubbed his fingertips together. "I've been given charge of the Orchid Saddle and the Bamboo Stave. And Jacques is right. I'd love a look at the Blaze and the Cascade. Though they must all be returned to their rightful places."

"Eventually," said Argent.

Sinder spoke up to agree. "Eventually."

Jacques waved a hand toward the dragon in their midst. "Sinder speaks for Hisoka Twineshaft, who wants information about a rogue dragon who has been running amuck. Akira was under the impression that you can help us."

Hajime slowly inclined his head. "I believe so."

"Brilliant." Jacques smiled warmly at the tree. "And you want … Naoki Hajime."

"I do."

Argent sharply interjected, "And the dismissal of all charges with regards to the thefts of the Plum Cascade and the Chrysanthemum Blaze. As well as the attempted thefts of the Orchid Saddle and the Bamboo Stave."

Jacques glanced Sinder's way. "Understandable."

"*And*," persisted Argent. "All the personhood and rights afforded to every member of Amaranthine society."

"A bold move," accused Jacques. "Are you championing the rights of Impressions now, my lord?"

Suuzu lifted a hand. "He should also insist upon all the provisional rights and courtesies afforded an Amaranthine grove. Including the rights to succor, secrecy, and proliferation."

"Noted," said Jacques, with a sidelong look in Fumiko's direction.

Oh. Were these rights she and Zuzu were meant to have?

She glanced at Diva, who patted her leg and murmured, "Noted."

"*And* Tabi-oji needs a passport," blurted Akira. "Because this tree likes to travel."

Laughter rippled around the room. And for the first time, Fumiko realized that none of those gathered were even trying to drive a hard bargain. This wasn't like hammering out a treaty. It was more like Argent Mettlebright was making sure that everyone had the chance to ask for what they needed.

When no further conditions were proposed, Jacques turned to Fumiko and Diva. "Which brings us to the members of this enclave. What is your part in this parlay?"

Fumiko stood and said, "Juuyu."

He dragged his gaze from the tree in Zuzu's arms to meet hers. He looked stunned. Maybe even distraught. Would he understand what she was doing? Again, she wished her words could reach him—*trust me, trust me, trust me.*

"I have a gift for you."

Juuyu's stance shifted, and he waited in silence.

Fumiko had been with Akira when he asked Portia, Melody, and Antigone about the pollen of Amaranthine trees. He'd tried more than once to tell Juuyu's team about the things he'd seen at the museum, and even though those conversations had taken place in Japanese, Fumiko had caught the gist. It had been confusing, seeing the guys ignore Akira's warnings. Until Hajime revealed himself to her.

"You gave me a gift that wasn't yours to give, nor mine to keep. Priceless and beautiful and perfect. The flute is uncommonly fine, and it's song is now a part of me." Fumiko held her head high. "I had no idea how to find a courting gift to match yours, and yet ... I've also found something priceless and beautiful and perfect. He isn't truly mine to give, nor yours to keep. But you can still catch him. Isn't that why you came?"

Moving to Zuzu, she carefully took the bonsai—which was surprisingly heavy—and brought it to Juuyu. She softly added, "This time, we are the beggars at your door. Here is the enormity of our trust."

Juuyu took the low earthenware pot, supporting its bottom, cradling its sides. He somehow managed an entire cascade of notes before hurrying to kneel before Hajime. Setting the ancient bonsai across his knees, Juuyu said, "Peace, father of ancients and kindred to time." Reaching for Hajime's hand, he kissed it and asked, "Are you well? Do you need anything I can provide?"

"Let me have a look," grumbled Argent. "I have some experience with bonsai."

"Some?" scoffed Akira. "Argent has dozens in his conservatory and fusses over every last one of them."

"They have a certain dignity. And I have a certain sympathy." Crouching at Juuyu's side, the fox lifted his hands to Hajime and asked, "May I touch?"

Lashes fluttered, and the tree tentatively nodded. And as

if they'd entered into their own negotiations, Hajime quietly countered, "May I see Tsumiko again?"

Argent tested soil, touched bark and caressed a tiny leaf. "I would demand it, if it were not so presumptuous. Come to us if you will, and find welcome."

Diva growled then. "We are not finished."

Argent and Juuyu remained where they were, seated at Hajime's feet.

With an apologetic bow, Jacques said, "A thousand apologies, Fumiko. Please, continue."

This was it.

Fumiko said, "Hajime and I have already come to an agreement. He will not cooperate with you unless you cooperate with us. Indeed, he would not be here at all, if not for the thing that Zuzu and I want."

"Also bold! I am giddy with anticipation." Jacques' smile was encouraging. "What are your demands?"

"Zuzu and I want a grove."

Into the sudden silence, Juuyu spoke. "Amaranthine trees require a great deal of room. This setting is less than ideal for expansion."

Fumiko stood her ground. "I know Hajime's story. I know what I'm asking for."

All eyes turned to the tree.

"I am Hajime. I am the first." His hands caressed the earthenware pot that defined both his limits and his freedom. "I was not the last."

Juuyu asked, "There are more trees like you? Like this?"

"Yes. Many more." Hajime sought Sinder's gaze. "Kodoku and

his kin have long toyed with the lives of Impressions—mingling and mangling."

Sinder sucked in a breath and swore in an almost reverent tone. "A name. We finally have a name."

Everyone was talking at once, an eager, urgent jumble, but Diva's growl cut through, and the group sheepishly gave their full attention to Fumiko.

"Rescue those trees, and bring them here," Fumiko begged. "Let us become their safe haven. Let them become our grove."

Argent formed a simple hand sign, which was quickly matched by every person in the room.

"So it has been agreed. So let it be done." Jacques softly clapped his hands and bowed to Fumiko. "Leave the rest to us."

53

TRADE WITH ME

The Farroost brothers were in fine form, perched together amidst Zuzu's topmost branches, piping their way through a song Akira was sure he'd never heard them sing before. In fact, the longer it went on, the surer he was that Suuzu didn't know it either.

Relaxing alone in one of the larger hammocks, Akira listened as the melody jumped from one phoenix to the next. Juuyu led, teaching his younger brother his lines. As lessons went, it was lovely. By the time they split into harmonies, the moon was on the rise, which reminded Akira to check his pockets.

He really wasn't expecting to find anything, yet his fingers bumped a small box that hadn't been there earlier. Curious as he was about what Rafter had found, Akira would have to wait for more light to inspect the potential gift.

Just knowing he had an option was ... good. He'd need to see about paying for it in the morning. He wasn't sure he wanted to owe another favor, even to someone as easygoing as Rafter.

Akira was still awake hours later, when the song ended in a lilting cascade and Suuzu transformed and slowly slipped down between the branches, gaze locked on his. Lifting a hand in welcome, Akira softly called, "You guys are amazing."

Suuzu settled on his knees at Akira's side and fidgeted with the creases in the quilts.

"Are you glad to sing with Juuyu again?"

"It is different now." He glanced toward the lighthouse tower. "He sings for her."

"Are you jealous?"

"No." Suuzu plucked and smoothed, gaze downcast. "I do not begrudge Brother his new bondmate."

"It's pretty amazing, if you think about it." Akira poked Suuzu's arm, trying for eye contact. "Both of you growing up in a grove. Both of you getting attached to tree-kin."

Suuzu frowned. "I did not know ...! And that is not why I ...!"

"How could we even guess?" Folding back the quilt, Akira said, "Come on. Zuzu went to the trouble to smuggle me up here. And I saved you a spot."

Side by side, they stared up through the leaves. Akira knew it was up to him, so he started with something simple. "This is nice. Being in a tree. I could get used to it."

"Mmm."

"If we had a treehouse, we could live in a tree. Do you think any of the ones on the estate are big enough?"

Suuzu turned his head. "Perhaps."

"Maybe while I'm away, you could find a good tree. Put dibs on it or something."

"You want a treehouse?"

"Well, a hammock is good for summer, but it's a little precarious. Four walls and a ceiling, may be a few windows ... it would be more like a home." Akira kept his eyes on the stars above. "Maybe something like the house we stayed in while we were visiting your colony. The one in Letik's branches."

"Are you asking me to build you a house?"

"Couldn't we build it together? When I get back?"

Suuzu sighed softly. "Do you know what you are asking?"

"Enough to know you probably want to." Akira rolled toward him. "I've got my room in Stately House, but it might be nice to have our own place, too. Kind of like Ginkgo's bolt holes, but ... off the ground."

Easing onto his side, Suuzu pulled him close and quietly declared, "I sing for you."

"I know."

"I would build for you."

"I know that, too. And once I'm home for good, we can figure out what shape our home should take."

Suuzu asked, "How long will you be away?"

"Nobody's said," Akira admitted. "I mean, if we're going by the amount of Uncle Jackie's luggage, it'll be months."

"I do not think he should be used as any kind of standard."

Akira snorted. "It's going to be a while. Boats are slow, and once we get there, I'm sure there are a lot of things to organize or synchronize or something. If Tabi-otosan thought he needed the

Four Gentlemen to pull this off, it can't be easy."

Suuzu warbled unhappily.

"Hey," said Akira. "Suuzu, you know I love you, right?"

"As friends."

"We're more than friends," protested Akira.

"Best friends."

"Well, yeah. That's how this started. But wouldn't you say we're more than that?"

Suuzu tucked his chin and said, "Certainly. We are lifelong friends."

Akira winced. He'd said all of those things so many times, trying to put their connection into human terms. By attempting to qualify their relationship, had he placed limits on it? Looking back, he guessed he'd been defining boundaries. And over the years, Suuzu had always respected them.

"Isn't there more, though?" Akira asked. "We're still growing, and what we need changes over time."

"Akira," Suuzu said softly. "I do not think I could refuse you anything."

"Did you know Juuyu thinks I spoil you? Little does he know that you spoil me."

Suuzu warbled weakly.

Akira hated how sad he sounded.

"Hey, since you can't refuse, how about you let me touch your hair?"

When he finally answered, Suuzu quietly repeated, "Do you know what you are asking?"

"This isn't anything new."

"It feels new," Suuzu murmured, though he draped himself across Akira's chest, the same way he did for a long sleep.

"Yeah, I think so, too." Akira patted Suuzu's shoulders and admitted, "I *do* know what I'm asking, but that doesn't mean I know what I'm doing. So bear with me."

"I will."

Akira worked his fingers through loose curls, tugging and kneading and combing. It really wasn't anything new, because this was how he helped Suuzu settle in for a long sleep. But their little routine changed up when Suuzu adjusted his hold in order to slide his fingers across Akira's tattoo.

Soon, Suuzu began to croon softly.

Smiling crookedly, Akira asked, "Are you singing to the sigil, or letting me know this feels good?"

"Both."

The hour lingered late, and still Suuzu made little bids for his soul's attention. And in exchange, Akira made a thorough mess of his hair ... and tickled his ears, which may have also been a bid for attention. And before long, Akira thought that maybe—just a little—he could hear distant music. As if the stars themselves had picked up Suuzu's song and were humming along.

Akira had no idea why it hadn't occurred to him that Tabi-otosan was using illusions. But Juuyu had been filling out forms for the last two days, and the details on one of the registration papers caught his eye.

"This part's wrong. His eyes are brown. Like mine."

Juuyu paused to check his work. "Not so."

Akira looked to Suuzu, who'd been focused on his tattoo for the better part of an hour. "What color are Tabi-otosan's eyes?"

"I could not say," Suuzu murmured distractedly. "Too much camouflage."

"Really? Are they actually red?" Akira next appealed to Sinder. "How was I supposed to know he was disguised?"

"When you look at Hajime, do you see flowers?"

"Nooo," admitted Akira.

"Yet he scatters flower petals wherever he goes. You never gave a thought to where they come from?" Sinder's tone turned teasing. "And I suppose when those dragons potted him, they docked his ears?"

"Oh. Well, when you put it like that ...." Akira asked, "How much am I missing?"

Juuyu said, "Ask him to show you. I have little doubt he would indulge your interest."

"*Leafling*," added Sinder.

Akira stood to do just that, only to have Suuzu catch his arm with an impatient sound that was decidedly new. At least to Akira. "Are you clucking at me?"

Sinder said, "First time? The chicken noises have always felt negative to me. And impolite. He's definitely scolding you."

Juuyu coolly asked, "Chicken noises?"

"Careful," warned Sinder. "You wouldn't want to say anything that might insult our cozy friends."

Similarly miffed, Suuzu grumbled, "I was not finished."

Akira shook his head. "Just ask Michael about it once we're home."

"Argent probably knows more than he has mentioned," said Juuyu.

"Understatement of the century," said Sinder, waving them off.

When Suuzu didn't let go, Akira simply towed him out of the guesthouse and along the sidewalk toward the crystal gate. Ever since yesterday, Argent had taken over the back room of Flutterbys, turning it into some kind of bonsai clinic. Apparently, Tabi-otosan was overdue for some pampering.

Rapping lightly on the screen door, Akira let himself in.

Argent spared them an impatient look, then went back to comparing sketches of complex sigilcraft with Jiminy and Rafter. Tabi-otosan sat on the counter a short distance from them, kicking his heels and looking bored.

"Come out and play?" whispered Akira.

The tree perked up, shot a moody look at the well-meaning cabal, and vanished. He tapped Akira's shoulder from behind and included Suuzu in his plea. "The beach?"

They trooped down onto the sand and settled together before Akira asked, "Would you let me see you? Really see you?"

With a small nod, Tabi-otosan ... changed. And tensed, as if awaiting criticism.

The differences were relatively small. Typical stuff that any Amaranthine in hiding tweaked in order to fit in with humans. His ears now came to points. Fine lines traced his skin, which seemed more luminous somehow. Younger. Ageless. But the real showstoppers were his flowers. Tiny red blooms began at the crown of his head and cascaded over straight black hair in a lavish display. And his eyes.

"You have red eyes," Akira whispered.

The tree quickly lowered his gaze.

"No, no! It's not bad. In a way, it's perfect. Say, can I reintroduce you to the family?" Bringing out his phone, he suggested, "It's about time we told Tsumiko the good news."

"Please."

Akira tapped, explaining, "Time difference won't matter much. Sis keeps odd hours because ... oh, hey! You okay to talk for a little while? I'm here with Tabi-otosan. Or ... Haji-oji, if that's more comfortable for you."

"You found him?"

"Yeah. He's safe, and Argent's getting him ready for travel." Akira asked, "Any chance Kyrie is close by?"

"Right here."

"You okay with switching to video? I think Kyrie needs to meet his grandfather."

"I'm giving Kyrie the phone."

And then the boy's light voice carried through. *"Uncle Akira?"*

"Right here! You good?"

"I am well." And then a chime sounded, inviting Akira to chat face-to-face.

"There you are!" Akira aimed his phone a little to the side. "Suuzu made it here."

Kyrie waved.

"And this is ... I guess it'd be Tabi-jiji, yeah? I found the family tree."

The tree eased into view, caught sight of Kyrie, and gasped.

Kyrie's eyes widened, too, and he looked to his mother. Tsumiko leaned in, blinked, and broke into a warm smile. *"So that's how things are! Haji-oji, this is my son Kyrie Hajime-Mettlebright."*

"You gave him my name?"

"We did. Although Argent and I didn't realize it at the time."

With another small wave, Kyrie asked, *"Are your eyes red? Like mine?"*

"Does that please you, young dragon?"

Kyrie blushed and nodded.

"Will you be coming home together?" Tsumiko asked.

Akira hesitated. He wasn't sure how much to say.

The tree patted his shoulder and said, "My arrival has become increasingly inevitable. Your bondmate has been laboring over safeguards. He fusses as much as Naoki ever did."

Tsumiko's expression softened, and she asked, *"Is there any word of dad?"*

This time, Suuzu stepped into the awkward silence, his arms around their shoulders. "Argent will bring Hajime to you as soon as he is ready to travel. Meanwhile, Akira will help to collect Naoki. Have faith in their return."

Akira had a plan. He wasn't sure it was a good plan, but it was the only way he could think of to give Suuzu a promise without actually … making the promise. And finding the right moment had been honestly impossible. Privacy wasn't any easier to come by here than it was at Stately House. So with one thing and another, it was the morning he had to leave for the airport with Uncle Jackie.

Begging ten minutes, Akira dragged Suuzu outside. Pointing to the top of the lighthouse, he suggested, "Gallery?"

Suuzu carried him to the overlook and immediately began fussing with Akira's hair, as if at war with the wind.

Taking a deep breath and releasing it shakily, Akira began, "Trade with me in the manner of friends."

Although he was startled, Suuzu immediately took a receptive posture. "I am willing."

"I'm not sure what's going to happen, and I'm not sure when I'm going to be home again, so I was wondering if I could borrow your nest."

Suuzu undid a few buttons and withdrew the necklace from its usual spot. He loosened and lifted, and with all the solemnity of a coronation, he secured it around Akira's neck.

Akira quietly suggested, "And you can hold onto my ankle bracelet for me. So we each still have a part."

Without hesitation, Suuzu dropped to his knees and lifted Akira's pantleg. And stilled.

"I thought it'd be good to have something of each other's. In case the trip gets long."

Very gently, Suuzu slipped the knot and claimed the length of braid that held a small, tuned stone … and the pretty bit of jewelry Rafter had found.

Best Akira could tell, it was some kind of scarf pin, the sort of thing favored by dragons, phoenixes, and any other clan whose traditional wardrobe involved an excess of draping cloth. The craftsmanship was definitely Amaranthine, because the ornament was comprised of a ring of nine tiny eggs, each a different color.

When Suuzu finally looked up at him, his eyes were enormous, and his lips were trembling.

"Nippet eggs," Akira managed.

Suuzu stood and swayed closer.

"Did you know I can see nippets now? It's something really small, but ... it's something." Akira was supposed to be letting the gift speak for him, but he couldn't help adding, "It's a start."

"This is ... yours?" Suuzu checked.

"Yeah. For now."

"May I wear it?"

Akira cracked a smile. "That's the idea. Since I'll be wearing yours."

Suuzu bent until their cheeks touched. "Do you understand ...?"

"Do you?" Akira pushed closer and hugged him hard.

"I believe so. May I formalize our exchange in the traditional manner?"

There was another formality involved?

Akira's confusion must have shown, because Suuzu took his time arranging and aligning. His thumb brushed Akira's lower lip, which made his intention abundantly clear.

"If you want." And because he intended to match Suuzu in every way he could, Akira added, "I am willing."

54
TENTH CHILD

Suuzu remained with the enclave even after Argent departed for Stately House. The remaining members of Juuyu's team scattered, and the enclave grew quiet. Suuzu's schedule had been cleared, which allowed him to fulfill a traditional role for his brother. While Juuyu was much occupied with Fumiko, Suuzu spent time with her tree-twin. It was meant partly as guard duty—though this place was thoroughly secure—and partly as a distraction, meant to keep Zuzu from barging in on the intimacies of the nest.

Not that she needed distracting. Sinder had set the sisters up with a phone, and Zuzu spent hours chatting with trees from the Farroost colony.

With time on his hands, Suuzu had turned his attention to Fumiko's gift. She'd said it was a puzzle box, and fiddling with it kept him from fretting over Akira.

It was more complicated than he anticipated.

And intriguing, once he realized that some of the inset tiles weren't shell, but crystal. Pale blue and potent. Had someone warded the contents?

"Zuzu?" he called.

She joined him in the hammock. "Yes, Brother?"

"Did this box belong to Soren? He was a ward, was he not?"

"Soren was, but this is not his box." Zuzu smiled. "Sister chose even better than she meant to when she gave this to you."

"Why?"

Zuzu tapped the box's gleaming surface. "This was Hajime's box. Sister promised to keep it safe, but she forgot. Sometimes she does."

"Should I return it?"

"No. When he found out it was you, he said, 'close enough.' And smiled." She patted his arm. "It is yours to do with as you please."

She winked away, and Suuzu renewed his efforts, but the box was reluctant to let go of its secrets. However, on the third day, he met with sudden success.

The tricky box swung open, revealing a shallow tray filled with flowers of several varieties. They had to be quite old, yet they looked and smelled fresh. Carefully lifting the tray aside, Suuzu found a deeper recess in which lay three leathery lumps.

Recognition slammed into him, and Suuzu trilled a sharp summons.

Leaves rustled, and Juuyu appeared on the nearest branch. Juuyu draped in orange silks. Juuyu with purple flowers in his hair. Juuyu whose forehead shimmered with the mark of an imp's good opinion. "Suuzu?"

"I have found ... a treasure. And I need your advice." He lifted his little finger, letting Juuyu know that this was a matter for tributes. For certain secrets—and duties—only belonged to the tenth child of each clan.

Juuyu joined him, kneeling so close their knees touched. "Fumiko's gift?"

"This *is* what I think it is, yes?"

"Without a doubt." Concern flashed through Juuyu's eyes. "Our duty is clear."

"*My* duty." Suuzu extracted one of the objects, which was withered and brown. Inserting the tips of his claws into the leathery mass, he gently pushed and pried, revealing the old fruit's single seed. Golden.

"Without a doubt," Juuyu repeated, inspecting the array of flowers. "Which variety ...?"

"Zuzu confirmed it. These are Hajime's fruit. Beyond rare."

"They *must* be protected." Juuyu extended his hand. "I will do it."

Suuzu only wavered for a moment. "You are needed for the battle ahead. I am the one who was set aside for peace. This duty is mine."

Conceding with a low warble, Juuyu stalled him with an upraised hand. "Will you hear my advice?"

He could only nod.

"Let the other two remain hidden. Reseal the box and allow me to add to its securities. Then I will carry you to Stately House." Juuyu was already replacing the tray and closing the lid. "By spring, there will be a Scattering. Once established, you could fulfill your remaining duty by entrusting these to that grove's protector."

Suuzu trembled at the thought. "Argent."

"Yes."

"He would give one to Akira."

Juuyu pressed his forehead to Suuzu's and thrummed a low, satisfied note. "Without a doubt."

Suuzu looked out to sea and trembled to think how far Akira had gone from the answer that was suddenly, dazzlingly here.

"He *will* return to you," Juuyu soothed. "I will make certain."

"May it be as you say."

For several long moments, Suuzu searched his brother's face, needing reassurance.

Juuyu's gaze softened, and he touched his cheek. "May the scent of flowers linger in your dreams. May the blessing of trees linger in your embrace."

With a small nod, Suuzu placed the golden seed in his mouth. And swallowed.

Abundant thanks to all who lend their support by reading, rating, and reviewing my stories, wherever they may be found. ::twinkle::

ALSO BY FORTHRIGHT

AMARANTHINE SAGA

Tsumiko and the Enslaved Fox
Kimiko and the Accidental Proposal
Tamiko and the Two Janitors
Mikoto and the Reaver Village
Fumiko and the Finicky Nestmate
Pimiko and the Uncharted Island

SONGS OF THE AMARANTHINE

Marked by Stars
Followed by Thunder
Dragged through Hedgerows
Governed by Whimsy
Hemmed in Silver
Captured on Film
Bathed in Moonlight

AMARANTHINE INTERLUDES

Lord Mettlebright's Man

PATREON EXCLUSIVES

Bard & Barbarian

When I reach 400 patrons, I'll begin publishing a new subscription-based storyline on Patreon. Loosely based on the old Amaranthine tale, "The Wolf and the Moon Maiden," this serial will involve three sisters, twelve pledges, and the long-awaited stirring of a sleeping landmark.

Kimiko and the Cycle of Moons

Become a patron at https://www.patreon.com/forthrightly

He leads and elite taskforce.
She did, too. On television.

PAMIKO
AND THE
UNCHARTED
ISLAND

Boon can almost taste his prey, he's *that* close. If only he hadn't run up against a barrier in the middle of the ocean. He puts out a call and calls in a favor. There's a plan in place, and reinforcements are *en route*, but Boon is restless to run the Rogue to ground. Taking a risk—definitely his style—lands him with a couple of responsibilities he *really* didn't need, and both of them are female.

After the finale of her dazzlingly successful television drama, Pim Moonprowl packs her bags and books passage to a secretive resort that makes alluring claims. She'll pay anything, promise anything, do anything to find out if they're true. On an island that's not on maps, Pim encounters a silver-tongued doctor, a kindred soul, a caged star, and a clever monkey. This is her big chance to put into practice the skills she gained from eight seasons on an elite taskforce.

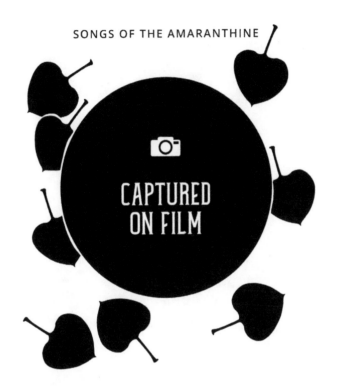

CAPTURED ON FILM

One brother believes in impossible things.
One brother denies he can see them.

When Caleb Dare's younger brother shows up out of the blue, he's immediately suspicious. The two of them live in totally different worlds. But Josheb threatens to camp in the middle of Caleb's urban loft for as long as it takes to convince him to take a nice, long hike into the woods. They can camp. Swap stories around the fire. Just like old times.

Yeah, right.

Josheb's true motive is a major hassle. If not a hustle. He's always believed in absolutely everything, from extraterrestrials to the paranormal. On a hot tip from an undisclosed source, he's chasing a myth into the mountains, sure he'll be the one to prove the existence of an elusive cryptid. It'll be the story of the century, and Caleb is the only one who can give him the edge he needs.

Yeah, he's right.

BATHED IN MOONLIGHT

Some courtships follow all the rules.
Some courtships bend them.

As the Seven Score Moons cycle through their phases, the appointed time for the Queen's Festival draws near. Wolves from all over will gather at a site that the packs count as sacred, to sing for the Moon and her maidens. Rinloo is part of an allotment of dexes sent to guard the Circle, which has long been anchored by an Amaranthine tree. There he encounters a girl-child spirited to safety by imps and an unhappy maid from the Luminous Court.

never more than
FORTHRIGHT

a teller of tales who began as a fandom ficcer. (Which basically means that no one in RL knows about her anime habit, her manga collection, or her penchant for serial storytelling.) Kinda sorta almost famous for gently-paced, WAFFy adventures that might inadvertently overturn your OTP, forthy will forever adore drabble challenges, surprise fanart, and twinkles (which are rumored to keep well in jars). As always... be nice, play fair, have fun! ::twinkle::

FORTHWRITES.COM

CPSIA information can be obtained
at www.ICGtesting.com
Printed in the USA
BVHW061957121021
618743BV00010B/393

9 781631 230752